SNAFU

"Soldier, it's an honor to know there are men like you around to volunteer for missions like this one. It's going to be hell, but hell is nothing you give a damn about, right?"

"I didn't volunteer," Simon said.

"Corporal, I *know* what you think. You think this is a stinking war and you hate it. Nevertheless, you're proud to be a part of it, you're doing your bit."

"No, sir," he responded to Trask's question.

"Not proud?"

"I mean yes, sir. Very proud. But I think a mistake has been made."

"No mistake, Corporal. Understand, this is no run-of-the-mill commando raid off in the bush country... this is the real thing, where we separate the men from the boys. You're lucky to be in on this one. In the old days, when they weren't afraid of calling a spade a spade, this is the kind of enterprise they would have characterized as a suicide mission."

"Did you say suicide mission?" Simon asked.

"I sure did, soldier. Does that turn you on?"

"This really is a mistake," Simon said.

Nicholas Rinaldi

Bridge Fall Down

St. Martin's
Press

ST. MARTIN'S PRESS TITLES ARE AVAILABLE AT QUANTITY DIS-
COUNTS FOR SALES PROMOTIONS, PREMIUMS OR FUND RAISING.
SPECIAL BOOKS OR BOOK EXCERPTS CAN ALSO BE CREATED TO
FIT SPECIFIC NEEDS. FOR INFORMATION WRITE TO SPECIAL
SALES MANAGER, ST. MARTIN'S PRESS, 175 FIFTH AVENUE,
NEW YORK, NEW YORK 10010.

BRIDGE FALL DOWN

Printed in the United States of America

First St. Martin's Press mass market edition/August 1986

ISBN: 0-312-90085-6
Can. ISBN: 0-312-90086-4

10 9 8 7 6 5 4 3 2 1

For Tina, Paul, Steve, and Dave

Simple Simon met a pieman
Going to the fair,
Said Simple Simon to the pieman,
"Let me taste your ware."

Says the pieman to Simple Simon,
"Show me first your penny."
Says Simple Simon to the pieman,
"Indeed, I have not any."

Life is, in fact, a battle. Evil is insolent and strong; beauty enchanting but rare; goodness very apt to be weak; folly very apt to be defiant; wickedness to carry the day; imbeciles to be in great places, people of sense in small, and mankind generally unhappy. But the world as it stands is no illusion, no phantasm, no evil dream of a night; we wake up to it again for ever and ever; we can neither forget it nor deny it nor dispense with it.

—from the essay "Ivan Turgenieff"
by Henry James

❑ PART ONE

1 ❑ Meyerbeer

SIMON WAS IN LOVE with the war. Before he was in the war, he hadn't thought much about it one way or another, but now that he was there, on the ground, moving through jungle, through swamp and across low hills covered with wild, lush foliage, he knew with a strange definiteness that the war was something he would never have wanted to miss. He was fresh out of City College, and if the war hadn't come along he would have been back home in the Bronx, living in an apartment on Tremont Avenue, close to the neighborhood he had grown up in. He would be eating in the Bronx, sleeping in the Bronx, dreaming in the Bronx, blowing his nose in the Bronx. Instead, he was sweating it out in the jungle, advancing steadily through palms, groves of gutta-percha trees, past drongos and macaques, knowing it was going to be a hell of a long time before he got to the bridge they wanted him to blow up.

Hot sun filtered through the trees. His boots made a sucking sound in the mud. Do I love this war, he wondered, or do I hate it? He despised the mud and the dampness, and the insects, the mosquitoes and ticks, and the slime, the slugs. Nevertheless, there were moments when the jungle was an amazing place, moments when the trees and foliage came brilliantly alive: sudden red flowers, smells of cinnamon and orange, immense thick leaves spreading out like friendly green blankets. The vines, the moss. All in all, it was a great place to slum around in with a thirty-five-millimeter camera, or even without one—if you didn't have to worry about the snipers and the incoming mortar.

3

For a few hours they had been in the trees, under a dense canopy of leaves and branches; then, briefly, they were moving through an open field. Simon studied the sky, horizon to horizon: he was looking for Meyerbeer, wondering when he would come highballing in again, in the rainbow chopper, with his camera and the big zoom lens, immortalizing them on film. There was a zany madness to it: you go to war, sweat your way through the jungle, shoot and get shot at, and Meyerbeer is up there in the chopper, making you a movie star. He was a cool number, smooth and unflappable, taking small arms fire from the peasants on the ground, dodging around, evading, turning up at the oddest moments and doing his utmost to get under General Trask's skin. Trask hated him. And, now that he thought about it, Simon hated him too. In fact, it was hard for him to say which of the two he hated more: Meyerbeer or Trask, they were both bad news. The trail took him up onto a rise, and far ahead he could see Trask striding along, vigorous, well over fifty but powerful, big, with the energy and drive of a man half his age, awesome in his determination to get to the bridge. Simon had the uneasy feeling that before the mission was over, Trask would get all of them killed, it could happen. If not Trask, then Meyerbeer, because as different as they were in temperament and style, they both had the same quality of recklessness about them, a flamboyant disregard for the precariousness, the essential fragility, of human life.

The open field was behind them now, and again they were into the trees. Tess Pollaiuolo trudged along beside him, and he noticed how she was practically the only one who wasn't a nervous wreck about being nearby. The others kept far ahead or far behind, giving him a wide berth because of the pyroxene-T that he carried in his pack. It could get touched off by a mortar blast, or an exploding mine, and if the pyroxene-T went it would blow them all sky high. The kill radius, for the amount he was carrying, was a few hundred yards. Simon suspected that even General Trask was a little terrified, though he was tough and hard, with a rugged, weatherworn face and opaque gray eyes that showed no fear. Sugg, Studdwin, and Vain also showed no fear, yet Simon noted how they had a way of keeping their distance. He couldn't blame them. There were times when he wished he could walk away from himself—simply turn and move off, the way the others did, and be somebody else. But wherever he went, whatever grass or earth he stepped on, he was a potential ground zero.

"It's a lousy war," he complained to Tess. "I know it's a good war and I should be infatuated with it, but right now I think it stinks." It was like everything else: the hate becomes love, the love becomes hate, and you're stuck in a jungle with a bomb in your pack and mosquitoes homing in on you like enemy attack planes. The pyroxene-T wasn't a bomb exactly, but it could go off like one. Long strips of sticky black gauze wound on a spool, like adhesive tape, powerful enough, when correctly placed, to demolish the bridge they were heading for. Simon swatted a mosquito on his cheek and nailed it, leaving a smear of blood across his face.

"You want the spray?" Tess said.

"I look that desperate?"

He had given up using the spray because it didn't work. It would work for half an hour or so, then the bugs would be at him again. A few days earlier, in something resembling a fit of rage, he had thrown his spray canister into the trees, and it was good riddance because he hated the smell of the stuff. It was the smell of a cheap deodorant with a bold, minty scent—but in the background, beyond the mint, if you bothered to sniff for it, there was, implausibly, a faint but unmistakable odor of urine.

"Take it or leave it," Tess said, coming on in a brisk, saucy manner that turned him on. "If you want it, I'll dig it out of my pack." She had large brown eyes that stirred something deep in him. Her hair was thick and brown, braided into a pigtail hanging halfway down her back. Her fatigues were sweated through, clinging to her breasts and thighs. "Well?" she said. "Do you want it or not?"

He swatted another one. "Fucking mosquitoes. Not even God cares."

"Don't blame God."

"You think God cares?"

"If God doesn't, who does?"

"I think Sugg cares. And Studdwin." It was meant, thoughtlessly, as sort of a joke, but it was grim, in bad taste. Earlier that morning Sugg had raped one of the women in a village they were passing through, and Studdwin had gunned down a few peasants with his M-16. It was an unlucky village, they had been collaborating with the enemy. Tess had been appalled, barely able to contain her anger, and now, hours later, her feelings still hadn't cooled. She came to a halt and gave Simon a blank, hard stare: furious, and he couldn't blame her.

"Simon, you're so full of bullshit. You know that? If you were floating on a raft, on a river, you'd think you were drowning. And if you were drowning, you'd imagine you were up to your ears in flowers and on your way to paradise. With you, Simon, it's all upside down. Isn't it the truth? Tell me. Tell me I'm right."

She was right, what could he say? It had been dumb of him to mention Sugg and Studdwin the way he had, and he wanted, somehow, to apologize, to unsay his inane remark—but there was nothing, no words. All he could do was shrug.

She turned in a huff and marched on, and for a while they moved forward in an unfriendly silence. The trail narrowed, and he slowed and fell back, a few yards behind her. She had good chunky buttocks, which he wanted to get his hands on, but he doubted that that was ever going to happen. "Why are we fighting?" he finally brought out, feeling that something had to be said. "I don't want to fight with you. You're the only person around who doesn't think I'm going to blow up. I *know* I'm going

6

to blow up, and it's nice that you don't think so. So why are we having this altercation?"

"You're not going to blow up, Simon," she said matter-of-factly.

"I'd like to believe it."

"Believe it. It won't happen." She was still up ahead of him, pushing through twigs and branches as she forged forward on the overgrown trail.

"Maybe I *want* to explode. It would be a way to forget this damn jungle."

"Don't do it."

"You mean if I concentrate on not blowing up, I won't?"

"Sure."

"That's crazy."

"Simon," she said wearily, "there are some things you just have to believe."

"There are?"

"You better be*lieve* there are."

He shrugged, not eager to argue the point. Still, it sounded a little mad, not blowing up just because you believed you wouldn't. She was losing her mind. She had wanted to be a nun, but now she was a sharpshooter instead, hiking through the jungle, and, like the rest of them, she was going off her nut. One way or another, they all were. Studdwin and Sugg were clearly deranged, feasting on a homicidal urge that Simon suspected had been incubating in them for quite some time. And Eikopf, anybody could see, was far gone, though in a different way, with a brand of lunacy entirely his own. Signs of insanity were creeping up all around. Even me, Simon thought. Why should I be immune? Vain and Smudge were insane, and Trask too. Simon could see it in his eyes: the intense, iron-gray gleam. Firmness of the lips. Never a hesitation, never any doubt. The Ahab-like monomania. He wore contact lenses, and Simon knew, from scuttlebutt floating around, that as a young man he had wanted to be a pilot in a supersonic bomber, but the option was denied him because of a problem with his eyes, so he settled instead for a life in the field, and quickly became a Corps legend. There were stories, wild tales: how he went off on impossible missions and got himself killed, murdered, shot, blown to pieces, but in every instance he had managed somehow to rise from the dead and find his way home. Close calls with Muslim fanatics in Iran, headhunters in Africa, left-wing guerillas in Central America. He had survived nineteen days in the Gobi Desert without food. Somebody stuck a bayonet into him in Guatemala, and he lived. He had a wife that he rarely saw, a son who had died of a heart defect, and a daughter he had married off to a submarine commander. He didn't smoke or drink, and made a religion of starting off each day with knee-bends, waist-bends, and thirty push-ups. Simon found him irresistible—so wonderfully mad, so powerfully and mysteriously out of his mind, that it was impossible not to adore him. I will follow him wherever he leads, Simon thought. Through swamp and jungle and mud and hell. I will reach that bridge and blow it apart!

"Damn it," Tess said with a bittersweet lilt, glancing back at him over her shoulder, "do you want it?" She was digging into her pack for the can of insect repellent. "Here—take it."

"It's poison," he scoffed. "It doesn't kill bugs, it kills people. By the end of this tour, they want us all dead, nobody around to mouth off about this class-A supersecret covert incursion."

She jammed the container back into her pack. "Simon, you have a diseased mind."

"I practice," he said buoyantly.

"You practice too hard."

"I have to. I don't have much natural talent, so practice is essential."

She stared straight ahead. "Simon, I'm going to pass gas."

"Be my guest."

8

She passed gas, a low snorting sound.

"Well done," he said appreciatively.

"Watch your mouth, Simon."

"I spoke?"

"You have a nasty good-for-nothing mouth and one of these days I'm going to punch your teeth in."

"I'll punch back."

"You think so? I punch hard when I punch."

He liked it, the way she bantered, coming on strong. She was shorter than he was, and pretty, with luminous brown eyes and a dimpled chin—but she was sturdy, with wide shoulders and solid hips, and he figured she could pack a wallop. Again he wanted to touch her, rip off her clothes, make mad, passionate love to her, but it wasn't in the cards.

They walked on for a while in silence, through mud, matted grass, over rocks, gnarled roots of trees. Up ahead, Thurl was laboring along, tall and bulky, black, from Harlem, his powerful left hand carrying his automatic weapon as if it were a toy. A pink earphone was saddled to his right ear, feeding him tunes from a cassette. He was a lieutenant, but it was hard to tell, because he had long ago lost any enthusiasm he might have had for being a lieutenant, and now was more or less just going through the motions, waiting for his tour to be over. In a firefight he was ferocious, because he was convinced that his best chance for staying alive, when they took fire, was to fight with all the hell and fury he could muster. But when the shooting was over, he didn't give a damn about war or nonwar, discipline or anything else; he just shuffled along, his own man, amiable and easy, trying to survive the jungle. When he talked to the General, he almost never used the word *sir*. Trask couldn't help but notice, yet he put up with it because Thurl was so reliably fierce under fire—and that, Trask knew, was what mainly mattered, though he did make a mental note to kick Thurl's ass as soon as they got back to base.

A few yards ahead of Thurl was Merlin, who almost never

talked. But it didn't matter whether he talked or not, Simon thought, because when the pyroxene-T went off they would all be dead, great gusts of heat and flame radiating off from the center, reaching out, consuming. And he, Simon, would be the center: raging blades of fire grabbing hold of Thurl, and Merlin, reaching beyond them for Sugg, Studdwin, Vain. Even the General would not be safe. When I blow up, Simon figured, not without a twinge of satisfaction, they will notice, they'll never forget. The pack on his back seemed heavier every day, the straps biting into his shoulders. The pyroxene-T was barely ten pounds, but it seemed to weigh more as they got deeper into the jungle: cumbersome, a burden. Then again, maybe Tess was right. Maybe he would not blow up and they would make it to the bridge after all. It was out there somewhere, beyond the trees, silent, waiting for them, cool and arrogant in an unseen distance: lofty, smooth, desirable, forever theirs.

Tess lifted her head and listened. "Is that a chopper?"

Simon heard it too, the eggbeater sound. Distant, but drawing close. He thought it might be Sugarman, but it was too early yet for chow, and it wasn't Sugarman's sound—the engine with too much bass in it, not enough treble.

"It's Meyerbeer," Tess said.

"You think?"

"It has to be. Who else?"

They continued walking, straining to see through the overhead foliage. The trees thinned, and they glimpsed the rainbow-colored helicopter that Meyerbeer flew around in: not drab, standard, green-and-brown military camouflage, but bursting with color, vivid and wild, a psychedelic fantasy. Meyerbeer had picked it up from an Arab who dealt with both sides. The Arab had a hangar full of choppers left over from when the French had been around, and he specialized in Day-Glo jobs. Simon couldn't believe it hadn't been shot down yet. Such an easy target, sooner or later it had to go. He hated Meyerbeer, but he was also amazed by him. He was such an implausible shark, wheeling and dealing, flying around with his camera, shooting reel after reel, then taking off, disappearing. "I'm going to make a star out of you," he had told Simon back at Base Blue. "I'm going to make stars out of all you QUIF people—but out of you, Simon, I am going to make a superstar." And when Simon simply turned and walked off, not interested, Meyerbeer followed him anyway, with the camera. Simon could feel it zooming in on his back, as if it were drilling right into him, X-raying him, penetrating his clothes and skin and seeing right through to his vital organs, into his heart and brain, his darkest thoughts, making him feel a dim form of rage. If Meyerbeer ever got shot down, maybe Simon would grieve, but there was a good possibility that he would rejoice.

A few minutes more and they were out of the trees. The trail bent away across an open field, wide flat acres of knee-high grass. It was Meyerbeer all right, up there in the rainbow chopper, getting them all on film. The blond kid, Henry, not twenty yet, was at the controls, and Meyerbeer, in a flashy Hawaiian sportshirt, was leaning casually out of the hatchway with the camera anchored against his shoulder and an unlit cigar wedged into the corner of his mouth. Simon knew it was unlit because Meyerbeer never lit his cigars. He would walk around, lean, calm, relaxed, a slight stoop in his shoulders, and when the cigar started to unravel he'd throw it away and break out a fresh one. He used Ben Franklins, though every now and then he treated himself to a Soledad, or a Cuesta Rey. From the first moment they met, Simon knew he was an untrustworthy son of a bitch, of a special kind. There were some sons of bitches who came on like an M-60 tank, all guns blazing, but there were others who were smooth and easy, casual, laid-back, irresistible, who would cozy up to you, and before they were done they'd have your wallet, your watch, your pants, even a few pubic hairs, and when they strolled off, leaving you a little the worse for wear, you felt pleased and honored, as if somehow you had been granted a privilege. Meyerbeer

11

was one of those. Always cool and easy, with soft hazel eyes, wavy chestnut hair, a thick brown mustache that had a quality of artlessness about it, illusion of candor and bonhomie. The expression on his face almost changeless, close to a smile, as if the lips were about to part in a broad grin—but somehow the grin, the smile, only rarely materialized, kept in reserve for special occasions. Simon's mistrust ran so deep that he knew, despite his misgivings, despite his apprehension and doubt, that they were going to become hopelessly involved. They would punch and kick and stab at each other, yet they would get along, maybe even survive each other, because under it all there was an invisible bond: they were both from the Bronx, bound together by the inextricable fate of geographical origin.

The trail led up onto another low rise, and there was more than a mile to go before it hooked back again into the jungle. No trees, and not many shrubs. Simon felt naked. He could see Smudge far ahead, leading the way at point; then Sugg and Vain, Emma Sue with her medical kit, and Trask, Major Kleff, Merlin, Thurl, Studdwin. He glanced over his shoulder toward the rear, but Eikopf and Lieutenant Schlumm hadn't come out of the trees yet. The chopper hung stationary while Meyerbeer panned up and down the line, then it moved far ahead for some closeups of Smudge. Eventually it drifted slowly back and hovered at an angle behind Simon and Tess. It made Simon nervous. He didn't like helicopters, especially when they were behind him. He kept glancing back at it, checking it out, trying to assure himself that it wasn't about to come crashing down on him. It hung uncomfortably close, and he found himself wishing that Meyerbeer would go away forever: vanish, die, disappear, never come back. It would be a lucky day. Suddenly, as if Meyerbeer were somehow aware of his unkindly thoughts, the chopper swung around in a bold and risky arc, and Meyerbeer came on the horn, loud and brassy, booming down to him for all the countryside to hear. "HEY SIMON, CAN'T YOU PICK IT UP A LITTLE? MOVE YOUR ASS!

GIVE IT SOME SPARKLE! YOU'RE WRECKING MY WHOLE GODDAMN SEQUENCE!"

"What's wrong with my ass?" Simon, flustered, called out to Tess, his voice strident, shouting to make himself heard above the thumping roar of the chopper. "Do I have piles? Cancer of the rectum? Is my ass that bad?"

"You have a terrific ass," she sang out.

"I do? Really?"

She stopped walking for a moment and studied his rear. "Well, maybe not terrific, but not bad. An ass like that you could save for a rainy day."

He wasn't sure if he should be grateful or pissed off. "What's in an ass," he said philosophically, and, as he said it, Meyerbeer came on the horn again, the decibels showering the countryside like sudden rain. "COME ON, SIMON, CAN'T YOU IMPROVE THAT WALK? GIVE IT SOME LIFE. YOU'RE CARRYING THE PYROXENE-T. JESUS, YOU'RE THE SINE QUA NON OF THIS WHOLE SCENE. WITHOUT YOU, WE DON'T HAVE A SHOW. DON'T YOU KNOW THAT? CAN'T YOU DO SOME-THING FOR AMERICA? MAKE THEM REALIZE YOU'RE REALLY EAGER TO BLOW UP THAT BRIDGE!"

It was true—there was something wrong about the way Simon walked, and he knew it. It wasn't an abominable walk, but it was there to notice if you were looking for it: a slight wobbling motion from side to side, as if he had spent a lot of time riding a horse without knowing anything at all about how to ride, and now he was off the horse, making up his mind never to ride again. It wasn't quite as desperate as a Charlie Chaplin walk, or a Groucho Marx walk, yet it was plain that when Simon was on his feet he didn't have any moves that were about to win him any prizes. And it really burned him that Meyerbeer had noticed, and that he had the cheek to blare it to the world.

"I'm going to shoot the bastard down," Simon said with sudden abandon, unholstering his .44. Because he was in demolitions, lugging the pyroxene-T, they let him use a .44 Magnum instead of an automatic rifle, but at that particular moment he wished it were an M-16 that he had in his hands. He stood firm, legs spread apart, and held the gun with both hands—aimed, and, aware of his own absurdity, squeezed off a round, knowing the bullet would go nowhere, just spend itself through empty air. He was a lousy shot.

"SIMON," Meyerbeer agonized over the horn. "YOU CAN'T DO THAT. WHY ARE YOU SHOOTING AT ME?"

Simon squeezed off three more rounds.

"I'LL CUT YOU OUT OF THE PICTURE, SIMON. YOU WON'T APPEAR. YOU'LL BE SCRAP ON THE CUTTING ROOM FLOOR!"

Again Simon fired, but as he did so he heard another noise, and saw it: a burst of mortar in the open field, some fifty yards away, and then another burst, closer, clumps of dirt and grass flying in the air, the mortar thumping loud and vicious, louder than the sound of the chopper, and he saw them all running—the General, Sugg, Emma Sue, hustling for the trees that were too far away. He ran and Tess ran, and a round of mortar hit square on the trail up ahead of them, where Studdwin was running, and Studdwin was suddenly gone. When they passed the spot, they saw what was left of him: ruined meat and bone, his head smashed in, one arm gone, the torso wet with blood. They raced on, there was nothing to stop for, nothing there but the raw, brutal butchershop fact: flesh torn, garishly ripped away, bare bone showing through, vividly white. Simon had hated him for killing the peasants that morning—and, now that he was dead, he hated him for being dead. What he felt was a deep, rageful anger: anger at Studdwin, anger at the unseen enemy hurling mortar from God-knows-where, anger at Trask and Sugg, and at Meyerbeer who was somehow incongruously mixed up in it all, the seething, pounding madness, the steady thump-thump-thump of mortar dumping randomly all around them. He was gasping, sucking for breath, a pain in his chest and a sharp, stabbing pain in his side, a wild sense of panic, thinking he would never make it to the trees—his body hot, feverish, but inside his chest a rasping coldness like ice stabbing into his lungs, and he pushed, pushed, knowing any minute it could be him there on the ground like Studdwin, blood and splintered bone. A shell burst close by and the blast knocked Tess off her feet. He grabbed her and yanked her up, pulled her along, running.

Above them, Meyerbeer's chopper veered crazily, evading enemy fire—weaving, moving close and then pulling off, up then down, sideways, headlong, grazing the grass then swinging away. Meyerbeer was still in the open hatchway, strapped in, leaning out and getting it all on film: the mortar bursts, Studdwin's ruined body, Simon running, Tess running, the General running, mortar shells ripping the earth, gouging deep holes. "*ZOWWWW-EEEEEEEE,*" he yelled over the horn. "THIS IS IT! THIS IS IT! KEEP RUNNING, SIMON! MOVE THAT CRAZY ASS! BEAUTIFUL! BEAUTIFUL! WHAT A SEQUENCE! JESUS, IT'S A FUCKING WET DREAM!"

When he reached the shelter of the trees, Simon was panting wildly, dizzy with pain, groaning as he sucked air. He felt as if he had been hit in the chest with a sledgehammer. The mortar shells were still thumping away. He looked for Meyerbeer, wanting to fire another round at him, but the chopper was gone.

2 ◻ General Trask

SIMON'S EYES were dimly blue. His nose was slightly arched, and he had a small scar on his chin from a high school brawl that he had got the worst of. His lips were wide and full, the lips of his paternal grandfather who had been born in Cracow, from whom he also got his eyes, his nose, his thick, heavy eyebrows, and his hair that seemed willfully ambiguous, too light to be brown, but a shade too dark to be blond. He had never blown up a bridge before—not an enemy bridge, only the ones in training, in Alabama, puny old railroad trestles on condemned freight lines that had been out of service for fifty years. But at Camp Alpha they had called him in and said, "Simon, this one is yours, you're going to blow this bridge." They gave him the photos and specifications, and the pyroxene-T on flat spools, like rolls of black adhesive tape, then they delivered him to Base Blue and turned him over to General Trask. A bridge, an authentic, actual bridge: it was no Golden Gate, and no Verrazano, but it was a hell of a lot more impressive than the Willis Avenue Bridge that crossed from the Bronx into Manhattan. "Do I have to do this?" he asked.

"You sure do," they told him.

"Then I will," he said, accepting the photos and the pyroxene-T. He was ready and eager, but not exactly thrilled. A bridge so magnificent, it was a crime to knock it down. And yet the knocking down, the destroying, was itself a form of beauty. "Why not? This looks fantastic. I'll do it, it's mine!" Imagining what it would be like, the steel girders ripping apart, twisting, bending, the whole structure yanking loose and flying off, hurtling down into the gorge. Such a splendid bridge, out there in the sun, sturdy and big and yet light as a bird, the metal arch soaring from one rim of the gorge to the opposite rim, gleaming, and he would rig it with the pyroxene-T, send an electronic signal, and suddenly there would be nothing, empty space. He could do that, uncreate all that blissful metal: it was in his power. And they were sending him out to do it.

From Camp Alpha they got him by jeep over to Base Blue, more than an hour away, a rough, nerve-wracking ride, bouncing along

16

on dirt roads cratered from rockets and mortar. He dropped his gear at Barracks T, where the QUIF force was being assembled, then headed over to C Shack, where General Trask was headquartered, and waited a full hour before Trask would see him. He sat on a hard chair in a sun-filled room in which an acne-afflicted private was hunched over an old Remington, grinding out requisition forms. The room buzzed with flies. At first Simon was restless, fidgety, but then resignation set in and he allowed himself to be lulled by the slow clacking of the Remington and the buzzing of the flies. When Trask finally came to the door and signalled him to come in, he was in a mild stupor, almost asleep.

Trask filled the door frame, tall and hefty in his field fatigues, and to Simon, gazing drowsily, he seemed not an ordinary human being but an apparition, something swiftly delivered out of a dream. Simon snapped to attention.

"At ease, Corporal," Trask said, scanning him from head to toe, with no sign that he was pleased with what he saw. His voice rumbled like a rusty old pickup truck that needed a muffler. "You can come on in now." He withdrew into the bare barracks room he was using for an office, and Simon followed. It was a large room, with a couple of metal folding chairs and a plywood table, nothing on the table but an ashtray and a stack of pink computer cards. There was a topographical map tacked onto one wall, so big it extended right across one of the windows. Near the table, in dress uniform, sat Major Kleff, paring his nails and smoking a pipe, a wide band of sweet-smelling smoke curling up from the bowl. His eyes focused narrowly on his nails. Simon saw him, but hardly noticed him, because his whole attention was riveted on Trask. Trask was imposing, with puffy eyelids and plenty of lines across his forehead and at the corners of his mouth. He was heavy, but heavy in a muscular way, the way a linebacker is heavy, the kind of heavy you would never want to run smack up against. He'd been promoted in the field—and the field, he knew, was where he belonged. He liked the open air, sun and sky, and wasn't looking forward to the time when they might pull

17

him out of action and hide him away at a remote headquarters installation, behind a desk. Standing there now, in his battle fatigues, he seemed to be chomping at the bit, eager to get going, even though it would be a couple of days yet before they'd be ready to move out. Simon felt dwarfed in his presence.

Trask reached out and shook his hand, gripping it in a firm, possessive manner that made Simon feel uneasy. "Soldier, it's an honor to know there are men like you around to volunteer for missions like this one. It's going to be 'hell, but hell is nothing you give a damn about, right?" He spoke with soldierly directness, deep-throated, plenty of gravel in his vocal chords.

Simon hadn't volunteered, and it disturbed him, now, to hear that he had. If he had to blow up a bridge, he would blow it up and do it gladly, but if he had to volunteer to blow it, that was another thing altogether. "I didn't volunteer," he said.

"Is that a fact," Trask replied blandly, releasing Simon's hand.

"I *think* it's a fact," Simon said tentatively, realizing, as he said it, that it was the wrong thing to say.

Trask eyed him sharply. "Corporal, I *know* what you think. You think this is a stinking war and you hate it. Nevertheless, you're proud to be a part of it, you're doing your bit. Correct? Isn't that how you feel?" He had a way of opening his mouth wide and peeling his lips far back over his teeth when he talked. Simon noticed a lot of gold in his mouth, and, with the price of gold fluctuating as it was, he fleetingly wondered what Trask's mouth might be worth at that particular moment.

"No sir," he responded to Trask's question.

"Not proud?"

"I mean yes, sir. Very proud. But'I think a mistake has been made."

"No mistake, Corporal, no mistake at all. You're burning up and ready, eager to stick it to the monkeys where it hurts. You're ready to kill that bridge, aren't you?"

"Yes, sir. If that's what I have to do."

18

"Soldier, that's what you volun*teered* to do."

"If you say so, sir."

"Understand, Corporal, this is no run-of-the-mill commando raid off in the bush country, toss a few grenades then cut and run. This is the real thing, where we separate the men from the boys. You're lucky to be in on this one. In the old days, when they weren't afraid of calling a spade a spade, this is the kind of enterprise they would have characterized as a suicide mission." He glanced across to Major Kleff. "Right Major?"

"Right," the Major said, still paring his nails. He had a pale, sour face, a dilapidated look about the eyes. His mustache was like a fine pencil line drawn across his upper lip. The pipe was still in his mouth, but there was no more smoke issuing from the bowl. The tobacco had gone to ash, and Simon had the feeling that the Major, too, in some ways, had gone to ash. There seemed to be a deep inner sadness in him, a loneliness that would never be explained.

"So when you come right down to it," Trask said, leaning toward Simon, "we're glad to have you aboard. Men of your skill, with your talent and guts—you're what we need. We're glad you had the good sense and decency to offer your services."

"Did you say suicide mission?" Simon asked.

"I sure did, soldier. Does that turn you on?"

"This really is a mistake," Simon said.

"Corporal, the only mistake in this room is this here nonsense about your name."

"Which nonsense is that?"

"The nonsense on this card." He picked up a pink computer card and waved it. "It says here your name is Simon—" He began to pronounce the surname, but faltered, and contented himself with spelling it out: "G-R-Z-E-G-O-R-Z. Now that's what I call a mistake."

"That's my name, sir."

"It is?" Trask seemed partly surprised, and partly insulted. The Major cleared his throat. "It's a computer error," he inter-

19

jected, staring now not at his nails but at the sheetrock ceiling, which was in bad shape, covered with water stains. "Nobody's name begins with G-R-Z." He clucked his tongue. It was an odd, forlorn sound in the nearly vacant room, the clucking of the Major's tongue.

Simon pronounced the name for them. "Grzegorz. My name is Grzegorz." Trask asked him to say it again, and he did. Trask listened closely, his hand to his ear, then he made a stab at it, and mauled it badly. He looked to the Major, but the Major didn't even give it a try.

"Is that a Jewish name?" Trask said.

"No. It's Polish. My grandfather was from Cracow. He ran a furniture shop in the Bronx, on Jerome Avenue. He changed the name to Gregory because he thought Gregory's Furniture sounded like a better money-maker than Grzegorz's. But six months after he changed the name he went bankrupt, and the family went back to using Grzegorz. He made some pretty nifty furniture, all hand-made."

Trask stroked his chin. "I've had plenty of wild names under my command, some real doozies. Bladderpuss, Mastercock, Applestalk. There was a weasel-faced bastard named Kunthandler." He glanced at the Major, his eyes narrowing with reminiscence. "Remember Kunthandler? Wasn't he a prick? It was a great day for humanity when that tank rolled over him and ground him into sausage." He looked again toward Simon. "But a name like yours, Corporal, a G-R-Z tongue twister, forget it, I won't have it. As far as I'm concerned, for this mission, your name is Simon, first name and last, the only goddamn name you need. When I call you Simon, don't imagine I'm being chummy."

"I won't, sir," Simon said, wondering what name the General would choose to call him by if he ever did want to be chummy.

They were all standing, Simon at ease, and the General by the table, with the computer card in one hand and the other hand in his pocket. Major Kleff was working on his pipe, knocking out the ashes. Trask stared at Simon's face, examining it as if it were a thing, an object brought in for his inspection. There was no friendliness in his hard gray eyes. "Very complicated," he said, "this thing about your name. I should warn you, Corporal, I do not relish complicatedness. In all likelihood we are not going to get along, you and I. I look in your pasty blue eyes and see the eyes of a person I don't like and have no intention of ever learning how to like. If another demolitions man were available, I wouldn't touch you with a ten-foot pole." He put the computer card down on the table, setting it at a distance from the other cards, as if it might contaminate them. Then, with a brisk change of mood and a sudden smile, he added, "Nevertheless, hats off to you. I think it's a hell of a thing you've done, volunteering to come along. We need more men like you, Corporal, even though I can't stand your guts and hate your smell. Major, take him to the briefing room."

Simon didn't understand the remark about the smell. The only smell in the room was the smell of the Major's pipe tobacco, Mixture No. 79. Simon had smoked a pipe once, in high school, and it had made him sick. He had smoked a cigar too, and it had also made him sick. For a while he was busy with cigarettes, but he eventually got off them because he was convinced he was going to die of lung cancer—and lung cancer, from everything he'd heard about it, was a rotten way to go. Occasionally he smoked marijuana, and still did if a joint were being passed around, but it wasn't something that was a passion with him. He figured maybe it was time to try a pipe again, or at least a cigar. Because this was, after all, an occasion: heading into the jungle in the company of a genuine, legitimate, two-star, bona fide general. A general who was a hero-general. Out on the same trail together, tramping through the same mud, cutting through thickets, sweating, getting chewed by the same insects. It appealed to him, there could be something in this, something to remember. The General in all his moods, eating, defecating, sneezing, coughing, blowing his nose. His feet sinking into muck and compost. Muttering, losing his temper. Revealing his true self, whatever the true self of a two-star, raw-mouthed general who was a living, walking legend might possibly be. For better or worse, an occasion. An opportunity, even though he hadn't volunteered.

"Is that right?" Simon said, turning to Tess as they moved along on the trail. "Is this an opportunity, or is it a hideous, ballbusting, imbecilic mistake?" They were at a point where the trail went down into a hollow and ran parallel to a creek. Old trees cloaked in moss and hanging vines, the creek a narrow trickle, a low gurgling sound. The memory of Studdwin's exploded body was still fresh in their minds.

"It's a mistake, Simon," Tess said wearily, "and you should be glad. It isn't every day you run into a mistake that gives you a chance to die for your country." She hadn't volunteered for the mission either, not many of them had. Smudge and Studdwin had volunteered, and Sergeant Sugg, but not Thurl or Eikopf, and not Emma Sue. They were just there, random errors. Simon never found out if Merlin had volunteered, and figured Merlin probably couldn't say for sure whether he had or not, and probably didn't care.

"Mistakes are terrific things," Simon said with relaxed irony. "I never knew they could be so filled with delight." He remembered overhearing his mother mentioning to one of her friends once, when he was eight or nine, how his getting born had been sort of a mistake, though she hastened to add, in caressing tones, when she saw that he had overheard, that the mistake had not been altogether unwelcome. She'd been practicing rhythm, trying to avoid a pregnancy, using litmus and a thermometer, but something had gone wrong, bad litmus or a bad thermometer, and when she finally realized why her periods had stopped coming, she snapped the thermometer in half and flushed it down the toilet.

"What the hell," Simon sang out, kicking a stone and sending it bounding up the trail. "If getting born could be a mistake, why shouldn't the rest of it be a mistake too? We're in the wrong country, the bridge is a mistake. I'm a mistake. I don't belong here, I'll blow up by mistake and we'll all be dead."

Thurl, walking along nearby, turned and looked him up and down. "The only mistake, Simon, is yo' ass, like that turkey Meyerbeer said. Look at that piddly thing. You should be ashamed. I am em*bar*rassed to be part of this here mission with yo' ass."

Thurl grinned, Schlumm and some of the others laughed. They were beginning to get used to the idea that if the pyroxene-T in Simon's pack blew up they had no chance of escaping the fireball, so they weren't so cautious anymore about keeping their distance. It was variable, erratic. Sometimes they worried and stayed away, and other times nobody cared.

"His eyes too," Tess giggled. "His nose, all of him. His whole *body* is a mistake!"

Simon trudged along, failing to see the humor, but what the hell. A mistake is a mistake, he figured, you learn to live with it, even if the mistake is yourself. He began to whistle. The important thing, after all, was that they were winning the war. That, at least, was what Trask and the Major kept telling them. If they weren't winning, they would be losing, but that couldn't be, because losing was not one of the things they knew how to do. He wondered, though, about Trask, if he too might be a mistake. There were rumors that his last trip out had been a disaster, half of his force wiped out, and Simon wondered if he might be nothing but a has-been, washed up, rushing into the jungle just to prove he still had some of the old fire left, thumping his chest and ready to charge into hell if necessary, because otherwise they might put him on a shelf somewhere in Podunk, Iowa. In which case he was a mistake indeed, of the most dangerous kind. Studdwin was a mistake, dead back there on the trail, and it was altogether possible that Trask was not just a mistake but a nemesis, a wholesale aberration from which none of them would ever recover. Simon heard the sound of mortar rumbling in the distance, and felt an instinctive urge to hit the dirt and dig in. But it was miles away, far off, somebody else's worry.

3 ◻ The Old Man of the Lake

THE FORCE was code-named QUIF, an acronym for Quick Ununiformed Incursion Force, a name Trask had come up with back at Base Blue. The "quick" part of it was simply a misnomer, as they were traveling on foot. The "ununiformed" part referred to the fact that they were out there without dog tags or any of the standard equipment that might serve to identify them as an American commando force, because it was an officially maintained fiction that no American ground operations were in progress in the country they were headed for. The fatigues they wore had been manufactured in Hong Kong, and their ponchos and sleeping bags were Cuban issue purchased through an agent in Mexico. Their weapons were a mixed bag—Russian, American, Israeli, whatever. Sugg carried an Uzi, and Smudge used an AK-15. Trask used a British Armalite AR 18. Thurl had a Swiss SIG.

They had been out on the trail for three days, coping with mud and webbed vines, dense undergrowth, and now they came up against a mountain. It was a big one—not exorbitantly big, but not small either. The trail led up onto the flank and around to the other side, through landscape that was stark and rocky, difficult to negotiate. The trees thinned, and for a while they were out in the open, exposed. "If you get captured," Trask said, "don't tell them your name. Tell them you're Russian. Or Albanian. If you don't want them to pull out your fingernails and stick ice picks in your ears."

It had been meant as a joke, and Simon knew it was, yet he couldn't help but take it seriously. Could I pass for Russian, he wondered. Do I look Russian? People often thought he was Jewish, that he looked Jewish, so maybe it was not impossible he might pass for Russian, a Russian Jew. On the other hand, maybe he looked more like a Bronx Jew than a Russian Jew, and he was out of luck. Somebody would notice. At City College he had labored through a year of Russian, and now he scrambled to recall a few of the words and phrases he had learned. *Da, nyet. Baba, yolkla. Idyot snyeg. Idyot dozhd.* It was useless; he'd never pass.

A cloud leaned against the mountain, and for a while they were inside the cloud, wet and strangely warm. Then the cloud lifted. They followed the trail down off the mountain and into a shallow valley, where there was a lake. In a clearing there were thatched huts, about a dozen of them. Some livestock, a bunch of natives in baggy old clothes, straw hats. Old men and kids, women with babies. Smudge, at point, led the way, and the people by the huts watched, not moving, just standing there, waiting.

"Monkeys," Sugg said.

"But they're *our* monkeys," Lieutenant Schlumm was quick to point out. Meaning they were mountain people: monkeys, yes, but of a different strain, no friends of the monkeys who were swarming in from the north and causing all the trouble. And maybe more than just a different strain: a different race, a different brand.

"A monkey's a monkey," Sugg grumbled. "I say shoot 'em all."

"And I say maybe you oughta shut yo' hole," said Thurl, who could get away with talking that way to Sugg because he was big, powerful, and if they got into a brawl it was clear that Sugg would not have had an easy time.

Still, Sugg didn't back off easily, he rarely did. He snapped open his knife, a sizable switchblade, and darted it at an oak about five yards off. It stuck, and quivered. "Sure," he said, retrieving the knife and caressing the blade, "there are holes and holes. Right, Thurl? Which side is your hole on? You with the monkeys or with Uncle Sam?"

"I'm hungry," Smudge said. "Where the hell is Sugarman?"

Sugarman should have been there already, waiting at the lake. They had expected to see his helicopter idling there, on the open grass, and Sugarman himself, with his big round face, smiling because he always smiled, waving at them with his thick, pudgy arms. But no Sugarman, no food. They went close to the lake and put down their guns, unburdened themselves of their packs, and stretched out. Emma Sue took off her clothes and went into the water. Simon had never seen her naked before. She was beautiful. A lean, long body, with ample breasts, and slender thighs. It turned him on, looking at her. During the night she had slept with Vain, and the night before that she had been with Thurl. Simon wondered when it would be his turn, if ever. She splashed around a lot and mostly was underwater, so he didn't see too much of her for too long. Tess didn't take off her clothes. She took off her boots, rolled up her pants, and dipped her feet. She slept alone, and had a reputation for being a virgin.

"Right up there," Vain said, pointing with his comb to a high spot across the lake. He was always busy with the comb, running it through his thick black hair, which was a little fuller than regulations allowed, but nobody objected because he was good with a gun and had killed plenty of monkeys. For a moment he stopped combing and used the comb to point with: "That's where we put the hotel, right up there on that knoll." He was making plans for after the war, figuring he'd come back and make a million. He had in mind a nine-story lakeside hotel with a rooftop band playing twenty-four hours a day so the lake would always be filled with the sound of music. Music, and people swimming, splashing around, having a good time.

"Who the hell is that?" Trask said, pointing toward an old man about forty yards off, sitting on a rock at the edge of the lake. His feet hung down in the water and he was leaning forward, elbows on his knees, head forward and down. He wore only a white loincloth. His skin was yellowish bronze, his legs skinny. Even from that distance they could see how gaunt he was, ribs protruding, cheeks sunken the way the cheeks of old people collapse when they have no teeth. His hair was mostly gone.

Lieutenant Schlumm studied him through the distance, and nodded slowly. It was coming back, something he'd read about, something he had researched. "It's a holy man," he said, a scholarly gleam lighting up his eyes. "This tribe keeps a holy man, they call him the Holy Man of the Lake." Schlumm was thin and angular, not much with a gun, but he knew about the monkeys and was even able, in a halting way, to speak their language. That was why Trask had brought him along. He knew about the mountain monkeys and the monkeys from the north, as well as about the tree monkeys, the town monkeys, and the monkeys from the south, and the other monkeys, the ones that moved around in tunnels under the jungle floor. He had learned about the monkeys while he was studying anthropology at the University of Chicago.

"Looks like a common ordinary orangutan to me," Trask said.

They moved closer, going slowly—Trask, Schlumm, Sugg, and the Major, and Simon not far behind. "Careful," Trask warned. "The bastard might have a grenade."

As they drew near, they saw that the old man was spitting. He spat in the water, and, a few moments later, he spat again. And again. The spitting was being done with regularity, the old man moving his tongue in his mouth, working up the saliva, and expectorating at what appeared to be fixed intervals. "What the hell," Trask demanded, turning to Schlumm for an explanation.

"He's spitting in the lake, sir."

"I can damn well see that for myself."

"It's a ritual they have. Once a week, every week, they send their holy man out to spit in the lake. Otherwise, they think it will dry up. It's an ancient custom. Before there was this holy man, there was another, it goes back a long time. There have been holy men spitting in this lake for centuries."

Trask frowned. "The lake would dry up? Is that what you said?"

"That's what they believe, sir."

"No wonder these people are in the trouble they're in. How long do you figure he sits there spitting?"

"I don't know."

"All day, I bet. When he runs out of spit, they roll out another old man. Maybe they have a little old lady who spits." There was an inscrutable cast to Trask's expression, at once wrathful and sardonic, rancorous, indignant, yet strangely calm, the serenity of someone who knows clearly what he is about.

They approached cautiously; then, a slight distance away, they simply stood and watched. The old man seemed not to notice. His posture was unchanged from the time they had first seen him.

"What a dreary son of a bitch," Trask said, darting a glance at Simon, who had come alongside. "How old would you say he is?"

Simon looked hard at the old man and shrugged. "About seventy," he guessed.

"I bet he's over ninety," Trask said, not taking his eyes off the old man. "Give him a burst. Put the bastard out of his misery."

Simon was stunned. "Me?" He stared incredulously, looking for some sign from Trask that the order was not an order but a joke, a mere flippancy not intended to be taken seriously.

"No, not you," Trask grunted. "We're saving you for the bridge. Schlumm, you do it. You're the expert on these people."

Schlumm paled, his voice quavered. "Sir, the man is a civilian."

"I can see that. Do it!"

"I can't, sir."

"Damn you, Schlumm. *Do it*."

28

But Schlumm remained immobile, less from choice than from simple paralysis, a sudden and incomprehensible inability to move. Something deep inside him had disconnected. While Schlumm hung there, Sugg stepped forward, raised his weapon, and fired. A sudden splotch of blood appeared at the old man's temple and he pitched forward into the lake. His head and arms went under, but his torso came to rest on a rock and his rump projected up out of the water. The water reddened with his blood.

Trask had been right about the grenade. It was there on the flat rock where the old man had been sitting. It had been concealed under a fold of his loincloth. He had not pulled the pin.

Trask glared at Schlumm, his hard gray eyes beaming out of his wrinkled face like electronic sensors. "Cross me again, dammit, and it'll be you down there in the water with a hole in your head." Schlumm was still motionless, rooted, and Trask leaned toward him. "Understand?"

Schlumm said nothing, and Trask broke away, heading back toward the huts. "Now these people will realize that a lake is a lake," he said, loud, pontifical. "It's about time they were ripped out of their superstitions and brought into the twentieth century. A lake is a lake, and a dead old man is a dead old man. It's time these doughheads learned to shift for themselves."

Schlumm was still dazed, looking as if he'd been shot in a vital organ but somehow had managed to avoid falling down. Sugg stood relaxed, easy, an implausible smile on his wide, fleshy face as he stared down at the body in the lake. Simon looked at Schlumm, and at Sugg, then headed back to where Tess, Thurl, and the others were. The day was unchanged, cloudless. The villagers stood by their huts, they hadn't moved. They'd seen the shooting, but their faces, deadpan, registered no reaction. The sun still burned in the sky, low on the horizon, as if nothing had happened.

Emma Sue came out of the lake, her red hair dark from being wet, made almost black from the water. Slender thighs and beautifully contoured buttocks, her belly handsomely flat. Arms and shoulders sprinkled with freckles, water running down her spine and legs. Simon watched as she dried off and pulled on her clothes, and he felt nothing, no desire. He wished it were Sugg dead back there in the water, or Trask—anybody, even himself, anyone but that pathetic old man.

Sugarman was half an hour late with the food. The big green helicopter lumbered in noisily, scaring the livestock. Back in New Jersey, in Trenton, he had run a delicatessen. He had a round face and wore thick, wire-rimmed glasses that gave him an owlish look. Always smiling, the smiles coming up from some inner well of good feeling that was deep inside him. "Better late than never," he called, climbing out of the chopper, but already he was catching abuse from Smudge. "You think we got all day? Chrissake, time is time. You know about busting your hump on the trail and marching against a schedule?"

"I'm so damn hungry I could eat a water buffalo," Thurl said.

Sugarman opened the food canister and silenced them all with the aroma of sirloin in an onion sauce. The previous day it had been swordfish, and the day before that it was veal scaloppine. "Eat," he said. "Stuff your mouths. For you guys, nothing too good." They lined up and dug in, loading the food onto paper plates, and settled down on the grass, at a distance from the thatched huts. They felt a little uncertain about the mood of the natives, who were still standing around in the vicinity of the huts, looking on. Along with the steak, there were boiled potatoes, pickled beets, warm rolls with plenty of butter. And, for a finish, Sugarman rolled out a pile of chocolate éclairs. "Do I deliver," he said, "or do I deliver?" While they filled their plates, he stepped over and had a few words with Merlin; then, still smiling, he got back into the chopper, and was on his way, skimming across the treetops, low across the flank of the mountain, and was gone.

Simon saw Sugg coming out of one of the huts, a satisfied expression on his face. His helmet off, his hair carrot-colored, cropped so close his scalp showed through. He was buttoning his pants, ambling over to where the rest of them were spread out on the grass. "These female monkeys," Simon overheard him saying to Smudge, "they wrestle like hell, but once you get inside 'em they can't get enough. What's for dessert? Is that éclairs? Jesus, I lose my fucking mind over éclairs." He went over to the bin of éclairs that Sugarman had left behind, picked up three, and wolfed them down. Then he picked up another one and stepped over to Merlin, who was sitting on a log, alone, done eating, his paper plate on the grass near his feet. He was narrow-shouldered and small, and strangely withdrawn.

"Hey Merlin—want an éclair?"

Merlin looked at it in a distanced manner, as if it were a piece of hardware, something that might be useful, or perhaps might not. "No," he finally brought out. "I don't think so."

"Too bad," Sugg said. "Anyway—good luck." He reached out and pushed the éclair into Merlin's face, cream oozing out onto his nose and eyeglasses, across his mouth and chin. Merlin didn't react. He merely sat there, yellow cream covering what was otherwise a blank, expressionless face. Slowly, he reached into his pack for his roll of toilet tissue, and wiped himself clean.

Thurl approached Sugg and looked at him with disgust. "What the hell'd you do that for?"

"For good luck," Sugg sneered. "Didn't you hear me say *good luck?* He's a good kid, he'll be all right. Just needs some roughing up to bring him around." He lifted a leg and cut wind, and headed back to the bin for another éclair. Thurl was left standing there, thumbs hooked into his cartridge belt.

Sugg had grown up on an onion farm in New Jersey. His mother was still alive, living on the farm, though the farm wasn't much of a farm anymore. She had suffered most of her life from diabetes. Sugg's father died when Sugg was fourteen, but Sugg had already been involved in the run of the farm, and, even though his father was gone, he had been able, with his mother's help and the help of a few transient workers, to keep the farm going at least on a marginal basis. Besides the onions there were chickens, about a hundred of them. Sugg had been in charge of the chickens from the time he was seven, feeding them, keeping the coop in repair, gathering the eggs, and, for Sunday dinner, catching two or three, chopping off their heads, plucking the feathers and ripping out the inner organs, getting the birds properly disemboweled. It was something he enjoyed doing. For a while, when he was seven or eight, he used to walk around the house giving out with a squeaky singsong: "Chop the head, chop the head, make the chicken pret-ty dead." His mother had it on tape, on an audio cassette, and the cassette was still there in the old rotting house, lost somewhere in a closet filled with old magazines, faded photographs, yellowed newspaper clippings, socks that needed mending, insulin needles, old shoes, back issues of *National Geographic*, shirts that nobody wore anymore, tulip bulbs, bent spoons, moth-eaten sweaters, old Christmas cards. *Chop the head, chop the head*, his seven-year-old hands going deep inside, wrenching out the intestines.

The QUIF force finished their meal, and the villagers were still over by the huts, standing, looking on. An elderly man, gray-haired but sturdy, tall, came forward, leading a girl out of the hut that Sugg had been in. She wore a faded blue dress, soiled and torn, black hair hanging down over her shoulders. The man might have been her father, or an uncle. He led her to an open space between the huts and the QUIF force, and pushed her to the ground. He stepped away from her, picked up a stone, and threw it hard, hitting her shoulder as she turned away. Then the other villagers came forward, with stones, and Trask, seeing what they were about, stood up and fired a burst above their heads. They froze, but didn't drop the stones, just stood there, staring at Trask. "Talk to them," Trask said to Schlumm.

Schlumm went over to the gray-haired man and had an exchange with him. The man pointed at Sugg. When Schlumm returned, he said, "They want Sugg to kill her. If he doesn't, they will."

"Tell them to go back in their huts," Trask said.

Schlumm told them, but no one budged.

Trask moved toward them, firing on the ground, bullets from the Armalite skipping about near their feet. They drew back, slowly, stepping backward, then turned and broke for the huts, disappearing inside. "Now let's get the hell out of here," Trask said, "since these bastards are so damned unfriendly." They gathered themselves together and moved out, leaving the girl on the ground, in her faded blue dress, gazing after them. The sun went down, and in the light that remained they made a three-mile march before they bivouacked.

"They'll kill her anyway," Schlumm said to Simon, as they hiked along. "If not now, tomorrow. Some of these tribes have some strong ideas about virginity." Sugg, nearby, cleared his throat, gathering phlegm from deep in his lungs, and spat, just missing one of Schlumm's boots. Schlumm didn't notice, or perhaps did, but chose to let it pass.

4 ❑ The Tree

MERLIN'S REAL NAME was Gary Alfalfa, but everybody called him Merlin, including the General, because he carried the black box, which wasn't black but a dark shade of gray. He was short and slight, blond-haired, with a long bony nose and black-rimmed glasses, and a smooth, beardless face. Most of them, if they could have been somewhere else, would have been somewhere else, but Merlin seemed not to care. He had a quiet, un-

33

ruffled manner, never showing any anxiety or stress, even when they were under fire—his blue eyes coldly remote behind thick, tinted lenses, his face exhibiting no emotion, only a numbness, a dreamy preoccupation. The only time there was ever a spark of life in him was when he was working at the box, keying messages into it and waiting for it to talk back to him on its miniscreen. Major Kleff could do some primitive playing around with the box, getting locational data out of it and using it as a communications device, and Simon, having had an APL course at City, suspected that in a pinch he could probably work some basic functions on it; but Merlin was the only one among them who knew the box from the inside, how it worked and moved, the only one who could reach its soul and put it through its paces, making it think, talk, speculate, analyze, calculate, make it ponder and dream.

The box was the nerve center of the mission. It told them where they were and how to get where they were going. It warned them when there were monkey patrols nearby, and it detoured them around monkey strongholds. It was a microcomputer with a fix on a communications satellite stationed overhead—it received and processed any strategic information the satellite had to offer, and it could also bounce signals off the satellite and establish contact with headquarters in the southeast quadrant, or with the command base at Alpha. Through the satellite hookup, it was in touch with memory banks around the world, and there were bundles of functions it could perform either in combination with its support systems or on its own. It kept time, clocked the days, gave them compass direction, computed distances, planned the bivouac points where Sugarman was to helicopter in with their meals, functioned as a two-way radio, and kept a watch on the weather. It could also play chess, translate Sanskrit, predict an eclipse, name the director and lead actors of any Hollywood movie, and list the annual batting averages of anyone who had ever played in the major leagues. It weighed about ten pounds, and Merlin carried it in a satchel equipped with a shoulderstrap.

Simon wasn't particularly comfortable with Merlin's abstract manner, his habit of almost never talking, but it was something he could put up with. As far as Simon was concerned, Merlin could sit in a tree with his black box, if he wanted, and never be heard from again, and if he didn't want to sit in a tree, that was all right too. Live and let live, Simon figured. Merlin was only Merlin—drab, dim, dull, no ball of fire, but harmless enough. Eikopf, though, was convinced that Merlin was a menace. For reasons that never became fully clear, he had conceived the notion that Merlin was a monkey in disguise, and that the black box was an insidious device that was going to get them all killed. "The tight-lipped bastard," he said, quietly furious. "Five days out on the trail, and where the hell's the bridge?" His dark eyes blazed with a strange, preternatural brilliance. "That damn black box is taking us down the throat of hell—that's where we're headed. But before this is over, mark my word, God will fix that fucker's ass. If God doesn't, I will."

Eikopf was plainly insane; Simon had spotted it the first time they met. There was a weird radiance in his eyes, a hint of mania crudely emphasized by the sinister slant of his crooked nose and the bulging prominence of his bony forehead. He carried his head tilted slightly to one side. "Do you believe in the resurrection of the body?" he had asked Simon back at Base Blue, when they first met, and, when Simon hesitated, a little surprised by the question, Eikopf rushed at him with an avalanche of verbal abuse, reproaching him for being godless, gutless, mindless, an unthinking dupe of the forces of sin and corruption. "I can tell from your eyes," he said, "and the shape of your mouth. You know what you believe in? You believe in mud and insects, and the goddamn jungle. You believe in getting blown to pieces and getting the rest of us blown to pieces with you. Ever since you were a punk kid, you've been planning this, putting it together. This hell is something that's been on your mind a long time. I know you, Simon Grzegorz—*I see right through you.*"

Eikopf was the only one in the force who could utter Simon's last name correctly, without mauling it and torturing it to death, and, perhaps because of that, Simon felt a lot more comfortable with Eikopf's madness, his hate and paranoia, than with Merlin's eerie silence. There was something about Eikopf that was oddly appealing, something that Simon couldn't quite put his finger on. Whatever it was, he found it very comforting to hear his name pronounced correctly, even if the mouth that did the pronouncing belonged to Eikopf, whose mind was adrift in another universe.

As they moved deeper and deeper into the jungle, it became obvious to all of them that Eikopf was an anomaly, he didn't belong. The rest of them each had a special reason for being on the mission. Simon because he could handle the pyroxene-T, and Emma Sue because she knew about lyncomycin and tri-methoprim. Merlin because he carried the black box, Sugg because he loved to kill and was so good at it. The General because he was a general, and the Major because he was a major. Schlumm because he could talk monkey-talk. Tess because she was a sharpshooter. But with Eikopf there was a lacuna, a gap: no reason whatsoever why he might be there. He was no good with explosives, and was useless with a gun. He had spent three years in the Corps Band, playing piano and glockenspiel, and how or why he had ever got transferred out of the band and into action, onto this mission, was simply unfathomable. Just another one of those things, Simon figured. Another mistake.

One night, in bivouac, while most of them were asleep, Eikopf stole over to where Merlin was stretched out, and got his hands on the black box. He was planning to go off into the trees with it and smash it to hell. As he bent down and grabbed it, Merlin's right hand came flashing up with a screwdriver, and the hard metal stabbed into Eikopf's thigh. Eikopf gave out a yell that woke the camp—and lucky it did, because his hands went fast to Merlin's throat, he would have killed him if he hadn't been dragged off.

The wound in Eikopf's thigh proved not to be serious, and

Emma Sue was able to fix him up with an antibacterial agent and a few stitches. Major Kleff was all for sending him back to base, but Eikopf was bent on staying with the mission, if only to get another chance at Merlin's throat. After giving the matter a moment's thought, Trask, reluctant to diminish the size of his force, decided to hold onto him. He had already lost Studdwin, and even though Eikopf was incompetent with a gun, he was at least something, a moving body. In a firefight he could pull a trigger and make noise.

They pressed on, through trees and undergrowth, smells of rotting leaves, birds erupting into flight out of gnarled and twisted branches. Then—suddenly, it seemed—they were out of the trees and onto a low rise. It was two days after they had been at the lake, where Sugg shot the old man. A vast, grassy plain spread out in front of them for a couple of miles. There was nothing on the plain, just grass, and, in the far distance, a single huge tree. "Jesus," Simon said, with boyish amazement. "Look at it. Just look at that tree! Isn't it wild?" They moved onward, the plain was deserted. No animals, not even any birds circling around. No snakes or fowl rustling in the grass. An immense, lonely calm, and the tree in the distance looming like something that had surfaced out of a dream. They all felt the strangeness. Eikopf was in a dazed silence, walking slowly. He seemed rapt, possessed.

It was an extraordinary tree, tall and round, dense with leaves, spreading out like an immense green cloud. So perfectly round that it looked as if a gardener had been trimming it and taking care of it for years. There seemed to be strings of white flowers hanging down from the branches. "It's so beautiful," Emma Sue said. "I didn't know they could make trees so beautiful." When they got closer, though, they saw that the flowers were not flowers but skeletons, each hanging from a noose around its neck. The bones had been picked clean by buzzards and other scavengers.

No clothes, no shoes, nothing, no ID tags. It was a tree full of death. The only things left on the skeletons were wristwatches.

There was a low, rumbling sound, and Meyerbeer's chopper rose into view above the far edge of the jungle. It crossed the plain and closed in on the tree, circling slowly while Meyerbeer worked with the telephoto lens. Then the chopper landed and Henry jumped out from behind the controls, and Meyerbeer also got out, slopeshouldered and tall. In his slow, shuffling manner he strolled over to the tree and got some close-ups from the ground. "What a fantasy," he said in a subdued tone, with the oddly muted enthusiasm that Simon was beginning to recognize as part of the Meyerbeer style. "A tree like this, it really has meaning. Doesn't it sock you? Important footage. Really important footage. If you tried to invent something like this, you wouldn't come up with it in a million years. Maybe two million." He shot a few frames of Eikopf, who was still entranced, gazing at the tree with a peculiar mixture of awe and disgust. And he also got some footage of the General as he circled the tree with a bold stride, surveying the skeletons with matter-of-fact deliberateness, the expression on his face severe, firm, glowingly defiant. Sugg cut one of the skeletons down, and Trask examined the wristwatch. It was Swiss. He looked at the teeth, and spotted a stainless steel crown. "They're not ours," he said. "Probably Russians, that band of armed advisers we heard was in the area. The Russians are pretty big on stainless steel." He glanced away, gazing toward the horizon, where the edge of the jungle rose like a low, green hump, and for a moment Simon saw him in silhouette against the sky, the stern jaw, broad shoulders, thick body: big-chested, brisk and classy in his black beret, his more than fifty-year-old face alight with vigor and earnestness, a mysterious sense of urgency and drive welling up from deep inside. "On the other hand," he added, "maybe they're Cubans. I hear the Cubans have been using Russian dentists lately. Maybe they're Bulgarians, or that team of Albanians that flew in last month. Whoever they were, somebody didn't like them. Good riddance."

Simon walked around the tree and counted twenty-seven skeletons. Tess counted twenty-nine. Major Kleff counted thirty-three, and that became the official count that went into the log. Merlin plugged the information into the black box. The box was good for that too: it was their diary, their journal, the electronic tabulator of their daily plight. Everything went into it, even the flap with Eikopf, his attempt to destroy the box, though Merlin coyly suppressed the part about his stabbing Eikopf in the thigh with a screwdriver.

"It gives me the creeps," Tess said. "That could be us strung up there on that tree."

It made Simon uneasy too. There was no knowing who was responsible. The mountain people, probably, or the monkeys from the east who had a reputation for sadism, or the monkeys from the south, or one of the jungle tribes that were part monkey and part something else. The tribes were unreliable. They could be your friends one day, you could be fighting side by side with them, then they could turn on you and you could be cutting each other to ribbons.

"Whoever it was," Tess said, "I hope we don't meet up with them. Why did they take the clothes and the IDs but leave the watches?"

It was peculiar. But everything was peculiar, one way or another. "Maybe they had watches of their own and just didn't need any," Simon said. "Or maybe they don't use watches, because they don't know how to tell time. What do they need time for? They have all the time they need, and they know time stinks."

Eikopf nodded slowly, staring up at the skeletons. "God gave those deadbeats what they deserve," he said. "God takes care. He knows who his friends are."

They moved out, leaving the skeletons in the tree. They headed across the plain toward the far line of trees where the jungle began again. Sugg and Vain stayed behind and caught up with them later. They were up in the tree, grabbing the watches. They got some Bulovas and a few Seikos, a Timex, but mostly it was unfamiliar brands from Eastern Europe—a few gold pieces, but not many.

As they neared the jungle, Simon looked back at the tree, far off, and again the skeletons looked like long, cumbersome chains of white flowers.

5 ❑ The Storm

GENERAL TRASK hated the jungle, and he often said so, with undisguised loathing. "I hate it. The only redeeming thing about being in a jungle is that you know there will come a time when you will be out of it and someplace else. If you're lucky." He liked being out of doors, active, part of a ground operation—but the jungle, with its insects and vermin, dense leaves and constant threat of ambush, and the persistent, maddening humidity and sweat, didn't exactly square with his notion of being in the field. There had been better times, better places. The jungle connoted a deviousness, a shadowy, underhanded kind of warfare alien to the straightforward, blustery approach to strategy he had always been comfortable with. He could die there, and the thought that his body might become part of the rank mud and clay that he sloshed through, compost, turned his stomach.

Major Kleff hated the jungle too. So did Thurl and Schlumm. But Simon, at moments, was enthralled. Trees! Mud! Strange, mind-boggling flowers! It beat running up and down the charred staircases in burned-out tenements in the Bronx, something he had done quite a bit of when he was a kid. And it beat playing around down by the tracks where the Amtrak trains came barreling through, which was something else he had done a lot of. He wasn't sure it beat the egg creams and smell of chocolate malteds and candy mingling with the aroma of Mr. Marx's cigar in Marx's Candystore on a corner of the Grand Concourse, but it came close. It beat Freshman Comp and Chem 100 at City College, and it was a hell of a lot more exciting that Psych 248, Math 246, History 231, and Soc 241. Nevertheless, he had enjoyed the course in English Romantic Poetry—Blake, Keats, Shelley, and the rest of them, though he recalled, vaguely, that he had been practically the only one in the course who was getting a kick out of it. Maybe, Simon wondered, maybe there is something wrong with me. It lingered for him, always, as a possibility, at the edge of consciousness, the suspicion, fear, that he might be odd, different, unlike the others. And, for that reason, he wondered if it was time for him, possibly, in the wet, stinking wilderness of the jungle, to step on a land mine and explode.

"Trust no one," Trask said, drawing a moral from the skeletons they had found strung up on the tree. "That's the lesson to learn. Somebody with a strange face comes up to you, don't trust him. Somebody you know turns up, don't trust him either. Somebody runs out of one of these straw huts and offers you free tea, free coffee, French fries, a hamburger, free sex—don't trust them. Don't trust the guy walking next to you. Don't trust yourself. Check and doublecheck. Your mother and father turn up, be suspicious. The pediatrician who delivered you when you were born turns up, don't trust him either. God turns up, think twice about it." Eikopf, removing a leech that had attached itself to his leg, nodded to himself and smiled.

Check and doublecheck, it was a mean war. A sniper fired, and they lost Smudge. He took it right through the head. He had

41

been up there at point without a helmet on, the bullet tore away a portion of his skull. Sugg got the sniper, and when he fell out of the tree, dead, Sugg went close up and emptied the clip into him, firing nonstop, and then another clip. Smudge and Studdwin were the only ones in the force that he had felt at all close to. Back at Alpha, they had been drinking buddies, sloshed on beer, bombed out on bourbon. Studdwin gone, and now Smudge: Sugg blasted away and the sniper's body ripped apart, shredded, raw meat for jackals, vultures, anything that happened along.

They buried Smudge in a shallow grave, then Sugg took over at point. They pushed on along the trail, and when they were about an hour out from where Smudge had been killed, Simon realized that he couldn't remember what Smudge looked like. He worked hard at it, trying to recall the eyes, mouth, nose, but it was all a blur. Smudge had disappeared from view. It bothered him. Studdwin too. Try as he did, he couldn't remember Studdwin's face.

He looked at Thurl, and wondered if he would forget him too if he got killed. He liked Thurl, he didn't know exactly why. He wouldn't want to forget him. Big and overweight but solid, not blubbery, just big. His features coarse, large: wide nose, massive jaw, the skin a dark shade of brown, gleaming with sweat, lips thick and purplish. And teeth, too, terrific teeth. Simon's teeth were riddled with cavities, filled again and again with silver, but Thurl's were white and straight, and, like everything else about him, big. When he opened his mouth, laughing, yawning, it was all white in there. Simon figured that if Thurl ever got killed, it would be the teeth he would remember, and the pink earphone, the way his mood lightened when he plugged in one of his cassettes. He had three cassettes that he played over and over: the Dugan City Diggers, a Cape Cod group with a tightly crafted blues idiom; the Everhearts, a smooth, quiet sound with weirdly mystical reverberations; and the Ash Berries, who specialized in a complicated, postmodern type of jazz, pieces like "Riverhouse Days" and "Pied Piper," very pyrotechnical stuff. Thurl had lent

Simon the headphone once, and he enjoyed listening. The Ash Berries were into something abstract and difficult, but they had feeling, there was something there.

When Meyerbeer caught up with them again, they were in bivouac, settling down for the night. The smell of gun oil, wet boot leather. It was dusk, the last light in the sky vanishing fast. Meyerbeer wanted some footage of them in camp: the way they bedded down, the conditions they had to cope with, night animals and such. The cigarettes they smoked. Fireflies, hum of crickets. Sleeping bags made of lightweight synthetic, protection against mosquitoes and rain.

They were spread out on a grassy slope at the edge of a large pond. Behind them was a cliff honeycombed with small caves. According to the black box, there were no monkeys within a twenty-mile radius—not, at least, in any sizable concentration. The rainbow chopper came in with landing lights ablaze, a wild, alien bug, noisy and horrific. It was risky stuff, flying around in the near-dark, with very little space to put down in. Simon expected sooner or later the chopper would smash into a tree and Meyerbeer would go up in a ball of flame. He was waiting for it to happen. Not hoping for it, exactly, simply waiting, expecting.

The first time Simon met him, back at Base Blue, he thought he was with a network, or with MGM, because of the slacks, sportshirt, the unmilitary manner in which he walked and talked. But Meyerbeer was no civilian. He was a master sergeant attached to Outgroup M, the media subcommand of the Corps' Communications Unit. Officially, he was at work on a documentary to be used as promotional material for the Corps' recruitment program. And as a sideline, Simon learned, he was selling action footage to the networks—to network cameramen who were shy of getting too close to the action—and was raking in a tidy profit for himself. But that was only a small part of it. The really big thing he was into, what he sometimes referred to as his major opus, was a full-length movie, a private venture that he pursued obsessively, collecting footage for a wide-screen feature that he figured for a blockbuster at the box office. He planned to distribute it on the international market as a private citizen, and hoped to reap a few million out of it. It was a movie about the bridge—the struggle to reach it, and the struggle to destroy it. The bridge as a symbol, an emblem of heroic effort and achievement, but also as an expression of despair, though the despair part of it was something that had only transiently flickered in his mind.

It was a complicated enterprise. With the help of a lawyer friend who had an office in Toledo, he had set up Vidwar Incorporated in Hollywood, Bomburst International in West Berlin, and Fission Unlimited in Tokyo. The plan was for Vidwar to make the film, Bomburst to distribute it, and Fission to promote it and eventually arrange the television rights. The three corporations were a kind of shell game, Meyerbeer's way of keeping the GAO off his back while he spent Corps funds on a project that was essentially a piece of private enterprise. And farther down the line, when the receipts came rolling in, the existence of the three corporations would serve as a handy mechanism for keeping the tax people confused. For the present, he was using Corps film and Corps equipment to make the movie, and the only investment expense he had was the five thousand dollars that he handed to General Trask, from Vidwar, in return for a written release giving Vidwar full rights over any footage that was shot during the march to the bridge. Trask signed the release and passed the five thousand along to Corps headquarters, and the GAO congratulated both Trask and the Corps high command for their foresight and prudence in the management of Corps revenues and resources.

It had not been easy, though, for Meyerbeer to obtain Trask's signature. Besides the five thousand that was to go to the Corps, Trask wanted fifty thousand for himself, in cash, deposited in a Swiss account. When Meyerbeer heard that, he threw away his unlit cigar, which was getting unraveled, and broke out a fresh one. Trask was a tough man. They were back and forth for a

44

while, offer and counter-offer, and Trask eventually compromised, agreeing to accept the fifty thousand not in cash but in the form of shares in Vidwar. Meyerbeer phoned his lawyer friend in Toledo and arranged to have the transfer made, but not before he exacted from Trask a stipend of ten thousand in cash for his role as intermediary in arranging the transaction. Trask gave him the ten, never realizing that Meyerbeer was not an intermediary but in fact was Vidwar, the whole of it, lock, stock, and barrel, except for the shares that Trask himself now owned. When they were finished bargaining and it was time for Trask to gather his men and gear and start off into the jungle, Meyerbeer had not only recovered the initial five thousand he had paid Trask, but had actually succeeded in doubling it. "Just stay the hell out of the way when the shooting starts," Trask growled. "You hear? Don't get in my way!"

"Sure, sure," Meyerbeer answered in a sanguine tone. "Look at it this way—when you hear the rainbow chopper on its way, it means the camera is rolling and it's money in your pocket. As soon as the box office receipts start pouring in, you can retire on dividends." What he didn't tell Trask was that he was planning on running Vidwar into bankruptcy as soon as the finished film became the property of Bomburst (Meyerbeer was also Bomburst, the whole of it, lock, stock, and barrel), and the General would be left high and dry with a lot of worthless stock that he could wallpaper his latrine with.

When Meyerbeer arrived at dusk, at the bivouac, lights blazing, barely missing a tree, narrowly avoiding a boulder that jutted up out of the grass, Trask went charging over, and when Meyerbeer emerged from the chopper, in a freshly laundered Hawaiian shirt and a pair of checkered black-and-white slacks, Trask chewed hell out of him for not signaling before he came in. "*I'm* the one who runs this outfit," he bellowed, "and *I* say when you come in and when you don't. Next time signal for permission before you sortie. And watch the way you and that kid spin this damn chopper around. I've seen some wild flying in my time, but never anything as asinine as what you two lunatics do."

"Henry is a good pilot," Meyerbeer said with subdued cheer. "I trust him with my life."

"But I don't trust him with mine. One of these days, Meyerbeer, you'll get us all blown to hell."

"Sir, I get the impression you don't like me."

"I abominate you. Weren't you aware? Too bad you're not more like that son-of-a-bitch corporal they gave us for demolitions—then I could just plain despise you, without the total revulsion I feel for you now." He still held it against Simon that he had had the effrontery to tell him to his face that he hadn't volunteered. Very few members of the force had volunteered, but the ones who hadn't at least had the sense not to go around boasting about it.

Meyerbeer maintained his attitude of serene forbearance. "You mean you hate that polack porcupine less than you hate me?"

"The word *hate*, Meyerbeer, is not equal to what I feel for you. It's something else—something they haven't thought up a name for yet."

"Sir, that's a terrible thing to say. I don't hate *you*, General."

"Maybe you should try. A solid dose of well-aimed hate can have a cleansing effect like nothing else I know. It clears the sinuses."

Meyerbeer grinned. "You have a nifty sense of humor, sir."

"Meyerbeer, I don't have a sense of humor. The only reason I'm concerned about keeping you alive is because I have a cash investment in you. If it weren't for that, I wouldn't mind seeing you smashed like a bug."

Meyerbeer's eyes narrowed. "That's beautiful," he said, studying the expression on Trask's face like a connoisseur inspecting a work of art. "I like that look of anger. Can you hold that look? There's a lot of strength in it, a lot of ferocious masculinity. This will go over great with the folks back home." He got the camera rolling, and he moved around, getting the General front on, then in profile. "Terrific. Terrific. That's it. You're doing fine. I got some footage of Simon's anger, a while back, but your anger is a lot better. I think we'll scrap Simon's anger and use yours instead."

Trask glared, a splendid fury in his eyes, in the corners of his lips, his tensed nostrils.

"Good God," Meyerbeer cooed, "this is just wonderful." Then he pulled away, the camera still grinding, and he moved around the camp, getting shots of everyone—Major Kleff, Lieutenant Schlumm, Merlin working at the black box, Emma Sue cleaning her fingernails. Trask stood motionless, still glaring. After a while, though, even he was not sure if the fury was real, rising up out of an authentic pool of anger, or just something he had managed for the camera.

Meyerbeer used fast, sensitive film because of the dark, and he had a few floodlamps rigged on a crossbeam, on battery. "Act natural," he kept telling them. "Just go on doing what you're doing. I want the American public to see what a bivouac is really like." He caught Schlumm washing his feet at the pond, and Vain combing his hair. Tess using needle and thread to sew a rip in the thigh of her fatigues. Sugg picking wax from his ear. He roved slowly through the camp, caressing them with his smooth baritone. "Don't pose, just be yourself." He was suave and chipper, smelling of aftershave. He caught Simon, Thurl. And Eikopf, bony and thin, his eyes deep-set, his face a memento mori. "Beautiful, beautiful. When they see this back home, it'll really warm their hearts. That's what this war is all about, folks. Right? Being able to sit around a campfire with your friends. Even if there's no campfire."

Merlin looked up from the black box, which he'd been poring over with a flashlight, and turned to Major Kleff. "We've got weather on the way, sir." His flat, mechanical voice stabbed out like a dull knife.

Meyerbeer heard. "What kind of weather?"

"Bad."

"Bad, huh? That's not good." He switched off his floodlamps. "What a bummer. A cyclone, you say?"

"Just weather," Merlin said. "A lot of rain."

"Well, we'll hope for the best." He grabbed Henry, and they anchored the chopper down with guy wires, in case it really began to blow.

Moments later, there was a hush in the air, a noticeable silence. It was not unlike the silence on the plain, where they had found the tree loaded with skeletons. But somehow it was different, more ominous. A heaviness was moving in on them. The moon and the stars were gone, layered over with clouds, and the air became oppressively warm. It was dark, the moon hidden, yet the night seemed strangely alive with an eerie luminescence. "It's not going to rain," Emma Sue pleaded, lifting her green eyes skyward. Her face—long and lovely, heavy red eyebrows, a straight nose and pointed chin, and full, sensuous lips—was scrunched with childlike disappointment. "It *can't* rain," she insisted. But the rain came, swiftly, big heavy drops splashing down, and they went scurrying for their packs, yanking out ponchos as they scrambled for shelter, up onto the wall of the cliff, under the ledges, into the caves. There was no wind, only the straight, driving rain, heavy and warm. The pond was aboil.

Simon got in under a wide ledge of overhanging rock at the mouth of a cave. He wondered if there were any animals inside, any snakes or lizards. Snakes made him uneasy, they were a feature of the jungle that he didn't relish. He dug a flashlight out of his pack and, staying where he was, threw the beam around. The cave wasn't wide, but it was deep, running about thirty yards into the cliff, and he couldn't be sure if what he took for the rear actually was a terminus, or if it was just a turn at the far end, the cave bending, possibly, and continuing on. For a moment he thought he saw a pair of eyes staring out at him from the far end. It startled him—the eyes intense and glowing, the pupils catching the beam for the briefest instant as it swept across them. Then they were gone. He played the beam back and forth, searching, but there was nothing. Just the cave, bare rock. If they had been eyes, they weren't a snake's eyes, they belonged to something big, a mountain cat or a bear—or a man. But he knew that couldn't be, because the cave was empty. He flashed the beam all over, and there was nothing. He had simply been imagining. Perhaps the beam had glinted off some mica. Still, it was an eerie feeling, thinking there might be something back there, watching, and it was a feeling he couldn't shake. He unrolled his sleeping bag, but he didn't lie down, he sat, leaning back against a cool slab at the mouth of the cave.

The rain poured down, noisy, like the grinding of a machine. "Mind if I come in?" Meyerbeer called, stepping in under the ledge. He was drenched, the rain rattling so loud he practically had to shout to make himself heard. "I'd stay in the chopper, but those seats are so damn cramped, they're hell to sleep in. I've got long bones that like to be lying flat when I snooze."

"I snore," Simon said in a tone that was less than welcoming.

"Don't give it a thought," Meyerbeer answered, sitting down and leaning back against a boulder.

"I won't."

"You know, Simon, that was fancy shooting, a few days back, whipping out your pistol the way you did and firing at the chopper."

"I missed."

"Damn lucky you did. It was great on film, though. You have a terrific inner meanness. It'll come up beautifully on the screen."

There it was again, Meyerbeer's friendly impertinence, his sheer cheek. Or was it mere disdain wearing a very thin disguise? But always easy and mellow, and it was hard for Simon to dislike him entirely, even though he disapproved of him from top to bottom.

The rain continued to pour down, and they still had to lift their voices to be heard. "This film you're making," Simon said. "What are you calling it?"

"I'm calling it—*Afrique*."

"*Afrique?*"

"Right. You don't like it?"

Simon hesitated. "Sure, nice. But—this isn't Africa."

"Oh?" Dark as it was, Simon could sense the hint of a smile on Meyerbeer's face. "Nevertheless," Meyerbeer went on, "look at it this way: it's theater, Simon. Film. Make-believe. Illusion. Don't you know about illusion?"

"*You're* an illusion," Simon said.

"You're right. Positively correct."

"We made you up. We have sick minds and we invented you."

"Right again."

"Hell, Meyerbeer," Simon said, exasperated, "you're just Meyerbeer. You're not God."

"I know, I know," he answered with a lazy drawl. "But that's only because film is God. Film knows all, Simon. You don't fuck around with film."

Simon rolled out a long belch, by way of commentary, and for a few moments neither of them said a thing, Simon sitting and Meyerbeer sitting, the rain hammering down, punishing the earth, the wash and rush of water condensing out of a steamy cloud. Rivulets and narrow streams gushed downhill across the slope in front of the cliff, rushing into the pond.

"Well," Meyerbeer chirped up, "I'll tell you one thing that is no illusion, Simon. This damn rain. I'm never going to get any sleep hanging around in this joint. Thanks for the hospitality. I'm heading for greener pastures." He rubbed his hands together, getting the blood moving as he readied himself to move out.

"You can't fly in this kind of a storm," Simon said.

"Henry can fly in anything. I can fly a pretty mean helicopter myself. Did you know I can fly?"

50

"No."

"Well, I can," Meyerbeer said, and again Simon sensed a hint of a smile in his tone. "Next time you shoot at me, be careful not to miss."

Simon stared back in the dark. "I won't."

Meyerbeer stepped into the rain, and clambered across the face of the cliff, among the caves and ledges, looking for Henry. He found him, and the two of them moved down onto the slope and ambled over to the helicopter. Simon watched. They didn't run— they moved easily, a leisurely stroll, with flashlights, letting the rain wash down over them. They undid the guy wires and climbed into the chopper, and Henry flipped the ignition. Still there was no wind, just the straight rain pounding down vertically. Simon saw Major Kleff running out with a flashlight, shouting something, waving his arms; but whatever he was shouting, it was lost in the sound of the rain and the roar as the engine turned over. Henry flicked on the landing lights and lifted off, high into the storm, and Simon watched as the lights were swallowed up in the furious night. Then there was only the sound of the rain, striking with a terrible anger, and the Major standing there, wet and frustrated, the flashlight down at his side. He turned and came back up onto the cliff, to the shelter of a cave.

6 ◻ Glacial Rock

WHAT MAJOR KLEFF had been shouting at Meyerbeer, out there in the rain, was that he was flying off into a grade seven hurricane. The black box had estimated, earlier, that the storm was just a storm, but now it knew better and it passed the news along to Merlin, who passed it to Major Kleff, who was trying to get it to Meyerbeer. But Meyerbeer never heard him. Or, if he did, he didn't give a damn.

After the rain, they were hit hard by heavy winds that hammered away for close to an hour. Simon, usually a sound sleeper, was startled by an unearthly sucking sound, as if the whole area were about to be siphoned up by a gigantic vacuum cleaner. A loud, swooshing roar growing more and more intense—a swift crescendo, but no climax, no surcease. He thought, for a moment, that it was part of a dream, a nightmare. But it was real, a hot blast of air gripping his body, howling in the rocky crevices of the cliff. Blinking awake, he saw that the rain had stopped and the overcast sky was dimly lit with a mysterious light, purplish-brown. Trees lashed and bent, leaves scattering, branches ripped loose, sailing in the wind like dark, ponderous birds. He checked his watch: it was just after four. The wind seemed to intensify, and he simply lay there, huddled in his sleeping bag, trees falling, branches hurtling wildly. A canteen blew by, bouncing across the ground, kicked by the wind. A poncho, and a sleeping bag, tossed madly. Then he saw someone moving around out there, stumbling, pitched and blown, buffeted, knocked to the ground, then up again, standing. It was Eikopf. He was stark naked. For a moment he just hung there, leaning against the wind, arms outstretched, leaning, and the wind held him, an image of crucifixion. He was shouting. Simon saw the jaw moving, the face, scraps of words, but the wind cut the words off and he couldn't make it out. Something about God, death, terror. *"God sees . . ."* he heard. *"Fucking God . . . He knows . . . knows . . ."* Eikopf fell, prone in the mud, and lay there a long time, motionless. Then he crawled off, slowly under the wind, back toward the shelter of the cliff.

The wind abated. Simon closed his eyes, and again he slept. He dreamed of Tess. In the dream he was caressing her thighs, touching her warm, mellow flesh. He knew in his dream that he had never touched her that way before, this was the first time, and he also knew it was only a dream. He wondered, in his dream, if it would ever really happen. When he woke again, it seemed he had only just shut his eyes—but it was much later, after six. The others were up already, preparing to move out. The place was a shambles, wreckage everywhere, debris floating on the pond. Nobody talking. They moved about in a grumpy silence, getting their packs together. The sky had cleared, though there were still some lumpy clouds around. The sun wasn't up over the horizon yet, but the sky was ablaze with light, a sea of pastels. Sugg stood at the edge of the pond, dragging a load of phlegm up from his lungs.

"Where's Vain?" Major Kleff called out. He had been taking count, Vain wasn't there.

They looked around, and, over by a pile of fallen trees, Simon spotted a bare arm sticking up from a bunch of leaves. Vain was unconscious under a mass of tangled teak and ebony. He looked dead, but they dragged him out and Emma Sue worked on him and brought him around. He had a broken leg and a few broken ribs—it was clear they would have to leave him behind. Merlin sent out the position, and a rescue chopper was reported on its way to pick him up. Emma Sue put a splint on his leg and wrapped some tape around his ribs. They made him as comfortable as they could; then, not without misgivings, they moved out, leaving him at the edge of the pond, with a flare gun to signal with when the chopper showed up, and his M-16. In fact, it was a lousy feeling, leaving him behind. He could die there, and they knew it. Vain knew it: they could see it in his eyes, a bleak, pained silence, a wordless terror gazing out at them. That was the kind of mission it was—if you couldn't move out, you were left behind. What it boiled down to, simply, was that the bridge was more important than Vain was, more important than any of them.

As they headed down the trail, Tess glanced back at him.

"Shit," she said, and Simon said nothing, because she was right, shit is what it was.

For a while it was slow going because of the wreckage the storm had left. Whole trees were down, blocking their way, vines and branches bent and twisted into surreal webs. Mud everywhere, puddles, whole pools of water that hadn't had a chance to drain off yet. Emma Sue fell face down into a puddle and got up black with mud, cursing furiously. Then Thurl went down, hard on his rump, a solid jolt jamming his spine. They had to help him up. "It's that damned black box," he shouted. "Eikopf is right—it's got us all fucked up. How many days on this dumbshit trail, and where the hell's that bridge?"

"We're getting there," Major Kleff said, irritatingly calm.

"Maybe we gettin' there," Thurl said, "but it's the long way aroun'. A damn week already. Before you know it it'll be a whole fucked-up month." His thick black face looked like puffy rubber. He was still massaging the base of his spine.

"You complain a lot," the Major observed.

"Why shouldn't I? I'm just a nigger, right? Niggers are allowed to complain. Whut else is a nigger good for?"

Simon had never thought of Thurl as a complainer. He did complain, but not that much more than anybody else. Actually, Simon had the impression that he was a pretty good soldier, despite the fact that he was just hanging on until his tour was over. If he had to pick someone to be on the trail with, Thurl was one that he would have picked. Thurl, and maybe Schlumm. Schlumm was tolerable. And maybe Eikopf, just because he was so weird.

"I think I broke my back," Thurl said.

"You didn't break your back," the Major responded sharply, a flash of impatience dashing his composure.

"Are you a fucking doctor?"

"I'm your fucking superior officer. Move your ass, you nigger."

54

"I've got a slipped disk," Thurl moaned.

"*Moving on*," the Major called aloud.

Thurl glanced about with beseeching eyes. "Anybody got a stretcher?"

The Major walked on, muttering, shaking his head.

"If I had a stretcher," Tess said, "I'd lend it to you, Thurl. But somebody else would have to do the carrying."

"That figures," he said sexily, with a big wink.

She drew back stiffly. "What do you mean *that figures?*"

"Whut y'mean, *whut do you mean?*"

Tess twisted her face with annoyance, and Simon smiled, thinking it was nifty the way she did that, it brought out her dimples.

"Stick it up your nose," she said to Thurl, her glance sweeping in Simon too, and she went stamping on ahead.

Thurl looked to Simon. "Tough broad. Ain't you bein' nice to her?"

"I try," Simon said.

"Shit, you gotta do more than try, man. A lot more than jus' *try*."

Up ahead, Tess was maneuvering around puddles, climbing nimbly over fallen logs and branches, her pigtail bobbing, bare neck visible and tempting, green fatigues still damp from the previous night's rain, clinging to the tender eloquence of her smooth, round bottom. Simon suspected that all she was really interested in was teasing him out of his mind.

Later that day, replacements were helicoptered in for Studd-win, Smudge, and Vain. The new men were Polymer, Falling Stone, and Mickey Kabuki. Simon was glad to see Falling Stone. They had gone through boot camp together, and Simon liked him. He was sensible, sound, a good person to go soldiering with. And big, as big as Thurl, though not as heavy, with dark, piercing eyes that seemed, to Simon, to be searching always for some hidden truth that would remain forever inaccessible. Mickey Kabuki he didn't know at all, and Polymer he was getting to know very fast, because as soon as he got out of the chopper he went gladhanding around, introducing himself. He was thin and bony, grinningly obnoxious, saying to everyone, "Hi, I'm Polymer, from Plastic, Idaho." It sounded like a bad joke, but it was true, he really was from Plastic. Merlin checked with the black box, and it was right there in Polymer's datafile, in bold letters: PLACE OF BIRTH: PLASTIC, IDAHO.

Simon overheard Trask grumbling to the Major. "I lose three good men, three hot guns, and for replacements they send me a Jap, an Apache, and a bigmouth from Plastic. What the hell is the Corps coming to?" An Apache and a bigmouth from Plastic he could put up with, but a Japanese he wasn't ready for. His older brother and two of his uncles had been killed at Pearl Harbor. Everyone knew about the brother and the two uncles, and, in certain quarters, Trask was known as the Pearl General, an epithet he neither endorsed nor encouraged, but which he was secretly rather proud of.

He called Mickey Kabuki over, and looked him up and down. Kabuki was short, with a round, moonish face and small eyes. "You're of Oriental extraction, aren't you," he said.

"Yes, sir. Japanese. My mother was from the Island of Okushiri and my father was from Osaka. They met in California."

"What does that make you?"

"A mongrel, I guess. I was born in San Luis Obispo. I grew up there." There was a flat, nasal tone to his voice, as if he were suffering from sinus congestion.

"San Luis Obispo, huh? That's good enough, I suppose. If HQ has confidence in you, who am I to complain? Just don't let me catch you making any sly moves. You're here to kill monkeys—you like killing?"

"It's a living."

"Ever kill any monkeys?"

"I collected seven ears in the fighting in the southeast sector."

"Seven? Not bad, that's pretty straight shooting. If we run into any monkeys, I'll expect you to collect seventy times seven. Ears or assholes, I don't care which. Just so long as any monkeys I set eyes on are dead monkeys."

"I'll do my best," Mickey Kabuki said.

"And remember—God's on our side."

"I'll remember, sir."

"Do you believe in God, soldier?"

"To be perfectly honest, sir, I think I'm an atheist."

"Goddamn, another one." Trask seemed genuinely upset. "We've got too many atheists in this force. Studdwin—he was an atheist, before they blasted him. And Merlin—all he believes in is microchips and motherboards. And that Eikopf, the one who's mouthing off about God all the time—deep down he's an atheist, but he doesn't know it yet and imagines he's still a believer. And that bastard, Simon—I suspect he's an atheist too, but he's smart and doesn't brag about it the way some of the others do. And that nigger Thurl—an atheist through and through, but he hasn't screwed up the courage to declare himself yet. Probably never will. All this atheism, it's bad image, bad for morale. You sure you don't believe in Buddha, or some crap like that?"

"In San Luis Obispo I was a Methodist. But not any more."

"Yeah? Too bad. Well, soldier, we can't win them all. Since you're such a hotshot, seven ears, I'm putting you up at point. How does that grab you? Let Sugg have a rest. Give 'em hell, soldier."

After that, Trask avoided Mickey Kabuki as if he were the bearer of contagion. There were times when he went up and down the line, checking the men, asking them how they were, but he made a point of never approaching Kabuki. When they camped for the night, he'd like to sit around and peel oranges and pass them around, handing half an orange to Sugg, half to Emma Sue, then peel another, half to Schlumm and half to Thurl, but never an orange for Mickey Kabuki, who was quick to notice how thoroughly he was being ignored. "At first I thought it was the color of my skin," he told Simon, at bivouac one night. "And then

I thought it was because I had been so straight-out with him about my being an atheist. Well, right now I'm not so sure. It looks to me, right now, like what he's really bugged about is that I'm from San Luis Obispo. He's from Fort Worth, and I figure he's got it in for California. You know how it is, the place you come from can be a pretty big deal. For some people, where you're from is deeper than what race you are. You could be queer and mongoloid, even a dwarf, but if you're from the right place it doesn't matter. You don't happen to have a toothpick, do you? I got this screaming toothache."

"Better have Emma Sue take a look at it."

"What can she do? Pull it?"

"You want it pulled? I'll pull it."

Simon carried pliers, wire cutters, and a couple of screwdrivers, standard equipment for demolitions people. He took a pair of pliers out of his pack, but Mickey Kabuki wasn't interested. "Some other time," he said, walking away, and Simon figured it was a smart move. Maybe he would get killed at point, so why go through the hell of having a tooth pulled? It would be a waste, an uneconomical use of pain. And pain, Simon was beginning to understand, was a precious commodity, not to be squandered, not to be spent profligately, under any circumstances.

They went across a low hill, through dense undergrowth, then across some level ground. The trail brought them through a cedar grove, and led to a clearing in which there was an immense boulder. It was the biggest rock Simon had ever seen. He had come upon one roughly like it on a camping trip in New Hampshire, but this one was much larger, shaped like a huge egg, about twenty feet high.

Sugg climbed a tree and got himself up onto the rock. For a moment he just stood there on top, arms akimbo and legs spread wide, helmet off, carrot hair vivid in the sun, his beefy face smug and self-assured. He was king of the rock, it belonged to him. He opened his pants and urinated, the long, steady stream brightly yellow, splashing off the hard, pitted granite.

Emma Sue climbed onto the rock, and some of the others followed. Eikopf, Thurl, Mickey Kabuki. Trask and Major Kleff stayed below, huddled over the black box, trying to radio HQ. Merlin turned the dials, searching for the right frequency, but was having trouble getting through. He thought the rock might have something to do with it.

Under a bush at the base of the rock, Polymer found two black snakes twined around each other, copulating. He watched, grinning, then grabbed a stick and beat away at them. They uncoupled and one swiftly slithered off, but the other was stunned and just lay there. With his knife he cut off the head, and, still grinning, called up to Sugg. "Hey Sugg—you dig raw snake's head? This one's the female. The male got away."

He tossed the head and Sugg caught it in his left hand and held it up in front of his face, studying it close. He touched the eyes. He opened the jaws, examining the fangs. "Don't look like no female I ever met up with," he said, and flipped it over to Mickey Kabuki. "You Japs are big on snake food, ain't you? Have a snack on me."

Mickey Kabuki made no effort to catch it. The snake's head struck him in the leg and fell to the rock. He kicked it away.

Simon was still on the ground, looking at the rock, admiring it. He remembered that the rock in New Hampshire was known to be something out of the ice age, transported on the back of a glacier. He figured this was the same thing. "A glacial boulder," he said to Schlumm. "Right?"

"That's what it is," Schlumm said, nodding. "Glacial rock."

But Simon suddenly wasn't so sure. "I didn't know glaciers had moved down this close to the equator."

"A glacier's a big thing, Simon. It goes where it wants."

Simon rapped his knuckles against the rock. "I think it's an egg," he said. "It made love to itself and begot itself in its own image."

Schlumm snapped his fingers. "Actually," he said, "in a way, you're right. It *is* an egg, and it did beget itself. It's what they call in anthropology a cosmogonic egg. In the old days, the natives probably gathered around and worshiped here."

Simon floated a dark look in Schlumm's direction. He was hard to take sometimes, he was so insufferably smart. The bastard had a photographic memory.

Schlumm's enthusiasm mounted. "A rock like this, they would have thought of it as the sacred egg out of which the universe was born. Come on, let's check it out." He set out on a quick tour around the base of the rock, looking for signs of ancient worship, and Simon followed along. They looked, searched, inspecting for marks, symbols chiseled into the rock. But they found nothing.

At the black box, General Trask was having a problem. He had established contact with HQ, finally, but the message he was getting wasn't something he was ready to live with. He was agitated, his beret was off and he held an earphone pressed against his ear. He was talking into a microphone connected to the black box—it seemed a small silver lollipop in front of his quivering lips. Simon had come full circle around the rock, with Schlumm, and when they heard Trask barking into the mike, they moved closer to catch what he was saying.

"What was that? What? . . . I said put a stop on it! You hear? Did you get that? . . . This is General Trask speaking, and I said put a stop on it or there will be hell to pay!" He handed the mike and earphone to Major Kleff, saying, "Tell that son of a bitch who he's been talking to and make him put a stop on that flight or I'll have his liver ground into chopped meat and fed to the hogs back at Alpha."

Major Kleff took hold of the mike. "Again. Again. Running Fox here on Scrambler Code Seven. Our ground force is on your grid. Repeat. Our ground force is on your grid. Abort your overfly. Abort your overfly. This is Special Force Major Kleff relaying direct command of Special Force Running Fox Field Commander General Trask. Come in and reply. Come in and reply."

As he listened to the response, his face showed no emotion. He glanced up toward General Trask. "He says they're committed."

"Well tell them to uncommit, dammit."

"He says they can't do that when they're at commit status. They won't acknowledge or respond."

"Just tell that flat-nosed sonofabitch colonel there is no such thing in this entire command as a nonrescindable commit status in the air. Who the hell does he think he's talking to? Did you tell him who I am? Tell him to send the abort signal on a Code Six Trout Four. That'll stop them."

Major Kleff relayed the message and awaited a reply. When the response came through, his face was still deadpan. "He says, sir, that Code Six Trout Four was rescinded as a code two weeks ago when they installed the nonrescindable commit status as a functionable mode. He advises we dig in."

Trask seethed. "Dig in, hell!" He grabbed the microphone from the Major and shouted into it. "Do you know who you're talking to, soldier? This is General Trask in the field. You send that abort signal any way you know how and stop that overfly. Send up an intercept if you have to. But stop it and stop it now! If I lose one man on the ground here I will personally search you out and put a bullet up your ass." He tossed the microphone back to the Major.

The Major still had the earphone and listened for the response, his face expressionless, his dark eyes blank. "He's telling us to dig in," he said.

Trask looked to Merlin. "How much time do we have?"

Merlin checked the screen on the black box. "From this moment, exactly . . . fourteen minutes to fly-over."

Trask's face was swollen, mottled with barely suppressed rage.

His eyes darted wildly, then fastened on the Major. "Tell them to dig in. Right here. Against the base of the rock."

"Pass the word," the Major said to Sugg, who had come down from the rock.

Sugg passed the word. "Shovels out—and fast! We're digging in!"

Emma Sue and the others who were up on the rock scurried down. They got their shovels out of their packs and started digging. Even Trask grabbed a shovel. "On the double," he said to Major Kleff, and the Major repeated the command to Sugg. It went down the line.

As they dug in, they heard the sound of Meyerbeer's chopper approaching. Suddenly it was there above them, hovering. It hung balanced in the air, then slowly descended and landed on the rock. Meyerbeer jumped out with his camera gear.

"Get that chopper the hell out of here," Trask shouted.

"You bet," Meyerbeer called down, reaching into the cabin for a tripod. He got it out, then signalled Henry to move out, and the helicopter lifted and went speeding off. Meyerbeer stayed.

"Don't you know how serious this is?" Trask roared. "Do you know what's happening here?"

"I know. I know."

"*How* do you know?"

"Sir, in my business we *have* to know. Let's just say I found out. I was lucky. I wouldn't miss this show for the world. It isn't every day, General, you get a view of one of these things from underneath. Do you know how valuable this footage is going to be?" He was still up on the rock, setting the camera onto the tripod.

Major Kleff waved his shovel at him. "You better dig in before you lose your ass."

"Just as soon as I get this motor rigged." The tripod was equipped with a drive that could rotate the camera a full 360 degrees. Meyerbeer attached a remote-control extension cord that would enable him to control the camera's position, then he caught onto a tree limb and got himself down. He grabbed a shovel and dug like hell, socking in between Eikopf and Falling Stone.

"Three minutes," Merlin called out in a loud, flat monotone.

Tess was dug in beside Simon. "I'm scared," she said.

"Who isn't?"

"Two minutes," Merlin called.

They waited, looking skyward. A loud, long hush, sounds of jungle animals in the trees. Intermittent cries of birds, chimps, jackals.

"One minute."

They listened, and then they heard it, the whispering in the sky, the whisper becoming a high, shrill whistling sound as the bombs neared the ground, and the whispering and the whistling got lost in a searing roar as the bombs went off, one after another, far out but moving close, detonating with fierce regularity, kettle drums struck in measured time. Tess burrowed into the loose soil. She had her helmet on, and Simon had his. They were all in helmets, except for the General, who had his black beret, and Falling Stone, who wore a red headband. Simon looked skyward, and there they were, the B-52s, far up there, miles away, small in the distance, barely visible through the haze and humidity. He counted seven, eight, nine. They had already passed over, had unleashed all their bombs, and the bombs were only now arriving, the explosions moving closer, shaking the earth. He buried his head, one arm around Tess, the other arm reaching up around his neck, covering the back of his neck with his hand. His pack, with the pyroxene-T, was under the loose pile of dirt he had shoveled when he dug in. He lay hunched there, with Tess, braced against the shaking earth, the bombs marching toward them like thunderous footsteps.

He heard someone yelling: "Yaaaaaaaaaaaah! Yaaaaaaaaaaaaaaa-aaah!" And suddenly the bombs were on them, all around them, trees ripping apart, tossed in the air, the air hot with flame and incineration. Simon was lifted up and thrown on his back. A loud ripping sound—then, for a while, he could hear nothing, only a hum, a loud hum inside him. He rubbed his ears, trying to get his hearing back. Slowly, he moved his jaws, opening his mouth.

He saw Tess, her face scarred with dirt, dazed. He tried to stand and go to her, but was unable to move his legs. He tried again, but still nothing, and he felt an inner panic over his helplessness. Gradually the hum dissipated, the deafness passed. He could hear again. His legs were numb, but feeling was beginning to come back to them. With considerable effort, he managed to push himself up off the ground and, with a slight dizziness, was able to stand. Tess was also up, she was all right.

The bombers were gone and Trask was on his feet, looking things over. Trees were cracked, split open. The air reeked with the smell of fire and burnt explosive. Major Kleff moved about, making a count.

Thurl was looking skyward, eyes glazed with disgust. "Our own bombers. Our fucking own!"

"Send a telegram," Sugg said.

"We're dead," Eikopf muttered in a ghostly tone. "We died. This is death." He had a cut on his forehead that needed stitches.

Mickey Kabuki had fouled his pants. He was cleaning himself off.

Simon climbed a splintered tree and went up onto the rock. Meyerbeer was already up there. The tripod was down and the camera had disconnected from the remote-control cable, but the film was still rolling. The lens was cracked. "I figured this would happen," Meyerbeer said, with no real sign of distress. "What the hell. If we only get a few frames, it'll still be sensational." He gave a casual shrug.

Simon walked around on top of the rock. A bomb had struck on the side opposite where they had been dug in, and a huge crater was scooped out at the base of the rock. Blackened trees, burnt vegetation. That was the blast that had tossed him into the air. Had the plane been slightly to the left instead of to the right, the bomb would have hit the other side and they would all have been wiped out. He got down off the rock, and urinated on a bush that had burned and was still smoldering.

They milled about groggily, a little dazed, astonished that they were still alive. Emma Sue moved among them, making repairs. Her helmet off, dark red hair neatly bobbed. Bending, turning. Her slender body an appealing blend of angles and curves, even in fatigues. "Nice having these nurse-types around," said Thurl, who had slept with her twice since they left Base Blue. Actually, she was not a nurse; she had spent a few years taking a degree as a physician's assistant, poring over medical books, learning emergency ward procedures, so she was more than a nurse but less than a doctor. She wasn't licensed for surgery, but if she had to pull out an appendix she knew how to do it, and if your testicles fell off she could sew them back on. A comforting thought, knowing she was around.

Then they found Polymer. The Major found him. He had been thrown headfirst into the trunk of a big beech, they found him at the base of the tree with his head turned completely around. He still had his helmet on. When Simon saw him, his first instinct, when he saw the turned-around head, was to laugh, because it was silly, dumb, clownish, Polymer lying there in the bushes like a broken doll, his face where the back of his head should have been. Simon didn't laugh, but the impulse was there, definite and strong, and it troubled him, filled him with a sense of self-loathing, because he saw, now, that something inside him was changing. He felt, vaguely, that he was someone else, someone he didn't recognize.

"What was that colonel's name?" Trask said.

"Tremolo," Major Kleff remembered. "Colonel Wolf Tremolo."

"Write it down," Trask told Merlin. "Key it into the box. That's a name I want to remember. I have business to settle with that man."

Merlin's helmet had been knocked off during the bombing. He had been flipped in the air and thrown hard, and had fallen against the edge of a shovel. There was a deep gash on the back of his head. Emma Sue applied antiseptic, and gave him a few stitches. As she drew the needle through his scalp, getting the sutures in, Merlin keyed the colonel's name into the black box, storing it in computer memory.

The rainbow chopper reappeared and set down on the rock, and Meyerbeer climbed in. The chopper lifted off, and for a while it circled lazily as Meyerbeer filmed the devastation from the air, using a backup camera that had been stowed in the chopper. Circled and dipped around, did a lot of hovering, then scooted off, heading south, back to Base Blue. Simon wondered how he had known the bombing run was going down. He seemed to have his hands into everything, he knew too much. One way or another, it appeared that he was always involved somehow, but the extent of his involvement was never entirely clear. Initially Simon had considered him merely a slick—a shark with a camera, a con artist whose moves were, for the most part, fairly obvious; but as the days wore on he sensed increasingly that Meyerbeer had dimension—a con artist yes, but with unfathomed depths that were shadowy and strange, whole areas hidden from view, and Simon wasn't at all sure that he wanted to poke into the shadows and see what was there, though he did at times wonder. There were times when Meyerbeer wasn't around, whole days when he didn't show up at all, and Simon imagined that he was probably off filming the monkeys: talking with them, making friends, consorting, splicing them into the movie. Maybe even trading information. Nothing seemed impossible. If there was an angle in it, something to be gained, it was meat for Meyerbeer. Maybe he had even arranged for the B-52s to unload on them, so he could get those special-effects shots from down under—though that did seem a little outrageous, even for Meyerbeer, and when his speculations reached that point, Simon drew back, figuring paranoia was beginning to set in. He noticed that, the way paranoia kept getting in the way, becoming something of a habit. And recognized, too, that it was a habit he felt strangely comfortable with.

"I was trying to sleep," Eikopf said, a glazed look in his eyes, "but they took sleep away. Now I don't need sleep anymore. I'm the one who stays awake."

It was true, Eikopf wasn't sleeping anymore. He resisted sleep, as if he had a fear of it, a fear that he might fall into a deep slumber and never awaken. He seemed more and more gaunt. "You need rest," Simon told him. "You should sleep."

"Why should I sleep? What does sleep have to do with it?"

"I don't know. Everything. *Some*thing."

"They took sleep away," Eikopf repeated, and Simon knew what he meant. When you had lived through enough bombs and mortar, the noise got locked in the back of your head, it was always there, hidden, lying in wait, ready to snap you into wakefulness—you never knew what dream it would interrupt, sending your heart racing with dread. It wasn't dying that Eikopf was afraid of, it was the noise of the bombs and mortar, which he had internalized, detonating in his skull.

They were moving out, leaving the big rock. Simon looked back and saw Falling Stone standing there, very straight, his two hands up against the rock, as if the rock had some deep, religious meaning for him. In his headband were two green feathers he had plucked from a bird that had been killed in the bombing. Just standing there, hands against the rock, as if communicating with some obscure power secreted deep in the rock's interior. Maybe Schlumm was right after all: the rock wasn't a rock but an egg, a cosmogonic egg. Why not? Maybe, one way or another, they would all be reborn—Thurl, Tess, all of them. Even the ones who were dead, Studdwin and Smudge, and now Polymer. All of them. Even Vain whom they had left behind. Even Meyerbeer, damn him. Redeemed and delivered. Maybe. He wasn't so sure about Meyerbeer. And Eikopf, yes, whose mad despair was a shining form of sanity. There was this tremendous surprise waiting for them, for all of them: good luck, more than they could hope for, too big to handle, they would be breathless and amazed.

7 □ The Queen of Skulls

THE SPOOLS of pyroxene-T that Simon carried were wide and flat—they called them pies, because each spool was roughly the size of an apple pie you might buy in a bakery. "Hey, Simple Simon," Thurl called, "how many pies you got in yo' pack?" He had three, and that was enough. One day Meyerbeer had him take them out of his pack and pose with them. Thurl and Falling Stone each held one, and Simon held the other. In some ways, Simon noted, they were more like donuts, big donuts, than like pies.

He hiked along with Eikopf for a while, then with Schlumm. Then he was with Thurl and Falling Stone. Tess had been up ahead, with Merlin and the Major, and now she dropped back, with a piece of bad news. The chopper they had called in for Vain had never made it. It had been shot down before it got to him, the pilot and two medics killed. Her voice was tense, as if the words were weights that she was straining to lift, too heavy for her to manage. "Merlin just got it on the black box," she said, repeating herself compulsively. "It was shot down, Vain is still out there. On his own." It was rotten luck for Vain. With one chopper already down, it was unlikely that Command would risk sending in another.

Odd, Simon thought, that the report was reaching them only now, days after they had left Vain behind. They all thought it odd—even sinister, unnerving—because the tardiness of the message meant that the black box wasn't as thorough as it was cracked up to be. One more piece of strangeness in a growing mess of strangeness. Maybe Vain was still out there, alive, but by now the monkeys would be swarming all over the place, and his chances, by anybody's calculation, had to be slim. They knew that it was probably all over for him already, but somehow they didn't think of him as dead; they thought of him as holding on, in pain, at the spot where they had left him, with his broken bones, waiting for the monkeys to move in on him. He would use the rifle and the grenades, giving them hell; then, when there was no point to it anymore, he'd use the last grenade on himself. Better that than the torture cages and things they'd heard about, pulled fingernails, amputated toes, needles through the eyelids.

They reached a stream, and they took off their boots and cooled their feet in the water. Five minutes of that, then the Major gave the signal and they were on the move again. They detoured east to avoid a monkey brigade, and south to avoid another B-52 bombing run. Mickey Kabuki was up at point, thinking about the beaches in California—sand, surf, girls. Schlumm thought about his fifty-eight-year-old mother, who was slowly dying of cancer in Brooklyn. Falling Stone thought about a ranch in Montana that he wanted to buy. Emma Sue thought about the baby she had given up for adoption the year before she enlisted. She thought about Vain, too, abandoned out there, on his own. They all thought about him, but tried not to.

The trail went slowly downhill, into farm country. It wasn't a trail anymore, it was a wide dirt road, with open fields to the left and right, acres and acres planted with low crops. It was good to be out of the jungle. Tess had the feeling that at last they were getting somewhere. The climate seemed suddenly dry, no more humidity. "I feel like I'm in Kansas. Kansas, or is it more like Minnesota?"

Simon leaned close to her. "I think it's Rhode Island," he said, just above a whisper.

"Stuff it," she said. "If it isn't Minnesota, why are there all those sheep up there, on that hillside?"

There were sheep: definite, palpable sheep. "They look like sheep," Simon said, "but they're something else."

"They're sheep," she answered in a ringing voice. "I did a report on sheep when I was in the sixth grade at P.S. 69. I wrote a term paper on sheep at Mary Magdalene High. I *know* those are sheep!"

"We must be in the wrong country," Simon said. "We should talk to Merlin. He's led us clear into another world."

They walked on, and they came upon a field where there were some women and old men, children. The men and women were dressed festively, the women in long, multicolored gowns, green and lavender, aquamarine. The men in white pants and shirts. The children were playing, kicking a soccer ball, but the men and women were slowly busy at something else, wandering about, peaceful and calm. Tess and Simon stopped, with Schlumm and Falling Stone. It was a strange scene, magically quiet. An old woman sat in a chair on a raised platform, dressed completely in white; a child stood close by, fanning her with a palm branch. Beside her on the platform was a brass chest, the lid open.

"It's the Festival of the Skulls," Schlumm said, lighting a cigarette. He smoked too much; he knew someday he would have to quit, it wasn't something he was looking forward to. "It's an important festival, I've heard a lot about it. The woman in white is the Queen of Skulls. A friend of mine was out here a few years ago and did a study, I remember the photographs."

"She's very beautiful," Tess said. The woman was old, but her features were extraordinary: a small, delicately shaped nose,

70

large eyes, high cheekbones, a broad forehead. She wore flowers in her hair, dahlias and orchids.

The General had called a halt farther up the road. He was conferring with Merlin and the Major. They were reading data out of the black box.

"Every year they do this," Schlumm said, gazing at the people in the field. "They keep the skulls in a brass coffer, and once a year they come out here and set the skulls up on poles. Today is their New Year's Day, this is how they celebrate. Their way of saying good-bye to everything that's old and dead in the old year."

Simon saw some poles that he hadn't noticed before, planted vertically in the ground, in the distance. There were skulls on top of them. That's what they were doing—setting the skulls on tall, slender poles. A woman took a skull from the chest and handed it to two men who were holding a pole. One of the men attached it to the pole, and they walked off and drove the foot of the pole into the ground. The poles were randomly placed, there seemed to be no logic in the way they were set up.

"This is holy ground for them," Schlumm said, "it's their cemetery. The skulls are the skulls of their dead relatives. They bury the bodies, but they save the skulls and go through this ritual every year. When a relative dies, they cut off the head and let the scavengers eat the flesh away. They save the skulls in that brass coffer."

Sugg had come up from the rear, with Thurl and Eikopf, and had overheard what Schlumm was saying. "That's fucking weird," he said. "Like cutting off your sister's head, or your mom's. Letting the ants get at it. Those skulls are their goddamn relatives?"

"That's right," Schlumm said.

"Thank God I'm from the good ole U.S. of A." Sugg said. He went off into the field, over to the woman in white sitting in the wicker chair. He looked at her, inspecting her up and down. A few men and a woman drifted over to him, smiling. He smiled back. They bowed, and he bowed. The woman offered him a flower, and he stuck it in the top buttonhole of his fatigues. Then he went over to the children who were kicking the soccer ball around, and he kicked it around with them. Schlumm and Falling Stone moved along up the road, and Tess went also, but Simon waited. He was fascinated by the skulls, the unusual ritual. He struck out across the field, as Sugg had done, and bowed to the woman in white. He looked in the coffer and saw the skulls, five of them. The woman in white smiled at him. The other woman, the one who had given a flower to Sugg, came over and gave him a flower also. He bowed, and she bowed, smiling. Then he saw Sugg, in the distance, heading into the woods with one of the kids. For a moment, nothing registered: it was just Sugg and a kid, the green field, the woods, the lady passing out flowers, the poles with the skulls on top. Then something opened up inside him, a sense of something sour and wrong, as if a trap door had sprung open underneath him and he knew he was falling, sinking—but he wasn't falling, he was running, racing along toward the trees where Sugg had disappeared with the boy, and when he reached the trees he was gasping, out of breath. A big bird flew out of a pile of green leaves, passing close by his face. He pushed through the shrubbery and reached a small clearing beside a rushing stream. As he stood there, in the shrubbery at the edge of the clearing, he saw Sugg and the boy standing by the stream, facing each other. The boy was stark naked. He had large dark eyes, and, from where Simon stood, he didn't seem frightened or terrified, merely perplexed, the eyes signaling something that looked like curiosity mingled with confusion. Sugg had unburdened himself of his pack and was stepping out of his pants. His legs were long and thin, matted with dark red hair, the legs paradoxical, seeming somehow too slight for his thick, robust body. The stream gushed noisily through a bed of rocks, and neither Sugg nor the boy had heard Simon coming through the trees.

Simon hung motionless, observing the scene, looking on as if watching something unreal, a movie, a depthless image projected on a screen. Then, quickly, he got his pack off his back, sucked in a deep breath, and leaped into the clearing, racing across the small stretch of grass, and jumped Sugg from behind. It was not something he had given any thought to, just a swift, impulsive lunge, and he knew, as he hurtled through the air, that it was a piece of insanity, utterly mad, because Sugg was bigger than he was—stronger, heavier.

He got his arm around Sugg's neck and pulled him down, and Simon got the worst of it because Sugg, coming down backward, fell on him with all his weight. They rolled around on the ground, and Sugg was swiftly on top, punching away. Simon pushed him off and then they were both up, fists going, Sugg landing two or three blows for every one that Simon managed to get off—the chest, arms, stomach, then square on the nose and Simon heard, felt, the cartilage crunching. He reeled backward and Sugg was quickly after him, grabbing him before he fell. He gripped the front of Simon's shirt with both hands, holding him up, then he let go and smashed both fists into Simon's midsection. Simon doubled over and went down, tasting blood in his mouth.

He lay creased with pain, and Sugg stood over him, breathing hard, fists clenched and ready to strike again. Their eyes met, and for a long moment they just stared at each other, a black depthless silence filled with fury and physical hurt. Then Sugg spat at him, a thick glob of saliva landing on Simon's forehead. Simon's hands clutched at his stomach, he didn't move. He watched as Sugg went back to where the boy was and got back into his pants. He picked up his pack and went stalking off, into the trees, back toward the road.

The boy looked at Simon and said nothing. He hadn't moved from the spot where he'd been when Simon first saw him. His clothes were in a heap at his feet. "Go," Simon said. "Get out of here." When he waved his arm, the boy seemed to understand. He picked up his clothes, an undergarment and a tunic cut out of a flour sack, got into them, and went off into the trees. Simon lay there a while longer, letting the pain in his gut subside. Then, cautiously, he got up. He went to the stream and washed the blood from his face. He was down on the ground again, at the edge of the stream, at a spot where there were no rocks and the water collected in a natural basin, his face hanging down in the water, the cold water easing the pain in his nose. Then he stood up, feeling the soreness in his ribs, face, stomach. He picked up his pack and headed off through the trees, across the field and back to the road.

8 □ Shadows on a Screen

"WHAT HAPPENED to your nose," Falling Stone said as Simon caught up with him.

"I walked into a tree."

They moved along at a slow but steady pace, and Falling Stone looked at the nose again, dubiously. "If you have to walk into something, a tree is a good thing to walk into." His voice was resonant and strong, powerful. Simon thought of it as the kind of voice that might have belonged to a warrior chief or a medicine man back in the old days of the Indians, when they were still hunting buffalo. "What kind of a tree was it?" Falling Stone wondered.

Simon looked away. "The kind that hits back." He still felt the pain of Sugg's fists on his body. He wanted to lie down on a soft bed and forget the world.

"That's very handsome," Tess said, dropping back from up

ahead and looking at his nose. "Did you do that yourself, or did someone do it for you?"

"I fell off a cliff."

She turned to Falling Stone. "There are cliffs on this road?"

"Only the ones you fall off of," he said.

Simon waved a hand in disgust. "All right, all right. I was in the woods taking a leak. I tripped on a rock and fell on my face. It's a war, isn't it? I'm entitled to break my nose." He stopped walking. "I'm going to vomit," he said, and went to the edge of the road, leaned against a tree, and retched. They waited for him, watching while he hung there, arms stretched forward, both hands on the tree, head down as he disgorged. When he was done, he rejoined them and they moved on again, pushing along steadily.

It wasn't long before the wide dirt road became a jungle trail again, and they were gone from that soft country where there were sheep and low hills covered with red and blue flowers. They were back in the mud and dampness, with the geckos, skinks, pythons, chameleons. Simon borrowed a mirror from Tess and looked at his face. It was not a face he recognized, the eye a rich shade of purple, his nose swollen and discolored, his lips puffed. There was a cut on his chin from the onyx ring that Sugg wore on his left hand. He felt stupid and a fool. His gut was in a state of ruin.

They were only a few minutes into the trees when a sniper opened up on them, rapid fire from an automatic weapon. They dove for cover. Simon was caught in an exposed position, slugs chewing up the ground all around him. He froze, feeling suddenly helpless, a dumb, frightened animal sensing the imminence of pain, death. Tess spotted the sniper and quickly squeezed off three rounds, one or all of which found their mark. The sniper tumbled out of the tree like an old ruined branch the tree didn't need anymore.

Simon saw where the bullets had ripped into the ground only

inches away from him. He looked at Tess, gazed intently at her, feeling an odd blend of lust and awe, gratitude, simple amazement mingled with desire, the desire muted but nonetheless real, part of his astonishment as he lay there on the ground, studying her eyes, her firm but sensuous mouth. Strange, he thought, how desire could quicken in the midst of peril and bodily pain. She was soft, sexy, mysterious—and weirdly magical, a terror with a gun.

After the sniper attack, they marched for less than an hour, then made their bivouac. The food came in, but Simon, still suffering from his encounter with Sugg, ate nothing. He drank some cold milk, sipping it slowly. He thought he might have a ruptured spleen, or a damaged pancreas—he could die in his sleep, and dying did not seem unattractive. He was off by himself, apart from the others, in view of them but not too close. He had unzipped his sleeping bag and spread it out on the grass, brown polyester, insulation between himself and the ground. Moss and fungus grew on his boots and fatigues, eating at his socks, but there was no fungus on the polyester. He wondered how long it would be resistant. The ground cool, wet with an inner dampness. The days could be hot, baking, but at night there was always that dampness; he imagined the core of the earth not as molten and hot, but cold, wet, maliciously sodden. There were tunnels down there, the monkeys rooting about, digging, carving chambers and passageways. An ammunition cache could be directly below: it could detonate, blow him sky high, his ass bombed out of the world, blown toward the stars.

He had an eerie sense that the monkeys knew exactly where they were. As if they were watching, looking on. As if they were toying with them, hitting them with mortar one day, an ambush the next. Enjoying the pursuit—not ready, yet, to move in for the kill. He remembered the eyes he'd seen, or thought he'd seen, back in the cave, during the storm—they had become a kind of symbol for him, luminous, staring, intense, flashing in his mind at random moments. Always watching.

Sugarman had flown in with a bin full of veal scaloppine, and Sugg wolfed down three helpings. Then he got busy on the rolls. He smeared them with butter and stuffed them in his mouth, chewing monstrously. He let out a deep burp and went on eating. There wasn't a mark on him, not a bruise that showed. "You think the monkeys eat like this?" he said. "You think they feed their faces on mashed potatoes, butter rolls, and veal scaloppeen? Roots and grass, that's what they get. Huh? That's what this war's all about. They're sick of the fungus and maggots they eat. If they could get their hands on some of this veal scaloppeen, that's all they're really after."

Tess brought an orange over to Simon, and peeled it for him, but he had no appetite. He was on his back, gazing at the darkening sky. A pale quarter moon, a few stars. She sat close to him, pensive, neither of them saying much. Simon flat on the ground, and Tess sitting cross-legged, the uneaten orange on the grass.

Simon lifted his head. "I think I'm losing my mind."

"That's news?"

He pointed. "That star up there. It just moved."

"Which one?"

"The bright one. It's not there anymore."

Tess studied the sky. The moon was there, and a handful of stars, not many.

"I was watching it. Then *zap*—it moved. Now it's gone."

"You better sleep. You want some painkiller?"

"I hurt, but not that way. It's not like a damned toothache."

"Something to help you sleep."

He closed his eyes. "I can sleep."

She got her backpack, took out her sleeping bag, and spread it out next to his, on the damp ground. They slept that way, beside each other, not touching. It was the first time they had been so close in the night. Simon figured she knew she was safe, what with all his bruises and smashed nose. And she was right, she was perfectly safe. He didn't make a move.

He awoke with the smell of smoke stinging his nostrils, and, opening his eyes, he saw a great spurt of flame in a stand of trees nearby. Tess, too, bolted awake. Behind them, more flame, the whole jungle going up. Screeching of birds and animals, and above the terrified screams of the animals he heard the *zsssst-zssssssst-szsssssst* of incoming rockets, thump and roar as they landed and blew up. Incendiaries, loaded with napalm or god-knows-what, and by now there was so much fire in the area it was as bright as daylight. The flames blotted out the stars.

Simon was still hurting from Sugg's blows, pain tearing through his ribs and arms, but despite the pain he moved fast, grabbing the pyroxene-T and slipping it onto his shoulders. They were all quickly up, coughing, gagging, on their feet. Merlin clutching the black box, Eikopf, Thurl, Falling Stone, all pushing around, getting hold of their weapons—looking for a direction, a way to run. Trask had his black beret on his head and his rifle gripped in his left hand. Simon was a few feet away from him. The flames lit up Trask's face, his gray eyes: the face intense, fierce, yet strangely calm, self-possessed, his eyes searching the perimeter, probing for an exit, a way through. "This way," he shouted, pointing a direction with his weapon, his voice rough and strong, creasing the air, cutting through the roar of the flames and incoming rockets. "Close it up. Push through and follow me. This way!"

He charged off into the jungle, into a gap between the flames, and they followed: into the mess, the raging nightmare. It was dumb obedience, an act of blind faith in his ability to find a way. The heat intolerable: Simon felt as if he were being cooked, baked, knowing that if it got any hotter the pyroxene-T would go off. He experienced a quality of terror he had never felt before, desperation, knowing that something had to be done but there was nothing, no help, only the heat and the running, and the waiting, wondering if the next degree of centigrade would push the pyroxene-T over its limit. They plunged into swamp and the swamp was burning, wet wood blazing, giving off steam and smoke, clouds of vapor. Tess gasping and coughing, and Sugg shouting "*Yaaaaaaaaaaaaaaaaaaah!*" and Thurl shouting "*Yaaaaaaaaaaa aaaaaah!*" and Simon thinking that this was hell, because hell is what it was, heat and terror, Trask taking them God knows where, deeper into the heat and flame where their flesh would melt and the pyroxene-T would detonate and smash their bones into atoms, wiping the earth clean of everything they had done and dreamed, dark moods, lust, anguish, fear, and there would be nothing but ash and a gaping hole where Simon had stood, ground zero. He imagined it: the explosion rupturing into flame as he ran, catching him in midair as his legs pumped and strained. A simple snap of light and sound, so sudden he would not even hear the roar of the blast. His frenzied running would be in the past tense, nobody alive to recall the terror, nobody who had lived it, sensed it, known the madness and the breathless, gasping, headlong rush to escape and survive.

But the pyroxene-T held. They reached water. Trask stood at the edge and waved them in, pushed, shoved, getting them into the wet safety beyond the flames, and they splashed in: Tess, Eikopf, Sugg, Simon, Major Kleff, every last one of them. It was swamp water, murky and sulfurous, waist-high, dense with algae and dead fish, mud, swirls of slime on the surface, lit up by the surrounding flames. Simon dipped down to his chin, getting his pack wet, cooling the pyroxene-T. A snake darted past him in the water. A burning branch from an overhanging tree fell into the water and sizzled, a noisy gush of steam and vapor. Simon kept his knees bent and stayed neck-deep. Tess was nearby, also neck-deep. A dead fish, belly-up, floated past her chin. Flames licked out over the water, and Simon saw her eyes, blank and lifeless, the eyes of someone who was scarcely functioning, the body still going, but everything else down, switched off. He grabbed hold of her, putting his arms around her, her face close to his. It seemed impossible they were still alive. Trask had saved them, the son of a bitch. He stood knee-deep in the water, defiant, painted red by the flames: a great, fiery god. He had run them through hell, and now they were in the stink and putrefaction of dead swamp water, safe.

The rockets were no longer coming in, and they waited in the water while the jungle fires burned themselves out. Thick, juicy leaves giving off smoke and steam, sizzling as they flamed. Merlin held the black box over his head, keeping it dry. When the biggest fires had died out, they ventured back onto land, and it was like walking through a set for an expressionistic film. Tree trunks gone to ash, blue and gray, lit by the first light of dawn. Heaps of ash and cinders on the ground, hot, they could feel the heat through their boots. Rocks blackened, empty spaces gouged out where there had been thick vegetation. Smoke curling up from the hot ground. The spot where Simon and Tess had been sleeping looked as if a blow torch had scoured it. In places the ashes were banked and sloped like snowdrifts. A few sleeping bags still intact, a couple of backpacks. Sugg, in his underwear, found his pants but not his shirt. Emma Sue found her medical kit. They would have to call Sugarman in to resupply them.

Simon looked at Trask: the way he moved, the confidence in his face, in every gesture. The black beret, smear of black ash across his face, darting gray eyes. Simon hated him, yet he wanted to go down on his knees to him. What a wild and damnable man he was, powerful and vain, aloof and definite, terrifyingly determined. He had saved them, and that was all the more reason to hate him, because now they were his, their lives belonged to him.

Eikopf was in an oddly cheerful mood. "See? You guys want to fuck around with God? He fucks back. Didn't I tell you? Don't say you were never warned."

"Who's been fucking with God?" Thurl said.

"Not me," Mickey Kabuki protested. "This trip out, I haven't even had a chance to fuck with the girls yet."

Eikopf still had that odd, otherworldly smile on his face, balanced between anger and delight, joy and self-righteous contempt. "You guys, say what you want. Talk and talk. But now you've seen it. Now you *know*."

"Have we been warned?" Thurl wondered.

Falling Stone nodded gravely.

"Where the hell is Meyerbeer?" Mickey Kabuki said. "How'd he miss a show like this?"

At the mere mention of Meyerbeer's name, the rainbow chopper pulled into range: they heard it and saw it. It was as if Mickey Kabuki had turned a piece of magic. "How'd you do that," Thurl said. "You said Meyerbeer, and there the fucker is."

Mickey Kabuki blew on his fingertips. "Basic," he said. "Very basic stuff. Actually, I've been learning from Eikopf. He knows some very sound tricks. Stick around, I'll show you a few other things."

Meyerbeer landed and got out of the chopper, cradling the camera in his left arm. Smoke was still curling up from the burnt grass and trees. "What the hell happened here," he said in his mild, calm manner.

"We figure *you* to know," Thurl answered, his tone lazy and accusatory. "We figure you the one who laid it on us."

"They gave it to you with the old incendiaries, huh? Tough. Real tough. Almost as tough as those B-52s. You think it was monkeys did it or some of ours?"

"We figure it was you," Thurl said. "Y'got some good footage out of it, no? Up there with the old infrared, immortalizing our asses while we hightailed for our lives."

Meyerbeer took out a fresh cigar. "Jesus, you folks never give a guy a break. I'm just a common working man, trying to make a living. Is there anything wrong with that? Tell them, Simon. Tell them how hard I work. What's wrong with that, huh?"

Simon looked over at Meyerbeer, but he was looking through him, beyond him. Wrong? There was wrong and wrong, more wrong than anyone could count. It was where they were, the air they breathed. It was the country they were in, ticks nestling in the meaty parts of your legs. Lice, vermin. The night was wrong and the moving star that had suddenly vanished was wrong. The sense of being watched, hunted, zeroed in—that was wrong too. The stink of burning trees was wrong. Meyerbeer was wrong, and wrong was Meyerbeer: he was the full meaning and definition of it. And *they* were wrong, all of them, Tess and Thurl and Eikopf and Falling Stone, because they had become a part of Meyerbeer, targets for his zoom lens, playing the roles he laid out for them: they were nothing anymore, images on celluloid, shadows on a screen, and even the shadows were wrong, shadows of shadows. Meyerbeer with the camera up to his face, his eye on the eye-piece, moving among them, getting all of them. Burnt trees, mounds of ash. Sugg in his skivvies, muttering. Trask in his beret, his face blackened with soot. Thurl, shirtless, scratching his chest.

"Boy, do I feel horny," Thurl said.

"Me too," Mickey Kabuki said. "Horny as a barn owl."

Simon wondered if that was true, that barn owls were horny creatures. Horny as a toad, horny as a goat, horny as a rooster, horny as a Tasmanian dingo. He looked at Kabuki. "Barn owls? Horny barn owls? Kabuki, are you making this up, or do you speak from experience?" Kabuki glanced haughtily at him, and gave him the finger. Meyerbeer got that too, the Kabuki finger: caught it, locked it in, about fifty frames, preserved for posterity.

❑ PART TWO

9 □ The Falling-Down Disease

WHEN TESS finished her senior year at Mary Magdalene High, in Philadelphia, she decided that what she really wanted was to be a nun, so she left home and went to the Sisters of the Holy Passion. At the novitiate, she worked hard at the things they gave her to do: she prayed, washed dishes, prayed, scrubbed floors, prayed, raked leaves, and prayed some more. She sorted laundry. After six months of that, she was no longer sure that the convent was the right place for her, so she left, with mixed feelings, and went on to college at Marymount, where she started out as a philosophy major and later switched to political science. She was restless, not sure of herself, feeling a need, a craving for something she could commit herself to in a deep and total way. She often wondered if she had made the right decision when she gave up on the convent.

Then the war began to heat up and she enlisted, thinking she might do something there, make a contribution. She could be a medic, or a typist, a clerk in a warehouse or in a supply depot. When she went through boot camp, though, it turned out that she had a fantastic knack with a rifle, and they made a marksman out of her. It was something that came naturally. She had never touched a gun before, but now, when there was a target in front of her, it was hard for her to miss. "What am I doing with a gun?" she complained to Simon. "I hate guns. I don't mind shooting at a target, but I don't want to shoot people. I want to be a nun, not a sharpshooter."

Before they assigned her to QUIF, they had used her in the

eastern sector for long-distance sniping with a high-power rifle equipped with a telescopic sight. They put her on a ridge overlooking an enemy encampment, and in less than a week she accounted for nine kills, including a colonel and two captains. "Every time it happens I feel a terrible sense of wrong. But I know it's something that has to be done, somebody has to do it. And I'm the one. It's so hateful, though. Sometimes, when I hit, for the barest fraction of a moment I feel good about it, and that makes it so much worse. You know how it is—you take aim at something and you hit, you score, and you feel good, you can't help feeling good, because hitting is what you were trying to do. It's the feeling good that's so terrible. It makes me feel guilty and wrong, as if I were in a state of . . . mortal sin."

They were on the trail, moving along side by side. Simon scratched at a mosquito bite on his chin. "You should have stayed with the Passionists."

"That's what my mother said in her last letter."

"That monkey colonel would still be alive. And all those other poor suckers. I'm glad you're on our side and not theirs."

"I asked them to transfer me to the secretarial pool, but they wouldn't listen. When I said I didn't want to shoot anymore, my CO just leaned back and laughed. Laughed, Simon. Then they gave me to Trask because he needed firepower." She pulled at her braid. "Firepower, Simon—that's all I am anymore. That's all I'm good for."

"When this is over, you should try the Franciscans," he suggested wryly, resisting her somber mood. "They have a very good feeling about animals. You like animals, don't you?"

"I hate animals."

"They could put you in a grammar school, teaching the eighth grade, you could impress the hell out of them with stories about the jungle. When the local cops need a sharpshooter, they call you in and put you on salary—you could support the whole damned convent that way."

She wasn't amused. "If I ever do become a nun again, I swear, Simon, I'll never pray for you. I'll say antiprayers, whole rosaries to make your life miserable."

He tilted his head cockily. "It figures. That's the kind of girl you are. That's how you repay a favor."

"What favor?"

"Didn't I ever do you a favor?"

"Simon, you don't know what a favor is.".

"Oh yes I do."

"Oh no you don't."

"I don't?" His face collapsed in a mock display of wounded pride. He shrugged, and kept on walking.

They marched through swamp, and then on high ground. In the rain. In the hot, sticky sun. Simon was tired, dreamy, suffering at odd moments from a sluggish form of lust. He lusted for Tess, and for Emma Sue. Lust was lust, what was the big deal? If an adequate-looking hippopotamus crossed his path, he would reach out and make a grab. But those were only odd, random moments. There were other times, whole hours, when he felt nothing at all: dead, empty, a machine that walked.

Tess was up ahead, and now it was Thurl beside him, pink earphone to his ear feeding him the subtle rhythms of the Ash Berries.

"Forget it," Thurl said, referring to Tess. "I could have told you the first day out—you want action, she is not the place to go. There is meat to dream about, an' meat to forget, an' that particular broad is meat to put on the shelf an' walk away from."

It amused Simon, the way everyone was waiting for him to make a move on Tess. It had sorted itself out that way, that somehow she belonged to him. But she did not belong, she had other things on her mind. Simon plodded on, and, while he was thinking about Tess, Eikopf materialized alongside, ghostly and intent, striding forward strenuously, with undisguised fatigue. "God has his ways," he said in his odd, enigmatic manner.

"What ways are those?" Simon wondered.

"Ways and ways. If anybody knew, then God wouldn't be God."

"He would be somebody else?"

Eikopf's face lit up, he snapped his fingers. "Exactly! That's the whole point. He can't *be* anybody else. That's why he's God!" It flowed along with a seeming show of logic. Eikopf was mad, beautifully and deliciously unbalanced, and often now, when they talked, Simon enjoyed letting go, allowing himself to be seduced into thinking the same moonstruck thoughts.

They heard the rumble of mortars far off in the valley, like distant thunder, but not with the randomness of thunder. A regularity, a steady humdrum beat. Somebody was getting clobbered. A monkey village that had to be wiped out because monkey guerillas were hiding in it—or maybe the other way around, monkey guerillas wrecking the village because the monkeys who lived there weren't loyal monkeys and had to be wiped out so they could never again be disloyal. The bombardment went on for almost an hour.

They made their way through oak and rosewood, through miles of rubber trees, pushing far into enemy-controlled territory. It was too risky, now, for Sugarman to carry the food in by helicopter, he would have been easy prey for the monkeys shooting from the ground. Instead, he now made high-altitude fly-overs in an old twin-engine transport and parachuted the supplies down in prearranged drop zones. Merlin would send a signal, and minutes later they'd hear the droning of the plane's engines, and the parachutes came sailing down like slow, lazy flowers. Occasionally a monkey patrol opened fire with automatic rifles, or with rockets they shot from hand-held launchers—but Sugarman was far up there, the monkeys in the field didn't have anything accurate enough to touch him.

Meyerbeer, though, was still whirling around in the rainbow

chopper, and they were taking bets now on how long he would last. A lot of IOUs were trading hands. Mickey Kabuki was at the hub of it, giving odds on the day and the hour. Sugg bet fifty, and Eikopf risked twenty-five. Major Kleff put up two hundred, and Emma Sue came up with thirty. Anybody willing to gamble that Meyerbeer would still be alive three days after bet time was getting four-to-one odds. Thurl took the four-to-one, and Schlumm got eight-to-one by picking a kill date that was six days off. It was a joke: with the amount of enemy firepower in the area, it was impossible that Meyerbeer would survive more than twenty-four hours. Yet somehow he did, spinning around, in and out, arriving, departing, again arriving, suddenly there above the trees. Sometimes it was the blond kid, Henry, at the controls, but frequently it was Meyerbeer himself flying the craft. Uncanny, the way he stayed alive.

Mickey Kabuki took special pleasure in setting up the bets on Meyerbeer, because he knew Meyerbeer had been giving odds on him. Day after day it was Kabuki out there on point: maybe he would still be alive by the time they reached the bridge, but nobody was putting any money on his chances of making it back. In fact, as they moved deeper and deeper into the jungle, not many of them were willing to risk anything on him at all.

"Hell," Meyerbeer complained to Thurl. "Is that all I'm worth? Four-to-one for me to make it through to next Friday? And fifty bananas are all you've got riding on me? I tell you, it's hard times. If you don't think I'm worth twice fifty, and if you can't get better than four-to-one out of that little jap—hell, that's demoralizing. On Kabuki, if you put up two hundred, I'll give you ten to one he doesn't make it through to next Saturday."

"Shit, man. Where do I come up with two bills?"

"Give me a note. If he's still on point next Saturday noon, I'll pay you off in Vidwar stock. When this movie hits the screen, Thurl, you'll be a rich man. That stock is going to skyrocket. Tell your friends. Tell Simon what a great deal I'm making you. I'll make the whole damn bunch of you rich."

Thurl wrote a note for the two hundred, and when Mickey Kabuki survived to noon of the following Saturday, Meyerbeer gave Thurl a note for two thousand dollars' worth of Vidwar stock. "You've got it made," he said. "All you've got to do now is stay alive. When you get back to the States, you can retire and live off the dividends."

Thurl stuck the note in his boot. He figured it was worth holding on to, though he had serious doubts that he'd ever collect on it. He figured either he would get killed or Meyerbeer would get killed, or both of them would get killed—and if both of them made it through, Meyerbeer was such an oily specimen he would just disappear and the note wouldn't be worth a damn. "That's a good place to keep it," Meyerbeer said. "Right there in your boot. I stick things like that in my boot all the time."

Meyerbeer flew off, and, as his chopper sped away, monkey artillery opened up on him from a mountain across the valley. Mickey Kabuki doubled the odds, and while the chopper was still in sight they were grabbing for pencils, writing notes like crazy. The rainbow chopper dodged around for a while, doing ellipses and spirals, then it disappeared into a low, blue cloud. The monkeys were throwing everything they had, but never touched him.

Later that afternoon, they were up on another mountain. They moved across the flank, and on the other side of the mountain they found that the trees had no leaves. The leaves were on the ground, wrinkled, gone brown and dead, as if the whole area had been hit by blight. Below the mountain there was a village: open fields, some farm animals moving about, cows and horses, a few water buffalo, bamboo huts roofed over with straw. The animals rooted about lazily, but among the huts there was a suspicious absence of activity. They approached cautiously, spreading out, moving in from different directions. At a signal from Trask, Sugg and Kabuki charged in across an open space and got to the huts. They prowled around, inspecting, then Sugg signaled for the rest of them to come on in.

The villagers were in their huts, most of them lying down, not moving. A few were on chairs, some were cross-legged on mats. Even the children were inactive. Simon peered inside a few huts, and everywhere it was the same: the people on cots, or on mats that were spread on the floor—motionless, yet they seemed alert, staring with large dark eyes.

"Let's get on with it," Trask said to Lieutenant Schlumm. They stood in a grassless clearing at the center of the cluster of huts. "Talk to them. Find out what's going on."

A middle-aged man came out from one of the huts and walked slowly toward the General. He wore dungarees, but no shirt. Simon was struck by how thin he was, his ribs visible like the lines of a musical staff. A string of beads hung around his neck, jade and turquoise, a red bandanna around his head. There were ivory plugs inserted into holes in his earlobes. Small, unsightly warts covered his chest and arms. From a distance the warts appeared to be an eruption of pimples. He walked a few yards, then fell, collapsing like a marionette whose strings had been cut. He raised himself and tried again to walk, but again he fell. He gathered himself together and managed to stand, and now simply stood there, smiling, hands extended, palms up, as if in apology for his desperate condition.

Schlumm approached him and they talked, and the man answered Schlumm's questions with extraordinary animation, nodding and gesturing. He was some sort of a chieftain. The mayor, the tribal headman. "He calls himself Willie Mays," Schlumm said, turning to Trask. "He says they're suffering from the falling-down disease."

Trask cleared his throat in a noisy, assertive manner. "What the hell is the falling-down disease?"

"They're not sure. They just keep falling down. Every time

91

they try to walk, they lose their balance and fall. He thinks it's from a bad crop of mushrooms. Mushrooms are a pretty big thing in their diet. They boil the mushrooms in water and mix them with ground-up roots. They're not sure if it was the mushrooms that were bad, or the roots. They fall down, and they've got these warts all over their bodies."

"The cattle aren't affected?"

"A few water buffalo died, but the rest of the animals seem okay."

"And everybody's got the warts?"

"Even the kids. The women too."

"Chemicals," Trask said. "Ask him if they've been hit by chemicals."

Schlumm posed the question, and the man who called himself Willie Mays talked for a long time, with expressive gestures. He drew a diagram in the ground with his index finger, a shape that looked like a bomb. Schlumm asked more questions, and Simon saw how Schlumm seemed to assume the characteristics of the man he was speaking to—quick motions of the hands, nodding and smiling, shifting rapidly from a smile to a frown and back to a smile again. Then he turned to Trask and was himself again, sober, no expression on his face, and very little inflection in his voice. "He says he's been living on this mountain all his life and they've been hit by all sorts of chemicals. The B-52s were here with Agent Orange, and the Russians were here with their Yellow Rain. Long ago, when the French were here, there was something they never learned the actual name of, but they called it the Blue Terror because it came at them like a blue fog. They liked the Blue Terror more than the Yellow Rain because it had a sweeter smell. There were some Albanians around with a T-2 toxin they got from the Russians, and some Cubans with a mycotoxin they got from the East Germans, who got it from the Russians, who stole it, he thinks, from the West Germans. He says he's the

Chief of this village and he knows about these things, he makes a point of keeping his eye on what's happening to his people."

"Ask him whose side he's on. I thought these mountain people were friendly with the Albanians. How come the Albanians are shooting T-2 canisters at them?"

Schlumm talked with the Chief, then turned again to Trask. "He says they're friendly with anybody who's willing to be friends. They're even friendly with their enemies. They have no guns and they know they'd lose any war they got involved in, so for them, he says, war is a bad idea. He wants to know why the B-52s were here last week dropping Agent Orange all over the place."

Trask was close to losing his temper. "Tell him I didn't send the B-52s. Tell him if I knew why they were here I wouldn't tell him because it's none of his business. Ask him if he knows why the B-52s put blockbusters up our assholes back there three days ago. Or was it three weeks? Tell him I'm a fucking two-star general and don't have to answer any of his mountain-monkey questions."

Schlumm interpreted, and the Chief smiled. He didn't appear to be put off by anything Trask had said. He smiled, and bowed.

"Ask him if they all fall down, or only some of them."

"He said they all do, sir."

"Show me. Tell him to roust them out of their huts and get them moving around."

The Chief was dismayed.

"Tell him I insist. It's necessary. Tell him if he doesn't roust them out, I'll have Sugg do it." He pointed toward Sugg, who stood with his thumbs tucked into his cartridge belt, leering.

Schlumm didn't have to translate. Trask's tone was belligerent enough for the Chief to understand. He shrugged, then turned and started toward the nearest hut, but he fell. Schlumm helped him up and walked with him, supporting him, and they went from hut to hut, telling the people to come out. There was murmuring, complaining. Low, astounded voices. But one by one they got up, and the ones inside the huts came out, into the clearing, where Trask stood, arms folded, observing intently. They walked, and they fell. They dragged themselves. They would take a few steps, then they'd lose their balance and go down. Women in long gowns with brightly colored waistbands, hair tied in a bun, or loose, flowing. Men in old, worn-out Levis and baggy cotton shirts. Kids with no clothes on at all. They all had small warts on their bodies, and they fell down. Trask stood in the center, watching. Soon there were bodies all over, twisted and contorted. People struggling to stand, and others no longer struggling, just lying on the ground. Schlumm brought the Chief, who was barely able to move, back to Trask.

"That's what it is all right," Trask said matter-of-factly. "It's the falling-down sickness. How long did he say they've had this?"

"Ever since they ate that last batch of mushrooms. Two weeks ago."

"Anybody die from this yet?"

"Just one old man who cracked his head open when he fell and hit a rock."

Trask glanced about at the fallen bodies. "These people are in rough shape," he remarked sternly. "They can't work their fields and they can't take care of their animals. It looks to me like they're starving to death. Ask him if he wants us to put them out of their misery."

Schlumm spoke to the Chief, and the Chief considered it. He said something in a low tone of voice.

"He says they'd like to live for a while longer. He wants to know if we can leave them any food."

"We don't travel with food," Trask said, his eyes rigid, firm. "Tell him the food comes to us out of the sky. Tell him if he's lucky food will come to him out of the sky, but I make no promises. Tell him Uncle Sam can't feed the world. Tell him we have no food but we have explosives. We can leave them some grenades for when they want to commit suicide. When the pain gets too bad they can blow themselves up."

Schlumm didn't know how to say Uncle Sam in monkey talk, but he relayed the gist of what the General had said. The Chief smiled with gratitude. He wanted the grenades.

While Schlumm and the General were busy with the Chief, Sugg picked up a girl who had fallen down in front of one of the huts and brought her inside. Tess saw it, and so did Simon. Sugg's animal vigor was unbridled, he would grab for anything within reach—old ladies, boys, and now this young cripple who was wasting away, couldn't stand on her feet, probably still a virgin. Trask saw it, but he made a point of not noticing. Major Kleff saw it and turned the other way. Tess looked to the General and the Major, and when she realized they were deliberately not noticing, she headed over in the direction of the hut. Simon went after her, to stop her.

"You don't want to go in there," he said.

"Why not?"

"He'll kill you."

"I'll kill him first."

He had his hand on her arm, gently restraining her. "There's no future in it," he said. He still had a black and swollen nose from when he stopped Sugg from taking the boy, pains in his bones.

She faced him, exasperated. "They know," she said, meaning Trask and the Major. "They know and they're letting it happen."

"Of course they know. Didn't you know they knew?"

Sugg was fearless and fierce: in a firefight he was raw, demonic energy. If a few rapes were the price Trask had to pay for that kind of toughness and reliability, he was willing to pay.

"It isn't right, Simon. It's foul. And wrong."

"I could shoot him," Simon suggested, surprised to hear himself say this. "Out on the trail, next time we run into a monkey patrol. They'll think the monkeys got him."

She looked at him. "You're serious, aren't you."

"Sure I am. Why not?"

She studied him, uncertain. Simon, too, was uncertain. He had never killed anyone, not even in battle. It was his job to blow up bridges, not people. Nevertheless, he felt a terrible anger, a frustration that tore at his insides. Was it anger, he wondered, or something less noble, less grand. Maybe it was just revenge he was after, getting even for his smashed nose.

"You don't even know how to shoot," she said.

"Sure I do. Just pull a lousy trigger. I could shoot Trask too," he added impulsively. "And Kleff." But as he said it, he knew it was empty talk, bravado, because you just didn't go around shooting people, not when they're your own, no matter how much you hated them.

Or did you?

Tess was looking away, toward the hut where Sugg and the girl were. She made a move toward the hut, then checked herself, and walked off in the opposite direction. There were people all over, lying on the ground. Long, bony faces and sunken cheeks, their large dark eyes patient and suffering, filled with a quiet pleading. They were dying, that was plain. In a couple of days, a week or two at most, they would all be gone. Tess moved slowly among them. She took a nectarine out of her pack and gave it to a pregnant woman who was holding a baby. The woman took it and bit into it. She stared up at Tess for a drawn-out moment, a look in which anguish and gratitude were painfully commingled. Tess lingered briefly, then she moved off and headed up the path, away from the huts and the people on the ground.

Emma Sue moved around among the natives, examining them. She had never seen anything like the warts before. The warts were on their arms and shoulders, and on the abdomen, the chest. She passed out aspirins to a few who had fever.

"The vital signs aren't good," she reported to Trask. "The blood pressure is low, and their pulse seems to be fading. Some of them are running a temp. I imagine the fever is preliminary to the final stage."

"Move the men out," Trask said to Major Kleff.

Emma Sue flinched, her green eyes fierce, rebellious. "You mean you'll do nothing for them?"

Trask was sharp with her. "You have a cure for them in that kit of yours?"

"No."

"Then buzz off. I left them some grenades. When the pain gets too bad, they can blow themselves up."

She glared, then turned and walked off, incensed.

"Get it moving," Trask said to the Major.

The Major turned to Merlin. "Report our position to HQ." Then he called to Mickey Kabuki. "Let's go, you're at point. Get it moving."

Simon picked up his pack, still bruised, still hurting from the beating Sugg had given him. Back to the trail. He felt powerless, caught in the grip of a blind, voiceless rage. He hated the war, the jungle, the defoliated trees. Hated Sugg, and hated Trask and the Major for making Sugg possible. And now he hated Tess too, because he knew, with a flat and tortured finality, that she was never going to sleep with him. Why should she? He was useless, of no consequence. Against Sugg, the loathsomeness of Sugg, he was irrelevant, and against the loathsomeness of the war, he was nothing, a cipher. As he pushed on along the trail, his hatred deepened, and finally it turned against himself. He thought it would have been lucky if he were not himself but something else, a dumb thing like a stone, or a swamp, with no mind, no feeling, nothing to imagine or remember. He wondered what that would be like, being an object, a clump of dirt, simply subsisting, without consciousness. People could walk all over him, spit on him, he wouldn't know, wouldn't care: it would have no meaning for him.

He thought he caught a glimpse of something moving in the trees to his left. He stopped and peered carefully, gun in hand, but saw nothing. He stared hard, feeling again what he had felt before, that they were being watched, that there was someone or something out there, tracking them, following along. But it was nothing, nothing that he could see. Up ahead, Falling Stone had also stopped, but now he was on the move again.

10 ❑ Crazy Wildflowers

MORNING, ANOTHER DAY. They had just moved out from their bivouac. "You know what I think?" Simon said to Tess, turning to her as they passed through a grove of mahoganies. "I think none of this is real. It's all a fantasy, make-believe." The anger and self-hatred that had been fermenting inside him had turned into a whimsical form of defiance, and he felt now a keen if temporary satisfaction in lashing out with jocular irony, denying existence to realities that he could no longer cope with. Trask, the jungle, Sugg. The war. "They're unreal, nonentities. And what I'm positively sure is *not* real," he added with special indignation, "is that damn bridge they want me to blow down. If it were real, we would be there already."

Tess looked at him blankly, and Major Kleff, walking close enough to overhear, made a clucking sound with his tongue. "What you lack, Simon, is confidence," he said, his voice flat and bloodless in the morning air. "The bridge is there, you know it is. You saw the recon photos."

At Base Blue, when Simon first met him, the Major was sour-faced and drab; he seemed depleted, out of shape, and Simon had simply assumed he would not be going into the field with them. He was still sour-faced, and still had that lonely, depleted look about the eyes, but he was by no means out of shape; day by day, on the trail, he seemed to strengthen, his body hardening, toughening. He was a quiet man, a plodder, conscientious and not unintelligent, but slow, inward, not ambitious, content to toil away in Trask's shadow. He had a problem with his kidneys, or with his bladder, and needed to stop often to urinate, but apart from that he was holding up well. He had survived three divorces, and if he could do that, Simon figured, he apparently could survive anything.

The Major's first wife had left him during the heyday of women's lib, going off, in a fit of feminist fervor, to live with another woman. His second wife had been a field reporter with a television network, and when it became clear to her that she could advance her career by becoming the mistress of one of the network's vice-presidents, she seized the opportunity and leaped to her new role with sweet abandon, though she did have the decency to sever her bond with the Major before her involvement became a public embarrassment for him. She was now in an anchor slot on a weekend news program, and the Major, partly out of curiosity, and partly out of a reluctance to jettison his past completely, made a point of tuning in whenever he had the opportunity. The third wife was psychotic. She had come at him three times with a knife, twice wounding him, and had to be put away. Plainly, the Major was a man unhappy in his choice of women, and, recognizing that fact, he had, in recent years, tried his hand at male companionship, though this was not something that was widely known. Simon learned about it from Schlumm, who seemed to have no end of information about the gray side of people's lives. Schlumm was discreet and sober-minded, hardly a gossip, yet if there was something dark to know, he had a knack for finding it out.

They were still among the mahoganies, Simon staring hard into the Major's eyes. "Confidence?" he asked in an agitated tone. "Is that what you said? I lack confidence?"

"We go the safest route, Simon. Not the shortest or the swiftest, but the best." The Major had a dry, formal way of speaking, as if he were not conversing, but reciting from memory. "The black box knows where the monkeys are—we detour, circle around, go left to go right, up to go down. Believe it—we're getting there." As he spoke, his mustache, a thin pencil line of black hair across his upper lip, wriggled obscenely. It was the wrong lip for that kind of a mustache, the wrong mustache for that kind of lip, and Simon wondered why the Major had never realized. "Trust the black box, Simon, it knows what it's doing. It'll get us there."

"I think we should kick the box to pieces," Simon said. "After that, we can all stand around and pee on Merlin's boots."

Merlin was about ten yards ahead, his feet badly afflicted with fungus, struggling along. He darted an anxious glance over his shoulder. "Keep away from my feet," he shouted, and Simon could see that he was genuinely concerned. He marched ahead at a quickened pace, as if he truly believed his boots—his feet— were in danger.

"Simon," the Major said, rather stiffly, "you are not a person of goodwill. Nobody should talk to you." He turned to Tess. "Why do you talk to him?"

"I'm never sure," she said in a bemused way. "I like his doubt, I guess. I like his misery and confusion."

"They told me there's a bridge to blow," Simon said with a flash of anger. "Where the hell is it?"

"The bridge exists, Simon," the Major answered. "We're getting there."

"When?"

"As fast as we can."

"I'll believe it when I see it."

"You will see it, Simon, when you believe it."

100

"Does that make sense?"

"Of course it does."

"It does?" Simon stopped dead—gave up walking, just stood there, glancing about wildly, a crazed look in his eyes. He called aloud: "Eikopf! Eikopf! Where are you? I need you!" But as he stood there, shouting Eikopf's name, he heard the familiar *pok-pok-pok* of automatic-rifle fire. Bullets ripped past him, tearing up the earth a few yards from where he was. He jumped for cover, down behind a tree that had a wide trunk and massive, protruding roots, and Tess went down beside him. Merlin was behind another tree, and the Major dashed ahead in a half-crouch, firing in the direction the first shots had come from.

"Didn't I tell you?" Simon shouted across to Merlin. "Put your life in the hands of a black box and it'll get you killed."

"Hush!" Tess said in a harsh whisper.

Simon looked at her, surprised by her absorption. The firing had stopped and there was, for a moment, a fearsome stillness. Tess rolled slowly away, and got a fix on a position halfway up the hill to the left of them. There was a big boulder up there. Before she fired, though, the monkeys opened up again, pouring it on. Simon kept his head down. He had his helmet on, but it was small comfort, one of those heavy slugs could rip into his skull as easily as if he had no helmet on at all. He hugged the ground, bullets ripping through the trees all around him. He had his Magnum in hand, ready, but didn't fire. The monkeys were blasting away, and the QUIF guns blasted back: Sugg, Thurl, Falling Stone, Mickey Kabuki, firing away, bullets spitting off in all directions. Tess was motionless, staring out coldly, searching for another target. She found one and fired, but from where Simon was he couldn't tell if she had hit or not.

The firing stopped and there was a lull again. Sugg and Falling Stone circled around and got into position on the left flank of the big rock. Thurl and Major Kleff flanked it on the right. Simon sensed that the monkeys were moving around too. The silence was tedious, as unnerving as the rage and noise when bullets were spattering all around. He looked to Tess, and then to Merlin. Tess waited calmly, her eyes scanning the trees. Merlin had the black box tucked underneath him, protecting it with his body; he seemed to be muttering to himself. Usually, under fire, he was composed and steady; but now, Simon noted, he seemed tense, barely under control.

Simon glanced toward the branches up above—they were webbed with vines that were loaded with purple flowers, the flowers giving off a rich, heady fragrance. Only now did he become aware of the sweet odor. Crazy wildflowers, he thought. He didn't know their name. Giving off that wild, crazy smell, smack in the middle of a firefight.

He heard a faint rustling behind him, a snapped twig, and swiftly rolled onto his back and blasted away with the .44. The monkey pitched backward, stopped by the impact of the slugs, and collapsed, a crumpled heap. It was a boy, sixteen or seventeen, in dark green fatigues. One bullet had hit him in the chest, another in his head. The face smooth, beardless. It was the first time Simon had ever shot anyone. For a moment, a brief, icy moment, he felt nothing. He was aware that he should feel something—guilt, or joy, or pride, or remorse, perhaps something on the order of postcoitum triste; but for that one moment, an instant of intense lucidity and calm, he felt nothing. Then, swiftly, the moment dissolved, and he saw the dead boy not as someone who had come at him with a gun, but simply as a dead boy, and the enormity of it hit him. He felt a fierce, stinging sorrow, and it was all mixed up somehow with the smell of the purple flowers in the tree above him, the sweet, pungent scent, mingling with the odor of spent cartridges.

"I didn't know you knew how to shoot," Tess said.

"Everybody from the Bronx knows how to shoot," he said glibly, hiding his feelings. He looked across to Merlin. "Merlin, are you still alive?"

102

"I think so. Yes." His left arm, grazed by a bullet, was bleeding.

Another monkey came up from the same direction the first one had come from, and Tess fired a burst, cutting him down. Then all hell broke loose, Sugg and Falling Stone firing on the big rock from the left flank, and Thurl and the Major hitting it from the right. The monkeys fired back wildly. Bullets sprayed through the trees, gouging trunks, shredding leaves and branches. After a few moments, Sugg got in close enough to toss a grenade, and that finished it. Eikopf was still firing, shooting madly at the rock. Schlumm had to stop him.

Falling Stone made the count. There were nine dead monkeys, all of them young. In another country they would have been schoolboys.

Emma Sue moved among the wounded. She treated Merlin's arm, which had only been grazed. Eikopf had tripped on a root and bit through his lip, and Schlumm's left ear had been shot off. She put a whole bunch of stitches into Mickey Kabuki's face. A bullet had gone through his left cheek. He must have been shouting, his mouth wide open; the bullet had gone in through the mouth and out through the cheek, or the other way, in through the cheek and out through the mouth. His face was wrecked, but Mickey Kabuki understood that he had never been much to look at anyway.

Simon went up behind the rock to see what Sugg's grenade had done, and he found Sugg bent over one of the corpses. He had slashed the pants open with his knife and was cutting off the foreskin. It was a grisly spectacle, but Simon wasn't shocked, there was little Sugg could do to shock him. Sugg kept a collection of foreskins which he carried in a small jar with a preservative in it. There were people who cut off ears, and others who cut off thumbs. Simon had heard of someone in the east sector who cut off toes. Sugg saw him watching. "What the hell are *you* looking at?" He glared jealously, as if at any moment Simon might try to claim one of the corpses for his own. His face was flushed, contorted. "How many'd you kill? Huh? How many? Get the fuck out of here, you bastard—or one of these days I'll cut off yours." He waved the knife menacingly.

Simon didn't move, simply stood there, looking on. They had fought once already, and he realized, with a sinking sensation in the pit of his stomach, that it was far from over. It was something deep, in the blood, and by the time they got to the bridge it would simmer up again, boil over.

Sugg put the foreskin in the jar and screwed the cap back on, and Simon turned and walked off, going back to the tree that was loaded with flowers, their powerful fragrance reaching deep inside him, a dizzying perfume sweetsick with death. The boy he killed lay on his side, knees bent, one arm twisted awkwardly behind his head. A few yards away lay the one that Tess had killed, face-down in the grass, a splotch of blood between his shoulders, where the bullet had exited. It was all a madness, a wild, blistering insanity that he didn't understand, and wanted desperately to get away from.

He took off his pack and went over to a dry creekbed, lined with rocks the size of baseballs. He picked one up and threw it at a tree. Then another, and another, as fast and hard as he could. He threw at a tree named Sugg and hit it square, Sugg's face collapsing, smashed, bloodied. He threw at a tree named Trask, a tree named Kleff, a tree named Meyerbeer, rock after rock, the rocks rebounding wildly. He kept throwing until he wore himself out, arms hanging down, sweat pouring off, his whole body limp with fatigue, too exhausted to think. Tess had come up behind him, and had been watching, waiting for him to finish. "Are you okay?" she asked.

"Yeah," he said. "Yeah. I'm okay." But clearly he was not. He went back and got his pack.

When Emma Sue was done with the wounded, they moved out, with Mickey Kabuki at point. Major Kleff had wanted Sugg to take over, because of the wound in Kabuki's face, but Kabuki wouldn't hear of it. He was determined, bent on carrying on, eyes burning with a mysterious resolve. The Major shrugged and sent him forward. They were lucky, nobody was dead, they could all still shoot. They were bandaged, bruised, in pain, but they pushed along quickly, eager to cover ground.

11 □ The Bear

THE NEXT DAY, Thursday, they put in a hard day's march, past cane fields, irrigation canals, then back again into palms, teak, mahogany. It was Thanksgiving Day. Simon was alone for a while, moving forward mechanically through the jungle mist. He felt again the same uneasiness he had felt before, as if they were being hunted, pursued, but the hunter was tracking them cautiously, waiting for the right moment to close in. At one point the feeling was so strong he stopped dead and took a good look around, peering into the trees, the foliage, even studying the sky. But nothing, just the feeling, and he pushed it aside, thinking he was coming unhinged, as bad as Eikopf. It seemed just a matter of time before it caught up with them, all this mad killing in a strange land. The mist was seeping into his brain.

He kept steadily on, through rocks and mud, and it struck him, suddenly, that the march was not just arduous, not merely hard, fraught with danger, but actually foolish—a wrong plan, an outrageous piece of silliness. Why, he wondered, was he carrying the pyroxene-T? If the food could be parachuted in, the pyroxene-T could also have been flown in at the time when it was needed—a lot safer that way, instead of this daily risk of annihilation. And not only the pyroxene-T, but the whole damn strike force—they could have been dropped from a plane close to the target. It came at him with blinding clarity, so obvious, so simple, he couldn't understand why he hadn't thought of it before.

"What about that," he found himself saying aloud. And now it wasn't Falling Stone walking along beside him, and not Tess, but General Trask. Simon had been too deep in thought to notice, and when he saw who it was, he didn't care, went right on saying what he had started to say. "What about that, huh? Why couldn't they parachute us all in? It would have saved a hell of a lot of boot leather."

Trask took it in stride, not at all bothered by the way in which the remark seemed to surface out of nowhere. "Parachute in," he said, "and we could land ourselves smack in the middle of an enemy regiment. Risky, Simon. Risky." He laughed, a raucous, throaty laugh that approximated a growl. Then the laugh stopped short, and it was as if he hadn't laughed at all. "This way, carving through the jungle, the worst we risk is stumbling into a few patrols, which we can beat the hell out of. Or getting bombed by our own B-52s. I'm not God, Corporal. I try to be, but there are some hazards I just can't protect you from. Look at it this way—if you weren't carrying that explosive on your back, where would be our esprit de corps? You're it, you're the center. This whole damn mission revolves around you, you son of a bitch. Think positive. It's your first big bridge, like deflowering a maidenhead. Didn't I overhear you saying something of the sort just a while ago? Well, that's the way to think of it." He took off his beret and scratched the top of his head. "Speaking of maidenheads, what kind of progress you making with that Pollaiuolo girl? She's a wop, ain't she? Or is she spic."

"She grew up in Philadelphia," Simon said. "Her father's from Venice, he was a glassblower. Her mother's Irish. One of her grandmothers was Lithuanian."

Trask stopped walking a moment and cut wind. Then he was

walking again. "Sounds to me like a pretty mixed-up girl. Have you nailed her yet?"

"No sir, not yet."

"She'll come around. They always do. If that's where your interest lies. The more they pretend not to want it, the hungrier they are."

"I'm sure you know better than I, sir."

"As soon as she makes up her mind," Trask said in a factual tone, but not without a degree of enthusiasm, "she'll start nibbling, then she'll get her hips up around you and you'll be right inside, where it counts."

"Is that how it happens?"

"That's how it happens. Though there are, you realize, plenty of other ways."

"Well, I'm looking forward."

"Things will happen that you never imagined. God help your organ, Corporal."

"God help it, sir."

"Frankly, I don't know why I'm giving you all this friendly advice. I hate your guts, Simon. You know that, don't you? I've disliked you from the first."

"You've mentioned that before, sir. Many times."

Trask frowned, his face seemed to darken. "And I'm telling you again, damn it, because it's something you should never forget. My point of view on you, Corporal, is that I feel toward you the way a man might feel toward a son that he never wanted to have, a son he hated and wanted to get rid of. A man who told his wife to have an abortion when she was pregnant with that particular son, but she didn't, and when the kid grew up the man knew more definitely than ever what a mistake it was not to have had that abortion. That's how I feel about you. So don't talk to me, I don't want to know you."

"Yes, sir. Anything you say, sir."

They moved along in a strained silence, side by side. They

107

crossed a narrow stream and followed the trail up across a low hill that didn't have many trees on it, then they came down off the hill and were in thick jungle again. Trask stopped to urinate, and Simon stopped with him. They were in a grove loaded with fuchsias, red and purple blooms, drooping, lush and tropical.

"The only good part about fighting a war in a jungle," Trask said as he urinated, "is that there is so much rot and shit around that you don't have any illusions. This is life, Corporal, rock bottom. As basic as it comes. Kill and get killed in all this rot. You hate somebody, you tell him to his face, like I just told you. The first monkey you see, you blast away and kill, or he'll kill you. That's life, in a nutshell. Pretty flowers, aren't they? Funny, the way they hang down that way." He cut wind again. "Simon, I like the kill you made back there in that firefight. Nice shooting. Make you feel good?"

"It made me feel like shit."

"That's because, deep inside you, shit is what you are. You were born that way, it's in the genes. Not to worry, though—we'll make a soldier out of you yet."

Simon finished urinating and buttoned his pants, but the General was still pouring it out, a long, steady stream. "God takes care of his own," he said. "If he doesn't, I can't figure who will. That's why I believe in God, you see. And that's where you atheists and agnostics have your face in the mud. If you don't have God to help you, how the hell you ever gonna find a place to pee in?"

"I guess that could be a problem," Simon said.

Trask buttoned up, and they were on the move again, on the trail.

They bivouacked early that night, an hour before sunset, because it was Thanksgiving Day. The early bivouac was Trask's gift to them. They were losing some marching time, but they'd make it up the next day, in spades. Merlin signaled their location to Sugarman, and Sugarman flew over and sent the food canisters parachuting down, three small pink chutes sailing down the air. Some days he used pink, other days he used green. One day he used white chutes and nearly got shot down, so he never used white again. He was superstitious about colors.

They went out and recovered the canisters, and once again Sugarman had been good to them. There was roast turkey, cranberry sauce, stuffing, candied yams. Creamed spinach and spiced apples. Two kinds of pie: pumpkin and mince. There was even some wine, a 1969 Barsac. The canister with the wine in it contained an apology from Sugarman for having failed to come up with a Château Haut Brion that he had nearly got his hands on. Sugarman was all right, he took care of them. He was better, in some ways, than a mother.

As they were fetching in the canisters and burying the parachutes, Meyerbeer showed up in the rainbow chopper, swooping in to get some footage of them in their Thanksgiving splendor. He put down in a snug clearing where there was scarcely any room, no margin for error, getting in with skill, nerve, and incredible good luck. He hopped out with his camera and started filming right away, as they were unhooking the canisters from the chutes. First a long shot, then moving in close, catching gesture, movement, facial expression. Then, somewhat abruptly, he turned off the camera and put it down on the ground, and told them about a stop he had made earlier in the day, at the village where the natives were afflicted with the falling-down disease.

"The place with that guy in blue jeans," he said, "the one with the red bandanna around his head and the ivory plugs in his ears. The Mayor. The one who calls himself Willie Mays." He seemed, for a moment, uncharacteristically pensive. "I got a lot of heavy footage, people falling down all over the place. The guy with the bandanna, Willie Mays, he took one of the grenades you guys left and blew himself up, himself and his family. It was quite a scene." Meyerbeer seemed genuinely moved. He began to gesture

109

with his hands, as if he were choreographing their last rites, showing a respectful concern that it be done correctly. "He sat down on the grass with his wife and kids, all close together. Three kids he had. They said good-bye to each other in monkey talk, then they leaned close together and he pulled the pin." He nodded soberly, seeming to see it again, vivid, as if it were happening now. "The people in that village, there's not much of a future for them. They're just lying around out there, waiting to die. Very thoughtful of the General to leave those grenades. As I pulled out, a couple of other grenades went off. There were grenades going off all over the place."

Eikopf, listening, seemed more thoughtful than ever, his eyes rapt in a blank gaze. Meyerbeer spotted him and picked up the camera. "Hey Eikopf," he called, in a chipper tone, "I like that expression on your face. Why don't you move right over there next to Schlumm and I'll get both of you together. I think your face and the bandage on Schlumm's ear make a dandy combination."

Eikopf didn't move, but Meyerbeer wasn't deterred. He got the film rolling and took some footage of Eikopf, then he panned over to Schlumm. "A whole ear?" he said. "No kidding. It must hurt like hell."

"Just part of the lobe," Schlumm answered. "I don't feel a thing, I guess it'll wreak havoc on my sex appeal."

"It'll make you more interesting. A ruined ear is a good conversation piece. It adds character. The girls will be full of questions."

The food was out and they sat around and ate, sweating and mud-splattered, smelling bad because it was days since they had been near any clear water they could wash in. But the turkey was good, the wine was terrific, and the spiced apples were delicious. Thurl thought the stuffing should have had more garlic and paprika, and Emma Sue thought it should have had less. Schlumm thought Sugarman should have tried harder to get the Château

Haut Brion. Nevertheless, it was Thanksgiving, and they had a lot to be thankful for: they were alive. They hadn't been wiped out by a monkey patrol, or a monkey minefield, or by the B-52s. The rescue chopper that had gone out to pick up Vain had been shot down, and that was too bad for Vain, but bad things were something you learned to accept, especially if they happened to somebody else. Once you accepted them, the bad things weren't bad anymore: they became good things. You could always accept, adapt, adjust, and move on, and if you were lucky you got the golden wound and were sent home. They had more turkey, more pie. They wanted more wine, but the Major wouldn't allow it. He didn't want any of them too drunk to pull a trigger. They had black coffee and chocolate bars, and before they were done eating, General Trask got up and made a speech.

"If there's one thing we Americans know about," he said, standing in their midst, one hand in a pocket, "it's the business of giving thanks. That's why we've got all this food here—turkey, and these yams, and wine. It's a tradition we have going back all the way to the Mayflower. Giving thanks is one thing we know about, and sticking together is another thing we know how to do. Through thick and thin. When I think of the days and weeks we've pulled together on this here mission, the sheer hell we've been through, I am amazed. I look out at all you sonsabitches, and I say to myself: I can't stand a one of them, and they probably can't stand each other, but we don't give a damn how much we hate each other—we stick together. We've got monkeys to kill and a bridge to blow down. That binds us together. I look out there at your fucking faces, and what do I see? I see a nigger, a Pole, and an Apache. There's even a Jap and a Jew. I don't see any Chicanos out there, but that's only because we lost Gomez to diphtheria back at Base Blue before we set out. There's even a couple of good old-fashioned white Anglo-Saxon Protestants with us, and I say to myself: How can a bunch like this function? How is it they can work together the way they do? Then I look at the

111

faces again, into the eyes, and I realize there isn't a nigger out there, not a Pole or a Jew, no Jap and no redskin neither: because what's out there is just red-blooded Americans. One for all and all for one. It's the Corps that makes us what we are, and it's America that makes the Corps. *E pluribus unum.* That may sound simpleminded to some of you folks that went to college, where they feed you all that relativity crap, but it's a fact. Hard rock fact. And that's what we give thanks for. So eat up and stuff yourselves, while you have the chance. What the hell!"

He raised his cup to his lips and tossed off what was left of his wine. They all picked up their cups, but most of the cups were already empty. Those who still had some wine left drank, and the others lifted their cups anyway. It was a powerful speech, something they would remember. Simon was impressed. The General was an amazing man. He would get them all killed—but if you had to get killed anyway, better to get killed with Trask than with somebody who didn't know how to stand on his feet and tell you about the Mayflower. He was stark raving mad, but his madness was resplendent, a form of beauty. He sat down and peeled some oranges, and passed them around.

The sun was low, igniting the sky into a bonfire of color—ocher, scarlet, fierce vermilion, streaks of lavender. Thurl leaned across to Schlumm and said, "You know what? I feel pretty bad about bein' a nigger, an' I apologize. If I coulda been a plain ordinary American without the nigger part, I would have arranged it. I really am sorry about that."

"Me too," Schlumm said. "If I could have been just a simple American without the Jew part, I would have set it up that way."

Mickey Kabuki scratched an itch on his thigh. "You can't imagine what hell it is being a Jap. If I could have been an unadulterated white American, just that, you can't guess what kind of a price I'd pay."

"Not me," Falling Stone said. "With me, Apache is just fine. If I could have been an Apache without being an American, there's

112

no complaint from me. We were doing just fine out there before the ranchers and the sheepherders and the cavalry came along."

"I think he's a communist," Thurl said.

Mickey Kabuki was still scratching at his thigh. "Sounds that way to me. A dyed-in-the-wool red. Shall we burn an Indian?"

Thurl made a lush, smacking sound with his lips. "I think we should. Burn an Injun. But first we should *flay him alive!*"

He leaped across at Falling Stone, grabbed him off the rock he was on, and they went rolling around on the ground. They were just about the same size, equally matched. Kabuki jumped into it, small and slight, yanking at Falling Stone's arm and twisting it, so Thurl could have a better go at him. Falling Stone broke loose, got a hold on Thurl, and tossed him on top of Mickey Kabuki. There was a solid, crunching sound. "That's what I mean about red-blooded," Trask said. Thurl and Falling Stone got to their feet, and somehow Mickey Kabuki managed to get up too. Some of the stitches had come out of his cheek, his face was a bloody mess. The three of them hung there a moment, eyeing each other, breathing hard. Then they were at it again. Falling Stone took a punch in his solar plexus, which doubled him over, and when he got his wind back he swatted Thurl on the jaw and sent him reeling backward, into Schlumm. Mickey Kabuki came up behind Falling Stone and got a stranglehold on him, but Falling Stone flipped him over and he landed on top of Major Kleff. Falling Stone was left standing there, alone, breathing hard, arms hanging down, bearish, panting. The Major disentangled himself from Mickey Kabuki, and walked calmly over to Falling Stone, as if to congratulate him, but instead socked him in the jaw. Falling Stone fell back on his head and went out like a light. Simon splashed some water on him and brought him around, and Emma Sue got busy on Mickey Kabuki's face.

That night, Simon slept for a few hours, then he woke up and lay for a long time in a vague state between sleeping and waking. He felt again a strange uneasiness, as he had felt several times before, but now the feeling was merged with dreamy images out of his past, random memories straying haphazardly. Memories of the Bronx, the slow years when he was growing up. Sunlight falling through a window in a library. A chemistry professor who committed suicide. His eyes were closed, then they were open, gazing emptily, and a large black shape detached itself from the darkness and hovered in front of him. It seemed unreal, he couldn't easily distinguish it from his drowsy imaginings. Something large and black, looming, pausing there as if wanting to be noticed. Then it backed off, vast and slow, part of the darkness, as if it were the darkness itself that had somehow taken form and was moving about, roving through the camp. Simon watched with drowsy curiosity, without alarm but not without a sense of jeopardy, as in a dream, when the dream begins to go bad and turns into a nightmare.

The black shape drew away, and then it returned, coming back now not to Simon, but to Emma Sue, who was asleep several yards away, under a tree. It nudged at her with its snout, first gently, then nudged again, aggressively, pushing her hard, and she screamed, jumped to her feet screaming, and Simon, hearing her shrill, piercing cry, knew it was no dream. He sat up, grabbed for his gun, and fired—once, twice, and the black shape slouched away in the dark. Simon quickly disentangled himself from his sleeping bag and charged out in his skivvies. He was all instinct, racing for the target, eager for a clear view and the chance for another shot. The animal was there ahead of him, in the tall grass, etched in moonlight. Simon raised the Magnum, aiming, and Meyerbeer snapped on his floodlamps and got his camera rolling. Simon was stunned by the sudden light, and so was the animal—it turned, facing him, an immense black bear, rearing up on its hind legs, forepaws spread wide, eyes ablaze.

Simon blasted away—four, five, six shots, and the gun clicked empty. He heard Meyerbeer behind him: *"Go, Simon, give it to him. Now, damn it! Shoot! Shoot!*" He turned, and Meyerbeer was just a few yards off, film rolling, floodlamps fixed to a cross-beam attached to the camera. If the cylinder hadn't gone empty, Simon would have shot at the lamps, or at Meyerbeer himself.

When he looked at the bear again, it was still standing. The bullets had gone into him, but still he stood, caught in the glare of the lights, a string of saliva hanging down from the corner of his mouth, breathing so heavily Simon could hear him, a hoarse, rumbling sound, raspy and deep. And then it was Falling Stone's turn, leaping out at the bear with his knife, wearing nothing, only his undershorts, no boots, no pants or shirt, the knife aloft and flaming in the lights, going home deep into the animal's chest, finding the heart—the bear and Falling Stone caught there for a moment in a fierce embrace, an instant of seeming stillness while the knife found its way home. Then the two of them went down, the dead bear crumpling backward, Falling Stone holding close, the bear's paws still clutching him.

When Simon got to them, the bear was dead. Falling Stone was disengaging, getting back on his feet, his back scarred with claw marks. He stood for a moment, bruised and tall, then he bent over the bear and dipped a hand into the hole he had carved, into the heart, and took out a handful of blood, which he lifted to his mouth and drank. Meyerbeer pushed Simon out of the way and moved in for a closeup.

When they examined the bear, they found three broken arrows in its hide. There were old scars, wounds that had healed over. The animal was immense, and Simon was in awe of it: its toughness, the way it had stood its ground as he fired on it. It had been through more wars than this one, an old survivor, and now it was dead meat. He felt odd, off balance: as if, somehow, the beast were sacrosanct, and by shooting at it he had unwittingly become involved in some ancient wrong. It was a feeling he couldn't shake, a mood he couldn't explain. Nor could he explain or clar-ify what he felt about Falling Stone, who suddenly seemed some-

115

one else, not the Falling Stone he had gone through boot camp with, but a stranger, someone he didn't know or understand, a man wielding a knife, going naked to the bear, reaching into its heart and drinking of its blood. It was an old ritual, stark and primitive, and, face to face with it, Simon felt timid, uncertain.

Trask, flushed and surly from having been wrenched out of sleep, took a look at the bear, kicked it to confirm that it was dead, then raised hell with Simon for having fired while they were in bivouac. He was apprehensive about rousing a monkey patrol. Luckily, the nearest concentration of the enemy was well over twenty miles away, and if the reports they got off the black box were to be trusted, there was little likelihood of a patrol operating in the area they were in. Nevertheless, Trask was uneasy. He went into a huddle with the Major, and in the end, though he was inclined to break camp and move on, he decided to stay put. He did insist on doubling the watch, though, and with undisguised malice appointed Simon to do guard duty till they broke camp at dawn. "Who the hell was on watch when this damn thing came in," he asked growlishly.

Schlumm had been, and Merlin. The bear had slipped right past them. Trask looked at them, cleared his throat, and moved his tongue around in his mouth, as if preparing to spit, then simply turned and headed back to his sleeping bag.

Merlin worked at the black box, feeding it questions, taking answers, feeding it more questions. He sat on the ground, cross-legged, the box in front of him, and suddenly he looked up. "That isn't a bear," he said, speaking to no one in particular, but loud enough for Simon to hear even though he was quite a distance away. "It's something else. There are no wild bears in this area. There are no wild bears anyplace in this entire country." They heard him, but he was merely part of the background, he had lost all relevance. They were looking at the bear.

Emma Sue took out the antiseptic and went to work on Falling Stone's back. Then she went over to Merlin and checked his feet, which were still afflicted with fungus. Simon watched as she dug into her bag of medicines, and it struck him how little he knew her, how little he understood her. She was bright, good-looking, and yes, sexy, but with problems and passions that seemed foreign to his life, as if she were from another time, another age, and he realized now, with a twinge of sadness, that she was a person he would only see from afar and never really know. She was down on her knees, looking at Merlin's bare feet, applying ointment. Busy over fungus. And Merlin, blind to her, was busy with the black box, wondering, if the bear wasn't a bear, what it might possibly be.

12 ◻ The Grand Concourse

"IT WAS the mince pie," the Major shouted from behind a tree.

"The creamed spinach," Merlin called out from behind another tree.

"Damn that Sugarman," Thurl muttered. "He fed us poison, green mold in the stuffing. Baked bacteria."

"Gastroenteritis," Emma Sue said.

Lieutenant Schlumm was doubled over with cramps. "It was the wine, that lousy Barsac. He should have got the Château Haut Brion."

Even Mickey Kabuki, who was notorious for his chronic constipation, was suffering from a steady flow. They were helpless, unable to move out of camp. Merlin sent a signal to Sugarman to fly in a few liters of Kaopectate and a load of toilet paper.

"Christ, is my ass sore," Thurl complained.

Trask was furious: they were losing one day, maybe more. "What are our chances," he asked Emma Sue. "Is it shigellosis?" If it was shigellosis, the mission was in abort.

"Probably just an *E. coli* thing," she said hopefully. "Montezuma's revenge. Delhi belly."

"Antibiotics?"

"No, no. Contraindicated. We don't want to unbalance the intestinal flora. Let's go with the Kaopectate and hope for the best."

Thurl lay stretched out most of the day with his earphone on his ear, listening to the Everhearts. He'd disappear into the trees for a while, then he'd be back in the same spot, on the grass. Merlin sat leaning against a rock, with the black box next to him. When he ran off into the trees, he carried the black box with him.

The bear lay sprawled in the tall grass a short distance from the encampment, where Falling Stone had brought it down. There was a gaping hole in the chest where the knife had carved through into the heart. Smears of dried blood where the bullets from Simon's .44 had gone in. Simon could see where the slugs had struck—he counted five hits, two near the right shoulder, two in the abdomen, and one in the right thigh. Flies buzzed around the wounds, and already ants and other insects were at work on the massive corpse. The black fur swarming with maggots and vermin. Vermin were also inside the body, having entered through the wounds and orifices. The abdomen moved and surged with the motion of the foreign life within. From a distance, it seemed the bear was alive and breathing.

Vultures had been busy at the carcass early in the morning and had ripped out part of the flank, but Falling Stone shooed them away. All day he sat there, keeping the vultures off by flinging stones at them. They were in the trees, waiting. Other birds were up there too, scavengers with black and brown feathers. A few hawks circling high up. Falling Stone kept the birds and animals off, and the maggots and vermin worked furiously under the hot sun.

Merlin worked the black box, monitoring the movements of the monkeys, making sure there were no patrols in the area. Then he checked again about the bear, and again he came up with the

118

same result: the bear couldn't be a bear, there were no wild bears in that part of the country.

"That's the biggest nonbear I've ever laid eyes on," Simon said.

Thurl nodded slowly. "It sure is. Back home every now and then we took a trip to the mountains, to hunt bear. Those were damn good times, huntin' bear. But I never hunted a nonbear. I wish I could have had a crack at this one."

Simon stepped over to Merlin. "You think there are any other nonbears in this territory? Thurl would like a crack at one."

But Merlin merely repeated, in a monotone, what he had said before, there were no wild bears in that part of the world.

"We know that. It's the nonbears that interest us."

"There are no nonbears either. That was the last one. It probably escaped from a zoo up north. Or down south. It doesn't belong here."

"Ask your black box if there are any zoos in the neighborhood. Maybe we can locate a nonzoo that has a nonbear in it that will make Thurl happy."

Merlin was gripped by intestinal pain. He clutched at his stomach, wincing, then grabbed the black box and rushed for the trees.

Sugg ambled over to where the bear was, and for a while he watched as the vermin worked away at the carcass. "Some job you did with that knife," he said to Falling Stone, with the barest hint of disparagement. "You probably did a lot of that when you were a kid, right? Is that what redskin kids do, chase bears with a blade?"

Falling Stone sat cross-legged on a high flat rock about twenty feet off from the bear. Beside him on the rock was a pile of small stones he was using against the vultures. He picked one up and flung it at Sugg, hitting him on his left boot.

Sugg roared: "What the hell'd you do that for?"

Falling Stone grabbed another and flung it, catching Sugg on his shin. Sugg jumped with the pain, and howled. "Fucking Indian! You're out of your mind! Crazy, stupid redskin!" He was ready to kill, but he hung back, because for the moment Falling Stone was untouchable: he had an aura, he had killed the bear. He was set apart, suffused with a mysterious, primitive power that Sugg didn't understand and chose instinctively not to challenge. He just stood there, enraged and shouting, and when he was done shouting he turned and walked off before Falling Stone took it in mind to throw another. "Crazy," he muttered, limping away. "Fuckin' redskin is out of his fuckin' mind."

Falling Stone said nothing, didn't even look in Sugg's direction. His eyes were on the dead bear.

It was shortly before noon when Sugarman made the fly-over and dropped the Kaopectate. They broke open the case and started pouring it down. "I hate this shit," Mickey Kabuki complained. "Do I have to take this?"

"Take it," Emma Sue insisted. They all took it, even Meyerbeer. They stood around, swallowing hard.

"I like the taste," Sugg said. Eikopf gagged on it and went off to vomit.

The Major went over to Emma Sue. "How long before it takes effect?"

She shrugged. "Hope for the best. The right amount of hope can work miracles."

Around five o'clock, Meyerbeer came out of the trees and announced that he was cured. Not really cured, he admitted, but close enough to be confident about taking off. He poured more Kaopectate down his throat, and got some final footage of the bear, which had been dramatically transformed by the action of the insects. Then he got into the helicopter, waved good-bye, and took off. Some of the others showed signs of improvement too. Thurl, and the Major, and Mickey Kabuki. Simon still had a few cramps biting at his gut now and then, but he found comfort, of a somewhat malicious sort, in noting that not even Meyerbeer was immune from the ravages of nature. He watched the rainbow chopper going up, hovering while Meyerbeer got his bearings. It hung there like a strange, ungainly bird, then moved off and was quickly gone.

Simon looked at Tess: she was tired, drawn. The long days on the trail had been hard on her. She had lost weight. Her pigtail was clotted with mud and her heavy eyebrows needed trimming. The weight loss, though, brought out her facial features to advantage—the high cheekbones, the sloping line of her jaw. She was lovely. He was used to thinking of her as adequate, not unappealing, pleasantly attractive, someone he would not at all mind going to bed with; but now he saw her as much more than that—not merely desirable, but in an odd, subtle way, quietly beautiful. It gave him pleasure simply to sit and look at her, even with the mud and sweat, the smear of dirt across her forehead. She had her boots off and was massaging her toes. Her feet struck him as being very small.

The afternoon sun did something with her hair. Her hair was brown, but the sun brought out a reddish gold tint that had, until that moment, escaped his notice. He had felt, ever since he first saw her, that there was something familiar about her; she seemed, somehow, someone he had always known, someone from out of his past—and now, suddenly, it came to him, he saw what it was. As she sat there, massaging her feet, the sun lighting up her hair, he realized that she bore an astonishing resemblance to a girl he had seen once, not many years back, when he was a freshman at City College. It was a terrible thing, an accident—the girl was killed. He was in his car, at a red light, waiting to cross the Grand Concourse. Traffic was heavy. He saw the girl coming out of a corner drugstore, and she was pretty. She seemed distracted, her mind very far away. Suddenly, as he watched, he had a sinking awareness of what was about to happen. It wasn't a presentiment, an intuition into the future—simply a fact, a view of the

121

total situation as it was occurring, a situation with its own unalterable logic. He saw how it began, and he knew how it had to end: it started with the girl stepping out of the drugstore, and he saw how it would unfold, how she was on her way across the sidewalk and into the street, into a moving line of traffic, as if she saw nothing, heard nothing, her mind somewhere else, her path taking her directly in front of a commercial van that was moving along at a pretty fast clip.

It was only a moment, yet it seemed to him an excruciating duration, everything clear, sharp, unbearably vivid. The van was a Mrs. Wagner's Pies truck. The girl came to the edge of the sidewalk and stepped off the curb into the street, and the van came bearing down on her. Simon wanted to blow his horn, but couldn't—he was caught in a momentary paralysis, unable to move, unable to do anything but watch. And part of what he saw was that if he blew the horn she might turn in his direction, and then it was almost certain that she would not notice the oncoming van. It was as if he were locked in a glass bubble, insulated, no way for him to get out and prevent what was in process of happening, what had to happen, what was predicated as having to happen the moment she put her foot outside the drugstore door.

The driver of the truck slammed his brakes on and turned sharply to avoid her, but it was too late. The girl and the truck were simultaneously at the spot where Simon had foreseen they would be. The girl bounced off the front end and fell to the ground some ten feet away from the point of impact. The van swerved into the curb and onto the sidewalk, and flipped over— the doors wrenched open, and pies went flying out all over, tin pieplates clattering above the noise of the traffic. Simon's paralysis was gone and he was in motion, out of his car, rushing toward the dead girl. Someone else was there ahead of him, bending over her. One of her shoes was off, and he was surprised to see how small her foot was.

The driver of the overturned truck managed to climb out, confused and shaken, a smear of blood on his forehead. On the street, dozens of pies were strewn about, broken and crushed. It couldn't have been more than a minute or two: from the time the girl stepped out of the drugstore, to the moment when Simon stood over her. Her face, her limbs, the dreamy way she came through the door and moved toward the street, and he could do nothing.

For Simon, it had all somehow disappeared, he had drawn a veil, and only now, as he sat there with Tess and saw her in the afternoon sun, did he remember, the particulars filtering through, vivid, wrenching. And, now that he remembered, he wanted to forget. Because it was a troubling thing, this sudden realization that his interest in Tess may actually have been fueled by his memory of the dead girl, a phantom buried in his unconscious. How alike they were, the dead girl and Tess—the color of the hair, shape of the face. The nose, forehead, chin. But at the same time that he thought this, another thought cut through, that it was quite possible the dead girl had not been like Tess at all—somebody else entirely, different hair, a different face, a face he could no longer accurately remember because it was simply too long ago, no link whatsoever between the two, other than his own arbitrary and baffling instinct to connect them. He wanted to tell her about it, wanted somehow to communicate to her the confusion that he felt, the distress, but he didn't quite know how to begin.

"You know," he said, "somehow you remind me—and don't get me wrong, don't misunderstand—you remind me, strangely, of a hideous accident I once saw. There was a truck and a dead girl, and Mrs. Wagner's pies all over the place. Up on the Grand Concourse."

It was wrong—he wasn't saying it right. Whatever it was that he had wanted to tell her, this wasn't it. He could see from the expression on her face how wrong it was.

"I remind you of an accident on the Grand Concourse?"

"Well—not in the way you think. There was this girl, this dead girl—"

"You knew her?"

"No. She was just a person I saw. She came out of a drug-store."

"And I remind you of her?"

"Yes. I think so. In some ways. I never knew her, you see. She was just a girl stepping into the street."

"You hit her?"

"Somebody else did. A guy in a Mrs. Wagner's Pies truck. There were pies all over the place. Cherry pies, pineapple pies. Lemon meringue. It was an awful mess."

"Simon, I don't think that's funny."

"Neither do I. I didn't mean it to be funny. Why did you think I was trying to be funny?"

"You have a peculiar expression on your face. Simon, really—I don't want to hear about this."

"It's something I want to explain to you. Somebody died. I think it's important."

"Somebody you never knew."

"Yes."

Her eyes took on a wild, crazed look. "Simon, people are dying all the time. We just came through a place where a whole village was dying."

"But this was different. It wasn't just anybody. And it wasn't just anywhere. It was in the Bronx, on the Grand Concourse. A girl I never met, and I watched it happen. There was nothing I could do, I just sat there and watched it happen. God knows—maybe, mentally, I made it happen."

"People die, Simon. There are accidents."

"But this one, somehow, seemed terribly, terribly important."

"Why do you remember it now?"

"That's what I'm trying to explain. I don't know why. She had small feet. Her shoes came off and I remember she had small feet. When you took your boots off just now, that's what I thought: You have small feet. Maybe that's the connection—just a stupid, random association."

She said nothing, merely stared at him, deeply, as if somehow she understood all the things he had wanted to say but had never uttered—about death, bonding, memory, about the past and the future, about holding on and connecting, about the great void that had opened up inside him when he remembered the dead girl, her dead face, and wasn't sure if it was her face he was remembering or Tess's face that he had mixed up with hers. She stared, gazed, seemed somehow to understand all of that, even though he hadn't explained a word of it—and he realized that he was projecting again, imagining that she understood when in fact she could not possibly have begun to guess what it was he had been trying to say. Or maybe she had. He wasn't entirely sure himself what it was, exactly, that he had been driving at.

She studied his eyes, gazing, then turned away suddenly with a twinge of pain, leaning forward, clutching at her abdomen. "Christ, Simon, I've got it again. Quick, get my boots on."

He shoved her boots on and tucked the laces out of the way so she wouldn't trip on them, and watched as she stood and shuffled off in a half-crouch, creased with spasms of pain, off to the trees.

He felt awful. There was death on the Grand Concourse, and dysentery in the jungle. He went off in the opposite direction, into other trees, away from Tess, and away from the dead bear that was slowly vanishing before their eyes, being eaten by vermin. Away from Merlin and the black box, and the General, the Major, away from Sugg.

He wandered among rubber trees and dieffenbachia, rosewood and eng. There were snakes, toads, drongos. Shafts of late afternoon sun filtering through the dense leaves. Chirping sounds, crickets. Green luminosity. He wandered around, figuring he was lost, and it was, for the moment, an amusing notion: lost in the jungle. Eventually, though, there were voices, thick and slurred, but familiar, and he went toward them, and found Thurl with Mickey Kabuki and Eikopf.

They were juiced. The Major had rationed the wine at the Thanksgiving feast, and they had got hold of what was left over, half a case of Barsac, and were swilling it down. they had a liter of Kaopectate with them and kept their stomachs well coated, though every now and then one or another of them had to retire into the foliage to relieve an urgency.

"Do you know which war this is?" Thurl was saying. "I can't remember which war it is. Is it World War I?"

"It isn't World War I," Mickey Kabuki said. He saw Simon stepping toward them through the foliage. "Hey, Simon—is this World War I?" He offered the bottle, and Simon took a swig. He passed the bottle to Eikopf. There were three empty bottles on the ground.

"It's World War II," Eikopf said. "We're in Burma." It was Eikopf as Simon had never seen him before, neatly lubricated. Eikopf mad, yes, deranged, bereft of reason, but Eikopf looped and glued, feeling no pain. Eikopf happy, his dark eyes burning in his skull in what Simon could only think of as a mild, serene frenzy. He had gone beyond hope into despair, and now he was beyond despair, drifting in the bliss and ease of an alcoholic haze. "Burma," he repeated, slurring. "The tsetse flies are getting on my nerves, but I think I have it under control. If I don't, God does. God is what is left over, He's not where you think he is. He's someplace else."

"What the hell does God have to do with it?" Mickey Kabuki wondered.

Eikopf shrugged, a queer smile slanting across his lips. "God only knows."

"This ain't Burma," Thurl said. "It's Africa. We're in the Afrika Korps."

"It isn't a war," Mickey Kabuki snorted. "It's a police action."

Thurl shook his head. "It ain't a police action, it's a military intervention."

Eikopf rinsed his mouth with a sip of wine, and swallowed. "It's World War III." His dark eyes fairly glowed with this insight.

Thurl took the bottle and gulped down more wine, then passed the bottle to Simon. "When the bombs start fallin'," Thurl said, "stick yo' head down between yo' legs and lick yo' hole."

"It's the war to end all wars," Eikopf called out as he moved off for another bout of diarrhea. "God invented it. He's the referee."

"It isn't a war at all," Mickey Kabuki said. "It's a piece of cake."

Thurl scratched his head. He still had his pink earphone on his right ear, and the cassette was going. This time it was the Dugan City Diggers. "I love war," he said, "'cause it makes us decent and clean."

Mickey Kabuki blew his nose. "If we're not decent and clean, how will we ever get to heaven?"

"That's what I used to be," Simon said, "when I was a kid. Decent and clean."

"What do you want to be a kid for," Thurl said.

Simon took more wine. "Who said I want to be a kid?"

Birds were busy up in the trees, making a racket, chirping, squawking, as if in the midst of a war of their own.

13 ◻ Tables Spread with Meat and Fruit

IN THE MORNING, there was very little left of the bear. The night scavengers had come in and done their work, jackals, hyenas, nothing left but bones and tufts of fur. In the vague light of dawn, the bones were invested with an eerie luminescence, as if possessed of some strange and mysterious power. Falling Stone stood gazing at them for several minutes. He touched them, and poured a cup of water over them. Then he turned and picked up his gear.

They moved out, eager to put behind them the place where they'd been sick. They felt like hell, and looked it too. Mickey Kabuki complained about the hole in his cheek, which was giving him pain, and Schlumm confided to Simon that he wasn't feeling too sensational about having lost an ear. It didn't hurt, he said, but he was beginning to feel a slight psychological disorientation from walking around with an empty space where his ear should have been. Simon thought it was too bad about Schlumm; he had a quiet manner, but under the apparent calm he actually was high-strung, and now, with the ear gone, he was beginning to show signs of distress. He was restive, fidgety, and Simon feared that he too, in his quiet way, was beginning to come apart.

For a while they were on a high chalk ridge, all white, with a few scraps of green vegetation on it, stretching out for more than a mile. Then they were off the ridge and back again in the jungle, on trails that carved baffling, elliptical patterns through trees and undergrowth. All morning like that, and on into the afternoon, the wet stink of the jungle, the air sour, stiflingly humid, nothing but trees. Then, toward midafternoon, they came upon a small village, thatched huts built up on stilts, and they spotted Meyerbeer's chopper parked in a field of beans. Up ahead, in the center of the village, there was a lot of activity, something was going on. The beat of drums, music from reeds. There was a bonfire throwing up a lot of smoke, and everywhere there were sprays of flowers—roses and lilies, and other flowers, vivid exotic blooms, red, yellow, purple, flowers whose names Simon didn't know.

Trask turned to Schlumm, but Schlumm was baffled. It was a festival of some sort, but not one that he knew about. The drums, the flowers, the fire, the piercing sounds of the reeds. Some sort of celebration.

128

As they drew closer, they saw that the natives were naked. A few of the men wore loincloths, and some of the women were girdled with belts of flowers, but most of them wore nothing at all. A large number of them were dancing around the fire, men and women, not touching each other, moving to the left, then stopping, then moving to the right—arms aloft, bodies weaving and undulating, swaying to the rhythm of the drums. Fresh palms had been thrown on the fire, giving off thick streams of yellow and white smoke. There were others, not dancing, couples lying about on the grass, making love. Bodies everywhere, it seemed, touching, embracing, lazily coupling. Simon had seen movies, underground erotica, with scenes vaguely resembling this, but had never imagined that he would come upon anything of the sort in real life. He was struck by the beauty of their bodies, women and men, the young ones and even the ones who were old, their bodies firm and taut, kept trim by the hard work they did in the fields. They were good-looking people, with broad foreheads, eyes set far apart, and finely chiseled features.

There were tables spread with meat and fruit—breadfruit, guava, pineapples, clusters of grapes. Nuts and cups of wine. Slow, unfrenzied beat of the drums, and the languorous melodies of the reeds. Men and women dancing, and others milling about, eating and drinking, and the ones who were making love. And, among them, casual and smooth, was Meyerbeer, in pink slacks and a Hawaiian shirt, with his camera, putting it on film. He was alone. The blond kid, Henry, was back at Camp Alpha—suffering from beriberi, Meyerbeer said offhandedly, as if it might or might not be true, or, in any event, was inconsequential. He moved slowly and deliberately, the camera anchored on his shoulder, getting it all: the dancers, and the ones at the drums, hands pounding the leather skin, and the ones in the grass, embracing. He roved slowly and gently, as if caressing them with the camera. He was the tallest one there.

The natives were neither distracted nor discomposed by the

arrival of the force. The drummers went right on drumming, and the others, looking over and noting their presence, went right on doing what they were doing. Trask marched straight for Meyerbeer. Meyerbeer saw him coming and got some footage of him as he approached.

"What the hell is going on?" Trask demanded. "Meyerbeer, did you arrange this?"

Meyerbeer switched off the camera and removed it from his shoulder, holding it down at his side in his left hand. He was as amiable as ever. "I arrange and disarrange," he replied indifferently.

Trask flared. "Like hell you do. *I*'m the arranger. And *I* disarrange. Any more crap like this and I'll disarrange you right out of uniform." It was off target, of course, the part about the uniform, because Meyerbeer never used a uniform. Yet it was plain that Trask had an anger inside him, and it was an anger that Meyerbeer couldn't afford to ignore.

"I apologize, General, sir," Meyerbeer answered. "I'd sure hate to lose my uniform. I truly would. But I think you'll change your mind, sir, when you see what I've got on film. I caught them in just the right light. A few minutes ago, the sun was fantastic—ripe, egg-yolk yellow. Unusual color tones. Apricot—and lush, tender gold. It'll blow your mind."

"I don't *want* my mind blown, Meyerbeer. I aim to keep my mind whole and intact, like God made it." Trask's square jaw seemed firmer than ever. His red face redder, more wildly furious. "Close it down—you hear? Close this operation down and get your ass the hell out of here."

"That's good enough by me," Meyerbeer said. "If that's the way you feel about it. Just remember, sir, you've got a lot invested in this film, I'd hate to see it go down the tube just because it doesn't have a few of the right scenes in it."

Trask's lips twisted as if he'd just rinsed his mouth with vinegar. His face was coated with a slick film of sweat. "This is war, dammit, not a parlor game. I won't have you exploiting the civilians." He hovered over the word *exploiting*, giving it its widest range of meaning.

"Sir, I haven't exploited a single one of them," Meyerbeer protested. "They're just out there doing what they want to be doing."

"You put them up to this."

"Well, a few suggestions here and there. They're fine people, General. Just look at them. Healthy human specimens, and they feel very good about all of this. They're really having a swell time. I wouldn't say I'm actually exploiting anything. In fact, it looks to me as if I've helped them start up a whole new tradition for themselves. Damn, I wouldn't be surprised if they decide to hold a festival like this every year. Or even every month. You don't have to look twice, sir, to see that they really are enjoying themselves."

"Either *you're* mad, Meyerbeer, or *I* am—and I know it's not me because *I'm* the one who gives the orders here. Do you hear that? *I'm still in charge*."

"I never doubted that. I was only thinking of the ten thousand dollars you have invested in this film, sir. All the shares you own in Vidwar."

Trask exploded. "I de-invest it! Cancel the shares and give me back my cash." His red, contorted face hung inches in front of Meyerbeer's, looking for all the world like a grotesque mask.

"It can't be done, *sir*. The money's been spent. There were expenses, I thought you understood about that. My man back in Toledo—there were trips to Paris and New York he had to make. The advance work is the whole thing when you're looking for a big success, *sir*."

Trask glowered, and took a step back. The gastroenteritis had left him weakened, with very little in the way of emotional resources, yet he had enough presence of mind to sense that he was operating on the margin, at the very edge. The dancers were still dancing, and the lovers were making love, languid bodies weaving in dreamy amorousness in the rich, golden light of midafternoon. The bonfire sent up great billows of white vapor and smoke. The women were lovely. He wondered if Meyerbeer had had his share of them before getting to work with the camera. He looked at Meyerbeer in a way that made it clear he wanted to punch him in the mouth, or shoot him between the eyes.

"Meyerbeer, this troop is moving out posthaste, this very minute. Before we reach the perimeter of this village, I want to see that chopper up in the air. Understand?"

Meyerbeer understood. All he had to do was take the chopper up, let the General see him there, then he could set right back down again as soon as Trask and the QUIF Force had moved on. He had won this round, it was all his. "An equitable solution," he acknowledged. "General, sir, I've always admired you for your brilliance and your sense of fair play. Your word is my command." He walked off in the direction of the helicopter, and when he had gone about ten steps, he turned and waved good-bye. "See you later, *sir*," he said, then hurried off at a trot to the beanfield where the chopper was anchored.

Thurl turned to Mickey Kabuki and said, loud enough for Trask and the Major to overhear, "What we got to go hustlin' off for? I don't see why we can't hang around a while and join in on some of the action."

"Because that's not the kind of action that wins wars," Trask said snappishly. "Discipline, that's what does it. It's in the mind, the will. Self-restraint makes all the difference. Don't you men see it? That's why these peasants are peasants. No self-restraint. We have it. That's why they're where they are and we're where we are. It's all the difference. Right, Schlumm?"

"All the difference," Schlumm said. Then he added, distractedly, as if unmindful of whom he was talking to, "But those melons do look tempting, they sure do. And that's terrific-looking bread, great loaves of bread these people make."

"Terrific-looking bread," Simon echoed.

"Move it out," Major Kleff called. "Kabuki, push on. Let's go."

"That crud Meyerbeer," Thurl said to Falling Stone. "He has all the fun. What a life." He called ahead to Mickey Kabuki. "Hey, Kabuki—here's twenty says Meyerbeer buys it tomorrow. In the A.M., between nine and noon."

"You're on," Mickey Kabuki shouted.

"I bet these people know nothing about birth control," Emma Sue said to Tess. "You think I should stay behind and give them some instruction? You think the General would mind?"

They could hear Meyerbeer revving up the engine, getting ready to lift off. Simon noted that Sugg was taking up a position in the rear, and he knew what that meant. As soon as the rest of them were on the trail, he'd be getting in a little quick action of his own before moving out.

Meyerbeer's chopper was up, hovering around in a tantalizing way. They went through a field planted with squash, then they were off into the trees, and through the branches they could see Meyerbeer circling around up there, swinging in a lazy arc, as if he owned the place, all of it, as if it were all his—the sky, the clouds, the jungle, the war. It was a kind of omnipotence he seemed to have, coming and going as he pleased, free, untouched, immune to monkey gunfire, as if he had made some sort of Faustian bargain with the devil. And if the devil was real, they figured he owned the devil too.

Owned all of it, yes, every last bit of it—but not for long. A few hours later, that same day, the tail end of the afternoon, Merlin used the black box to communicate with HQ, and word came through that the rainbow chopper had gone down, blasted out of the sky by small arms fire. The monkeys scored a hit on the fuel tank and the chopper exploded in a ball of flame, no survivors.

The news filtered down the line, and the march came raggedly to a halt. They all just stood around, loosely clustered, trying to absorb it. They were stunned.

"Get a confirmation," Trask said to Merlin.

"Sir, they did confirm."

"Confirm again."

Merlin raised HQ again, and the confirmation came through. Meyerbeer was dead.

"How could he be dead?" Simon said. "Meyerbeer doesn't die. It's not in the cards for him to go under." He had wished him dead so many times that now he felt culpable, as if, simply by wishing it, he had made it happen. He was Meyerbeer's executioner. Most of them felt the same kind of guilt, or, at the least, a twinge of self-doubt. They had been betting on his death so long, it was as if they were all somehow responsible, as if they had actually fired the shots that brought him down. Day after day he had been in and out of their lives, in the rainbow chopper, turning up when they least expected, zooming in with the zoom lens, selling them shares in Vidwar: they were used to him, the way you get used to a fly that keeps buzzing around your head. Hard to imagine a day, a succession of days, without him.

Trask had his hands in his pockets, a sober expression on his face. "He was a cool customer," he noted, sensing that something ought to be said. "Real cool, the kind they don't make many of anymore. A son of a bitch and a bastard, yes, but a son of a bitch with class. He had the Meyerbeer touch—which none of us, God help us, will ever forget." The tone was elegiac, but there was the barest hint of relief, a shade of triumph in the realization that Meyerbeer was finally and forever gone. "He was a wheeler-dealer, all right. Smooth as they come, with polyvinyl testicles. Hell, if he were still around, I figure any one of these days now I'd be ready to shoot the fucker down myself. But the monkeys got to him first, thank God for that. They spared me the agony of blowing a hole in one of our own."

They stood around for a while, a little dazed, not saying much.

134

Mickey Kabuki moved quietly among them, collecting from the losers. There were lots of losers and only one winner, Sugg. Days ago he had bet that Meyerbeer wouldn't get nailed until this particular afternoon, and Kabuki had given him long-shot odds. Sugg walked away from it with three big ones, in the form of an IOU that Kabuki wrote out in a scrawl that was barely decipherable. Sugg had never felt one way or another about Meyerbeer, but as Kabuki handed him the IOU he was delighted that Meyerbeer had had the good sense to select that particular afternoon on which to make his exit and pass from the scene.

Thurl took his Vidwar stock note out of his boot, tore it up, and flipped the pieces into the air. Falling Stone took out his, folded it into a paper airplane, and sent it aloft. The plane drifted in the warm air, making a wide arc, and came down on a pile of dung a passing yak had left behind. A yak or a llama, Simon wasn't sure.

"It's tough luck for Meyerbeer," Emma Sue said. "He was okay, he really was." She had never slept with him, and hadn't had any immediate plans, but he was someone she had thought about, someone she would gladly have obliged. It still seemed impossible, hard to believe: Meyerbeer. What an astonishing vacuum his death left. There was an unraveling, a sense of having been abandoned. If Meyerbeer could die, so could they all. His death seemed a warning, especially to Simon, who was baffled, thrown off balance. For all the suspicion and antipathy he had felt, he realized now that a peculiar form of dependency had built up, Meyerbeer like a bad habit, an addiction, and, even though he was well gone, there was nothing to replace him: they were in a state of withdrawal, made captive by the swiftness of his death. It was all there in Simon's imagination, vivid and whole, as if he had seen it, made it happen: the chopper bursting into flame, the fireball, the smashed wreckage, and now a smoldering, stunned silence, hollow-boned disbelief. Meyerbeer, and all the others who'd been killed since they set out from Base Blue. How quick, sudden, a ringing emptiness.

135

And yet, even though the crash had been confirmed, and even though Simon could actively visualize it in imagination, it remained difficult for him to absorb, hard for him to accept it as real: because Meyerbeer was too slippery, even in death, too cunning and elusive, and, as they pushed on through the underbrush and the white jungle mists, Simon felt an unshakeable skepticism, wanting something more definite, some sort of proof, evidence, wanting to see with his own eyes the charred and broken bones.

14 ◻ Happy Birthday, Eikopf

TOO MANY of them had been lost. Studdwin gone, Smudge gone, Vain gone. Polymer. And now Meyerbeer. And already it was apparent to all of them that they were going to lose Eikopf.

He refused to wear his clothes any more. He had taken off his shirt, pants, and underwear, and had thrown them away. Before he threw them away, he slashed them with his bayonet, ensuring that they were definitely gone from his life. He wore his helmet and boots, and carried his pack on his back, but other than that he was stark naked. It was something that nobody objected to, something they simply took for granted. Even Trask didn't object, though he did raise an eyebrow. If Meyerbeer could go around in pink slacks and a Hawaiian shirt, the way he had, there was no clear reason why Eikopf should not be allowed to walk around naked. It was, admittedly, something of a rationalization, because Trask knew he wasn't likely to get a replacement for Eikopf at this late date, and Eikopf naked was better than no Eikopf at all.

All that was expected of anyone was that he do his job and do it well. Eikopf was useless with a gun, and useless with respect to just about everything else connected with the mission, so in effect his job was to have no job, and he did that extremely well, with above-average competence. He was Eikopf—why should he be somebody else? Trask noted, wearily, that the hard logic on which he had always prided himself seemed to be bending more frequently now, more in line with the strange logic of the mission.

"He doesn't have the will to live," Tess said. They all knew about the will to live. Back in training they had been told all about it, how it was the thing that got you through when everything else fell apart on you. Day by day, now, things seemed to be falling apart.

They pressed on, cutting their way through a lot of dense foliage. Then they were out of the undergrowth, and the trail widened. "Hey," Thurl called aloud, "don't you know? Today is Eikopf's birthday."

"No kidding," Simon said. "His birthday?"

"Happy birthday, Eikopf," Falling Stone said.

"It isn't my birthday, you fuckers." He plodded on, carrying his pack and his gun. His body was covered by a lot of black moles and mosquito bites. The mosquito bites didn't seem to bother him, he never scratched. His genitals were small and shriveled, lost in a luxuriant growth of black pubic hair.

Thurl fell behind, then he came running up. "I was lookin' for strawberries, but I found these mushrooms instead. Ain't they beautiful? Eikopf, accept these as a token of my appreciation."

Falling Stone caught a glimpse of what Thurl had in his hand. "Those aren't mushrooms, those are toadstools."

"In that case, Eikopf, I offer you these toadstools."

"Bug off, you bastards!"

"Happy birthday, Eikopf," Emma Sue sang out. "How old are you today?" Merlin checked with the black box, and the box gave them an answer: twenty-six years, seven months, and three days.

"Christ, he's an old man," Thurl said. "Years, months, and days. How many hours?"

"The computer doesn't have the hours," Merlin said apologetically. "When they stored the bio data, they didn't record the time of birth."

"It isn't my birthday," Eikopf grumbled. Simon thought it was brave of him, the way he bore their taunts. There was a desolate dignity in the way he tramped along, almost as if he were beginning to come back to life. But they knew that was never going to happen, because Eikopf was already dead. He had been dead before the mission started, and if he wasn't dead then, he would be dead before it was over. He was a marked man; it was like traveling with a corpse.

"Let's sing for him," Emma Sue suggested. She started singing "Happy Birthday," and they all joined in. Simon sang, and Thurl sang. Even the Major sang, belting it out with his scratchy voice that couldn't carry a tune.

General Trask heard the singing and dropped back to see what it was all about. "So it's your birthday, is it?" he said to Eikopf. "That's pretty wonderful, having a birthday."

"No sir, it's not."

"Not wonderful?"

"Not my birthday, sir."

"Don't be shy about getting old, son. If you're not shy about walking around without any clothes on, you shouldn't be shy about a little thing like a birthday. It happens to the best of us. How old are you, Eikopf?"

"My next birthday, I'll be twenty-seven."

"That's a great age to be. When I turned twenty-seven, I was a captain in Korea. I remember that birthday well. I tossed a grenade into a bunker and blew the heads off four gooks that had us pinned down. Looking at you, though, I can see, Eikopf, there will be no such happy memories for you. You'll never make captain. It doesn't even look to me as if you'll ever make corporal. I can see from looking at you, your case is a hopeless one. What did they train you as?"

"I'm a musician, sir. I play in the Corps Band. I do piano, drums, and glockenspiel."

"What the hell are you on this mission for?"

"I don't know. I figure God has his reasons."

"Eikopf, you're big on God, aren't you. I've noticed that. I have a suspicion, though, that under that pious exterior you're a down-in-the-mud atheist."

"Actually, sir, when I joined the Corps, I was an atheist. I think, at times, I still am. There are moments, though, when God seems a correct idea. I can feel God. I know that what I'm experiencing is probably a delusion—but what I feel, I feel. When that hurricane hit us back there, that heavy wind, I could feel God in that wind. God is no fool, if you don't mind my saying so, sir."

"Eikopf, if you're still alive when we get back to Alpha, I'm putting you in for a special commendation. You're useless, but you've got moxie. I like that in a person. You'll probably get yourself killed out here, playing with the big boys, but you don't mind about that. You volunteered anyway."

"I didn't volunteer, sir."

"Sure you did. Everyone on this mission volunteered. Even that bastard Simon, though I can't for the life of me figure why he goes around boasting that he didn't. Anyway, happy birthday, soldier."

They were singing "Happy Birthday" again, and they were still singing when the eighty-twos started coming in on them. They were on open road, and they scattered and dug in. The eighty-twos ploughed up huge quantities of dirt, creating large craters. Emma Sue sang all through the bombardment. She was always terrified under fire, singing was a way she had of keeping calm. Merlin was hit in the head by shrapnel, but he had his helmet on, he was only dazed. Eikopf lost the tip of his nose. Major Kleff caught some shrapnel in his chest, but it was nothing serious. He

139

lost his left nipple. Emma Sue dressed the wound, and after a bit of rest he was able to hit the trail again.

"Thank God those monkeys don't know how to shoot straight," Trask said. He was weary, exhausted, but nobody could have guessed. An inner drive kept urging him along, a relentless instinct to push on until they got where they were going: hell-bent, crazed, pressing forward as if the whole war depended on his getting to the bridge and knocking it down. More and more, now, seeing what a dedicated monomaniac Trask was, Simon wondered if the top brass might not actually have sent him into the jungle just as a way of getting rid of him.

"Keep goin', keep goin'," Thurl mimicked. "That's all we ever hear from this fucker. Goddamn madman's gonna drive us right down into the ground." Not into the ground, exactly, but into the mud, the trees, the undergrowth, steadily, into the mist, the rot, ceaseless jungle noises, the stink of decay.

Thurl was tired. They all were. Drive, drive, drive, one foot in front of the other. "Juz' keep drivin," Thurl remembered his father saying. "The future is in cars, boy. The way to the new world is through auto-*mobiles*. America moves on wheels. You wanna get someplace, *drive*. You want that new world, get into *cars*." Thurl had been born in Alabama but had done most of his growing up in Harlem. When he was sixteen and seventeen, still in high school, he got away summers and lived with an aunt and some cousins in Detroit, where he worked at a Ford plant, hammering hubcaps onto Granadas. His father wasn't around to see it. He had taken off with another woman and disappeared into the deep South. Thurl didn't see him again until three years later, finding him back in Harlem, in a two-room flat infested with rats and roaches, above a hamburger shop, living alone, not with the woman he had run off with. There was a bare mattress on the floor and a pile of third- or fourth-hand *Hustler* magazines strewn about, and empty wine bottles. The stove and refrigerator encrusted with grease and dirt. His father was on the mattress, in rumpled black pants and an undershirt, about a week's growth of beard on his face. When he saw Thurl, he looked at him flatly and said, "Did you find that future you were lookin' for?"

"Yeah," Thurl answered. "I found it in hubcaps."

"Smart boy," his father said. "Now go back there and don't stop till they make you one of the bosses in the company. Tell 'em to make you Vice-President in charge of Negro Affairs." He put a green wine bottle to his lips and took a slug.

But Thurl didn't go back to the assembly line and the hubcaps. He went to college instead. An admissions officer from a mostly white college in Connecticut latched onto him and offered him a scholarship. It was tempting. "I don't think I'm the college type," Thurl said.

"You won a spelling bee, didn't you?"

"That was years ago. In grammar school." It had been when he was in the eighth grade, and he won it not because he had any special talent at spelling, but because the kid who should have won was out with the flu. They sent Thurl on to the city finals at the Hilton, and he washed out in the third round, on the word *bullion*, as in gold, spelling it *bouillon*, as in soup, because soup was something he knew about, whereas gold was something he had only dreamed of but never touched. "It doesn't matter," the admissions officer from the mostly white college in Connecticut said. "We like you. We like what we see." So Thurl accepted and moved into a dorm, and found that he was one of nine token blacks on campus, and the money side of it wasn't easy. The scholarship covered his tuition and gave him some cash for books and an occasional hot dog, but it hardly put him in velvet, and the summer money he had saved from hammering hubcaps onto Granadas disappeared faster than he could have imagined. So he teamed up with a white senior who was peddling pills and marijuana and making a bundle. The senior drove into Manhattan, to Third Avenue, and picked the stuff up, in a Thunderbird, and

141

Thurl did the pushing on campus. It worked fine for a few months, but then the senior turned up dead in an alley a few blocks away from Third, his hands tied behind him with wire, a bullet hole in the back of his head, and Thurl figured it was time to pull out, before whoever had done it came looking for him too. He took off from the college and went home to Harlem for a while, then on to Detroit, back to hubcap land. This time they had him mounting tires on LTDs. He spent a couple of years doing that, then the war began steaming up, and the recruiter from the Corps turned up, a black sergeant who offered him a package. "Sign up for five," he said, "and in this new program, in a couple of months time we'll make a lieutenant out of you."

"But I never finished college," Thurl said.

"It don't matter," the black sergeant said. "You won a spelling bee, didn't you?" Thurl didn't even bother to tell him how long ago the spelling bee had been. He signed his name on the paper, and a few months later they made him a lieutenant—which wasn't bad, for a while. But now, as he sweated his way through the jungle, through rotting leaves and fungus, he couldn't help but feel that his life might have been vastly different if he hadn't come up with *bouillon* when they had asked for *bullion*.

He was walking along with Simon, the trail cutting through open grass, then back into the trees again. Tess was about ten yards ahead of them, lugging her pack. A good, sturdy body, wide hips, strong thighs. Her fatigues wet with perspiration, clinging. The smooth, sweet articulation of thighs, buttocks.

"I'm gettin' hornier by the minute," Thurl said. "Simon, if you don't nail her, I will."

They walked on in silence, savoring the action, the way she moved. She was something to behold, even in fatigues. Plodding along behind her, watching, looking on with unvarnished lust.

Then, amazingly, she disappeared—dropped straight down into the earth. Vanished.

They dashed forward. She had stepped into a monkey trap, a

hole covered over with branches and leaves. The monkeys liked to put sharp sticks on the bottom, slivers of bamboo, razor sharp, stabbing into anyone who fell in. Sometimes, instead of the bamboo, the holes were rigged with explosive. When Simon reached the hole, he saw Tess on her back, on the bottom, brown eyes staring up at him, filled with a quality of terror he'd never seen in them before. It was a big hole, deep. There were no bamboo spikes, but her left leg was caught in a tangle of trip wires attached to a grenade. She said nothing, just the wide, stunned, terror-struck appeal of her eyes.

"Don't move," he said, quietly desperate. "Just *don't move*."

He quickly got his cutters out of his pack, and Thurl held him by the ankles as he reached down into the pit to clip the wires. Thurl was jittery. "Damn it, Simon, don't blow us all to hell." Simon traced the wires carefully, and some of them, as he had suspected, led not to the grenade but to a secondary charge buried a few inches down, a wad of C-4, put there to catch an unwary samaritan. He cleared the dirt away, and took a good look at the detonating mechanism. He had seen something like it in demo training, but his recollection was hazy and his confidence wasn't a hundred percent.

"C'mon, Simon," Thurl urged, adjusting his grip on Simon's legs, "get on with it, get it done."

Simon hesitated, looked it over again; then, with a tightening in his chest, he cut: clipped a wire leading to the charge, then boldly cut another, and when he saw that the device hadn't blown up in his face, he breathed easier, he had got the right ones. He snipped the trip wire to the grenade, and they were home free.

He looked at Tess. "Are you okay?"

"I don't know. I think so."

She stood up in the deep hole, moving slowly, feeling her bones.

"I don't think anything's broken. I guess it just sort of knocked the wind out of me."

But in her eyes he could still see the terror, the fright, as if she had passed through a door, and suddenly it was all different for her: she was vulnerable, defenseless, knew that she too could get killed, like the rest of them. Simon and Thurl reached down into the hole and pulled her out.

15 □ Piano Sonata and Mortar Death

THE NEXT DAY, late in the afternoon, they heard the sound of a heavy chopper moving in on them. It was something big. They scattered and took cover, suspecting it might be a monkey gunship. The monkeys didn't have many gunships, but the ones they had were pretty effective. Simon went up a tree to get a sighting. It was big all right, but not a gunship. It was a cargo copter from Camp Alpha, a CH-54. It hung in the air above an open field of grass about half a mile off. Cables hung down from it, and suspended from the cables was a white piano, a concert grand, swaying, huge and luminous in the violet sky. The chopper descended slowly, with infinite caution, setting the piano gently down on the grass.

"It's Meyerbeer," Simon told them, coming out of the tree. It had to be Meyerbeer, because only Meyerbeer was brazen enough, lunatic enough, to be flying around in a war zone with a concert grand. But it couldn't be Meyerbeer, because Meyerbeer had been shot down. So it wasn't. Yet it was, had to be. Because he was out there in the chopper, in the flesh, with a piano, committing a craziness that only Meyerbeer was capable of. He had risen from the dead.

"Goddamn," General Trask said in a sinking tone.

144

They headed up the trail and out through some tall palms, in the direction of the open field. The chopper was already down, cables disconnected, and Meyerbeer was waiting for them beside the piano. It was a different chopper that had crashed, not the rainbow chopper. Somebody else had died. Sugg was pissed off, because now his IOU from Mickey Kabuki was null and void, and Kabuki was delighted, he was in business again. Already he was scurrying around, taking bets on Meyerbeer's future.

Henry was there too, with Meyerbeer, by the piano. He hadn't been suffering from beriberi after all, but from something else—or nothing at all—and now he was on his feet, in one piece, present and accounted for.

"It's for Eikopf," Meyerbeer said, rapping his knuckles against the piano. "Am I a day late, Eikopf? Was your birthday yesterday? Anyway, it's the thought that counts. I also brought the chow, Sugarman is taking the day off, he's racking out in a sleazy downtown joint that he just discovered." He winked at Merlin, who seemed oddly distraught. "You know Sugarman, he has his needs. Anybody want chow? It's in the chopper. Henry, fetch the chow."

Eikopf stood trancelike, gazing not at Meyerbeer but at the piano. The lid was up. His eyes warm and sober, his face suffused with a quiet excitement that none of them had ever imagined him capable of. His nose, damaged in the last shelling, was covered by a white bandage. "For me? It's mine? I can play it?"

"It's yours, Eikopf. My gift to you. Play it. Keep it. Wear it in good health."

"I won't allow it," General Trask thundered. "Nobody is playing a piano in the middle of my war. Merlin, check the box, see if there are any monkeys around."

"But he's good," Meyerbeer urged. "More than good. He's terrific. It'll be great for morale."

Trask looked at Meyerbeer with loathing. "Meyerbeer, why didn't you just stay dead?"

"He's a genius, sir. You can't suppress genius, General. Genius needs to express itself."

It was a slight exaggeration, about Eikopf's being a genius. Nevertheless, he did have an extraordinary talent. He had been playing piano since he was three years old. At seven he was giving recitals in church halls and school auditoriums, and at fourteen he made his debut at Alice Tully Hall. At sixteen he began fooling around with drums and a saxophone, and his piano technique went into a decline. At eighteen he had his own rock band, and at nineteen he underwent a born-again conversion and joined a religious commune situated on a farm outside Poughkeepsie, and vowed, as a peace offering to God, never to play a musical instrument again. At twenty his conversion fizzled, and he left Poughkeepsie and enlisted in the Corps. He had told them he wanted to work in artillery, but instead they put him in the Corps Band and asked him to play the glockenspiel. They were short on glockenspielers that year. He mastered the glockenspiel, and in his spare time he fooled around with the piano, regaining some of his lost technique. He had messed up his life, he knew that. But it didn't matter, there was a war on. When his hitch was over, he reenlisted, because the Corps, he realized, was the closest thing to a home and a family that he would ever have. They had taught him how to fire a gun, and they gave him a glockenspiel to play. What more could he ask? When he wasn't busy with the glockenspiel, he was free to hit the ivories, which he did often, with a passion. Then one day somebody fed his computer card in with the wrong pile of cards, and his file ended up on the desk of a lieutenant colonel who turned him over to General Trask.

"A genius," Meyerbeer reiterated. "Wait till you hear him. The boy has talent."

"A freak, you mean. What the hell'd he enlist for?"

"He wanted to serve his country."

"Well let him serve it with a gun. No frilly, fancy-lace arpeggios on my turf."

146

"Let him play a little, I'll roll some film. Meanwhile, the men can have their chow. I realize it's a little before their usual suppertime, but what the hell. Four P.M. Sixteen hundred hours. What harm can it do? Think of it as dinner music."

Trask had a smashed-up look on his face, like the windshield of a car that had just plowed into a stone wall. He was thinking about time, the mileage he wanted to make before they lost daylight. The chow canisters were already unloaded. If they didn't eat now, they'd have to reload and meet Meyerbeer farther along the trail, and that would chew up more time. Besides, the men looked tired, and Trask calculated that if he were to let them rest and eat now, he could march them hard when they hit the trail again, straight on through to dark. "Dinner music, huh?" There was acid in his tone. He mulled it over for another moment, rubbing his chin, then grudgingly acquiesced, but not without a burst of temper. "Meyerbeer, you son of a bitch, if this were the good old days of British Admiralty Law, I'd have you tied to the mast for forty lashes. I'd do it personally, and rub in plenty of salt. But those days are done, damn it. This is the jungle, not the sea." He turned sharply to the Major. "Tell them they can chow, but get it down fast. We move out of here in half an hour. Merlin, make another check for enemy patrols."

"You're a terrific sport, General," Meyerbeer said. He looked toward Eikopf. "Isn't he a sport?" He gave Eikopf a white jacket and black bow tie, and Eikopf put them on. He had no shirt, so he put the tie on around his bare neck. He had no pants, and wouldn't have put them on even if Meyerbeer had brought a pair.

"I'll get your plate for you, General," Meyerbeer offered. "It's your favorite: chicken chow mein. Plenty of soy."

"If you had to bring a piano," Trask said, "why a Yamaha? That's Jap, isn't it? They've already got the market in cars and hifis. Now it's pianos too. Hell, Meyerbeer, if you had to buy, why didn't you buy American?"

"I got it secondhand, it was a deal. I could have had a brand-new Baldwin at discount, but it still would have cost double what I put out for this."

Trask scratched at his crotch. "It still sounds disloyal, dammit. Or at best only semiloyal."

They all lined up at the canisters, digging into the chow mein, loading on the rice, pouring on the soy sauce. Eikopf fumbled around at the piano, warming up. He had his helmet on, he almost never took it off. He ran a few scales, getting the feel of the Yamaha—then, abruptly, he sailed into it, playing, rolling it out of memory, and it was all there, flowing through his arms, his fingers. They sat around on the grass and ate, and listened.

Thurl turned off the Dugan City Diggers and tucked the earphone into a pocket. Trask sat cross-legged. Simon sat cross-legged. Tess lay on her belly, leaning up on one elbow, the plate on the grass in front of her. Emma Sue sat with her legs tucked under her, the plate on her thigh, her helmet off, her bobbed hair blazingly red in the sun.

"What the hell's he playing?" Trask said grumpily.

"An American piece," Meyerbeer answered, "a piano sonata by a guy named Carter. I heard him fooling around with this one back at base. He plays Liszt too, a great Liszt. Let him do Liszt for you someday."

Meyerbeer wasn't eating. He had his camera going. He sat next to Trask for a while, filming from that angle, then he got up and moved around. Eikopf was remarkable, wandering over the keys. He was not the Eikopf they knew. Sitting there in the white jacket and black tie, all tensed up, the helmet still on his head, nose bandaged in white, hands weaving vibrantly across the keyboard, fingers flying—he was a stranger, not the person who had brooded his way through the jungle, dark eyes, dark face, dark thoughts, dark loneliness. It was a different Eikopf, a different darkness, the notes rising up out of the Yamaha brittle as glass, striking the grass and trees, rising to the sky and doubling back again, touching the ground, bounding off again into the open sky,

148

an antimelodic bittersweetness raging through the opening maestoso.

"Not bad," Trask said, "not bad at all. An American piece you say? A guy named Carter? I'm not much for this kind of thing, you understand, but I know what I like. This is a piece that has guts and muscle. Not like that sulky fin-de-siècle shit, or that Pagliacci wop opera shit, or that flowery French shit, or that Mussorgsky Russian shit, or that Scott Joplin nigger shit, or that Wagnerian German Nazi shit, or that Gustav Mahler moody Bohemian shit. This is good, sound, reliable stuff. Solid American shit. I like it, it has potential. Should I promote Eikopf and make him a corporal?" He briefly considered it, and quickly decided against, feeling he didn't want to lean too obviously in Eikopf's direction, because Eikopf was, after all, stark raving mad. "We'll wait on that, put it on hold. What with one thing and another, we don't want to give him a swelled head. Genius proud of itself can be insufferable."

Eikopf continued to work away, the notes piling up in an atonal strangeness, the right hand wandering off, busy with a world of its own while the left hand seemed lost, estranged, wandering somewhere else. Icy excitement of keys in the high registers, and an overall heavy tug of middle and low tones. An odd, disjointed, otherworldy sweetness filtering up through it all, beauty caught in the middle distance, making Simon feel empty and odd-angled, utterly alone. Eikopf's hands raced, danced, and the music struggled toward a resounding, vigorous passage that seemed to be a climax. Soulful atonalities, busy complications of chords and rhythms, moments when it was almost jazz but was something wildly, profoundly different: haunting, peaceful, cheerful, wrenching, disturbing, and Simon waited for it to be done.

But before it was over, the mortars got busy again, zeroing in. They ran for cover, scattering, racing for the trees. Meyerbeer and Henry rushed for the helicopter and got it off the ground. All of them were quick to escape, racing for cover, except Eikopf,

149

who stayed at the keyboard and went on playing. From behind a tree, Simon saw the mortar shells bursting all around the piano, closing in, sending up clumps of grass and dirt. Eikopf was oblivious. Thurl and Mickey Kabuki shouted, but he went on. The flaming notes that had seemed a climax had merely been a bridge into something else. Eikopf played, lost in concentration, hammering at the keys, the ripe, rich sound blunted by the furious pounding of the mortars.

Then, suddenly, his hands slowed, and there was a final stillness. He was done. His arms hung down like heavy logs. He sat a moment, glancing about at the bursting shells. Then he stood up and slowly walked through the pock-marked and exploding field, toward the shelter of the trees. Thurl ran out and dragged him in.

A shell hit the Yamaha and it flew apart—keys, wires, sounding board, pedals, splinters of wood booming off from the point of impact. Simon felt an odd, acheful twinge. Never again would there be a piano on that particular spot, on that grass, never again the fury of intertwining chords raging in those blissful trees. Meyerbeer kept the helicopter hovering in the distance, safe from the bombardment, but close enough to catch it all with a telephoto lens.

The shelling lasted more than a quarter of an hour. When it was over, they assembled at the edge of the field to take stock of their losses. The food canisters had been wrecked, but Merlin's black box was still intact. They found Major Kleff by one of the craters. One of his arms had been ripped off at the shoulder, and his face had been bashed in by shrapnel. He was dead.

"War is hell," Trask noted, saying it as if it were being said for the first time. There was a quiet strength and deliberateness in his tone, as if he expected that somebody would be putting the words down in writing. And there was something else, too—a sharpness, an unmistakable anger.

"Shall we bury him, sir?" Lieutenant Schlumm asked.

Trask looked skyward, toward the chopper. "We'll have that

150

son of a bitch Meyerbeer take him back to base. If it weren't for him and that damn piano, the poor bastard would still be alive."

They put the Major's body in his sleeping bag, and zipped it closed. Thurl and Simon did it, the others looked on. Simon felt peculiar about the Major; somehow he had never thought of him as the sort of person who got killed. He had seemed exempt, a man in the shadows, doing his job—plodding, reliable. With that silly pencil-line mustache. Odd, that he had never realized how dumb he looked with it on his lip. He had been proud of it, trimming it every day, looking at it in the small mirror that he carried, not with vanity, but with the eye of an unassuming man who simply believed it was a good thing to spend some time every day putting his face in order. And now he was dead. But Sugg was still alive, and Simon thought there had to be some sort of an injustice in that. Meyerbeer brought the chopper down, and they put the Major's body aboard.

Simon strolled over to the crater where they had found the Major, and Meyerbeer, after chatting briefly with Emma Sue, came over and joined him, an unlit cigar in the corner of his mouth. "Too bad," he said to Simon. "He was a swell guy, he really was."

"Yeah."

"Not flashy, not one of your superstar types, but he knew how to hold his own. That's life—right? The good with the bad. Tough luck for the Major, real tough." He had his hand on the back of his neck, massaging a stiffness. "Anyway, that was a hell of a show, wasn't it?"

Simon looked up, puzzled.

"The show, Simon. The goddamn *show*. When that damn piano blew. Didn't you see it? The eighty-two hit the Yamaha, and the keys and wires flew off all over the place, all the way downtown. I got it in slow motion. Music, that's what it was—sheer, explosive song. That piano, Simon, is gonna make the film. I know just where I'll use it." He paused, dimly conscious of Simon's distress, and glanced toward the crater, which was still wet with the Major's blood. His tone softened. "Yeah," he said. "The Major. Too bad about him, he was a decent guy."

Simon looked at the crater, and then at Meyerbeer's face. It was then, that weird, awkward moment, the air acrid with the stench of burnt explosive, that he had a sudden, ugly suspicion that Meyerbeer had somehow arranged it all—had not only delivered the piano, but long before that had set it up that Eikopf would be attached to the mission so there would be somebody to play the piano when it arrived. As he stood there, looking into Meyerbeer's face, the cigar, mustache, long jaw, the barest trace of a smile, he even wondered if Meyerbeer might not actually have arranged with the monkeys to zero in with their mortars so he could catch that shot of the Yamaha blowing to pieces, the slow-motion surge of wood and steel blowing sky-high when the shell went off—and, if the Major had to die for him to get that shot, that was too bad, unintended and apologized for, but an acceptable risk, one of the unavoidable hazards. It was, of course, too enormous to be true. So it had to be false, just another one of Simon's paranoid imaginings. Still, where Meyerbeer was concerned, paranoia was a safe bet, because with Meyerbeer there were layers and layers, it was always a shell game: black was white, up was down, left was right, dead was alive, and anything you wanted to imagine about him, no matter how paranoid or benign, it was all hit or miss, up for grabs.

But Simon didn't miss. His fist came swinging up from down low somewhere, and he smashed Meyerbeer square in the jaw, sending him stumbling backward, onto his rear end. He sat there in the grass, aghast and bruised, looking up at Simon with an expression of injured pride and innocence. "What the hell'd you do that for?"

"I don't know," Simon said, a little amazed at his own daring. "I truly don't know." There was nothing more to say or explain. He had simply let his imagination run away with him, that's all it was. He turned away and slowly walked off, through a patch of thick grass, back in the direction of Trask and the others. Some heavy clouds were beginning to move in. A flock of crows crossed the sky, black wings laboring in the warm, sultry air.

Trask signaled to Lieutenant Schlumm and drew him aside. "With things the way they are," he said, in a firm, matter-of-fact tone, loud enough for Simon, several yards away, to overhear, "I'm appointing you my second-in-command. I could give Lieutenant Thurl the position, but let's be frank about it—he's a nigger, and he's a lousy lieutenant. I can't say whether he's lousy because he's a nigger or just because he happens to be lousy, but I suspect both are true. The bottom line is, between a nigger and a Jew, I'd take a Jew any day, though I can't say it makes me happy—especially since the Jew is you. You crossed me once, Schlumm, when you didn't shoot that geezer with the grenade, the one that was spitting in the lake. But that's all right, you went chicken. You didn't have the guts to do what you had to, so you reverted to type. Cross me again, though, and you're dead. Got it? Watch your toes and don't fuck off, or I'll blast you in the back of the head and you won't be the first fuck-off I got rid of that way."

Schlumm wasn't at all thrilled about being Trask's second-in-command, but he didn't let on. "I'll do my best, sir."

"You'll do better than your best. I expect it." He paused, scrutinizing the side of Schlumm's head. "And by the way, Lieutenant, when we get back to base, see that you get something done about that ear. Plastic surgeons work wonders these days. Without that ear, you look like a donkey's ass."

Trask was in rare form, he had an edge on. Simon could see it, and so could the rest of them, it was an easy thing to spot. He seemed bigger somehow, taller, his body swollen by an inner anger smoldering deep inside. He wasn't happy about having lost the Major.

When he was done with Schlumm, he strode over to the chopper, the big CH-54, and caught Meyerbeer just as he was about to climb aboard. He told him to get back to base and not establish contact with the QUIF force again. "We're getting too close to the objective. I don't want you queering things for us with your bitch of a noise-mongering chopper. You've caused enough hell and damage as it is." He glanced about at the shell-gouged field, his eyes settling, briefly, on the spot where Major Kleff had been killed. "I'm canceling Sugarman, too. The next drop, he's dumping us a load of rations. Hereafter, we'll be on our own. Getting too deep into monkeyland, can't risk giving away our position with these goddamn fly-overs."

Meyerbeer objected—tried to object—but Trask was adamant, and Meyerbeer came as close to losing his cool as Simon had ever seen. "Shit, General, you can't cut me out now. It's not what we agreed. You've made a signed agreement with Vidwar." His voice was raised, tense, with a shade of anger; not enraged, not out of control—he was still Meyerbeer—but irritated enough and anxious enough so that for a moment it almost sounded as if he was about to fly off the handle and become not-Meyerbeer. "When that bridge goes down, hell, that's what the movie is all about."

Trask was livid. "Damn Vidwar! Damn the movie! Meyerbeer, you're on my ground, you bastard, and if you're on my ground you do what I say or I'll blow you down." He had his automatic rifle with him, the Armalite, and although he didn't exactly shove the muzzle into Meyerbeer's face, it was clear to Meyerbeer, and to all of them, that he was not disinclined to use it.

Still, Meyerbeer hung in there. "I know how you feel, General, I really do, and I respect your keen military judgment. I do. But you have to see it my way too, sir. Because there's a lot at stake here. If it's all the same to you, why don't we just sort of split the difference, if you see what I mean. I'll hang back a few days, keep in the background, but when that bridge goes, sir, I've got to be there—it's the finish, the grand finale. The goddamn climax."

154

"*Shove it*," Trask roared. "I want you to get the hell out of my war and never come back. *Comprende?*" This time he did push the Armalite up into Meyerbeer's face, and Meyerbeer, staring into the muzzle, just hung there, hazel-eyed and steady, gazing at the gun as if it weren't a gun exactly, just something dumb and unpleasant, but backing off nevertheless, because he was an expert in knowing just how far to push and when to back off, when to bow out and pull away.

"Oh, I understand, sir," he said, completely himself again, casual and easy. "I understand fine. Far be it from me, *sir*. Whatever you say." He smiled, and saluted, doing it in a slack, offhand manner that raked Trask's nerves and caused him to tighten his grip on the Armalite. "Whatever you say, General. You're the boss. *Sir*." Then climbed into the CH-54, and, with Henry at the controls, and the Major's body stowed in the rear, took off and headed back to base.

Simon watched as the chopper scudded along just above the treetops. He was still upset from his encounter with Meyerbeer, thinking Trask was merely insane, a megalomaniac, but Meyerbeer was worse: devious, untrustworthy; an ambiguity factor, a form of pollution. Maybe he shouldn't have punched Meyerbeer, maybe that had been rash, but all the same he was glad he wouldn't be seeing his face any more—for a while, at least. With Trask it was the pounding madness of the jungle, mud, death, smells of rot and decay, but at least you knew where you stood, knew what you were dealing with. With Meyerbeer there was no knowing—it was pianos in the sky, peekaboo games with a zoom lens in the midst of bombs and mortar, God only knew what he was up to, and maybe even God wasn't too sure. But Kleff knew, dead up there in the chopper, found out the hard way, and maybe, sooner or later, they would all know, the hard way, every last damn one of them.

"Get it moving," Trask said to Schlumm. There was still some daylight left, he wanted to squeeze as many miles out of them as they were capable of.

Schlumm gathered the men. "Come on, guys. Let's get a move. Kabuki, you take point. Falling Stone, take up the rear. Move it. Simon, don't get killed—we need you for that goddamn bridge."

I'll blow it up, Simon thought. *If it's there. I'll smash it down and I'll blow up with it.* He was thinking again of the jungle not as a jungle but as an immense green sea, hostile and vast, and, far off, the bridge like a great whale waiting for them, gleaming and malevolent, it would kill them all.

16 ◻ Chess Game

AFTER THE PIANO had blown up, Eikopf sank even deeper into madness. He wore the white jacket and black tie that Meyerbeer had given him, and his helmet, but still he wore no pants. He walked the trails that way, and at night he slept that way, the jacket scarred with mud and dirt, bare legs descending out of the jacket, so that he seemed a grim parody of a waiter in a Manhattan nightclub. He was obsessed again about the black box, convinced that somehow, through some dark, demonic power hidden in it, it was going to get them all killed. He wanted to grab it and smash it, shoot it full of holes. Thurl and Falling Stone had a hard time restraining him.

"God is less than you suppose," he said, with a queer, whimsical gleam in his eyes, but his face sober, dead serious. "Much less. But he's more than you imagine. Or nothing at all. Or everything!"

"Like trees," Simon suggested. "Like these damn trees we've

been lost in all these weeks. They're nothing at all, or everything."

"Yeah," Eikopf said. "Like trees."

"And toads."

"And vomit."

"And shit."

"*Especially* shit." Eikopf said.

Tess was not very far away. "Simon, you're as mad as he is."

"Are you mad, Eikopf?" Simon asked.

"The clouds are mad," he replied.

"See?" Simon said to Tess. "He's not crazy. And neither am I. If you want crazy, look at the clouds."

There was a dull heaviness in her eyes. "Simon, I'm tired. Very tired."

"We all are." But he knew, could tell from her tone, that she meant more than tired. Too many of them had died, one by one they were all getting killed off. There was fear, day and night, so real it was something you could taste; and, deeper than the fear, even harder to cope with, there was an emptiness, a fatigue of the mind and soul. It wasn't despair, nothing so grand as that, simply a blankness, like being in a room in which there was an absence of color and sound: no windows, no door, the same blankness that Eikopf had seen through to—and Eikopf had not only seen it, not only understood it, but had touched it and handled it, the great, sullen blankness at the bottom of life, had rubbed his face in it, and it had robbed him of his mind.

It rained, then the rain stopped. They marched a whole day, the next day, and the day after that. Sweating, stinking. Fatigues frayed and torn, limbs scratched from nettles. They stopped to rest, and Simon was on the ground, looking at Eikopf, who was standing, leaning against a boulder, gazing at the drab, cloudy sky.

"There's somethin' up there," Eikopf said.

"Where?"

He pointed, and Simon looked, but there was nothing.

157

"You saw something?"

"Yeah."

"When?"

"Last night. All lit up. It had its eye open, looking hard, watching."

Simon asked around. Tess, Falling Stone. Thurl. They hadn't seen a thing.

"It's up there all right," Eikopf said. "It's there, in the sky. It goddamn knows what it's doing."

Simon had the same strange feeling: there was something out there, somewhere, watching them, though he had thought of it as something on the ground, not in the sky. He had had that feeling through most of the long march. After Falling Stone killed the bear, the feeling went away for a while, but now it was back. He studied the sky, but saw nothing.

"That damn bridge," Tess complained softly. "Will we never get there?"

"Sure we will," Simon said, not really believing they would.

"I don't think so, Simon."

"We'll get there, then we'll go home." He turned to Thurl for support. "Isn't that right? We're almost there."

"Sure," Thurl said, rubbing his knuckles against his massive jaw. "That black box is takin' us right on in. Sweet an' simple."

"I hate that box," Tess said.

The box was guiding them, and it was also doing other things. Merlin was using it to play a complicated game of three-dimensional chess with an opponent in another part of the world. He had been reticent about the game, mentioning it to no one; but late one afternoon, for no apparent reason, as they were making their way through a farm and an orchard of almond trees, he started telling Simon all about it. Simon was a little surprised, it was out of character for Merlin to be so talkative. Usually he was cautiously private, walking alone, easy not to notice, advancing steadily on short, sturdy legs, blue eyes small and uncommunicative behind thick, black-rimmed glasses.

158

The game had begun three days before they set out from Base Blue, and Merlin had a feeling, he told Simon, that it was now nearing its climax. He admitted to being slightly nervous about the outcome. He was playing against an opponent in Georgia, and it was hard to say, at that moment, which way the game would go. As Simon listened, he saw how right it was that Merlin should be into three-dimensional chess. He was a smart little fellow—quantitative rather than verbal, but nevertheless bright. He had been playing with computers since he was seven years old. The chess game explained his long silences, Merlin spending hours, whole days, analyzing the game and planning his next move.

"Do you ever cheat?" Simon wondered.

Merlin's small blue eyes were vacant. "Cheat?"

"With the computer. The black box. Aren't you ever tempted to have the computer work out the moves for you?"

"Sure, but that's not cheating. My opponent in Georgia has his computer going too. The two computers are talking to each other all the time."

Simon wrinkled his forehead. "If this is a game between computers, why's it taking so long? I thought computers were fast thinkers."

"They are. They are. But it isn't just the computers that are playing. I'm playing, and this guy in Georgia is playing, Pyotr Trofimov. Having the computers in on it only complicates it. I talk to my computer and he talks to his. The computers talk to each other. We all talk back and forth. There's a lot of evaluation and reevaluation going on. It's not that simple, Simon, not that simple at all."

"Trofimov, you said? Pyotr Trofimov?"

Merlin nodded, and Simon finally understood. "This Georgia you're talking about—it's not Georgia the way Alabama is Alabama, or Tennessee is Tennessee. This is Georgia in Russia, the way Uzbekistan is in Russia."

"Of course, Russia. You imagined a three-dimensional chess player in Warm Springs?"

Simon winced. "You mean *our* computer, this black box here, is having a conversation with a computer in *Russia*?"

"Why not?"

"Christ, Merlin, the Russians are the fucking enemy. They're supplying guns to the monkeys. Who do you think is training the monkeys how to use the rockets and mortars they keep throwing at us? There are cadres of Russian advisors honeycombed all over the place. How can you trust a computer that's talking with the enemy?"

Merlin smiled. It was rare that he smiled, and his smile, now, had a touch of self-importance in it. There was so much Simon didn't understand, so much that so many people didn't grasp. "Simon, the computers are talking to each other all the time. The black box talks to the computer in the overhead satellite. The satellite computer talks to the mother computer in Washington. The mother computer in Washington talks to other satellite computers that are talking to the mother computer in Moscow. It isn't official, you realize, because it wouldn't look right, but unofficially it happens. We have our long-distance sensors picking up on their computer runs, raiding their memory banks, sneaking in and out of their RAM and ROM. Their satellites do the same to us. The trick in it all is to figure out if they'll make the moves their computers are telling them to make. You see, it's very like this chess game I'm playing. The computer gives you your best move, but it's always possible to do something else—feint, bluff, dodge around. In some ways, it's more like poker than chess."

Simon scratched at a mosquito bite behind his left ear. He had felt all along, like Eikopf, that the black box was bad news, but what he was hearing now was worse than anything he had imagined. "This is crazy," he said. "This is the true madness." And, when Merlin gave him a blank stare, he rushed on excitedly: "Because it means they know where we are, dammit. We've been fumbling through this lousy jungle almost a whole damn month, turning left, right, going north, south, doing everything the black box says—and everything it tells us it also tells them. We *are* being watched. The box is a fucking traitor. Eikopf is right—it should be put up against a wall and shot for treason."

"Simon, you exaggerate."

"I exaggerate?"

"All the time. It's one of your less endearing traits. The fact is, we don't always do what the black box says. You've seen the General with his compass. We revise the instructions. A few degrees east, a few degrees west. When those long-distance rockets come in, the monkeys never know for sure if we are where the computers say we are. It's a shell game."

Simon threw up his hands. "Then why use the box at all?"

Merlin was quiet for a moment, thoughtful. "Simon, if we don't use our computer, they'll use theirs, and we'll be up the creek. We use ours to negate theirs. If either side stops, the other side has the advantage."

There was in his tone a hint of condescension, and it raised Simon's blood. Merlin was a runt, an introverted blond runt with astigmatic eyes, and he was nervy enough to condescend. Simon came back at him sharply. "So why don't both sides just kick their computers to pieces? Or invent a father computer to monitor the wanton ways of the mother computers. That should be simple enough. Somebody ought to be able to come up with something like that. If I could think of it, why can't they?"

"Take the computers out of war," Merlin said, "and war would be a heck of a lot less interesting."

"Merlin, you're a creep."

"Simon, you're a primitive."

"I'm *not* a primitive. I try to be, but they won't let me. I may be stupid, dumb, and a fool, but primitive is not something I've had any success at."

"Don't pick on Merlin," Schlumm said. "He's just doing his job."

"Who's picking? He's picking on me. He called me a primitive. Nobody picks on Merlin. They pick on Eikopf, and Falling Stone, and Kabuki. And Thurl. And Polymer, who's dead."

"Nobody picks on Falling Stone," Schlumm said.

But Simon plowed on as if he hadn't heard. "Why don't they pick on Merlin, huh? Look at him. He's not even alive anymore. Right, Merlin? You're just an extension of that ten-pound box you carry around." They were passing a clump of bushes, and Simon grabbed a bunch of red berries and started throwing them. Merlin went hurrying ahead, a couple of quick, running steps. Then he was just walking again, glancing back over his shoulder. Simon threw more berries, and Merlin ran some more, putting distance between them. "Look at him. NANDs and NORs, that's all he is. He needs poking. It's about time. Picking and poking. It's time to paste tiny particles of nonsense on his skinny skin. Squeeze a few of his pimples. Horsehairs up his nose!" He threw more berries, but Merlin was too far ahead, moving fast. He didn't even bother to turn any more and look back. Simon didn't know why, but more and more, lately, Merlin brought out the sadist in him. He had never thought of himself as a sadist, but now he recognized it might be an interesting way of life, something he could make a career out of. With a little effort, he could become an expert, a PhD in evil ways.

At the end of the day's march, they made camp against a high rock wall, up on a hill. A stream flowed past the base of the hill, and they went down and got out of their clothes and washed off. Fresh, clean water, cool, flowing steadily. They splashed around, washed. Then back into their fatigues and up the hill, settling in against the rock wall. They had had their last hot meal from Sugarman, and now they were on rations—tidy, unappetizing meals sealed in transparent plastic bags. Sugarman had dropped a hefty supply in his last fly-over, enough to get them through till they hit the bridge. The sky was clear, the moon rising slowly above the humped, black trees on the other side of the stream. There was a soft breeze, warm and constant.

In the dark, after he had eaten, Simon went back down to the stream, and sat on a rock. He thought about Tess, feeling miffed over the way she seemed to take him for granted. She liked him, it was obvious—she was with him more than with any of the others. But he sensed that the very fact that he hadn't made a move on her was itself the thing that she liked most about him; she felt secure with him, safe, and little by little it was driving him mad. He was alone for a while, gazing at the water, lulled by the sound, then he saw someone emerging out of the dark, walking in the stream. It was Eikopf, in his muddied white jacket, with his helmet on. His nose was still bandaged, his bare legs badly lacerated from trekking through tangled undergrowth. He was engrossed, in something of a revery, and went right past Simon without seeing him. He moved slowly, water rushing against his shins, his carriage erect, stately, advancing down the middle of the stream, following the stream as it curved around the base of the hill. Simon watched as he disappeared into darkness and mist.

Simon was alone again. He stayed a while longer, on the rock, mesmerized by the sound of the water. Then tossed a stone into the stream, and went back up the hill, to the bivouac.

That night, toward midnight, Eikopf, as if sleep-walking, moved quietly across the encampment. He went over to Merlin, who was sleeping lightly, his left arm stretched out across the black box. For a moment Eikopf just stood there, looking down, calm, with a kind of majesty. Then he bent over and slipped the box out from under Merlin's arm.

Merlin bolted awake. Ever since the bear had intruded on their bivouac, he had been sleeping with his pistol at the ready, and now, when Eikopf lifted the black box, he whipped out the gun and fired off a round. It was mechanical, an act performed with the barest minimum of consciousness as he startled out of sleep. He got Eikopf right between the eyes.

There was commotion in the camp, everyone quickly up, snapped out of sleep by the shot. Rushing around, thinking it was monkeys. Then they saw Eikopf, and Merlin with the gun, bewildered, and when he realized what he had done he came unglued, trembling, hands shaking violently. "Jesus, I just shot. I didn't know it was him. It could have been a monkey in the camp. Or another goddamn bear."

"It's all right, soldier," Trask assured him, with a consoling tone that Simon hadn't thought him capable of—and, now that he heard it, in this context, it made him mad, mad the way he had been mad after he had killed for the first time, back at the creek, when in rage and fury he had thrown stone after stone at the trees. "You did what you had to," Trask said to Merlin. "You had the box to protect, and you protected it." He tugged thoughtfully at the small pouch of flesh under his chin. "Eikopf was on his last legs anyway, something like this was bound to happen."

Eikopf lay flat on his back, on rocky ground. In the vague, blue light of the moon, he seemed a blur. Simon bent over him and studied his face. It had been bony and ascetic, not handsome, but striking in the severity of its lines. Now it wasn't a face at all, the nose smashed, part of the forehead caved in, one eye not visible, the other eye bulging from its socket, glassy, reflecting the moon. The small bandage that had been on his nose hung down across his mouth. Mad, dumb Eikopf, still with the muddied white jacket, the black bow tie. He was out of it now, a dead pawn, safe from the demons that had tormented him. The jacket wasn't buttoned right, the button in a wrong hole. Simon undid it, then straightened the jacket and buttoned it correctly. He wanted to weep, but his eyes were dry.

17 □ UFO

THEY BROKE camp right away. There were monkeys in the area, in heavy numbers, and there was a very good chance that Merlin's pistol shot might have alerted a patrol. They left Eikopf under some shrubs, no time to dig a grave, and made off across an open field, stumbling in the dark. They traveled a few miles, then made camp again, bedding down for whatever sleep they could get before dawn.

Simon and Tess were too rattled to sleep, too shaken by the quick way Eikopf had been yanked out of their lives. They lay close to each other, Simon holding her, his arm around her, the image of Eikopf fresh and vivid: his ruined face, his pathetic, worn-out body abandoned in the night. Simon gazed at the stars, and wherever he looked it was Eikopf, Eikopf who had found fire in the keys of the Yamaha, making it come alive. Not even time to bury the body, just stash it behind some bushes, where the monkeys wouldn't see it. In a day or two it would be stripped clean by scavengers. So dumb and maddening, without reason. "Why do they pass out pistols to idiots like Merlin," Simon wondered angrily.

The warm breeze continued to blow. Tess closed her eyes, but Simon still gazed skyward, eyes ranging from star to star. Then, suddenly, the same thing happened that had happened before: a star detached itself from its fixed position and moved. Not fast, not sudden—a slow, gradual motion, defining an arc. It stopped, and he lost it in a cluster of other stars. It was a trick of the eye, an illusion. A falling star that never finished falling. His eyes scanned the sky, and his mind wandered, thinking of Eikopf, Falling Stone, the dead bear. If Falling Stone hadn't leaped in, would the bear have dropped anyway, killed by the slugs he had pumped into it? It bothered him, he wanted to know. Damn Falling Stone! Falling Stone was several yards away, bedded down in thick grass, with Emma Sue, making love. A lot of rustling around, some heavy breathing.

The star moved again, spiraling downward, growing larger. "Do you see that?" he said to Tess.

She opened her eyes and lifted her head. "Where?"

"Up there."

She saw it, it was hard to miss. "What is it?"

"It's not a plane or a chopper, they just don't move like that."

"It's getting closer."

"It sure is."

"It's not a meteor," she said.

"No."

"It's a weather balloon?"

"Could be."

It continued to move in a wide, spiraling motion, coming toward them. Then the spiraling motion stopped, but the object continued its approach, moving now in a straight line. Whatever it was, they didn't feel threatened by it; on the contrary, as it drew near, they felt a strange fascination, almost a euphoria. The object continued on course, and finally stopped, hovering large and steady, at what seemed to be only a mile or so away.

"But if it's a weather balloon," Tess said, arguing with her own theory, "why does it have all those lights?"

Plenty of lights, but no sound. The lights mostly white, though there were blips of red and green, and purple, orange.

They weren't the only ones awake. Merlin and Mickey Kabuki were up, and Thurl. Sugg was rustling around, though it was hard to tell if he was awake or simply having a nightmare.

"It's a UFO," Thurl said, pulling on his boots. "I seen one a coupla years back. But not this close."

"That's not a UFO," Mickey Kabuki said, sounding very authoritative. "It's a balloon the monkeys send up against the B-52s."

Tess nudged Simon. "See? I knew it was a balloon."

"They send them up by the hundreds. The lights are meant to scare the pilots. It's got electronic gear too, to confuse the navigational instruments on the bombers. If they get close enough to a bomber, there's a built-in sonar system that blows up a ton of TNT aboard the balloon and knocks the plane out of the sky."

General Trask was sitting up, gazing at the UFO and massaging his temples. "Where'd you hear that crock of shit," he said.

"I didn't hear it anyplace, sir."

"Then where'd you get it?"

"I made it up."

"You have a fertile imagination, Kabuki, loaded with manure. They should have stuck you in public relations, where they do a thriving business in manure." He cracked his knuckles, and stood up. "What you're looking at right now, folks, is a bona fide UFO. Officially they don't exist, but unofficially they're real. They're benign, they come and go. Nothing to get upset about. There's a rumor around about a UFO leveling a town in Siberia, but that's just malicious gossip. The truth is, the Russkies got careless with one of their nuclear reactors and it blew up on them. But that thing up there, it's a genuine unidentified. It may be real, or it may be a mass hallucination, a mirage. But if it's just a mirage, there's nobody can explain the powerful influence these things have on our electronic gear. Merlin, fiddle with the black box. Throw a signal to the overhead satellite."

Merlin, still agitated over what he had done to Eikopf, hesitant, his hands not steady, tapped some keys, feeding commands into the black box. But he got nothing. He realized, with alarm,

167

that the box was dead, and the realization gripped him with a kind of panic. He kept at it, not willing to accept the fact that the box was nonfunctional. Finally, frustrated, and obviously distressed, he looked up at Trask. "It's down," he said with a breathless, surprised voice, deeply perturbed. "It's dead as a stone."

"That's a UFO for you. It's powerful magic. The box will be back on power just as soon as that thing is gone. Get some shuteye, we shove off at dawn."

Trask slipped back into his sleeping bag, and Thurl did the same. Mickey Kabuki was still skeptical. "It's a balloon," he said to Simon and Tess, low enough so that the General wouldn't hear. "You ever hear a general say such a dumb, stupid thing as that there are real UFOs? He doesn't want us to know what it is. Those monkey balloons must be terrifying things."

"It's Eikopf's revenge," Simon said. "He's striking back at Merlin right where it hurts." He said it with full seriousness, but the way it came across it sounded suspiciously like a grim attempt at humor, which no one, least of all Merlin, appreciated. Slowly they dispersed, back to their sleeping bags, stretching out for a few extra minutes of sleep.

It wasn't long before the sky began to brighten. Simon opened his eyes and couldn't tell if he had been asleep or not. He had been close to sleep, but it seemed to him that he had not actually gone under. "Did I doze?"

"I think so. Yes."

"Did you get any sleep?"

"I'm not sure," Tess said.

They looked to the sky, to where the UFO had been, and it wasn't there. Simon rubbed his chin. "We didn't dream all that, did we?"

"I don't think so. No."

Trask was already up, standing by a tree, urinating. Kabuki was still asleep, and Sugg was kicking at his feet, waking him.

Emma Sue and Falling Stone were still together in Falling Stone's sleeping bag, both wide awake.

With the UFO gone, Merlin was able to work the black box again, and they got a heading. Schlumm and the General pored over a map for a few minutes, tracing out the route they would pursue. Mickey Kabuki moved out at point, with Thurl and Falling Stone close behind, and Sugg brought up the rear.

All morning they marched, pushing hard. Simon was thinking again about the bridge. The bridge, and Eikopf. Eikopf, and again the bridge. How he would climb out onto it, among the beams and cables, setting the pyroxene-T at the critical points. At first it had simply been a bridge, something to demolish; then it became a fantasy, a figment, and now it was a nightmare, because it was far off in another country: they would never get there. He remembered the pictures, the recon photos, and again he felt what he had felt before, that it was too beautiful to destroy. Too beautiful, he now wondered, or was it, rather, that he doubted his ability to do the job? Like lusting after a woman for six months or a year, and when you finally get into bed with her, impotence strikes. What if the bridge didn't go down? It could blow up and then simply hang there like a wounded bull in a bullfight, damaged but not dead, the matador unable to drive the sword home for a clean kill, and the crowd, outraged, blankets him with boos. Victory goes to the bull. It could happen. The bridge still there, a few girders gone after the pyroxene-T ignites, but the main structure holding. He remembered that happening once in training, when a trainee failed to get the charges rigged at the critical junctures, and the bridge didn't go down. It was a terrible thing, the bridge hanging there twisted and bent, a wounded animal crying out for the coup de grâce. Again he thought of Eikopf, flat on the ground, wrecked, and the bridge seemed to fade in importance.

"How far away are we?" he asked Schlumm.

"Not far, not far at all. We're getting close."

"Today? Tomorrow?"

"We have to detour around a couple of monkey brigades."

Schlumm marched along steadily. He was not enchanted with the idea of being second-in-command, but he was doing his best. Thin, alert, scholarly, one ear shot off, eyes dark and abstract. It had been clear from the start, from the time they set out from Base Blue, that he would have preferred being somewhere else, thinking other thoughts. At the University of Chicago he had read Derrida, Lacan, Spinoza, and Lévi-Strauss. When he finished his BA, he took a masters in anthropology, and that was how he learned what he knew about the customs and rituals of the monkeys, and how to talk some of the language. Simon had read Spinoza and Lévi-Strauss, but not Lacan; he had read Augustine, Voltaire, and Montaigne. Schlumm had not read Montaigne. He had read Eugenio Donato, whom he liked very much, and Radcliffe-Brown, whom he liked not at all. He was heavily into the structuralists, the writings of the structuralists, and he also liked crossword puzzles. He carried a book of crosswords in his pack and worked at them whenever he had a chance, favoring the ones that were hugely complicated, cluttered with foreign words, recondite geography, cryptic historical allusions. His taste in women, on the other hand, ran to the plump and the simple. He preferred women who were waitresses, salesgirls, and, for some strange reason that even he did not understand, he had very small tolerance for women who had been to college. He didn't dislike Tess, or Emma Sue, but they were not women that he felt any burning need to sleep with, or to be around and talk with. Simon liked him, respected his intelligence, but he felt somehow that he lacked solidity. He was there, visible, he talked, Simon heard the words, but somehow there was a vagueness about him, an insubstantiality, as if a strong wind might come along and blow him away, and after he was gone it would be hard to remember he had ever been there.

170

"If we detour around the monkey brigades," he said to Simon, "we might make it in three days. If we cut right through them, we could do it in a day, but we'd have a firefight on our hands and might never make it. The pattern keeps shifting, nothing is definite. It keeps changing and reshaping. I'm reminded of what Thales said. Do you remember Thales, Simon?"

"Sure," Simon said, amused to hear the old Greek's name invoked in the jungle. "Who could forget Thales?"

"Water. He said everything is water. Isn't that a wonderful insight? *Hudor*. That's what we're into, Simon. But at the moment it seems more like soup."

"I have to take a leak," Simon said.

"Have a good one."

They were on the trail for a little less than an hour when the UFO reappeared. It was behind them, off to the left, low in the sky, and large. At night it had been all lit up, but now, in the morning sky, it appeared dark, an enormous black ball, slightly flattened, like an egg. They stopped for a while and looked at it, then they pushed on. Every now and then Simon glanced over his left shoulder, and it was still there, as if keeping an eye on them. It seemed harmless enough, but it didn't escape any of them that it might have hostile intentions. Maybe not a UFO at all, but a new piece of technology the Russians had put in the hands of the monkeys. Observational stuff, or even firepower, some form of rotorless helicopter: it could open up on them, blow them away.

As the morning wore on, they kept turning, looking skyward, and still it was there. Even Trask, who had said it was benign, nothing to worry about, kept turning, looking. He wasn't nervous, exactly, not visibly worried, but it was getting to him, something there that shouldn't have been, and, like the rest of them, he showed signs of being on edge. Clearing his throat a lot, spitting; slapping angrily at mosquitoes. They moved across some hilly terrain, through undergrowth, keeping close to the protection of the trees, the UFO all the time visible through intermittent gaps

171

in the overhead foliage. When they reached the base of a low cliff, Trask called a halt, and he moved them in under the wide, overhanging ledge. He said nothing, and didn't have to, because they all understood. They were waiting it out, hidden, out of sight under the moss-clad lip of rock, tucked away behind thick strings of vines that hung down off the cliff.

After a half hour, Trask stepped out from under the ledge and looked up, and the UFO was still there, in the same position it had been in when they stopped. With a disgusted wave of his arm, he motioned them on, and again they were on the trail, pushing hard, under the trees. The UFO hanging dark and knowledgeable, seeming to follow, as if knowing all about them. The black box was nonoperational.

"What if the damn thing starts shootin'?" Thurl wondered.

"We goddamn shoot back," Sugg grunted. There was an eagerness in his eyes, a trigger-happy craving to get on with the encounter. Yet Simon thought he saw in him an uncertainty, an apprehensiveness—doubt, if not actually a hint of fear, something he'd never seen in Sugg before.

"I think it's a friend," Simon said casually. For some reason he didn't feel particularly threatened by the UFO; in fact, he felt rather comfortable about its being there, and it amused him to see the others becoming as disturbed as they were, especially Trask and Sugg. "I think it likes us," he tossed out, provocatively, "that's why it's hanging around. Like Eikopf said, it knows what it's doing."

Sugg gave him a dead stare. "You dumb fuck," he muttered, and moved off, putting space between them.

A cloud moved in, darkening the sky, and they caught some rain. It came splashing down, washing them, cooling them off. But it only lasted a short time. The cloud passed, and it was the hot sun again—the jungle steamy, thick with vapor. When they reached a clearing they stopped and took a good look at the sky, horizon to horizon, looking for the UFO, and, much to their surprise, it was no longer there. Simon stood a long time, head lifted, feeling a kind of sadness, almost a loneliness, wondering if it was gone for good.

That afternoon, early, shortly after they had stopped to rest and chow down some rations, word came through on the black box that Vain had been rescued and brought back to base. It was fantastic news. He was alive—only barely, according to the message Merlin got, but alive enough to be counted among the living. There was some doubt, apparently, as to whether or not it actually was Vain, since he carried no ID and was too much of a mess to be recognizable, and was close to catatonic, unable to talk. Nevertheless, they couldn't imagine who else it might be, lost and wounded, in that part of the jungle. So, until it was proved otherwise, the man they found was Vain. It was grounds for optimism: you could be abandoned in the jungle, be left for dead there, and a couple of weeks later you could have the good luck to get born again. A good omen, what the hell. It cheered them, gave them a lift, despite the fact that most of them couldn't remember exactly what Vain looked like, and didn't altogether care. For a while, before they moved out again, they stood around in a lighthearted muddle, arguing about the color of Vain's eyes.

❑ PART THREE

18 ◻ Wan Luk

THEY PUSHED ON, and before the afternoon was half
spent, they came upon a village situated between two low-lying
mountains that rose up off the flat country like two well-formed
breasts. There were no other mountains in the vicinity. The lower
reaches of the mountains were treeless, covered with grass and
great quantities of pink and purple flowers. Farther up, there
were trees, rosewood and pine. Not mountains, really, just two
large hills that had pushed up from the flat earth and then
stopped, as if satisfied, content to specialize in a few types of
trees and flowers.

They had a couple of miles of open road before they got to the
village, and, as they approached, an old man on a donkey came
out to greet them. He was short, slight, with fuzzy white hair,
wearing a white linen tunic that looked a little like a hospital
gown. He appeared to be a simple, homespun man, yet Simon
had an odd feeling about him, a sense that he was far more complicated than he seemed.

He told them he had spotted them through his binoculars as
they came out of the far trees, and since it was not often that
there were strangers in this part of the country, he thought he
would come out to welcome them and make their acquaintance.
His name was Wan Luk. At the point where he met up with them,
they were about a mile off from the village, and he got off the
donkey and insisted the General get on and ride the rest of the
way in. Trask complied, though he was clearly too large for the
animal, his feet almost touching the ground.

Wan Luk spoke almost perfect English, with a trace of a British accent. "You do not have to worry about the enemy here," he assured them. "The enemy don't come here. They passed through, a long time ago, but don't come back. We have nothing here for them. They don't deem us worth coming back to. They consider us, you see, bad luck."

Trask stared intently at him. "Why?"

"Because it is a fact. We are a village of bad luck. Perhaps you too will consider us bad luck and will never come back."

He told them that the village had sent him off many years earlier to get educated in England. He took a degree at Cambridge, then he went to the United States and earned an MBA at Harvard. "It was hard work, you see, but I was young in those days and did not mind hard work. I wanted to educate myself so that I might return one day and help my people." When he finally did return, however, holding true to his promise to come back, he saw that it was too late to do anything to help them. Their bad luck had become too much for them, and the measures they had taken to remedy their wretchedness only succeeded in bringing on more misery and misfortune.

"What kind of misery?" the General asked.

"You shall see. You shall see for yourself." It was a village, he said, that had learned to live with its unhappiness. As dreadful as things were, their bad luck was something they were beginning to be glad about, it was the only thing they lived for any more. As for himself, he in no way shared the views and feelings of his fellow villagers—but that, he understood, was because he had spent too much time in foreign countries, and his habits of thought had been influenced by foreign views and prejudice. He had given serious consideration to leaving the village forever, but it was an option that he finally rejected. His roots were here, he said, in the village between these two mountains, where he was content to live out the remainder of his days. He had a small personal library that contained the essays of Charles Lamb, the

178

Pensées of Pascal, the complete works of Dickens, an outdated *Merck Manual*, and a copy of *The Scarlet Letter*. With these he was satisfied. He read every night, by candlelight, and was just beginning *David Copperfield* for the third time. He had kept up with events in the world through a subscription to the *Wall Street Journal*, which used to arrive in the mail that came once a month via caravan from the country to the north. The war, however, had put a stop to that. He owned a windup phonograph and had a number of seventy-eights that he frequently played, including some Irving Berlin and Schubert's *Unfinished*. Somehow, he found great consolation in Schubert, playing the *Unfinished* over and over again, but now it was quite worn. He wondered if they might send some recordings to him, if any one of them might ever have the opportunity. He would, he said, be most grateful. He was ascetical in appearance, extremely thin, and short, with large dark eyes and a broad forehead. He wore iron-rim glasses, the kind that had been popular in the years when he was a student at Harvard. He walked with short, rapid steps.

As they moved along, they heard the sound of an approaching helicopter. Meyerbeer's rainbow chopper hove into view above a stand of trees. He circled around, looking things over, then pulled off and simply hovered, apparently with no intention of landing. Trask was furious. He sat astride the donkey, livid, aboil with anger, eyes riveted on the chopper. "Tell that son of a bitch to get the hell out of here," he shouted to Merlin.

Merlin fiddled with the black box, but couldn't get through. "I can't raise him, sir."

"Tell him anyway," Trask raged. "I've given that fucker face-to-face direct orders to steer clear of our operation. Tell him, dammit. Tell him to get his ass out of my sky!"

Merlin tried again, desperately, but with no success. Suddenly, as though aware of Trask's ire, Meyerbeer maneuvered the chopper off into the distance, though he didn't quit the scene. He just hovered around up there, far off, making with the telephoto lens.

Trask stared fiercely, as if by the intensity of his gaze he could knock the chopper out of the sky. "I'll get that bastard. Any day now. I'll blast him so good he won't even be able to locate his asshole."

As they neared the village, the road veered around toward the mountain that lay to the west, and a far flank of that mountain now came into view. Halfway up the slope, overlooking the village, was what appeared to be a large wooden cross.

"Is that what I think it is?" Trask said to Schlumm, still in a temper over Meyerbeer, but calmer, less discomposed, still chafing but no longer incensed, not quite so overwrought as to be unable to recognize a cross on a hill when he saw one.

"I think it is, sir."

"Is there somebody tied to that?"

"There seems to be."

Trask got down off the donkey and took a look through his field binoculars. "My God," he said. "What *is* this? What in heaven's name is going on?"

Wan Luk stood by in an apologetic attitude, eyes to the ground. "It is a village, you see, of immense misfortune. They have lost the desire to live. Life, to them, is not worth living. That is the conclusion they have reached. It is not a conclusion with which I agree, but that is what they feel. Death, now, is the thing they worship, because that is all they believe there is. Death, and dying—growing into death. They have erected the cross as a symbol of their belief." He paused, as if disinclined to go on.

"There's somebody hanging on that goddamn thing," Trask said angrily, still looking for an explanation.

"Yes, yes," the old man nodded, "every month there is a new one on the cross, hanging there. They fill him with drugs, and if one should live very long, they climb up and give him more drugs, and he hangs there until he dies. The next month, another takes his place, chosen by lot. Sometimes they moan and weep,

180

and one hears them through the night. Sometimes the drugs are so rich for them, they sing, or even whistle. They hang there and die, then we take them down and bury them. They are the heroes of death. We shall all be dead, they show us the way."

Trask made no effort to conceal his loathing. "What kind of people are you?" he fumed. "This is unnatural. Unnatural!" He pushed the donkey aside and began marching up the slope toward the crucified man, moving with a quick, determined step. It was a long hike. Schlumm, Emma Sue, and Simon went along, and Tess. Simon realized now what the flowers were that were scattered everywhere, and it surprised him that he hadn't recognized them before. Poppies. The place was an immense opium farm. Pink and purple poppies, ablaze with color in the rich green grass.

The man on the cross appeared to be in his mid-twenties. There were ropes around each of his arms, holding him to the cross, and also around his legs and waist. His head sagged off to one side, as if he were dead, but he was breathing, his eyelids half-open. They reached the foot of the cross and stood a moment, staring up at him.

"How long can a man hang like that before he dies," Schlumm wondered.

"A long time," Trask said. "Cut him down."

There was a wooden ladder nearby, on the ground. Schlumm and Simon went for it and set it up at the rear of the cross, and Simon went up and cut the ropes. Schlumm and the General stood at the front, catching hold of the man, and they stretched him out on the ground. Emma Sue bent down to examine him.

"He's dying," she said.

"He must have been there for days," Trask speculated. "Maybe a week. The crazy sonsabitches."

"I can't get a pulse," Emma Sue said. She took a stethoscope from her kit and checked for a heartbeat, but the man was dead.

Trask looked at him, then he turned his gaze toward the village. "This town is an opium factory," he said. "Where the hell is that Wan Luk character?"

Wan Luk was still back on the road, with the donkey. He hadn't moved. The white linen gown, and the sandals, and the fuzzy white hair on his head, like cotton. Trask fixed his gaze on him, glaring; then, with a burst of determination, he marched down off the hill, heading straight for him in a barely restrained state of rage.

"Opium," he said, "that's what this is all about. You're the agent, right? The merchant. You with your Harvard MBA, you arrange it all and make it move."

"I am a very old man," Wan Luk said with quiet dignity. "Older than you suppose."

"And that," Trask fumed, pointing up the hill toward the cross, "that's how you keep it going. How you keep them under control. Rituals of death, human sacrifice. You've made a goddamn religion out of it."

"You come from very far away," Wan Luk said. "You do not understand my people."

"Maybe I don't. You're right about that. But you I do understand. I know your kind."

Wan Luk stood motionless beside the donkey. He hadn't moved a step. "The opium," he said, "was here long before I was born. It will be here after I am dead."

"I suppose it will," Trask granted. "I suppose it will." He turned to Schlumm. "You and Sugg go in there," he said, pointing to the village, "and check the place out. Round the people up. I want to talk to them." Simon moved to go with them, but Trask called him back. "Not you, Corporal. I don't want you into any kind of a fracas with those demolition pies in your pack."

And then, in a swift, easy motion, as if it were all part of something he was saying, he unholstered his pistol, a Ballester Molina, swung it up toward Wan Luk's head, and shot him in the temple. The old man went down like a pile of old clothes.

182

It was done with amazing ease and swiftness, and it caught Simon unawares, took his breath away. He was shaken, but not deeply surprised, because that was how Trask was, quick and unpredictable. He had visions and acted on them impulsively, convinced of the infallibility of his judgment. Like the time he had led them through the burning jungle and got them out alive. And the time he had Sugg shoot the old man at the lake, and it turned out he was right, the old man did have a grenade.

"Sling him over the donkey," he said to Simon. "This place is an opium empire. That's why the monkeys leave it alone. He was shipping to the States, and they know it. They figure the more drugs going into American cities, the sooner we'll lose this war. Get him on the donkey and bring him along, I want to talk to these people." He went back up onto the slope, heading for the cross.

Simon picked Wan Luk up off the ground and was surprised at how light he was. It was like picking up a child. He laid him across the donkey's back, then led the donkey up the slope.

Tess and Emma Sue were still up there. They all waited around while Schlumm and Sugg checked through the huts and rounded up the people. Before long they all came streaming out of the village, up onto the slope, a motley crowd, about three hundred or so, most of them in linen gowns, though some were in jeans, and others in outfits that looked like satin pajamas. Sugg and Schlumm signaled with their weapons, waving the people on, and they slowly made their way up to where the General was. He stood at the foot of the cross, with Wan Luk dead on the donkey a few feet away. The villagers stood quietly on the slope beneath him.

"If you mean to talk to them, sir," Schlumm said, coming up to Trask. "I don't think they'll understand. I can't speak their dialect. I couldn't translate for you."

"It's not necessary for them to understand. It's only necessary for them to stand there and listen. I've got something I want to say. They'll get the gist, all right. Just get them all up on this hill."

Sugg got a few more stragglers out of the huts and moved them up the slope. It was as Trask had said: the place was a factory. Sugg and Schlumm had found clay pots filled with opium, and all the equipment necessary for processing. The General had his gun in hand and raised it aloft. He motioned toward Wan Luk's body, which was still slung across the back of the donkey. "That there is Wan Luk," he said in loud, powerful tones. His voice carried far, across the heads of the villagers, across the rooftops and off to the opposite mountain. There was a faint echo. "He's dead and I killed him. You don't have to be afraid of him anymore. Anybody wants to take his place, I'll come back and kill him too. You people are strong, healthy people. Forget poppies and work for a living. Plant cabbages, and soybeans. If you're hungry before the crop grows, eat grass. And as for this," he said, pointing toward the cross, "nobody has to die anymore. It was a lie. Wan Luk's lie. Now it's over. Forget dying, and learn how to live." He turned, then, to Schlumm and Sugg. "That's it, they've got the message. They know what I've been talking about. Now rip that damn thing down, and let's get out of here."

They put down their weapons and removed their packs, and got hold of the cross. It was planted deep. They worked it back and forth, loosening it. Trask moved Schlumm aside, and he and Sugg worked at it. They rocked it forward and back, pushing hard.

Through all of this, the people from the village were silent. Their faces showed no emotion. The sun was high in the sky, glistening in their hair. They had listened carefully while the General spoke to them, even though they couldn't understand a word. They had registered no reaction when he pointed to Wan Luk dead on the donkey, and they stood passive now as he worked on the cross with Sugg, rocking it back and forth, yanking at it. Finally it was loose enough and it went over, tumbling to the ground.

184

As the cross went down, a low moan went up from the crowd, such a moan as Simon had never heard before: a single, agonized sound, like the groan of a large animal dying, magnified many times. The crowd hung there on the slope, hovering in the mournful, convulsive sound; then, still moaning, they moved forward, advancing toward Trask and Sugg, toward Tess and Schlumm and Simon and the rest of them.

"Move it out fast," Trask said, grabbing his pack. "We don't want to tangle with these people."

"Move it out," Schlumm shouted. "Move it out!"

They backed away quickly, Tess and Simon, all of them, and Simon saw, now, that many in the crowd were brandishing knives, long blades glinting in the sun. They were advancing faster, still walking but moving rapidly, the air resounding with their long, terrible moan. The space between the crowd and the troop began to narrow, and Simon, with Tess and the others, broke into a run, though Kabuki, for some reason, hung back, moving backward away from the villagers, facing them, not turning and running until they were nearly upon him. Simon glanced over his shoulder and saw a few figures breaking from the crowd and running in pursuit, then others, twenty or thirty. Sugg fired a burst, and Trask fired. A few bodies fell. They fired again—more bodies went down, and, raggedly, the chase came to a halt.

The squad continued running till they were at a far distance. When they stopped and looked back, the villagers were gathered around the fallen ones, not moaning now, but shouting, arms over their heads, looking toward the troop and screaming, wailing, shouting angrily, words and phrases that could only have been curses, execrations, cries of despair. High overhead, Meyerbeer circled in the rainbow chopper, getting it all though the telephoto lens.

"This is *awful*," Tess cried aloud, huge sobs bursting from her, as if torn from her violently, sending tremors through her whole body. "*Awful. Awful.*" She stood alone, holding her weapon in

185

both hands, shaking her head from side to side, sobbing uncontrollably.

Then they saw Kabuki, the front of his shirt full of blood. He was on his feet, steady, looking toward the villagers, almost as if he were unaware that he'd been hit. It hadn't been only knives back there; someone had had a pistol, and Kabuki had taken a slug in his chest. He had been too slow to turn and run. They put him down on the ground, and Emma Sue got to work on him right away, while the others kept a sharp watch, in the event the villagers should attempt another charge.

19 ▢ Waterfall

"I'M OKAY," Kabuki kept saying. "I'm okay."

The bullet had entered high on his chest, near the shoulder, and was still in there someplace, a slug from a small-bore weapon. Emma Sue decided not to probe for it, it might be too close to something vital. She cleaned the wound as best she could and gave him some penicillin, then applied a bandage.

"We shouldn't move him," she said, wiping off a smear of blood that had got onto Mickey Kabuki's face. "He should be helicoptered back to base."

"Where's Meyerbeer," Falling Stone wondered, looking for the rainbow chopper. But Meyerbeer was already gone, the sky was empty.

"When we need the fucker," Thurl said, "he's never around."

Trask's face was contorted, as if in pain. The thought of calling Meyerbeer in, after the way he had cursed him out and ordered him to keep away, was mortifying. Still, with Kabuki wounded, it

186

would have been too patently inhumane not to grab for the only available help. Meyerbeer had just left the area, he couldn't be too far off. "Raise him," he told Merlin, grudgingly. "Tell the son of a bitch to come on in."

Merlin tried, but, as before, Meyerbeer was unreachable. Either his equipment was faulty, or he was flying with it switched off. Or maybe the UFO, which wasn't at the moment visible, was somehow involved. A lot of them thought that, but nobody actually said it.

"Try again," Trask said. And, when the result was still negative, the expression on his face balanced uncertainly between consternation and relief. He gave a snarling glance skyward. "If the bastard ever crosses my air space again, I'll shoot him down personally."

Kabuki was just lying there, looking up at them. "I'm okay," he repeated, perplexed by the fuss and bother. "I really am. It's all right."

"What happened," Simon asked, squatting down next to him. "Why didn't you run? Why'd you hang back?"

"I was talkin' to them."

"Talking? How do you mean?"

"I don't know. It just seemed the right thing to do. I was tryin' to talk to them."

"He shouldn't move," Emma Sue said to Trask. "It obviously didn't hit a lung, or his heart, but if that bullet starts pushing around in there, it could be nasty."

"He can move," Trask said. With Meyerbeer unreachable, there wasn't much of a choice—it was either move or stay where he was and wait to die. "Right soldier? Stand up, let's see you walk." There was no kindness in Trask's tone. He had never liked Kabuki, and had even less reason to like him now, feeling Kabuki was to blame for getting hit, he had been too stupidly slow when they were pulling back.

Mickey Kabuki got up on his feet. He stood motionless for a

moment, getting his balance, then did some walking around. "I can walk," he said pluckily. "I'm all right."

"He should have a litter," Emma Sue said.

"I don't need a litter," he insisted. "I can manage."

Trask stared at him, a long, studied look, as if X-raying the wound. If Kabuki didn't want a litter, that was fine with him. He turned away sharply. "Let's move it out," he said. "Before these people take it in their head to give us more trouble."

The villagers, in the distance, were still gathered around their wounded. They had quieted down, but many still looked toward the troop, across the open field. It was hard to know what their mood was, whether they might try another assault.

"Moving out," Schlumm called. Sugg led the way, taking over at point.

For a while they were in the open, crossing fields that were covered with grass; but before long they were in thick jungle again, on trails that were narrow and overgrown, trails that were only trails because sometime in the recent past the monkeys had been moving through on them, carving a path, whole regiments of monkeys. Mickey Kabuki seemed to be holding up, making his way. "I'm fine," he kept saying. "I'm okay." But he wasn't. He was sweating, oozing with perspiration. They were all perspiring, but Mickey Kabuki was suffering more than the rest of them, he was running a fever.

"He mustn't go on," Emma Sue warned the General.

"I can," Kabuki insisted. "I'm tougher than those monkeys any day."

She pumped him full of aspirins, and they kept moving. There were a lot of birds in the low country they were in, darting through the trees. Warbling, chirping. There were animals among the trees, tapirs and tree shrews, macaques. The sun sloped to the west, and they groped forward, tediously, toward their bivouac. The sky clouded over and it looked as if they might catch some rain.

188

That night, in camp, Kabuki's fever was still up, and it was going higher. He lay stretched out on top of his sleeping bag, his gun on the ground beside him, his pack under his head serving as a pillow. His shirt and pants off. Simon sat with him, wiping the perspiration from his face. He had gone cold, into a bout of chills, but now he was warm again, burning up. Simon wet a cloth, dipping it in a nearby stream, and spread it on his forehead.

"I want to go home," he said groggily. "Back to San Luis Obispo. You ever been there?"

"Sure," Simon lied, "I've been there."

"There's plenty of farms out there, and a bay. Some terrific bars. Places you can get fantastic abalone. You dig abalone?"

"Yeah," Simon said flatly, feeling guilty for not being more enthusiastic.

"My mother made incredible abalone. She'd do them up in butter and wine, like nothing else in this world."

"You like raisins?" Simon asked.

"Sure. Raisins are okay."

"Have some." He took a box of raisins out of his pocket and put a few in Mickey Kabuki's hand. Mickey Kabuki held them a moment, then he let them fall out of his hand, onto the grass. He looked at Simon. "You think we got far to go?"

"A ways yet," Simon said.

"I'm going back to San Luis Obispo."

"Sure you are."

"You never been there?"

"A couple of times."

Mickey Kabuki's eyes were closed. He stopped talking, and drifted off. Simon sat there a while longer, then he went over to where Tess was, but she was already asleep. Behind a layer of clouds the moon was faintly visible.

Toward morning, he was awakened by a shot. He grabbed his gun, thinking they were under attack, but the one shot was all

189

there was. It woke most of them. Wrenched out of sleep, they looked about cautiously. Simon went over to check on Mickey Kabuki, and, in the faint light of dawn, he saw that Mickey Kabuki had shot himself in the mouth.

"That was very sensible of him," Trask said. "He was slowing us down." Simon knew what he meant: they would have had to leave him there, or abandon him farther down the trail, and the monkeys would have got to him. If not the monkeys, the jungle animals, or the wound itself, which apparently was as bad as Emma Sue had said it was. "Actually," Trask added, "I'm not too sorry to see that one gone, hateful as it may sound. The fact is, I always had doubts about his loyalty. Those squinty Oriental eyes, and that scrunched-up look on his face. Isn't that a hell of a thing to have to say about a dead man?"

That's what it was, Simon thought. A hell of a thing to say. He helped Schlumm dig a hole, and they dragged Mickey Kabuki over and put him in, covering him with dirt and leaves.

"Maybe it'll rain," Schlumm said. He liked the rain, when it was a slow drizzle. Cooling, it washed them clean. But the rain held off. There was a small break in the clouds, and there, in the break, they could see the UFO. It was far off, much farther away than it had been the previous day, but still there, a nagging implication. Sugg was particularly unsettled when he noticed it. "We oughta shoot the damn thing down. That's monkey stuff up there. We oughta blast it."

"Sure," Simon said. "Why not?" Throughout the mission, he had been angry about Sugg, even afraid of him, but now, for some reason, he somehow felt himself at a distance, secure. In this bizarre, nightmarish world they were bogged down in, Sugg was, for all his tough bluster, as vulnerable as the rest of them. Simon smiled. "Go ahead, shoot it down," he said whimsically. Nothing they had could reach that far, it would take a long-range missile, and then some.

190

Sugg watched it fiercely. He seemed ready to lift his Uzi and cut loose. But he turned away, shifting his malevolent focus to Simon for a moment, and slung a wad of spit in a wide arc in his direction. Simon watched it sail past, and waited until Sugg was well up the trail before moving on.

He traveled along with Merlin for a while. Merlin said nothing, and Simon felt no obligation to say anything in return. Merlin worked away at a chunk of bubble gum, chewing and chewing, but not blowing any bubbles. He spat the gum out. "I lost the chess game," he announced.

"No kidding. That's too bad. The Russian was too much for you?"

"We'll get a rematch going. Sometime."

"You've got a better computer than he has, don't you?"

"I thought I did. Now I'm not so sure."

Simon despised Merlin for killing Eikopf, but he understood, remotely, that the hate and resentment were misplaced. It was the war, the madness of the jungle. Merlin was nothing, a jerk who slept with his hand on his pistol, ready to fire. Guardian of the box, this miracle they depended on in the trackless jungle, and he couldn't even win a chess game. "Maybe you'll win the rematch," he said.

Merlin gave a despondent nod. "Maybe."

They walked along in silence, then Simon kicked a stone. "That box of yours," he said, jabbing through Merlin's gloom, "it's a regular little grab bag, isn't it. What's it know about Vasco da Gama?"

"Why?" Merlin said, backing away from the question as if it might somehow do him harm.

"No reason. I just suddenly think Vasco da Gama is terribly important. All that Cape of Good Hope stuff—you think that was easy? If you want a hero, there's a hero for you."

Merlin shrugged, unresponsive.

"Gee, Merlin, you don't know much, do you. Is your black box

191

on an ignorance strike? I give you a hero, and you can't tell me what he used to eat for breakfast?"

The clouds started to break up, and the sun warmed through. They went across some hilly terrain overgrown with cedar and evergreen oak. And then they came upon a waterfall.

It was a big one, narrow but more than fifty feet high, the water cascading down into a deep, clear pool. Falling Stone pulled off his clothes and jumped in, and swam around for a while.

"Any crocodiles in there?" Thurl called. "Any snakes?"

If there were, they weren't showing themselves. Merlin checked with the black box to see if there were any big concentrations of monkeys close by. There weren't. Thurl undressed and jumped in, so did Simon. Even Trask jumped in. "You two keep guard," he said to Schlumm and Sugg. The girls jumped in. They all swam around for a while, and Thurl and Falling Stone got out and took watch so Sugg and Schlumm could get in. The water cool, fresh, clean enough to drink, the roar of the falls so loud that if any shooting started it would have been hard to hear. A wild churning where the water plunged down from high above, and, farther off, a calm surface dotted with water lilies, long-finned carp flashing red and orange in the beams of sunlight that pierced the water. Chunks of white limestone at the edge, and tall, ancient trees, densely strung with vines and moss.

Simon went deep under, down and down. The pool seemed bottomless. Then up, gasping for air. Tess went down and was gone a long time—then up, breaking through the surface, wet and gasping, her large breasts pillowing out on the water. She splashed Emma Sue, and Emma Sue splashed back. Then Emma Sue went down, deep, long gone, and came crashing through the surface. They splashed around some more, and Simon swam off, enjoying the motion of his arms and legs, his face in the water, the cool water over his body like another skin.

When he looked back, he saw Tess climbing out over the white rocks, the slope of her wet thighs, black bush of hair between her legs. She moved gingerly over the rocks, cautious of gashing her feet. Schlumm and Merlin were climbing out, also Sugg. Trask was waist-high near the edge, giving the signal. His gray-black hair pasted down on his scalp, the right arm waving. Calling them in. Barrel-chested. Fleshy but strong, his arms and shoulders knotted with muscle, white hairs on his chest glistening in the sun. He might have been somebody's grandfather on a picnic in the woods, on vacation in the Adirondacks. Shouting the kids in for hamburgers and Coke, eager to get his hands on the cold beer.

Simon plunged down again, deeper and deeper, among the carp and other fish, turtles, long streamers of underwater grass, and while he was down there he thought of Kabuki, who was dead, and Eikopf, who was dead, and they were at peace, in death, saved in a mysterious silence. He was moving toward them, into their silence, their slow dream. Then up, up, bursting through the surface, lungs straining, ready to pop, and swam to shore.

They bivouacked that night in a shallow bowl of land surrounded by shrubs and trees. They pulled out their rations and ate, packing it in even though they grumbled about the taste, the lack of flavor, and they were still eating, chomping away, when Meyerbeer came sailing in, in the rainbow chopper, alone. There was the barest glimmer of light in the sky, the chopper descending like a queer mechanical bug, noisy and bright, finding its way infallibly, with an instinct that seemed almost preternatural. Still the same mad Meyerbeer, jockeying the chopper around the worst time of day, loving it because of the danger. He put down on a small outcrop of rock about thirty yards off from the bivouac.

He hopped out of the rainbow chopper, and, as he ambled toward the bivouac, Trask got up off the log he had been on and stood up tall, in a state of masterfully controlled rage, raising himself up to his full height. He extended his right arm stiffly, pointing at Meyerbeer. "Sugg," he said with full-throated timbre, "write that son of a bitch up and clap him in the brig."

Meyerbeer stopped dead in his tracks, and Sugg, not entirely sure how to handle custody in the jungle, yet clearly delighted with the idea, whatever it might entail, displayed a vague, bemused smile and raised his Uzi, ready to blow a hole in Meyerbeer if he made a move for the helicopter.

"Jesus Christ, *sir*," Meyerbeer blurted, perplexed by Trask's order and a little nervous about Sugg. "What's this all about? What's *hap*pening here?"

Trask was still pointing, standing rigid, firm, and only now did he lower his arm. "When we get back to base, Meyerbeer, I'm putting you up for a general court-martial. For buzzing around in my sky yesterday when we were at that goddamn opium farm, and for not responding when we needed you to pick up Kabuki. You're in direct violation of orders being here right now, damn you. I warned you: *Keep away from my operation*. We're too goddamn close to the objective."

Meyerbeer stood rooted where he was, about twenty feet away from Trask. "Sir, can we dispense with the gun?" He nodded in Sugg's direction.

Trask, glancing at the Uzi, hung silent for a moment, seeming to take pleasure in Meyerbeer's discomfort. Then, scratching at the back of his hand, he spoke up crisply. "Since you're so damn eager about that bridge, you can march the rest of the way in with us, on the ground. And when we get back to base I'll personally plant you in the stockade."

Meyerbeer took it in stride. "Fine, fine. March to the bridge, huh? That's fine by me. But you ought to know, sir, I don't think General Zaster will be too happy about what's going down here."

At the mention of Zaster's name, Simon saw something change in Trask's face. Zaster and Trask had never been on the best of terms, and it was quietly but widely rumored that Zaster was not at all impressed with the derring-do style of Trask's performance in the field, and was in fact doing his utmost to shove Trask into retirement, or at least into an innocuous desk job stateside.

Trask stepped forward, toward Meyerbeer, and as he went past Sugg he gently pushed him aside, a signal for Sugg to lower the Uzi, which he did. Trask went right up to Meyerbeer. His eyes narrowed and he searched Meyerbeer's face, as if measuring him, testing to see just what the connection with Zaster might be.

"Zaster? Did you sell Vidwar shares to him too?"

"Not just yet, sir, but he's considering, thinking it over. And I tell you, sir, he has a real interest, he's really eager to see the Vidwar project go forward."

"I just bet he is," Trask said. He was still firm, erect, magnificent in his anger, but Simon noted in his expression, his tone, not just anger, not just vexation on the point of boiling over, but frustration, an awareness of his own inability to cope with Meyerbeer's slipperiness. Meyerbeer was indefatigable. He had angles, lines, connections. Zaster, and who else out there? The anger was still alive in Trask's voice, rich and voluminous, but something had changed, it was the anger not of conquest and victory but of stalemate, disappointment, because he knew now that his talk of arrest and court-martial was just that, talk, he'd have to back off and let Meyerbeer go his own way.

"Meyerbeer, the next goddamn time I see this chopper in the air, my men have orders to assume it's the enemy and deal with it accordingly." He turned and scanned the surviving members of his force, a slow pan, focusing hard on each of them, one by one, as if searching their faces for signs of allegiance. He nodded confidently, as if finding what he had been looking for, and turned again to Meyerbeer, sharply. "You're an excrescence, Meyerbeer. A boil. I'm on to you, you bastard, and don't you ever forget it. What the hell are you here for anyway?"

Meyerbeer smiled, relaxing in the knowledge that Zaster's name had done the trick for him. For the moment, at least, he was off the hook.

"I developed that last reel of film—and just at the end there, I saw Kabuki took a hit. Somehow I never noticed that from the chopper. I figure if he needs help, I can ferry him back to base."

"Kabuki is dead," Trask said bluntly, glad of the opportunity to disappoint Meyerbeer, if disappointment was what it was.

"Yeah? No kidding. Too bad, too bad about that." Meyerbeer said it, Simon thought, as if Kabuki's death were something he might have known about all along. "Kabuki, huh? That's bad news, sorry about that. I hate to mention it, sir, but there's some other bad news you should know about. We lost Sugarman. Did you know?"

Simon and the others drew close, to hear more. Merlin seemed to hover motionless on the periphery, suspended like a butterfly pinned on a mounting board.

"Yeah, Sugarman," Meyerbeer said. "He bought it a few hours ago. A swell guy like Sugarman." He leaned toward the General. "I figured it was something you'd want to know. Since you were counting on him to make your boat drop."

"Sugarman isn't dead," Merlin interjected, in a high, piercing tone that took them by surprise. They all looked at him, puzzled by his strange, anguished definiteness. "If he were dead, we would have had it on the black box."

"The black box doesn't know everything," Meyerbeer said.

"I *know* he's not dead," Merlin insisted.

Trask glanced at Merlin, then at Meyerbeer, looking at Meyerbeer not just with anger, now, but with stony bewilderment, because he was not just an excrescence, a boil, but an outright menace, interfering, playing with people's lives. There was no redeeming quality in him. Kleff dead, because Meyerbeer had flown in with the Yamaha, and, from the expression on Trask's face, it was clear that he was wondering what else Meyerbeer

196

might or might not have been up to, what else responsible for. If he could have had his way, he would have bashed Meyerbeer in the face and sent him back to base, a beaten dog. An appealing thought, to crash a fist into Meyerbeer's face. Trask hung there a moment, thinking about it, giving it serious consideration—then stepped away, just turned and walked off, fuming, stuffing his hands into his pockets.

Meyerbeer took out a cigar and spent a lot of time unwrapping it. "Sugarman, he liked to fly, but he really wasn't cut out for it. Very insecure at the controls, you know. He was blown out of the air right after he made a drop for C Group, on his way back to base. The monkeys have a few of these new Russian rockets they've installed, they can knock you down no matter how high you fly. Poor Sugarman, he must have seen the rocket on its way, but he didn't know how to take evasive action. That's the only way to stay alive up there, evade and evade. I flew over the wreck myself not half an hour ago—it's all burned out, a real smash-up."

"I *know* he's not dead," Merlin repeated, his eyes oddly unfocused. It seemed, for a moment, that he was on the verge of coming unglued. Nobody's death had seemed to bother him—not Studdwin's, Polymer's, or Kabuki's. Eikopf's death had upset him only because he had been the one who pulled the trigger. But death itself, that anybody should die, had never seemed to touch him. Now, though, he stood there in the grass, holding the black box, looking at nobody at all, unable to accept the news of Sugarman's demise.

"We all go sooner or later," Meyerbeer offered philosophically. "What the hell, that's life. I talked on radio-com with some guys at the base, and they're all broken up back there. What a blister, huh? Sugarman. Who would have thought? A delicatessen man."

They were all silent for a while; then Merlin, his eyes vacant, abstract, looked again toward Meyerbeer. "Is Sugarman really dead?" When Merlin said that, Simon looked across to Meyerbeer, and had a strange, bewildering sense that maybe Merlin was right: Sugarman was alive and well somewhere, and Meyerbeer was lying, making it all up, for some obscure, sinister purpose known only to himself. Or just passing along an unsubstantiated rumor, for the hell of it. Life was crap, Simon thought. Meyerbeer was crap.

"Only make-believe dead," Meyerbeer answered. "Don't worry about it. Anything you need to know about it will turn up on your little black box. Why do they call it a black box? In this light it looks gray."

"It is gray," Thurl said.

"It is? Really? There is no trustworthiness in the world anymore. Nobody is reliable." Meyerbeer hung there a moment, slope-shouldered against the darkening sky, hovering as if he had just articulated an important piece of wisdom. He shrugged, then went over and sat on a log, and motioned to Simon, calling him over. "I have big news for you, Simon. The real reason I'm here is because I wanted to tell you about the bridge. It exists—it's out there, waiting. I saw it this morning. Flew right over it. Over and around it. Under it. A while back, you were saying you were skeptical."

"I know, that was a while back. I changed my mind. I conquered my confusion. The last few days, I've been looking forward to blowing the hell out of that bridge. I'm a true believer." He paused. "But now that I'm hearing it from you, Meyerbeer, I have my doubts again."

"Doubt, Simon, is a condition of your soul. But doubt no more. I swear, it's the prettiest bridge you'll ever have a chance to blow. You should feel privileged." Simon shivered. It was like bartering with the devil, if the devil were a slightly shabby used-car salesman who was damn good at selling you things you didn't want.

The UFO was in the sky, far off but brightly lit. Impossible to

198

mistake it for a star. Simon wondered whose side it was on, if indeed it was a thing that took sides.

The others went off to sleep. Emma Sue was nestled close to Falling Stone. Merlin lay on his sleeping bag, eyes open, staring vacantly. The night resonated with the noise of crickets. The darkness seemed to grow, ripening toward a mysterious fullness.

Schlumm, one ear gone, weary, sat in the grass, smoking, leaning against a rock. "If you can't win a war," he said, "why fight it? This is not a war we are going to win." He felt the malicious absurdity of the mission, as Simon did, felt they were somehow being tracked, fooling no one, that if they got to the bridge at all it would only be because they were allowed to do so, and the result, for them, would be disastrous.

"It's all a matter of image," Meyerbeer said, not on the log now but flat on his back, one hand behind his head for a cushion. "Don't you know that yet? We're not going to win, but we're not going to lose either. That's the wonderful part of it. It's a new dimension that we're working with. Nobody wins and nobody loses: it's the face you put on it that matters. What ap*pears*."

"That's dumb," Simon said, cross-legged in the grass. "Tell it to Eikopf and Kabuki."

Meyerbeer pointed toward the UFO. "You think that's dumb? You fancy college guys. Tell me—is that a piece of ignorance?"

"It's an unknown," Schlumm said.

"An unknown? It's something you see, dammit. It appears. The way a beautiful girl in a movie appears, when she takes off her clothes. When you come right down to it, it doesn't matter what it is. It's there. It comes and goes. Who cares? It has its place. It's the ap*pear*ing that counts. Not the *what is*."

Listening to Meyerbeer talk like this made Simon nervous, he didn't know why. It was as if each time Meyerbeer was around, a forbidden room in his mind was opened to him, and the most terrible notions became real. What he felt, at the moment, was a disquieting suspicion that Meyerbeer may have arranged, somehow, for the UFO to be there. He had probably been the one behind it all the time, rigging the image with lasers. Simon had read about that: the way you could use lasers to create a solid-looking three-dimensional image in space. But if you reached out for it, to touch it, there was nothing there.

"God used to appear," Eikopf said.

"Appear and disappear," Meyerbeer answered flippantly. "That was God's way."

"And when he appears," Eikopf pursued, "he doesn't screw around. The eye of God sees all and knows nothing, and sometimes dreams."

Simon realized, suddenly, that it wasn't Eikopf talking, it was himself. Eikopf was dead. How dumb. Dumb of Eikopf to die, and dumb of Simon to be Eikopf. He wasn't Eikopf—at least he didn't want to be. Eikopf be damned!

"But if the image is insubstantial," Schlumm said, "only a dream, how account for the tangible aspects that can be measured and weighed? How account for time and motion, and death?"

Meyerbeer blew a fart. "I'm turning in, you guys. All you have to do in the morning is traipse through the faery forest. But in the morning Meyerbeer has to fly. You think flying is easy? Try it." He tossed his cigar into the night, then he went over to the helicopter, took out a sleeping bag, stretched out in it, and went to sleep.

It wasn't until the next day that Simon found out why it was that Merlin had reacted so strongly to the news of Sugarman's death. Merlin and Sugarman had known each other for quite some time before Camp Alpha and Base Blue. They had been stationed in Colorado together, and for almost a year they had shared an off-base apartment in downtown Durango. It was something that Schlumm told him about.

"You mean Sugarman was gay?"

200

"They both were. Merlin still is, I guess. But not Sugarman any more, unless there's sex after death."

Simon was surprised. Merlin was so withdrawn and antisocial, it had always seemed that he simply had no interest in things like sex. Simon had merely taken it for granted—thoughtlessly, he now realized—that Merlin was neuter, sexually nonfunctional. And Sugarman was such a straight-on masculine type, it was hard to imagine he was a homosexual. "There are surprises and surprises," Simon said, acknowledging that he had been the dupe of hasty assumptions and conventional thinking.

"Yes," Schlumm agreed. "There are surprises." Simon noted a curious inflection in the way he said it, and wondered if Schlumm, too, might be gay, though he was far from being about to ask. There were other things to worry about, like monkeys, like not getting killed.

20 ❑ The Lake

THE LAST BIG OBSTACLE they faced before getting to the bridge was the lake. Simon hadn't known about it, and the first he heard of it was when Trask rounded them up before they moved out in the morning and told them to gird themselves for the final leg. He remembered Meyerbeer mentioning boats, but it had meant nothing at the time, and only now did he make the connection.

"What lake?" he asked Schlumm.

"The big lake. It's a whopper. Didn't you know about it?"

It was very big. Bigger than Winnebago in Wisconsin. Bigger

than Okeechobee in Florida. Bigger than the Great Salt Lake in Utah. Too big for them to get easily around, so the plan was that Sugarman was going to drop rubber boats for them, with outboard engines, and they would get across in the night. But Sugarman was dead.

"I don't think there are any sharks in the lake," Schlumm said, "if that's what you're worried about."

"I'm worried about getting my feet wet. How do we get the boats without Sugarman?"

"He isn't dead," Merlin offered, brisk and assertive.

Simon turned and blinked. "Merlin, there are some things you just have to accept. You heard Meyerbeer: Sugarman went down."

"Meyerbeer was wrong, it was somebody else went down. It came through on the black box just a few minutes ago."

"You mean between the black box and Meyerbeer you choose the black box?"

"Between the black box and Meyerbeer, I choose Sugarman." There was, in his tone, an unwonted daring, a note of defiance. It was so human that Simon almost forgave him for Eikopf, for the black box, for being Merlin—but not quite.

"Merlin, is that an act of faith you've just made? I think you've undergone a conversion."

"It's an act of nothing," Merlin said, just short of cocky. "I believe in nothing."

"Nothing is a dangerous thing to have confidence in. Don't put your trust in nothing, Merlin. You hear? It'll bite back." But Merlin had already walked on ahead, in a kind of euphoria, basking in the knowledge that Sugarman was alive.

They went through a lot of mud and swamp before they got to the lake, and it took all day. But they got there. They didn't run into any patrols. The country they were now in was insulated from the war—there were occasional bomber runs, but the war on the ground was far off, and although there were swarms of monkeys around, they were not on alert, and it was relatively easy to get around them with the help of the black box. There were a few clouds, some hefty ones that periodically blotted out the sun—but the weather held, no rain. Late in the afternoon the clouds cleared away entirely. When they reached the lake, the sun was low, sinking toward the horizon.

The lake was extraordinary. They were on a high point, on a hill, and as far as they could see there was nothing in front of them but water. Below them it was all rock and boulders, the water lapping lazily against the shore. Off to the right, the shore-line curved, and there were white beaches and hotels. People on the sand, sunning themselves, baking in the heat, getting the last rays as the sun went down. In skimpy bikinis, some of them nude. A hundred miles to the east, whole armies were slaughtering each other; but here the lake and the lake life subsisted in a kind of vacuum, inviolable, untouched by the war, an ancient ritual of time and pleasure. Relaxing, swimming, taking the sun, sex in sun-filled hotel rooms. You had to be rich to vacation here. Rich, or part of the war—a general, or a diplomat. There were all kinds out there, Russians, Chinese, Italians, French. The Germans and the Japanese, a lot of them. Even some Americans. Swimming, or lying on the sand. Sitting on patios, sipping cock-tails, a prepranadial vermouth. Movie stars and TV celebrities, business magnates, executives. The monkeys out there too, in the sun, monkey generals and monkey colonels. Boats in the water. Sails. Waiters in white jackets and white gloves serving drinks on canopied verandas, moving quietly among the guests, like whis-pers.

Simon saw how daring Trask's plan was, and grasped its bril-liance. He had brought them into a country overrun with mon-keys, to an international resort area isolated from the war, a region where the monkeys were so much in abundance that se-curity was lax and negligible, because it was deemed unneces-sary. The perfect jump-off point to get across the lake. Daring, he wondered, or ingeniously harebrained? Whatever else it might be, it was damn risky.

Trask was on the crest of the hill, on his stomach, propped up on his elbows, scanning the area with binoculars. A few boats out there, sailing craft and fishing vessels. No gunboats that he could see, though a gunboat might be tucked away in just about any cove. He relished the sheer expanse of water, vast and purple in the setting sun. "Isn't that grand?" he said to Simon, who was down in the grass beside him. "You'd swear you were at the edge of the sea. You like it, Corporal?"

"I hate it."

"I thought you liked water. Back there at the waterfall, you seemed to be having a damn good time."

"Sure, a waterfall. A place to swim. But this kind of stuff is no joke. When I was a kid I was on a motor launch that went down on Long Island Sound. A couple of people drowned. Me too—I nearly drowned."

Trask continued to study the lake. "Simon, you're a depressing person."

The sun went down and the sky darkened, and in the ambiguous light of dusk Sugarman made his fly-over. Merlin had sent the signal, pinpointing their position. It was a tricky drop to make. The chute had to come down far enough inland to guarantee that a sudden wind wouldn't carry it out and dump it in the water. Risky too, with all the monkeys around. Trask was relying on the element of surprise and on monkey indolence, hoping they wouldn't notice the drop—or, if they did, hoping to get the boats in the water and across the lake before the monkeys could organize a significant pursuit. The twin-engined plane circled high above them. "That isn't Sugarman," Thurl said. "Sugarman never circled that way."

"That's Sugarman," Merlin said.

Tess squinted, keeping her eyes on the plane. "Let's see if he wobbles his wings." Sugarman had a habit of wobbling his wings after he made a drop.

The plane continued circling, and the chute came, a large blue one. The plane didn't wobble its wings. It circled again, the pilot wanting to be sure the chute fell on target. It was a mistake, he was hanging around too long. "Go home, damn you," Trask said, just under a shout, waving his arms angrily. "Merlin, signal that idiot to get the hell out of here." But it was too late. While the plane was still circling, a couple of rockets went up, from miles away, and one of them smashed the plane's tail section. Debris from the tail scattered, they could see big chunks of it falling.

Merlin was devastated. He watched the plane, his jaw hanging open. Sugerman had been dead, then alive, and now it seemed, incredibly, if this was Sugarman, he was on his way to being dead again. It was too much for Merlin to handle, something broke inside him—yet he hung in there, watching, hoping.

The front end of the plane hovered momentarily, then it nosed over and went into a slow spin as it headed down, swinging around on its own axis, looking a little like a boomerang thrown by an inept amateur. "My God," Emma Sue cried. "Poor Sugarman!"

A black speck detached itself from the plane, and it was hard to tell if it was the pilot or just another piece of debris. Then a chute opened. "Hot damn," Thurl called. The plane hurtled down, a great whining sound from its engines, and smashed into the water, exploding, sending up a huge geyser of water and steam. The figure dangling from the parachute was still far off, descending slowly, looking like a small toy doll swinging back and forth under the enormous chute. He was tugging at the lines, wrestling with the wind, getting the air currents to bring him off the water and over land. And then he was down, missing the water, coming down on the hill. It was Sugarman. Merlin was the first to get to him.

They helped him out of his chute, and they retrieved the supply chute, which had also come down on target, bearing a crate containing three inflatable boats and the outboard engines to power them across the lake. "You realize," Simon told Sugarman, "this isn't really you that we're talking to. Meyerbeer declared you dead. We've already performed a funeral."

"That bastard Meyerbeer—always connivin', drummin' somethin' up. He wants to bury us all. Hell, it wasn't me went down, it was a jerk kid that took off in my plane. Damn fool got himself killed and wrecked the plane to boot. It was a good plane, I liked the feel of it. This thing I was flying just now was a piece of shit, it deserved to get shot down. I guess I made a mess of things, huh? If they don't know where we are now, they'll never know. Tell me, how you guys been eatin'? Been subsistin' on rations for a while, huh?" Short, fat Sugarman with his round delicatessen face, wire-rim glasses, most of the hair gone from the top of his head, just that thick fringe over the ears. Food was his life. He loved flying, enjoyed it even though he was no good at it—but food was what he lived for, it was the thing he knew.

He wasn't on the ground five minutes before a gunboat turned up. With the sun gone, darkness set in swiftly, and the boat cruised up and down along the shore, playing its searchlight around, looking for Sugarman. They had seen his chute open, maybe had even seen the supply chute. On the ground, patrols were moving around, picking up the search. A couple of flares went up, less than half a mile off. The patrols were inching forward. If they had seen the supply chute, they knew it was more than just Sugarman in the area. The gunboat swept the vicinity where the plane had gone down, then it moved closer in and played its light along the rocky shore.

The flares died out and more flares went up from the patrols. The gunboat, too, sent up some flares. The monkeys were milling about off to the left and the right of the knoll, but not yet advancing on the knoll itself. Simon hunkered down close to the General, behind a chunk of pink granite.

"They're sweeping all around us," Trask said quietly. "Making sure we're neatly tucked away up here. Methodical bastards, aren't they?" He was silent for a moment, then he said, "You know what we need, Corporal? We need an aircraft carrier out there. Then we'd have a bunch of attack planes we could call in, and we wouldn't be in the mess we are in."

"An aircraft carrier? On a lake, sir?"

"You're damn right, on a lake. A prefab job, something they can take apart in sections and reassemble wherever it's needed. This is modern war, Corporal, there are plenty of lakes in the world where a carrier could make the difference. Fly the sections in and assemble them overnight. It could be done, American technology can do it. A whole fucking aircraft carrier right out there on that water. Invent it, Corporal. Go out and do it. Draw up the blueprints."

Simon wondered about Trask, what kept him going. Pride? Patriotism? Stupidity? At times he seemed simple and straightforward, a personification of sheer will and dogged resolution. But at other times he seemed opaque and inaccessible—his motivation, the engine that drove him, wrapped in a cloud. Still other times, like now, talking about portable aircraft carriers, he seemed quixotic, mad. Simon had heard the rumors about his debacle, last time out, and from Schlumm he'd got some of the facts. Trask had gone out with a dozen men to wipe out a nest of guerillas, but the guerillas outgunned him and he went home with only three survivors. ("A dozen," Simon noted. "That's what we were at the start.") And before the guerrillas, there had been another mission that went wrong, an assault on a radar installation. So if anything, Trask was out here now trying to prove himself, reaching into the old magic hat to see if there was still a rabbit around down there. But there wasn't, it was all going sour, and Simon couldn't help but feel that the brass might have approved this assignment as a mission impossible, in the fond expectation that this time Trask himself wouldn't return. It was a thought that had passed through his mind early on; but now, as more and more of them were wasted, his grim speculation seemed to take on the solidity of fact. Trask was a legend, but a legend nobody could afford.

The gunboat was still out there, and it didn't appear to be ready to go away. It cruised about a mile along the shore to the left, then doubled back and traveled a mile off to the right. Then it turned again, ready to keep sweeping up and down like that all night.

The flares died out and fresh flares went up. Trask motioned to Thurl, and Thurl crawled across an open patch of grass to get over to the granite boulder that Simon and Trask were crouched behind.

"If we get down there at the edge of the water, you think you can hit that boat with a rocket?"

Thurl looked at the boat and nodded confidently.

"I'll be down there with you," Trask said. "Wait for my signal." The patrols still slowly closing in, sending up flares to the left and right, to the rear. In front of them, where the hill fell away sharply, there was the flat expanse of the lake, and the gunboat. "Got to get our boats in the water before the goddamn patrols start buzzing us," Trask said. He signaled Schlumm, who darted over, and told him to move the boats quickly off the knoll and ready them for the water, while the patrols were still at a distance. "Before they come pouring down our throat," he grunted. "And leave Sugg and Falling Stone up here with grenades, to protect our rear. When they hear the rocket launcher blasting the gunboat, have them pitch frags toward all points of the perimeter, and come running down like hell. Move it fast."

Schlumm passed the word and started moving the boats, and Thurl and Trask wriggled down off the knoll, positioning themselves behind the rocks at the water's edge. Simon helped with the boats and engines, bringing them cautiously off the knoll, keeping under cover as much as possible, to avoid being spotted by the gunboat. They got down off the knoll and inflated the boats behind a row of high boulders, and attached the motors, Pratt & Whitney outboards, and prepared to push off into the lake. Sugg and Falling Stone stayed up on the knoll with a pile of fragmentation grenades. The others, below, gathered around the boats, ready to shove off.

The gunboat came cruising by again, about fifty feet offshore, the searchlight probing diligently. Thurl waited, taking aim with the launcher. Trask tapped his shoulder, and he fired. The first shot hit the bow, sending the sailor stationed at the .51 caliber gun to his knees. But he was quickly up, firing away—wildly, but firing. Trask loaded another rocket into the launcher and again Thurl fired, this time hitting the stern, boring right through into the fuel tanks. The boat detonated in a blaze of white flame that quickly darkened to red and green. Sailors were hurled high in the air like broken dolls; boards and panels from the cheaply constructed boat sprang out from the concussed area, spinning in the air, splashing in the water. Simon was deafened by the blast, he felt the heat of the flame. But he was up, rushing, shoving one of the boats into the water. He was knee-deep, getting Tess into the boat, climbing in himself, and Thurl came splashing aboard. As he yanked the starter, he could hear the grenades going off up on the knoll. In the glare of the burning gunboat, he saw Sugg and Falling Stone charging down off the knoll, Sugg leaping for Schlumm's boat, Falling Stone for Merlin's, and all three boats were pulling away. More flares went up. The gunboat was gone, a few burning planks in the water, an oil slick burning. Simon revved the engine. On the crest of the knoll, monkey troops appeared, sharply etched under their own flares, in helmets and uniforms. A flare went up over the water. The monkeys fired, and they fired back. Tess fired. Trask fired. Bullets sprayed wildly, pattering into the water. In Schlumm's boat, Sugg took a hit and doubled over, and in Simon's boat Thurl was hit. Tess was blasting away with her automatic rifle, Thurl too, even though he was hit, but the shooting was sheer bravado. At the speed they were making, the boat bouncing as it was, it was impossible to take aim. The flare over the water died out, and another went up, but no more bullets were reaching them from the shore. "We're out of range," Simon shouted to Tess and Thurl, and only then, as he shouted, did he realize his helmet was gone, knocked off his head, somehow, in the mad rush and flurry of getting the boats in the water. "You can stop shooting. We're out of range."

Tess looked at him oddly, a glance that was almost cross. It was the look of a woman who had been sitting at a machine in a factory all day, punching staples into pieces of cardboard, and the foreman has just walked over and told her she's been stapling the wrong pieces of cardboard together, they don't need her anymore, she can go look for another job. The expression on Tess's face was something like that, but not exactly. She cradled the weapon across her lap. Thurl also stopped firing, and was looking at his wound. He had been hit high on his left arm, but the bullet had merely grazed the flesh without hitting any bone.

"We're losing air," Simon said. "They hit us." A bullet had ripped through the bow and the bow had gone to mush. The sectional construction of the rubberized craft had prevented all of the air from going out, so they were not about to sink, but the flabbiness in the bow made the boat hard to maneuver and slowed them down. He signaled the other boats, and they slowed and rendezvoused. Thurl got into Schlumm's boat, which held Sugg and the General; and Tess and Simon climbed into Merlin's boat, which held Sugarman, Falling Stone, and Emma Sue. Sugg had been hit in the hand.

"Get us a course," Trask said to Merlin, and Falling Stone took over the tiller from him, leaving him free to work the black box. He tapped some codes into it and established contact with the overhead satellite. He punched out a few more signals, then got

210

an array of numbers on the miniscreen. They had a compass bearing, and Merlin checked it against the stars. "That star over there," he said. "That bright one on the horizon. If we head for that, we'll come ashore where we want to be."

"That's not a star," Schlumm said. "That's a planet. Isn't that a planet?"

"Who gives a fuck," Sugg said. Emma Sue passed a compress over to him, and he held it against his hand.

"It's Mars," Trask said. "We'll head for Mars."

They revved up, and the two boats separated and pushed on across the lake. A breeze was up and the water was choppy. Simon was cold. It had been a long time since he'd been cold, it was a good feeling. Tess was cold and huddled close to him. The breeze, the speed of the boat, the water. Tomorrow it would be heat and sweat again, the cold would be something they wouldn't even remember. Emma Sue crouched low, ducking away from the wind. Merlin's teeth chattered, he was close beside Sugarman. Falling Stone at the tiller, his face set, eyes on the star. His shirt was off. The weather seemed never to affect him one way or another. In the heat he had never complained, and now, in the cold, he seemed indifferent.

"What's on the other side," Simon wondered aloud. There could be more monkeys, waiting for them, firing from the shore, or no monkeys at all, just tourists, starlets, jet-setters with beautiful, bronzed bodies, trim, a little drunk, waving to them, cheering, offering a drink, some tequila, a margarita, bloody mary with a stick of celery.

"Let's get there first," Tess said, shivering, holding close. "Damn, let's just get there." She was worried about the gunboats. They all were. They had destroyed a gunboat and the signal must have gone out. By now the whole lake had to be alerted. There would be other boats on the prowl, hunting them down.

"It's a big lake," Simon said. "We'll get through."

"These damn, noisy motors," she agonized. "They can hear us miles away!"

It didn't matter, though, about the motors. There were other motors on the lake—yachts, launches. Close to shore, in lighted areas in front of the hotels, people were waterskiing. The war hadn't come here yet. The war didn't belong. They had brought the war with them, but they were merely passing through. There were boats with sails, gliding lazily under the stars.

"We'll get through," Simon repeated, and it wasn't something he said merely for the saying. It was something he felt, an uncanny sense that while they were on the water they were, somehow, implausibly, safe. Simon, who was afraid of the water, was thinking that.

They were less than fifteen minutes on the water when a gunboat turned up, heading in their direction. They cut their engines and crouched down, and the boat come slowly on, cruising. It came straight toward them—then, a quarter of a mile away, for no apparent reason, it veered, heading off on another course, without spotting them.

They revved their engines and moved on, and when they were about halfway across to the other side, another gunboat turned up. It was larger than the one they had just encountered, heavily armed with machine guns and small cannon. They cut their engines again and lay low, waiting. Thurl had the rocket launcher loaded and ready. Schlumm and Simon were ready with grenades. Tess aimed her automatic rifle. The boat came on steadily, sweeping the water with the searchlight on its bow. As they lay there in the two rubber boats, they were tense, poised, barely breathing, ears tuned for the first rush of machine-gun fire. They could hear the monkey marines talking, their quick, brittle chatter. The thumping engine.

The boat came to within a hundred feet of them, and passed by, the searchlight scanning off its port side while they lay bobbing in the water off to starboard. It was chance, an incredible stroke of luck, and, as the boat moved off into the night, engines fading, running lights vanishing in the dark, Simon wondered if their luck would hold. Maybe, he began to think, just maybe, they might make it to the bridge after all.

They waited a long time before starting up again. Not until the gunboat was long gone did they risk turning the engines over.

21 ❏ Zoo

ON THE OTHER SIDE of the lake they hit shore at a spot that seemed deserted. There were homes off to the right, on high ground, villas with lighted windows. But at the point where they put in, it was rocks and trees and darkness. They seemed to be in some sort of park—mowed grass and gravel paths, picnic tables. No houses, though, and no activity, no lights. Only the moon, making the lawn appear blue. Simon scanned the star-clustered sky, looking for the UFO. If it was there, he couldn't see it.

They moved off to a secluded spot, screened from the lake by a line of trees. They could see the lake, yet they had cover if another gunboat should come along. Trask sent Schlumm, with Merlin and Sugarman, to scout the place out, and Emma Sue got busy dressing the wounds. Thurl's was merely a flesh wound, she cleaned it out and applied a bandage. But Sugg's was more problematic. A shell fragment had shattered the middle finger of his left hand, there were pieces of bone sticking out through the flesh. The bone was too shattered. "It has to come off," she said.

He looked at her, just stared, didn't say anything. It was as if what she had just said hadn't registered yet. Or, if it had, what he felt, wanted to say, was beyond words, beyond thought, so there was just that dumb, hard stare. Emma Sue took two tranquilizers out of a plastic bottle and put them in his mouth. "Here. Swallow these." She injected a heavy dose of anesthetic into the hand, and while she waited for it to take effect she gave him a shot of penicillin. She made him lie down on the grass, on his back, so he wouldn't see what she was doing. When the hand was sufficiently numb, she took a scalpel and sterilized it with alcohol, and, while Tess held a flashlight, she severed the finger at the knuckle. It was quickly done. She sutured the wound and applied a bandage, then slipped a packet of pain-killers into one of his pockets. "You may need some of these later," she said.

Merlin and Sugarman emerged from a clump of trees, after scouting around. "It's a zoo," Merlin reported to Trask. "They've got zebras, elephants, all sorts of things. Schlumm is up at the house talking to the keeper. We cut the phone lines. The keeper lives alone up there with his wife. He's not a monkey, but he can talk monkey talk, so Schlumm is managing some conversation. He says there aren't many troops on this side of the lake. They're mostly down on the south side."

"I'm going to catch some sleep," Trask said. "Wake me if the dogs start barking."

Simon went over to Tess, who was on the ground, leaning against a tree. "Come on. Let's check out the orangutans."

"Are you kidding? In the dark? I'm sleepy."

He dug in his pack for a flashlight. "Never again will you have a chance to check out a zoo in this garbage dump of a country right after nearly getting killed on the world's third largest lake." He looked to Merlin. "This is the third largest, isn't it?"

It was not.

"Nevertheless—" Simon said, coming up with the flashlight.

Sugg lay on top of his sleeping bag, eyes open, in what appeared to be a stupor. His bandaged hand rested on his chest. Trask was out of his fatigues and in his bag, asleep already, or

214

well on his way. Emma Sue sat leaning against a tree, eyes closed. Tess still hadn't moved, sitting against a silver-skinned tree that looked like a birch. "Okay," she finally said, pushing herself up off the ground, and together they went along a gravel path that brought them eventually to the keeper's house.

It was a cottage, a single large room illumined by candles, the exterior fashioned out of wood and stucco, the same type of wood-and-stucco construction that characterized the hotels and villas on the other side of the lake. They paused by a window and looked in. The keeper was a small old man, slight, with heavy pouches under his large, dark eyes. His wife was also old, with thin gray hair. She sat in a rocker, nodding quietly as Schlumm and the old man talked. The old man was animated, his face full of energy and feeling. The woman wore red pajamas, with a knit shawl over her shoulders. The old man wore a green satin robe over his nightshirt. They had been asleep and Schlumm had got them out of bed. There was wine on the table. Schlumm and the old man were at the table, and when Tess and Simon came in, the old woman brought two stools over for them. She poured some wine.

"He says he's been the keeper of this zoo for some thirty-three years," Schlumm said. "When they started, they had a couple of dogs, some birds. A friend of theirs, connected with a French zoo, got them a wolf and a Siberian tiger. They went on expeditions all through this region and brought a lot of animals back with them. They even went to Africa a few times. They've got two bald eagles that they're trying to mate. It bothers them that the bald eagle may become extinct."

It was a tranquil domestic scene. A small bed raised slightly off the ground on low legs, a couch against one wall, a bookcase loaded with books. A porcelain lamp on a table, carved walnut chairs. A small wooden Buddha on the slate ledge jutting out above the stone fireplace. There was a coal stove in a corner of the room, where the old woman did her cooking. The sound of their talking was rich and musical. Even Schlumm, when he

215

talked with them, sounded musical. His voice was normally flat and dull, but in another language it was a different voice. His face seemed different too, taking on the same brightness that appeared in the old man's face.

"Ask him about the bear," Simon suggested.

"What bear?"

"Falling Stone's bear. What other bear do we know?"

Schlumm asked if there was a bear at the zoo, and the old man's face became grave, somber. Yes, he said, there had been a bear, it had been with them for many years. But now it was no longer there, it had escaped and gone away. They searched for it, but it was never found. It had been a foul old creature, moody, full of meanness, and they were glad it was gone. Yet they were also despondent. They had lived with that old bear a long time, and it saddened them that it had left and gone off somewhere else to die.

"Ask him to describe it. Tell him about ours, maybe it was the same one."

"Simon, this is crazy."

"Ask him."

Schlumm told the old man about the bear they had killed, and he showed great astonishment. As Schlumm described it, it seemed very much like their bear. The man talked animatedly to the woman, and they were both nodding eagerly.

"He says it's the same one, Simon. But for chrissake, a bear is a bear. How can you ever *know?*"

"We should tell Falling Stone," Simon said. "They might want to meet him." He drained his glass and set it on the table, then rose and bowed to the man and the woman, thanking them. Tess also bowed, and touched the woman's hand.

"I wonder if they have any bats," Simon said, when they were outside. "You think they have any trained bats?"

"Simon, people don't train bats."

"Sure they do. I knew a girl at the Bronx Zoo, she trained a bat

216

to stand on her shoulder. It stretched its wings for her when she wanted, and folded them when she gave the signal. She was written up in a science magazine."

"You have strange friends, Simon."

"She was a nice girl. What's so strange about a girl with a trained bat?"

They passed an aviary, but there was no activity in it, the birds were quiet. Simon flashed the light around, and the staring eyes of birds on bare branches beamed the light back at them. They passed a lion, some foxes, a few polecats. A camel, an elephant. The animals weren't moving around much, most of them were asleep. The elephant on its side, swishing its trunk restlessly.

"Are you Jewish?" Tess asked.

"No," he said, a little surprised at the question. "I don't think so. You *know* I'm not Jewish."

"With a name like Simon, why aren't you Jewish?"

"I don't know. Somebody made a mistake, I guess. Is Simon a Jewish name?"

They went across a wooden footbridge, crossing water, onto what appeared to be a small, man-made island. The grass was trimmed very short, like the green on a golf course. There were roses, and dogwood, and ornamental cherry trees in flower, lighted by the moon. A low wooden bench, and they sat, for a while, facing the roses. A stream ran around both sides of the island, a low rushing sound, the water glistening, fracturing the moon into pinpoints of light. The grass wet with dew, condensation dripping from the trees.

"You *look* Jewish," she said, sitting close beside him, their bodies touching. "I don't know if you're aware of that. I'm not sure I can say exactly what Jewish looks like, but if there is something that it looks like, I think I see it in your face. A faint resemblance."

"My father was Polish, my mother was Lithuanian. My grandfather on my father's side was born in Cracow."

"Maybe your grandfather was Jewish, and it was something he told no one. His secret. Even your grandmother didn't know."

"Schlumm is Jewish," he said, annoyed with the way she clung to the theme, "and I'm pretty sure Polymer was. But my grandfather, I don't think. Unlikely. I have an aunt who married a Jew, and a third cousin who almost married a Jew but married a Presbyterian instead, and then got a divorce." There had been a cousin who wanted to be a circus performer but ended up a clerk in a post office, and another cousin who taught botany in a small New England college, but neither of them was Jewish either, and they were not cousins that he saw very often. He didn't tell her about his mother who died when he was sixteen, in a car accident on the Brooklyn Bridge, or about his father who had been killed when a bomb went off in a litter disposal unit at the World's Fair in Flushing Meadow Park. He didn't like to tell people about his mother and father because it tended to make them pity him. Pity was fine, something he appreciated when he was in need of it, but when it came at him indiscriminately, unasked for, it made him uncomfortable.

"I want to blow up that bridge," he said. "I'm really looking forward."

"Don't you want to make love to me first?"

It sprang out at him, taking him unawares, though he quickly recovered. "Sure, why not," he said in a tone of mingled wonderment and delight, dazzled by her surprising straightforwardness. "But I thought you weren't interested in that sort of thing."

"If I don't do it now, I think I'm going to trigger a booby trap or get blown up by mortar, I'll die a virgin."

"We mustn't let that happen."

"No."

"Are you really a virgin?"

"Well, there were a few close calls." She unplaited her braid, tilting her head as she maneuvered the strands of hair.

"Why were you hoping I might be Jewish?"

218

She shook her hair loose and ran her fingers through it, and it radiated out around her shoulders. "I'm turned on by men that I imagine are Jewish. I don't know why. It's just a funny thing that happens."

It made him feel inadequate. "Do you want Schlumm?" he said, with a flash of irritability. "I'll get Schlumm. Or if you rather, I'll go back on the trail and dig up what's left of Polymer."

She put her hand on his leg. "I'm even more turned on by men who I think are Jewish but turn out to be angry instead."

His testiness slid away and he smiled. "You're too complicated."

"I try not to be," she said with soft irony, and leaned across, putting her mouth on his, her lips excitingly moist, the kiss slow and long, languid. Her heavy breasts pressed against him, and, as he held her, he felt the tense, magical heat of her body.

He had been close to her before, many times. On the trail, helping her on cliffs, across ravines, his hands touching her, gripping her, and it was nothing—mechanical, a simple matter of surviving the elements. He had seen her washing, swimming naked, splashing in the water, and he had lusted for her, wanting to grab her, take her, resenting the distance she imposed, the way her body was visible and public but inaccessible, guarded—and he had hated her for that, her physical aloofness. But all of that, now, was in the past, and it was as if the past had never even existed; there was only this sudden, vivid present, unanticipated, a moment desired and longed for but something he had ceased to imagine would ever come to pass. And, now that it was happening, it was different from anything he had hoped for or supposed: violent and warm, incredibly soft, silken, ravenous yet strangely gentle, and swift.

They held each other, touching, hands roving and holding, exploring, and then they were down off the bench and onto the close-cropped grass. They were fierce with each other, clothes quickly gone, and she was under him, legs up around him, and

219

he pressed hard against her, entering. She winced briefly in the thick moment of penetration, but then she was moving again, fluid and alive, a warm ocean. He was a fish inside her, in her terrible dark. It was not a war they were in, fighting and killing, a jungle, but somewhere else, sweetly furious with hands, mouths, flesh. Her hair in his mouth, the salt taste of it. Lips, tongue; her breath quick and warm. The way she moved, her pelvis tilting, rising to meet him: it was all a wild, sweet madness, silver and green, and he came, his semen gushing warm inside her, and he went on moving, riding inside her, and she came, her thighs clamping tight, mouth quivering, her body briefly, quickly tense, then relaxing, slipping away, moaning with the release.

He stayed, holding her, being held. Then he moved off and they were side by side on the grass, gazing skyward, breathing heavily. His hand on her thigh.

"I liked that," she said, her heart still racing. "Nice. Really nice. In fact, it was terrific."

"It was."

"More than terrific."

"Yes. Much more."

"Isn't it better than blowing up a bridge?"

He was quiet for a moment, then he said, lightly, "I guess I'm going to find out. I'll let you know after it goes down."

"Write me a letter," she said, jabbing him with her elbow.

There were drops of dew along a dogwood branch a few feet above them. Simon stared up at them—they caught the moon, reflecting it, looking like small pearls. So small, so fragile. He wanted to put them on a string and give them to her.

"Did it hurt?" he wondered, feeling a little awkward about asking the question. She was the first virgin he had ever made love to.

"It's hard to say," she said, after a moment's reflection. "A little. It did and it didn't. Mostly it was just pretty sensational. It was wild!"

Wild, he thought, and more than wild. It was sheer fantasy, lying there on the grass, naked. Nothing else, at that moment, had any solidity. Trask was unreal, and the war was unreal. The dead were no more or less real than the living, and the living were maybe less real than the dead. As he lay there, his fingertips roving across her thigh, across her slack, smooth belly, wandering through her pubic bush, he was filled with a strange and fathomless joy. All he wanted, all he wished for, was to remain in this garden, these few slow moments, with the roses and dogwood blossoms, and the drops of dew that looked like pearls, and the running stream gurgling over a bed of rocks as it ran downhill on its way toward the lake.

He leaned up on an elbow and looked at her. His fingers on her face, tracing the outline—her nose, forehead, lips, chin. Down across her body—her belly, thighs. He cupped one of her breasts in his hand, silk-soft and full, the nipple hard, distending as he touched it. He put his lips to it, his tongue, feeling the hardness. Then his lips were on her mouth again, quiet and long. Her hands roved across his body, feverishly, and her tongue was into his mouth, and again they were caught up in the slowswift ardor of their passion, touching and wanting, holding, grabbing, and again he was inside her, moving with a desperate longing, a tightness yearning for release, the sweet, tormented need that they had for each other.

22 ◻ Another Country

SUGG, in the morning, was alert and strong, his left arm in a sling, the hand bandaged, his mood as gruff and bullish as ever, as if his hand had never been damaged. Eager to get going. His pack on his back and his Uzi slung over his right shoulder.

As they moved out, they passed the zookeeper's cottage, and Schlumm stopped in to say good-bye. Tess and Simon also stopped, and Sugg followed them in. The keeper and his wife were old survivors, they had lived together a long time. For Simon, and for Tess too, they were a symbol, a feeling, though neither Tess nor Simon could say exactly what the feeling was, or where it came from. They were people who had worked with animals, feeding and caring for them. Close to the animals, and close to the land the animals were part of. Close to each other too; they had been together a long time, good times and bad, and now, in their old age, their life seemed to be aglow with a grace and simplicity, an ease and a naturalness that were quietly eloquent and moving.

Schlumm had told Falling Stone about the bear, and Falling Stone had gone to the cottage with Schlumm and had talked with the old man, with Schlumm interpreting. Then Schlumm left and Falling Stone stayed on alone, and somehow he and the old man got through to each other, talking and not talking, somehow communicating, deep into the night. The old man set up a cot for him to sleep on, and Falling Stone stayed there till morning. He was just about to leave as the others came in.

Schlumm said a few words and the old man responded. An excited smile lit up his face, yet it was a smile that bore a quality of sadness. The old woman had a food basket that she offered to Falling Stone—fruit, cheese, a bottle of blackberry wine the old man had made. Falling Stone accepted the basket and bowed to the old woman, and she bowed to him. He shook hands with the old man, then lifted his right hand in an old Apache sign, and went out the door.

"These people know who we are," Sugg said, after Falling Stone was gone.

Schlumm was quick to grasp his meaning. "We cut the telephone line," he said. "First thing we did when we got here. We'll be long gone before they ever see anybody."

"Who says?"

"Sugg, there are some people in this fucked-up world it's possible to be sure about."

"Yeah? What the hell do you know about it anyway?"

Schlumm bristled. "Get in line, soldier."

"Fuck off," Sugg said. "Don't pull rank on me."

"Get in line," Schlumm repeated sharply.

Sugg's right hand rested lightly on his weapon. The Uzi hung from a strap slung over his right shoulder, barrel pointed toward the floor. There was a pause, a slow, indefinite moment, and then it happened quickly, the faintest whisper of an instant. Simon and Tess were by the door and didn't see it in process of happening— but Schlumm saw it, the barrel of the Uzi lifting, casual and innocent, barely noticeable, and he leaped at Sugg to stop him, knocking him over. But Sugg had already got off a quick burst, and the old man and the old woman pitched backward as the bullets tore into them. One bullet smashed the carved Buddha on the fireplace, and another crashed into a pile of dishes that had been stacked on the table. The old man was on the floor, his back pushed up against the wall, eyes open, a trickle of blood from his mouth. The woman fell sprawling across a chair, a couple of bullets had ripped through her chest.

Sugg was on the floor, knocked over by Schlumm, but he was quickly up again. Simon and Tess were rooted by the door, in a state of shock. Schlumm bent over the old man, confirming that he was dead. The woman was clearly gone.

Tess turned away and leaned her forehead against the wall. Her eyes were closed. She was motionless, limp. She stayed that way a moment, dazed, her forehead pressed against the wall. Then, without looking back, she went out through the door, moving slowly, as if sleepwalking.

Simon thought that if there ever was a moment to shoot Sugg it was now—and he was ready to do it, his hand going to his hip for the Magnum. But Sugg was ahead of him, on his feet after Schlumm had knocked him down, holding the Uzi level, swinging it with lazy confidence from Simon to Schlumm, from Schlumm to Simon, ready to use it if he had to.

"I'm right," he said. "You think about it, and you'll know I'm right." Then he brushed past Simon and went out the door, arrogant and self-possessed, giving Simon his broad, square back for a target. Simon had his hand on his gun, but somehow the moment was over, defused. The thought of shooting anyone in the back, even Sugg, was too much for him.

He glanced at the old man and the old woman, and at Schlumm who stood motionless in the middle of the room, a crazed look in his eyes, numb. Broken dishes, the smashed Buddha. The slow blood at the corner of the old man's mouth, already congealing. A chair knocked over, the glass door of the bookcase smashed. He turned and went out, his boots crunching on the gravel path.

He walked alone for a while, looking in at the animals as he passed the cages and pens. A buffalo that looked mangy and old, ready to die. A llama with large, mournful eyes. A few sheep, some deer. An antelope. They seemed moody and uncertain, apprehensive, as if they sensed, somehow, that something was amiss. Everywhere Simon looked he had an awareness of death: in the trees, the shrubs. In the grass. In the animals. In the eyes of the animals, in the hair that covered their bodies, the slow way they moved. It was everywhere, in the rocks, the puddles, death in the air, the hint of it, something he could smell.

They were soon off the zoo grounds, and onto a dirt road that cut through an area that was heavily treed. Trask had said the bridge would be only a two- or three-mile march from the lake, but it was clearly more than that. When they passed the three-mile mark, the bridge was still nowhere in sight.

Most of the land was wild, undeveloped. Miles of timber, though there were a few farms they passed through, acres of oats and vegetables. The land above the lake, where they were now, was different from the land below the lake, where they had come from. It was something about the trees, the vegetation, though Simon couldn't quite put his finger on it. And it wasn't just the trees, the leaves, but the atmosphere, the quality of the light. The air cooler, drier, though still warm, and they perspired. But they were out of the oppressive, sultry atmosphere they had been laboring in through all the previous weeks.

"We're in a different place," he said, coming alongside Merlin and Sugarman, who had been together on the trail since the troop pulled out of the zoo grounds. Ever since Sugarman had parachuted in at the lake, they had been inseparable, and Merlin seemed, somehow, the better for it, less withdrawn, less intense, though Simon still found it hard to understand their relationship—Merlin a chess freak, his head into computers, basically an introvert, and Sugarman outgoing, always the smile, a man who enjoyed cooking and flying.

"It sure *is* different," Merlin said, with unwonted cheer. "It's another country." He grinned, even though his feet were in pain. The fungus had abated for a while, but now it was back with a vengeance, he had a hard time walking. Sugarman was also having trouble with his feet, raising blisters; not since boot camp had he been in the field, on a march.

"Another country," Simon said, in a lackluster tone. His thoughts strayed back to the old man and the old woman that Sugg had killed. He was quiet for a moment, then again he turned to Merlin. "You mean a different country from the last one, which was different from the one we started out in?"

"Right."

"When did that happen?"

"When we crossed the lake." Merlin halted and sat on a rock, pulling off his boots so he could smear some antibacterial oint-

225

ment on his feet. It was pathetic, even absurd, grotesque—Merlin sitting down like that, doctoring his scarred, fungus-ridden feet. The same Merlin who had shot Eikopf, Simon still blaming him for that, yet he recognized Merlin was just one more sap like the rest of them, ordinary flesh and bone, ill-equipped for the stresses of war.

"Whose country are we in now?" Simon asked.

"They're not monkeys," Merlin said, "just friends of the monkeys—which is better, I guess. From here on in we won't be running into any more monkey patrols. The patrols we run into will be patrols sent out by the friends of the monkeys."

Sugarman, hopelessly out of shape for a long trek, and not eager to run into a patrol of any stripe or color, tapped his forefinger against his chest. "Me, I should have stayed in the delicatessen business. You want herring, I give you herring. You want borscht, I give you borscht." Distinctions between the monkeys and their friends meant nothing to him. "Which reminds me, I gotta see the General. He wants to talk about a clambake he's planning for you guys when we get back to base. You know the General, he's always thinkin' ahead. A big blast, more than just clams. Simon, take care of Merlin for a while." He moved forward, double-timing so as to catch up with Trask, who was some distance to the front.

As it turned out, Merlin was wrong about the absence of monkey patrols. Barely five minutes after he got his boots back on, less than two hours out from the zoo, they walked smack into one. Monkeys, the real thing. Bullets flying everywhere. They ducked, ran. The force scattered. Merlin and Simon dove down behind the trunk of a thick mahogany that had been uprooted and lay stretched across the ground. Tess and Emma Sue were somewhere to the rear, with Thurl and Falling Stone. Merlin glanced about nervously, looking for Sugarman.

Bullets flew back and forth, ripping through the trees. Movement in the foliage—an arm, a leg. Simon held his fire. He watched as the others pulled together in what seemed, roughly, a circle. A lot of cautious movement from tree to tree. Falling Stone climbed up into a tall magnolia. Trask was behind an ironwood, and Simon spotted Tess firing from behind a boulder about thirty feet away. He stayed hunkered down behind the log, with Merlin. The heaviest firing seemed to be coming from straight in front of them, with sporadic fire from the left and right. A grenade went off a few yards in front of the mahogany and Simon began to feel desperate about not having his helmet. Another grenade burst a considerable distance behind them. For a few minutes grenades were popping off all over the place, Simon kept his head buried. When he looked up again, he saw Sugg, his left arm in a sling and his weapon in his right hand, racing through the trees off to the right, trying to flank the enemy position, and Thurl darting to the left. He looked to the rock that Tess had been behind, and she was no longer there.

Merlin was jittery. "You think we should move?"

"Hold tight," Simon said. "*Right here.*" He had got the pyroxene-T off his back and had it tucked safely underneath him. He peered out from around the end of the log. There was a lot of shooting, bullets shredding leaves, tearing bark from the trees, but still he couldn't get a fix on exactly where the monkeys were. A monkey got a fix on him, however, and began pouring it on. Bullets thudded into the mahogany, a thick, drumming patter. Other shots whizzed over the log and tore up the ground behind him. For a few moments it was a murderous barrage. Then the firing slowed, uneven and sporadic.

"I want to get out of here," Merlin said. And now, Simon saw, he was more than jittery. He was deeply agitated, frightened. Altogether unlike himself.

Simon glared. "For chrissake, don't move."

"*Where's Sugarman,*" Merlin said, shaking Simon by the arm. There was a desperate urgency in the way he said it, a note of frenzy that Simon had never heard before in Merlin's voice.

227

"*Where's Sugarman?*" And, when Simon didn't answer, he drew away, still behind the log but putting space, distance, between Simon and himself. He raised his head above the log and stared about fiercely, looking for Sugarman.

"Get down," Simon shouted, as bullets whizzed by, all around. But Merlin hung there a moment, searching the trees for Sugarman and not finding him. He ducked down again, fretful, and now his hand was on the black box, idly fiddling with it, tapping keys at random, aimlessly.

"Just hold on," Simon said, trying to maintain contact, doing what he could, knowing it was damn little, hardly enough, to keep Merlin from spinning off into never-never land. "Just hold on, sit tight." He glanced around, off to his left, and spotted Sugarman hunkered down behind a boulder, about forty yards out. "He's over there," he called to Merlin. "It's all right, he's okay."

"Where?"

Simon pointed. "Over there."

Merlin looked, but didn't have a clear view.

"It's Sugarman? You're sure?"

"He's okay."

"I better go over there. He doesn't have a gun." Sugarman had parachuted in without one—he never carried a gun, had never imagined he'd ever need one.

"Stay put, damn you."

Merlin stared at Simon in an odd way, like a wayward child who had just received a reprimand. He went back to fiddling with the black box, tapping at the keys in a peculiar, ill-affected manner. He had been on the trail too long. For days, weeks, he had seemed to be in perfect control, but now, all at once, he was losing it, going to pieces in a rush.

More bullets drummed into the log, a stuttering volley, and still Merlin toyed with the box. Then, as Simon watched, Merlin changed: something snapped inside him, and he crossed over,

228

traversing an invisible inner line. In a quick fit of rage, teeth clenched, completely unlike himself, he raised his head above the log again, the words coming from him in a strange, growling frenzy, between a snarl and a shout: "DAMN MONKEYS! DAMN FUCKING LOUSY MONKEYS!" And, before Simon could reach across and catch hold of him, he was up on his feet and running, leaving the box behind, darting off, heading for Sugarman.

He didn't get far. One bullet got him in the neck and another in the back. He crumpled over, down in the grass, not more than a few yards away from the fallen mahogany. Simon knew he was dead, he didn't have to touch him, or even look at him.

The firefight went on for another fifteen minutes, then it quickly came to an end. Tess killed a monkey, and Thurl killed one. Falling Stone killed two, firing from the magnolia tree. Sugg got the last one with a grenade. There had only been five of them.

Sugarman went over to Merlin, and for a while he just stood there, looking down at him. He put him on his back and straightened his limbs. He unfastened the helmet, then took off Merlin's glasses and kept them, slipping them into a pocket. Merlin seemed very small, dead. Sugarman reached down and closed his eyes.

"I'll help you bury him," Simon said.

"Thanks," Sugarman nodded. Simon had never seen him so somber. Something had gone out of him, the buoyancy, the verve. His face had a grayish cast. He seemed old, much older than Simon had thought. They dug a grave and got Merlin quickly under, and Sugarman heaped some leaves and branches over the freshly dug soil.

"Where's the General?" Schlumm said, suddenly aware of his absence.

They looked around, apprehensively, and found Trask by an old acacia, his right leg shot off and part of his left arm gone. His eyes were vague, but his voice was solid, firm. "Did you kill the fuckers?" he said. He glanced up at them, seeming to glare, then his eyes went slippery, rolling back in his head, and he passed out.

They looked at him, not quite capable of absorbing what they saw. He was as vulnerable as the rest of them, flesh and bone, he could go down like anybody else. But somehow they hadn't quite envisioned it coming to this, that they should actually lose him. He had brought them through hell, and as much as they might have hated his blood-and-thunder willfulness, his raw fury, they had nevertheless come to rely on him. As they stood there, gazing at his wrecked body, it escaped none of them that they needed him to lead them back to base after they hit the bridge.

Emma Sue got to work on him right away. "It's massive trauma," she said, as she began. "But he's tough, he really is an incredible specimen. I wouldn't be surprised if he lives." She cut the leg off at the knee, and took off what was left of the arm up to the elbow. She was a long time at it, working deliberately, doing her best to get it right. Falling Stone stood by and helped, and Thurl and Simon cut a couple of saplings and made poles out of them, and rigged a litter.

When Emma Sue was finally done, Trask's heart was still going strong, and she expressed a guarded optimism about his condition. Perspiring and mud-spattered, covered with Trask's blood, she seemed a creature from another world, telling them he had a fifty-fifty chance of making it. They lifted him onto the litter, and, before they moved out, Schlumm gathered them all together. "I'm taking command," he said, looking pointedly toward Sugg. "Till the General is himself again. We don't have far to go, so let's push and get it over with. We're going to hit that bridge. Today's the day, dammit. We'll smash it before sundown." He spoke with uncharacteristic firmness and vigor, sounding, Simon thought, more like Trask than like himself, yet there was somehow a weakness, a falling short, he couldn't quite bring it off.

Sugg made a rumbling sound in his throat and spat, then he stepped over to the litter and looked at Trask. Trask was flat out, unconscious, looking as if he was going to be that way a long time.

It was past noon when they got going again. Simon picked up the black box and carried it along.

"Do you know how to work that thing?" Schlumm asked.

"I doubt it. I had a semester of APL at City, but I don't think it's enough to work this monster."

"Hold onto it anyway. It's classified equipment."

Without anybody to operate the black box, they were fully on their own. They had no communications system, no way of getting in touch with base. Schlumm felt nervous about that, most of them did. The box had been, in its way, a great source of security for them—though Simon had always had his doubts, a definite uneasiness. He remembered how eager Eikopf had been to destroy it, and there had been times when he more than half hoped that Eikopf would succeed. And now he was carrying it, lugging it along, and it was worthless. Unworkable junk.

Thurl and Falling Stone struggled with the litter, and Simon and Schlumm spelled them. For a time all four of them carried, one at each corner, but it was awkward. Sugarman carried for a while, but he was out of shape, breathing hard, barely able to shift for himself. They hated Trask, he was meat and he was useless. He had taken them through fire and storm, but now he was a burden, and they secretly agreed that the most sensible thing he could do was die. He had brought them this far, and they needed him to get them back, if ever he regained consciousness; but it was hard to believe, as they struggled to carry him, that he was really worth the trouble. Better if he died, they'd find their way without him.

"Shit," Thurl said. "Where is Meyerbeer?"

Simon thought if Meyerbeer showed up now, he would go home with him. The hell with the bridge. Meyerbeer could ferry them out one by one. First the General, because he was wounded, then the women and children, and, since there were no children, the cowards could get in line right behind the women. Me first, Simon thought. Get me out of this. Sugg could hang around for the final trip out. He was wounded, but he wouldn't want to ship out until the last of the ammo was used up. Maybe he'd strike off on his own and rig the bridge with his one good hand, and blow himself up in the process. Proud to be a hero.

They emerged briefly from the trees and saw that the UFO was there again, dogging them. It may have been there all the time, but only now, for some reason, did they notice. Hanging there, dour and noncommittal, watching them as they sweated along.

When Sugg saw it, he went berserk. With his one good hand he raised his Uzi and blasted away, the gun shaking wildly, bullets hurtling randomly into the purple sky. He finished the clip and jammed another into the gun, and again fired, his lips tense, his eyes burning. Nobody tried to stop him, they moved on ahead as if they could just walk away and leave the madness behind.

They went through mud, and across dry road. They passed ditches swarming with larvae. Schlumm checking the compass all the time, nervous about their direction. They went through groves of teak, oak, camphor. Uphill. They noticed that: they were climbing. Sugg pushed on in a dazed way, talking to no one. Schlumm was short of breath. It was the cigarettes, he smoked too much. He knew he smoked too much and complained about it, figuring first it would be emphysema and then angina, or maybe he would die of a coronary before he even got within kissing distance of emphysema. Emma Sue was breathing hard, but she wasn't a smoker, she was just tired, worn out, it was a hard climb. Before long they were all breathing hard. Sugarman was close to passing out from overexertion. It was a joke, a travesty, that he should be in the field, he belonged back in a kitchen, at Camp Alpha or Base Blue, whipping up enchiladas, escargots.

They set the litter down in a grove of palms and rested for a while. Trask came to, moving his head around. His eyes were blurry, but quickly they focused and he glanced about. He saw Thurl, Schlumm. "Where the hell are we?" he demanded. His voice was surprisingly strong, fully in command.

"We're close," Schlumm said.

"How close?"

"It's not far now, maybe an hour." But he was guessing. "We lost Merlin, we can't work the black box."

"Lost Merlin, huh? Too bad." He cleared his throat, pulling up a lot of phlegm. He gave no sign of being aware that he had lost an arm and a leg. They were watching, waiting for his reaction, but there was nothing. It was as if he knew, as if he had known a long time and had accepted it, it wasn't something that mattered to him.

"What time is it?"

"Fifteen hundred hours," Schlumm said, glancing at his watch.

"Fucking three o'clock," Trask said. "I've always hated three o'clock."

From a distance there came the sound of a chopper, and they all fell silent, listening. The sound drew closer, and they recognized the familiar vibration of the rainbow chopper.

"Hot shit," Thurl said. "It's about time." Now they could unload the General, he was thinking. Meyerbeer could carry him back to base. They were all thinking that.

Trask lifted his head. "Is that Meyerbeer?"

"Yes," Schlumm said, seeing the rainbow chopper through the trees.

"Where's the rocket launcher?"

Thurl had it.

"Give it here," Trask said. But Thurl hung back, and Trask, angered, snapped thunder: "I said *give it here*, damn you." As Thurl passed it over, Trask grabbed hold, gripping it solidly with his one hand. He was still flat on his back, on the litter. "You got the rockets?"

Thurl nodded. There were three left.

"Give 'em to Sugg," Trask said. Thurl dug into his pack and passed them over, and, as he did so, Sugg gave a gratuitous sneer. He had never liked Thurl, and felt now a glimmer of triumph in the fact that Trask, for whatever reason, was playing out this scene of rejection.

"Now bring me out from under these trees, where I can get a good look at that son of a bitch. A goddamn traitor, that's what he is. A fucking enemy. That's all he ever was. He'd kill us all, the bastard, if he thought there was good footage in it."

Thurl and Schlumm exchanged glances, apprehensive about Trask's intentions. He sounded straightforward enough, his voice coming across with its usual gruffness, but in his eyes there was the barest glimmer of delirium. Thurl shrugged, and Schlumm wrinkled his forehead, hesitating. Trask raised himself up on an elbow and darted a wrathful look in Schlumm's direction, and Sugg, on cue, cradled his Uzi expectantly. For one long moment, it seemed as if the worst would happen; but then Schlumm relented, and with Thurl he lifted the litter and carried Trask to the edge of the grove, by an outcrop of rock that slanted away from the trees at a shallow angle. They were on a high bluff. Beyond the rock, the land fell away sharply, into a densely overgrown valley.

The whole force, what was left of it, moved out onto the rock. Trask waved them off. "Leave me, give me some room," he said. "Back away." He wanted only Sugg with him. The rest of them moved off, giving him room, but they were still on the outcrop, in the open—looking on, amazed, as Trask, with a strong, twisting movement, got himself up into a sitting position, propping himself against a tree stump that the litter was next to. He handed the launcher over to Sugg. "Here," he said, "you do the honors."

The rainbow chopper was far off, above the valley, at an angle of about fifteen degrees above the bluff, not moving, hanging steady in the distance, as if studying them, looking them over. Sugg, his left hand still bandaged, loaded a rocket and got the launcher up onto his shoulder. He took aim and, with the chopper low enough for him to get a shot off without his being burned by the backblast, he fired. Simon stood several yards away, and only when the rocket was actually launched, the searing flash raging from the back end of the tube, did the reality of it reach him. Trask actually wanted to shoot Meyerbeer down. And Sugg was doing it for him. *"Fire again,"* Trask roared, as the first shot went wide of the mark, and Sugg, puffing out his cheeks, loaded the second rocket and got the launcher up on his shoulder again, taking aim.

The rainbow chopper rose to a high altitude, then began descending, coming at them in a wide, swooping arc, and as it swung down it opened fire with a machine gun mounted under the nose, coming at them in a strafing run. Bullets ricocheted across the outcrop. A burst caught Sugarman in the midriff and cut him apart. The rest of them scattered, diving for cover in the trees, bullets whining all over the place, barely missing Tess's shoulder, Simon's foot, one whizzing past Falling Stone's ear. "What the hell's with Meyerbeer," Thurl shouted from behind a rock. "What the hell's he shootin' for?" They watched as the chopper veered off and pulled away, and they looked out onto the outcrop and saw Sugarman's body, ripped apart, a bloody mess, slowly rolling down the rock incline, jiggling in farcical, slow-motion mockery, then quickly tumbling away where the land fell off sharply. Dead, gone. The round face and bald pate, bringer of food, delicatessen mastermind. Nothing there anymore, only the long trail of his blood on the slanting rock.

Trask and Sugg were untouched, still on the outcrop—Trask propped up against the tree stump, and Sugg in a crouch beside him. He hadn't fired, hadn't been able to get a fix on the chopper as it zoomed in. The second rocket still in the tube. In the distance, the chopper hovered again, seemed to hesitate, then again it came at them, swinging in another wide arc. Bullets danced across the outcrop, and, as the chopper swung past, almost level with the bluff, Sugg launched the second shot. It blazed from the tube, creasing the stagnant afternoon air, and missed, ripping past the chopper just yards away from the tail rotor.

"Give me that," Trask said, reaching out with his one hand and grabbing hold of the launcher. With incredible doggedness, he wrenched himself around and got the tube into position, up over his shoulder. "Now load," he said. Sugg inserted their last rocket.

Far off, the chopper hovered, and suddenly they heard Meyerbeer's voice on the horn, loud, filling the sky with sound: "HEY SIMON, CAN'T YOU PICK IT UP A LITTLE? MOVE YOUR ASS! GIVE IT SOME SPARKLE! YOU'RE WRECKING MY WHOLE GODDAMN SEQUENCE." It was Meyerbeer's voice, all right, blaring the same thing he had blared at Simon early on, when they had first set out from Base Blue. They remembered, it was hard to forget.

"This is crazy," Simon said. "That can't be Meyerbeer. Meyerbeer is a lunatic—but this is *crazy*. Not to fire on us, dammit." But the voice was there to prove it.

"The lousy sonofabitch traitor," Trask said, with roiling anger. "I warned the fucker. I warned him!"

The chopper waited momentarily, then again it came swooping in. Trask held the launcher over his shoulder, steadying it with his powerful right hand, taking aim. This time the chopper came not in a long, wide arc but in a straight line, headlong, at a low angle, blazing away. Trask, out in the open, held the launcher firm, taking aim and waiting, holding his fire till the chopper got in low and close—just waiting, fiercely steady, while slugs from the chopper skipped and danced all around him. The chopper sped on in, powerful, noisy, and Simon, watching from behind a

236

tree, stood rooted, locked in place, looking on in a kind of dazed paralysis.

Trask fired. The rocket sped off and hit the chopper square on, piercing the nose and detonating in the cabin. The front end blew apart, pieces of debris scattering wide. The approach was cut off, as if the chopper had been snared in midcareer by an invisible net. What remained of it—the rotors, the whole back end—dangled uncertainly, clownishly clumsy, then tilted over and went down, missing the bluff and plunging into the trees below. It blew up on impact, a ball of flame and a funnel of black smoke, the force of the explosion sending out tremors they could feel all the way up on the bluff.

Nobody said a thing. It was too astonishing. Sugarman dead, and now Meyerbeer. Not just astonishing, but baffling, because Meyerbeer—not the calm, casual, cunning, manipulative Meyerbeer they had known, but a Meyerbeer who seemed crazed and unhinged, hopelessly flipped out—had come at them in a homicidal frenzy, shooting, bent on killing them. It was out of character, without any intelligible motive, and for all they could see, Trask in his delirium may in fact have been right about him: he was a traitor. They looked at each other—Simon, Thurl, Tess, Schlumm—and said nothing, because, whatever dark suspicions they may have harbored about Meyerbeer, this latest turn was beyond them, they couldn't grasp it. Again Trask had saved them. Trask, who by rights should have been dead, who was hanging onto life by his fingernails, had come back from the dead to knock Meyerbeer out of the sky and kill him, he hated him that much. His mad intuition working inscrutably, sending him onto the outcrop with the launcher, readying himself before the chopper had even made its first pass.

Baffling, Simon thought, and actually more than baffling: because death and Meyerbeer somehow didn't go together, it was a wrong mix. Meyerbeer filmed death, focused his lens on it, it was

237

all around him—but it had always seemed, somehow, that death could not reach out and touch him, he was privileged. Simon stood on the high bluff and watched the black smoke rising up from the burning wreck, and found it hard to believe, even though the evidence, the smoke and flames, was right there in front of him, in the valley.

"Now take me back under the trees," Trask said, letting the launcher fall from his hand. They helped him settle back into a recumbent position. "We'll blow that bridge," he said. "We'll blow it, and it'll change the whole damn course of this goddamn war." He closed his eyes, and again slipped away from consciousness.

Simon looked at Trask, then back at the black funnel of smoke, and thought he understood now why Meyerbeer had come in, the night before last, with the misinformation about Sugarman being dead. It was the boats. Sugarman had been due to drop the boats at the lake, and if Sugarman was dead, that meant Trask had to do some worrying about whether or not a replacement would be out there when they needed him. Meyerbeer jabbing at Trask's ulcer, if he had one. Just passing along an unconfirmed report, or an actual lie; whichever it was, the intent had been the same, to make Trask's heart valves work overtime. Apparently there had been a lot going on between the two of them—more, Simon now realized, than he had ever noticed. The boats, he figured. Or something else. And now Sugarman—poor, dumb, innocent, pathetic Sugarman—really was dead.

They moved along briskly, past moss-clad rocks, across narrow streams. Schlumm was worried that the crash of the chopper might bring on the monkeys, so they moved fast, pushing hard to put distance between them and the smoldering wreck. Schlumm was busy with the compass, checking and rechecking, nervous, because without the black box he wasn't entirely sure he was leading them the right way. "Keep it moving," he kept saying.

"Let's pull it together. Move it along." Simon could see that, given time, Schlumm could develop into a son of a bitch like all the other sons of bitches who had ever shouted orders at him.

They marched through sumac and cane, past rotting logs loaded with lichen. They pushed on for over an hour, then Schlumm called a halt, convinced they were headed in the wrong direction. They doubled back to a place where the trail had forked, and tried the other fork, but after going down that for a mile, the trail disappeared into dense jungle, they would have had to cut their way through. A dim sense of panic began to set in, an awareness that they were lost.

Schlumm brought them back to the trail they had been on, and it was frustrating, going back over ground they had already covered. A few miles on, the trail split off in three directions, and they stood around for a while arguing which one to take. Schlumm studied the compass, trying to apply reason to a situation that had long ago become reasonless, and finally, in a blind assertion of will, took them down the fork on the left. They were so close, but so far—perhaps only minutes from the objective, yet it might take them hours, or whole days, of dumb stumbling before they got there. And, what all of them knew, though no one was willing to put it into words, they might never even get there at all, because at any moment, if they were this close to the bridge, they might run into a whole platoon of monkeys. Simon glanced skyward through an opening in the trees, looking for the UFO, but it wasn't there.

They were climbing again, the trail taking them uphill, all of them laboring, sweating, breathing hard, Trask an impossible burden. A half hour of hard marching, and suddenly they reached a high place where the trees stopped, and there was a narrow margin of gray rock in front of them. Beyond the gray rock, the gorge opened up, vast and splashed with color—not gray, but purple, pink, red. And deep. The floor of the gorge covered, as

Merlin had said it would be, by trees, a dense, vaporous carpet, misty and green.

And, to their amazement, when they looked off to their left, they saw the bridge.

23 ◻ The Bridge

IT GLEAMED. The late sun danced off the wire cables, and when Simon saw it everything fell away: the hardship, pain, long weeks in the jungle, monotony, confusion, doubt, the firefights, the terror, the near despair. The bridge existed, suspended there in a rich, meaningful silence.

It was more splendid than he had imagined. He had seen the intelligence photos and had pored over the structural sketches the engineers had drawn up for him, showing him where to wrap the pyroxene-T—had lived with the bridge in his mind, in his thoughts, dreams, anticipations, a kind of fever burning inside him. And now it was there in front of him, barely a half mile off, spanning the gorge. All he need do was walk the half mile along the lip of the gorge, and he'd be there. But it was better, now, being where he was. Through the distance, he took it all in. The great steel arch leaping from one rim to the other, emerging out of a density of green trees, yearning skyward through the emptiness above the gorge, then down again on the other side into a wilderness of trees and vines. Cables strung from the arch supported the span that served for a roadway. A slender, articulate design, light and free, with the ease and fragile sureness of a ballerina—whimsical, playful, a statement in simplicity, easy conquest over distance and space. It connected.

240

The General came to. Emma Sue wanted to sedate him and put him back to sleep, but he refused. The litter was on the ground. "Are we there?" he asked.

"Yes."

"Prop me up. I want to see."

She propped him up, putting his pack behind his shoulders, using it as a pillow. He saw the bridge.

"So that's it," he said. "At long last. It's a big fucker, ain't it. Nice, the way the sun strikes those cables." Simon was close by. "That's it, Corporal. There it is. You think you can blow it?" There was something in his tone, as if the bridge were his, to do with as he pleased. As if he owned it, as if he knew all about it. Simon felt like telling him to buzz off.

"I can handle it," he said cautiously.

"We lost a lot of good men so you could do this. Do it right. You know what to do?"

Simon gave a slow nod, with no show of enthusiasm.

"Wait till dark," Trask said firmly. "When it's good and dark, go out there and blow it to hell." He was still in charge. One leg gone and one arm gone, propped up so he could see and talk, but the voice vigorous, his thinking clear and firm. Emma Sue was right: he was tough. There was nothing in his life but the thing he had been sent out to do, and he would see it done. Simon remembered his palaver about the need for goals, about defining an aim and driving like hell till you got what you were after. Basically, that's all Trask was anymore, and maybe it was all he had ever been: an appetite, raw ambition. His body gone, ruined, but the drive was still there, the will, the fiercely pumping heart, and it would still be there after he was dead—the crude, gravelly voice, urging them on.

"The bridge is deserted," Simon said. It was something that he only now became aware of: there was no one there. No cars, no people. Until now he had been too preoccupied with the bridge itself, the structure, the thing as thing, to notice that there was no one on it. But now he saw: there were no convoys going across, no guards were posted. The roadway was empty. Nobody even there to collect a toll. No Volkswagens, Datsuns, Toyotas, Fords. Nobody out there for an afternoon stroll.

Trask raised his eyebrows quizzically. "So?"

"Where are the convoys?"

"They stagger them. You don't expect tanks and trucks to be crossing every damn minute, do you?" His lips curled sourly. "Are you sure you know what you're doing with that pyroxene-T?"

"There are no guards," Simon noted.

"Get me my binoculars."

Simon dug them out of Trask's pack, and Trask scanned the bridge and the opposite rim of the gorge. He saw nothing. "They're there," he said. "They have eyes. If you get out on that bridge in daylight, you'll find out fast enough."

Simon gazed at the bridge, and had a deepening sense of its lack of importance strategically. It was useless, a superfluity. Another mistake. They had built it in the wrong place, so now it was there and nobody cared. A thing of beauty, untouched and unnecessary. "I don't know," Simon said, risking the General's wrath. "Is it possible, just remotely possible, they sent us to the wrong bridge?"

Trask blinked slowly, and turned away in disgust. "Simon, you do know how to disappoint." That was all he said. No thunder, no stormy outburst, just that quiet turning away, and it was then that Simon understood that, for all his will and drive, Trask was a dying man.

"After dark," Simon said.

"You bet your ass. After dark."

Simon moved away, and Schlumm tried to talk to the General about the escape route back to Base Blue. But Trask waved him off. He signaled to Emma Sue. "I'll take that sedative now."

242

Simon went over to where Tess, Thurl, and Falling Stone were, the seclusion of the trees. "It really is something," Tess said, looking toward the bridge. "It never crossed my mind that it would be so lovely."

Falling Stone said nothing. Simon noted that he had tended to be quiet, withdrawn, ever since he killed the bear. Thurl had his earphone on and was tapping his foot to the rhythm of the music—but his eyes were on the bridge, gazing at it through a thin screen of saplings. "Sweetest music ever," he said. "How big is that big mother out there?"

"Eighteen hundred feet. A little over a quarter of a mile."

Thurl let out a low whistle. "That's bigger than the Hell Gate Bridge. Damn, it's even bigger than the Kill Van Kull."

Tess was undoing her braid, combing it out. "They don't seem to use it very much."

"Some bridges are just for pretty," Thurl said. "A gorge like this is pretty enough by itself, but havin' a bridge there adds a little bit of an extra touch."

"Yeah," Simon said flatly.

They waited for the sun to go down, and Simon was restless. Mentally, he reviewed the plans, remembering the details, the measurements. Where to wrap the pyroxene-T. He lived it in anticipation, down to the moment of pressing the button. Trask slept. Sugg lay stretched out on the ground, the bandaged hand resting on his chest.

Schlumm drew Simon aside. "You fiddle with the black box yet?"

"No."

"See what you can do. Find out if you can handle it."

Simon took the box out of its satchel and looked it over. A bunch of keys on it, like a typewriter. A small display screen. Simon tried to remember the APL he had learned at City, but it was vague. He flipped a switch that lighted up the screen, then tapped some keys. The screen remained blank. He keyed in an-

243

other command, and still nothing. He rapped the box with his knuckles. "Maybe that UFO is still around, blocking transmission."

Schlumm looked around in the sky. "If it's there, I don't see it. I haven't seen it since after that last firefight."

Simon tapped away, trying some commands that he remembered, then inventing, plugging in random combinations. Suddenly the screen lit up with an array of numbers: 3.14159. "Where did that come from?"

"That's pi, Simon. Don't you know pi?"

"Sure I know pi. Pi is an old friend." He cleared the screen and again played around at random, and again he got pi. "Something's not working right. All it wants to say is pi. You think that means something?" He remembered hundreds of Mrs. Wagner's pies strewn across the Grand Concourse, when the girl was killed outside the drugstore. And the pies in his pack.

"It means you don't know what you're doing, Simon. We're in trouble. After you blow that bridge, I don't know how the hell to get us out of here."

"Back the way we came. You have the Major's maps, don't you?"

"Are you kidding? After the trail we've left? From here all the way back to Base Blue will be crawling with monkeys on the watch for us. We need a different route. Without the black box, we're up the creek."

"I think we were up the creek *with* it, but I realize that's minority opinion. Talk to the General."

"He's not talking."

"Wait till he wakes up, he'll be more with it. He knows we lost Merlin, doesn't he?"

"Yeah," Schlumm said. "He knows."

"Poor Merlin. He was playing chess against a Russian. He lost and it cracked him up." But as he said it, Simon knew it was more than that. It was the jungle, the war, it was thinking Sugar-

244

man was dead when he was alive, and then, when he was alive, seeing him get knocked out of the air and thinking this time, for sure, he was dead.

Simon used Trask's binoculars to study the bridge. A girl went across on a bicycle. Then no one for a while. A man leading a camel. Another man walking, and, much later, a woman on a motorcycle. "They sure do a big business, don't they. If they put up a toll gate on this one, they'd get screaming rich."

As the sun went down, he took Falling Stone and Thurl with him and set out along the tree-lined rim, keeping under cover in case there were guards scanning the rim from the other side. They carried flashlights for the trip back. The walls of the gorge were huge slabs of red sandstone, with massive intrusions of pink and white quartz, and patches of other rock, yellow and green. A cloud of vapor rose from a stream that was hidden by the trees on the floor of the gorge, and the setting sun played on it, creating a fantasy of light, as if, far down, there were a conflagration, flames of color swirling up from the depths of the gorge and flickering in the sky. As they moved along, Simon thought about their long weeks in the jungle, the madness and death, like a nightmare he couldn't shake loose from. The bear, the B-52s, the UFO, Meyerbeer's insane attack, Eikopf in his white jacket, and Kabuki dying, talking about abalone. Sugarman, Merlin, Polymer. And Vain who had been saved, if indeed that was Vain who had been plucked out of the jungle. It was coming to an end, now, the reason for all that death, and Simon felt a kind of dread, a terrible anticipation about the bridge. All those weeks it had seemed they were being watched, hunted—and it seemed impossible that they weren't zeroed in now, too.

They drew close to the bridge, close to the road leading onto it, and secluded themselves in a thicket. The sun was gone, and the gorge went black, but the sky was still suffused with color. The bridge's steel glowed rose, then crimson, then bronze. As the last light went out of the sky, another motorcycle crossed the bridge, its single light probing the semi-dark like an uncertain lantern. A woman walked across, and then there was no one.

There were lights at either end of the bridge, but no lights on the bridge itself. Simon opened his pack, and each of them took a spool of pyroxene-T. It had the appearance of standard hospital adhesive, one inch wide, but it was black, not white, and much thicker than ordinary tape, each spool holding a strip that was thirty yards long. When it was fully dark, they went out onto the bridge, cautiously, and Simon showed them the cables and beams he wanted the pyroxene-T to be wrapped around. Falling Stone and Thurl worked at one end, and Simon ran across the bridge and worked on the opposite end. It was a good night to work. A thin film of cloud stretched across the moon; enough light filtered through to enable them to see what they were at, yet it was dark enough so that they couldn't easily be spotted. With infrared, though, they would be noticed, and as Simon applied the pyroxene-T, he felt naked, felt he was being watched through the crosshairs of a gunscope. He worked quickly, methodically, ears tuned for the crack of rifle fire.

He heard the throaty roar of an old truck, and the roadway was suddenly lit up by headbeams. He rushed to get off the roadway, onto the outer structure of the bridge, into the shadows. But the light had picked him up, and he wasn't at all sure he hadn't been seen, nor did he have any idea if Thurl and Falling Stone had got out of the way in time. His heart pounded, racing furiously. As the truck came slowly along, he hung on to a network of criss-crossing steel, bracing himself as best he could. Beneath him lay the immense depth of the gorge, black and vast. The truck lumbered along, and then he saw what it was, an open vehicle stacked high with wooden cages holding chickens. The chickens squawking, as if quarreling with the broken-down rattle of the motor. Simon saw the driver, bearded, long-haired, a lit cigarette hanging from his lips, the sound of rock music coming from the

246

radio. As the truck went past, the driver turned his head and looked exactly at the spot where Simon was. The driver's eyes were right on him, but Simon, partially concealed by the criss-crossing beams and cables, went unnoticed.

As the truck neared the far end of the bridge, it hit a bump and three of the chicken crates fell off. The driver stopped the truck and got out, grumbling. A rooster got loose and the driver ran, chasing it halfway back along the roadway. Just as he was about to catch up with it, it flapped its wings and eluded him, giving itself enough lift to go over the railing along the edge of the bridge. Over, and then straight down. Simon watched as the rooster plunged, dead weight, into the darkness below. The driver leaned over the railing, confirming that it was gone, then shuffled back to the truck, talking aloud in a language that Simon knew to be monkey language, and in a tone that was recognizable, in any tongue, as hefty swearing. He got the loose crates back onto the truck, still cursing roundly, and finally drove off.

Simon waited before going back onto the roadway. So did Thurl and Falling Stone. When the noise of the truck was completely gone, and there was nothing but dead silence, only the breeze soughing through the gorge, they got back to work. They had to climb up into the arch, setting the tape at the structurally critical junctions. To each strip of pyroxene-T that they applied, they attached a fuse the size of a cufflink. The fuses could be touched off by an electronic signal from as far as a mile away.

Simon worked fast, applying the tape and attaching the fuses. One beam, then another. The cables. Getting the sticky tape laid out where it had to go. A few feet of it here, a few feet there. Wondering if he had forgot a fuse on the last strip and rushing back to check. The steel of the bridge cool to his touch. When he had used up his spool, he ran back across the bridge. Thurl was finished and had climbed down out of the arch, but Falling Stone was still up there, and he had started moving farther up, toward the topmost point at the center.

"No," Simon called in a shouted whisper. *"No! Come down!"*

But Falling Stone continued to climb. Simon and Thurl hurried off the roadway, back to the safety of the trees. They watched Falling Stone moving deftly toward the top of the arch. Simon was jealous. It was something he would have wanted to do himself. It was madness, unnecessary, a foolish risk, spending more time out there than had to be spent—yet he had an understanding of what it was that was summoning Falling Stone to climb, urging him far up to the pinnacle. It was like the moment when Falling Stone had killed the bear. Simon had blasted away with his .44, from a distance, but Falling Stone went right in there, barehanded, with a knife, driving home into the heart. Simon had felt cheated then, and he felt cheated now.

"Damn Apache," Thurl said. "He'll never learn."

Falling Stone reached the top. He had been in a semicrouch, moving along the sloped, tubular beam, and now, at the highest point above the gorge, he stood up straight, legs partially spread, a solemn figure, facing the moon. He held the spool of explosive in both hands and raised it high above his head, as if offering it to the moon, or to the barely visible stars. Simon could hear the light breeze echoing in the gorge. *"Get down, dammit,"* he said in a harsh whisper, realizing he couldn't be heard. *"Get down!"*

Falling Stone didn't move. He stood poised in the wind, facing the dim moon, timeless, as if destined to be there, locked in a frozen moment like a still photograph, the silver bromide exposed and fixed, unable to be changed ever. He could have moved, but he didn't and then, finally, it was too late.

A single shot rang out. Falling Stone hovered there a moment, poised, still standing, still holding the spool, then he pitched forward off the arch, his body stiff and unbending, the spool still gripped in his hands, head first into the gorge.

Neither Simon nor Thurl said anything. Their eyes were fastened on the spot where Falling Stone had stood: there was an emptiness there, an emptiness that had solidity, shape, force. It was as if he were still there, as if they might climb up and drag him back to safety. But it was merely an emptiness, nothing. On the road on the other side of the gorge, headlights appeared, moving toward the bridge. Noisy, a cluster of motorcycles, probably military, on their way to cross over.

"Detonate," Thurl said. Simon held the electronic detonator in his left hand, the size of a cigarette lighter. He did nothing. His eyes were still fastened to the spot where Falling Stone had stood, and he wondered now, in a moment of doubt, how much of the pyroxene-T Falling Stone had affixed to the bridge, if any at all.

"Damn you," Thurl said impatiently, punching him in the shoulder, "hit it and let's get the hell out of here."

Simon was jolted by the blow, but still his eyes were on the bridge. The way the moon illumined the girders. The cables harplike, played upon by the wind. The empty roadway where the bicycle had crossed, the man with the camel. And now the motorcycles approaching, a night patrol, nearing the bridge, getting damn close. Simon pressed the button just before they got there.

The fuses sizzled, acetylene-blue, and the strips of pyroxene-T burst explosively: a flash, a brightness like daylight, and Simon saw the steel beams wrenching loose. The ground shook horrifically. The multiple blasts echoed in a deep roar all up and down the far length of the gorge. It was fast, sudden, yet it seemed to be happening in slow motion: the bridge shuddered, moved, then seemed simply to hover, as Falling Stone had hovered, and then it slipped away, sinking from view and crashing in the dark on the floor of the gorge. The crash at the bottom set up another immense roar, the gorge rumbled and shook.

Simon was motionless, riveted by the noise, the glare of detonation. He felt nothing, blank. Then, as the long roar rolled up and down the gorge, feeling came back to him, and what he felt was loss, waste, depletion, as if he had witnessed, caused, the destruction of something whose meaning he could not fully grasp, and now the meaning was permanently gone. He felt contaminated, infected, as if he had consciously cooperated in something that was unclean. "We're nothing," he said, not knowing exactly why he said it, and seemed to watch himself saying it. As if someone else had uttered the words.

Thurl was on the move, eager to get away before the monkeys swarmed all over them. "We sure *will* be nothing if we hang around here any longer. Let's go." He hurried off into the trees that lined the rim of the gorge, and picked his way along, close to the edge, where he could see by moonlight, using the flashlight only when he needed it. Simon hesitated, then quickly followed. Thurl tripped once, and Simon helped him up. Simon fell too, tripping over a root, or a rock, spraining a wrist as he went down. Thurl came back for him, grabbing his arm, getting him up and moving again.

By the time they got back to the encampment, guns, big guns, were blasting away at the rim. "Get down," Schlumm shouted as they came through the trees. "Goddammit, get down!" The shells poured in thick and fast, a hellish storm. They were zeroed in.

24 □ "We Have to Get Out of Here"

SIMON HIT the ground, going down beside Schlumm, and quickly dug in. "They found us," Schlumm said. "They keep finding us." The monkeys were across the gorge, on a road leading to the bridge. "They've got a howitzer hitting us with one-fifty-fives, and we're catching a bunch of mortar."

"We lost Falling Stone," Simon said.

"Yeah? Falling Stone? That's lousy. *Lousy*."

"Where's Tess?"

"Back there," Schlumm pointed. "She's dug in."

More salvos came in, falling short, pounding into the gorge with a deafening roar.

"We have to get out of here," Schlumm said. But he knew there was no way to move out while they were pinned down, they'd be wiped out. He was frantic, losing his cool. "I figure they have somebody on the rim using infrared to spot us."

"The bridge is down," Simon said, abstractedly. "They can't cross over."

"They don't have to cross over! They're murdering us with their goddamn mortar!"

Schlumm was shouting, partly out of anger, partly out of frustration, and partly just to make himself heard above the whine and roar of the incoming salvos. But Simon wasn't thinking about the mortar, his mind was still on the bridge, puzzled by it, wondering why it had been left unguarded—just that single shot that took out Falling Stone, something not right about that. Peculiar, just one shot. A single guard, maybe, hidden in the trees— asleep, probably, until he woke and looked out, and there was Falling Stone up on the arch. If the bridge had had any kind of strategic importance, there would have been a whole corps of guards, a fucking platoon.

"They left it wide open," he said, thinking aloud, "they were somewhere else and now they come rushing down, but it's too late."

"Too late, Simon? You said too late? It's too late for us, dammit, if we don't get off this rim." But movement was impossible, shells were raining down all over the place, falling to the right and left of their position, and behind them. Many went into the gorge, detonating with long, thunderous echoes. Trees blew apart and tumbled, great wrenching sounds of cracked wood, roots

251

yanking loose. The ground shook. A few small fires blazed in the woods, and a tree burned nearby.

Simon lifted his head. "Tess? Tess?"

"Stay put," she called.

"Damn right, stay put," Trask thundered. Simon turned and looked up and saw Trask standing over him. He had fashioned a crutch for himself out of a Y-shaped branch. He stood there now on one leg, leaning on the crutch, his face painted red by the flames of the burning tree. He seemed demonic, something out of an old Norse legend. The right trouser leg pinned up, there was fresh blood on it.

"We've got to get off this rim, sir," Schlumm said. Not said: shouted. There was no talking, no saying. They had to shout to make themselves heard above the noise of the bombardment.

"And go where?"

"You better get down, sir. Those shells are getting close again."

Trask stood immobile on his one leg. *"And go where?"* he repeated.

"Back the way we came," Simon shouted.

Trask reared his head and let out a wild, scoffing laugh. The laughter slid about, curled and twisted. Then he was shouting again, punching the words out at them as if the words were fists. "Don't you know? Don't you know what's waiting for you down there? Khorbaks. Back the way we came. They've got Khorbaks down there. You know what Khorbaks are? Headhunters. Cannibals. You wouldn't know it to talk to them, they look and talk like damn civilized people. The chief wears a shirt and bow tie."

Simon and Schlumm exchanged glances. Hard to know, at that moment, if Trask was sane, rational, or if he was giving vent to fantasies, feverish ramblings of a doped-up amputee who was only hours away from having lost an arm and a leg, and maybe only moments away from death.

252

"Khorbaks, gentlemen. The monkeys have them mobilized. By now they have them spread out all over the place, looking for us. You want to run through that?"

"Is there an alternative?" Schlumm asked.

"An alternative? I give you an alternative," Trask said grandly. He lifted his crutch and pointed with it toward the gorge. He was all energy and drive, a tightly bound package of kinetic force, the great hulking torso balanced on one leg, the right arm extended, using the crutch as a pointer. "Into the gorge. It's the only way. Stay dug in here till morning, then down into the gorge and follow the stream, it takes you clear across to another country."

Simon was envisaging the sheer walls of the gorge, vertical slabs of rock he had seen flaming with color as the sun went down. "It's not possible," he called. "The walls are too steep. There aren't enough footholds."

"Damn you, Simon, nothing's impossible. That's what's wrong with you: no will. No vision. You fall down and die. If a cripple like me can do it, anybody can. What kind of dreams do you have? Pancakes and syrup? Is that what you dream about?"

Simon wanted to punch him. "I blew the fucking bridge. Smashed it to hell. A damn fine bridge. And what for? You tell me—*what for?*"

Trask planted his crutch in the ground and leaned heavily on it, bending down toward Simon, who was still on the ground, worried about the incoming salvos. They were only a few feet apart, Simon bareheaded, without a helmet, and Trask in his black beret. "So you blew the bridge, huh? And what for? Well I lost men, mister. Good men. Kleff, and Merlin, and Studdwin, Smudge. You weigh your bridge against that, mister, and tell me *what for*." He straightened, then cocked his head at an angle and went on talking, but it was as if he were talking now not to Simon but to someone else, someone not there. His eyes narrowed, his tone softened, his face went suddenly calm. "We smashed it, goddamn. Knocked it down.

253

I saw it. Saw it crack and plunge into hell. *We did what we came for!*" He turned sharply, a tricky maneuver with the crutch, and headed for the rim. It was an incredible thing to watch, the way he half-hopped and half-walked, using the crutch as if it were a leg, the crutch up under his right arm, the right leg gone, the left arm gone, a wild pathetic figure, distorted, ruined, yet willfully pushing forward, moving in a way that it might have taken an ordinary amputee months to learn. Miraculous, dumb, raving—stupid, and yet heroic, evoking in Simon a maelstrom of conflicting feelings and emotions. He didn't know if he admired the man or hated him, pitied him or resented him—wanted to hold him and thank him and care for him, or spit on him and throw him over the edge. The edge was where he was headed, right up to it, the light of the fire painting him, flickering shades of orange and red. He turned to them and called, the crutch raised again, pointing into the gorge— a ludicrous parody of a man, one leg, the one hand waving the crutch, the face and mouth going, shouting, all will and determination. "Out there, you sonsabitches—that's where. That's the escape route. We had it all planned. Out there! Thirty miles up there's a village of friendlies, they've got supplies, and a route out of this hell. Out there, dammit!" And as he stood there, the hulking torso balanced on one leg, he began to waver, side to side.

Schlumm leaped and ran for him, traversing the distance in long, swift strides. Emma Sue was closer and also ran for him, and they got there at the same moment, one on each side, stabilizing him, catching him back, the three of them lit up by the flames of the burning tree. They hung there, outlined against the black night—the stick, the crutch, still held aloft, and the voice still raging: *Out there! Out there!*" Simon could still hear the voice calling, booming, high above the whine of the incoming shell, and when the shell hit it struck right where they were, Schlumm, Emma Sue, Trask, the dust clearing slowly, and when the dust was gone there was nothing there, nothing at all, only night.

Simon stared at the spot, feeling he had been shot in the brain. All three of them. He went dizzy with it, wanting it to be wrong, a mistake, an error in perception, bad dream, but the darkness out there was all that was left of them.

Two more shells smashed against the bluff, close by, and he got his arms up around his ears, clasping his hands behind his head. He stayed that way a moment, breathing hard, in and out, in and out, making a conscious effort to breathe, controlling it, because he felt, that moment, that if he didn't make himself breathe, his breathing would stop. A few moments like that, simply blank, breathing. Then grabbed the black box from where Schlumm had left it, and raced across to Tess.

She saw him coming. "Get down, you idiot!" she cried in a frenzy. "Get down! Damn you! *Damn you!*"

25 ◻ Sweet Music

TESS HAD seen it too: the shell hitting, the bright flash, concussed earth and air, then nothing. Schlumm gone, Emma Sue gone. And Trask. It was too much for her. She buried her head against Simon's chest, and the hot tears came, wild convulsive sobbing. For weeks on end she had lived with the heat and filth of the jungle, leeches, mud, bombs, mortar. She had shot back and killed, holding up bravely, and now it all broke loose. Simon held her. She was dug in, in a hole, and it was deep. That's what she had been doing while the shells poured in: digging. The soil was moist and cool. She had pushed the rocks aside, digging wide and deep. Her face was wet, salty, he held on to her. Gradually, her sobbing subsided.

Sugg was dug in a few yards away, off to the left. Simon glanced about and spotted him. "Sugg? Is that you?"

"Yeah, it's me, you fucker. I'm on to you. Don't think you can lie to me." The words grating, close to a snarl. Sugg too had undergone a change, as they all had. He had always been belligerent, mean-spirited, full of military macho, but now it was more than that, different—he seemed weirdly unhinged, fanatic, seeing in Simon the source of all the hell they'd been through during their long weeks on the trail, his anger rising out of a violent mix of hate and desperation, defiance and simple fear, stark recognition of the apparent hopelessness of their situation. He needed a scapegoat, and Simon was it. "You bastard, you killed them all. *Every last damn one of them.*"

Simon looked at Tess.

"He's crazy, Simon. Out of his mind. I guess by now we all are."

"Where's Thurl?"

"Over there." She pointed off to the right.

"Hey, Thurl," Simon called. "Are you in one piece?"

Thurl raised his head, he had his earphone on. "Ain't it shit?" he said. "But I got the Ash Berries, the Everhearts, and the Dugan City Diggers to keep me company. It's a sweet, beautiful world, Simon." He wasn't shouting, just talking in an ordinary tone, and they all suddenly realized that the shooting had stopped. There was a lull. For quite some time there had been a pause. They thought of moving, getting off the rim, but if they did move, they knew the infrared would pick them up and the shells would start pouring in again. Better to stay dug in, hold where they were.

"Sweet music," Thurl said. "Wasn't that sweet music, that thing that Falling Stone did? Crazy, but it sure was a beautiful moment."

Simon told Tess about Falling Stone at the bridge, how he had

256

climbed the arch, how he had stood there, arms aloft, and a single shot had brought him down.

"You killed them all," Sugg called aloud, the words surfacing out of a smoldering meanness. He stood up, menacing, looking across to where Simon and Tess were dug in. "You slime, Simon. You got us all killed. The General, he was the best that was. *You buried him, you prick.*"

Simon said nothing. The moon was high in the sky, and the filmy cloud that had dimmed it earlier was gone. Trees were down all around them from the shelling. Far off, some trees were burning, and nearby a few were smoldering. The ash-gray light of the moon gave the scene an eerie, surreal quality. Sugg had snapped: Simon could see that now. He had watched it building toward this through the long weeks. He had always known that Sugg subsisted in a gray region at the edge of sanity, but now something had tripped inside him and he was more dangerous than ever. He could go berserk and shoot them all.

Machine-gun fire opened up from across the gorge, and .51-caliber shells struck home all around them. Instinctively, Sugg crouched down and took cover, and for the moment, at least, his attention was diverted away from Simon. The monkeys were firing at random, just for the hell of it, wasteful and sadistic, an effort to intimidate. A way of teasing and tormenting. Trying, maybe, to push them off the rim and back down the trail to where the Khorbaks were waiting.

For a while the firing was sustained, a rapid patter, but then it stopped and the gorge was quiet again, only the crackling of burning trees. Tess huddled close to Simon. Sugg and Thurl kept to their dug-in positions. A prolonged, unconvincing silence. Then the firing began again, steady and harmless, but unnerving, bullets spraying through the trees. Simon saw Sugg stand up, rising out of the hole he had dug. He was ash-blue in the ash-blue moonscape, his weapon in his right hand, his left arm out of the

257

sling, free and mobile, the bandage still on the hand. "Fucking monkeys," he raved. "I'll show you. Think you can fuck around—huh? Think you can fuck and spit and piss and shit? I'll show you!"

He advanced toward the rim, steady and unhurried, his weapon level, ready to fire. Bullets from across the gorge ricocheted off trees and rocks, chunking home into the humid soil—but he was untouched, tall and big in the vague light of the moon, like some strange, otherworldly alien, going to the rim, and he opened fire. The gorge echoed with the exchange. He emptied a clip and plugged another in. When that was done, he pulled a grenade from his pocket and, laughing, hurled it. It fell woefully short, falling into the gorge, exploding with a long echo, and he stood there laughing: large, sturdy, maniacal, obscene. The machine gun across the gorge was still active. A bullet caught his left arm. He plugged in another clip, and as he started firing he took a hit in his shoulder and a hit in his leg, and was spun around, firing now not across the gorge but at Simon and Tess and Thurl, his thick body bleeding under the moon—blasting away, shouting *"Kill, kill, kill!"*

Simon watched, saw him take the hits, and couldn't believe he didn't go down. It seemed he would go on forever, bullets from the Uzi spraying wantonly, tearing into trees, skipping off rock, ripping through foliage. Simon thought he saw Thurl moving in the darkness off to the right, but Sugg's barrage cut cleanly through that space, cleaving the night, and Simon wondered if Thurl had bought it. He crouched down, with Tess, and Sugg advanced steadily toward them, each footstep mechanical, robotlike, his face beaming with mad glee, shouting *kill, kill*, the gun shaking wildly as the bullets flamed from the barrel. Suddenly, his face shone with the fiercely lucid realization that it was not the monkeys he was firing on, but Simon.

Briefly he stopped firing, savoring the moment. *"Kill,"* he repeated, almost calmly. "You fuck, Simon. Now it's your turn!"

258

And began firing again, the gun hot and furious, tongues of flame where the slugs burst from the barrel, Simon thinking he was already dead, like Thurl, Tess too, the three of them gone, buried deep—by one of their own, and it didn't matter, because whether it was Sugg or the monkeys it was the same, pointless, without reason. At any instant now it would reach them, tear into them, the Uzi shaking, blazing—

But it stopped, and when it stopped Simon knew what it was: the clip was empty. The firing from across the gorge had also stopped, as if the monkeys somehow knew what was happening and were waiting for it to play itself out. In the sudden silence, Simon jumped up out of the hole and made for Sugg, thinking to overpower him, knock him down, which couldn't have been hard to do, with all the hits he had taken. But he was no sooner up, moving across the distance between them, then he saw that Sugg had already jammed in another clip. The Uzi was level, pointed straight at him.

"How about that," Sugg said, possessed of a strange serenity. His fatigues were drenched with blood. There was blood on his face and hands, a mad winsome gaiety in his eyes—barely alive but hanging on, deriving pleasure from the thought that there was still more life to take, and the life was Simon's. It was as if he didn't want to rush it, didn't want it to be too quickly over. "How does it feel? Huh? You like it? You like knowing you're gonna *die?* From the first I met you, you fuck, I knew, I *knew*." The muzzle of the Uzi was about five feet off, pointed at Simon's chest. Simon stepped cautiously sideways, drawing back, to his left, and Sugg turned, keeping the Uzi aimed. As Simon moved, Sugg moved with him, stiff-leggedly, enjoying it, Simon going in a circle around him, thinking *I am dead either way, either Sugg or the monkeys*, pulling slowly away, and Sugg going toward him, both of them edging closer to the rim. Then, in a moment of bravado, Sugg dropped the Uzi and whipped out his knife, the switchblade, holding it aloft in front of him. "Come at me," he taunted. "That what you want? Come on, come at me." And, when Simon made no move, he turned the knife around, holding the blade between thumb and forefinger, and Simon remembered how good he was at that, darting the knife into tree trunks on the trail. "Kiss off, fucker," the words swollen, ripe, pronounced almost with a joyousness, the hand already in motion, about to whip the knife through the dark, toward Simon, but a shot rang out, catching Sugg in the face. Thurl. Sugg hung there a moment, swiftly stopped, then staggered back, wavered, the knife still in hand, and sank backward over the rim, falling, not making a sound.

It seemed, for a moment, that they were in a void. The gunfire gone, the whine and racket of ricocheting slugs. And Sugg gone—wiped, deleted. The violence, lust, the sheer killing power that had been Sugg. Thurl had stopped him. Simon staggered back into the deep hole Tess had dug, to hold her, to pull her back, expecting the monkeys might start firing again at any moment.

For a long time no one spoke, they just stayed where they were, dug in, listening to the silence, feeling the absence of Sugg, and the absence of the others, as if their absence were a tangible thing.

Thurl, still off to the right, behind a mound of dirt, took the earphone off his ear and threw it across to Tess and Simon, along with the cassettes. "You guys can have it," he said. "I'm sick of this shit. The Ash Berries have some fancy rhythms, but after a while, when you hear enough of it, it gets strange. Real strange. Know what I mean?"

"No Thurl," Tess said. "What *do* you mean?"

"I don't know," he answered, in his indirect way. "I'm not too sure. I guess what I mean is that I'm movin' out. Back the way we came."

Simon bolted, alarmed. He looked across to where Thurl was,

260

heaps of broken branches on the ground between them. "Don't do it, Thurl."

"I got to."

"Why?"

"I just got to, that's all."

"There are Khorbaks down there." And, even if there weren't, even if the Khorbaks had merely been an invention of Trask's fevered brain, it was still an impossible route, because there had been too many firefights on the way in. The monkeys would be on the alert, searching. It was obvious to Simon, and it had to be obvious to Thurl too, but Thurl suddenly didn't give a damn.

"I knew about the Khorbaks long ago. They're big black fuckers. I learned a lot in this war."

"It's too risky, Thurl," Tess said.

"Look, I'm tired, tired of fightin'. I'm black, I can throw away my fatigues and decorate myself with paint or whatever, and put on some wild clothes, or no clothes at all, and pass for crazy. That's what passes in this world, ain't it? Crazy passes. So I'll be crazy too. If I can't pass, I'll at least blow a hell of a lot of holes in those fuckers before they get their hands on me. At least I'll be off this damn rim."

Simon listened, and saw, now, that it was Thurl's turn, his moment to crack and cave in. He didn't sound crazy, his voice, tone, but he was acting crazy, leaping to a reckless choice. Simon tried again, doing his best to reason it out with him. "Look, it's better if we stick together, no? Better for all of us. By dawn, if we sit tight, those nuts across the way will figure we're dead, or just not worth the shells they've been wasting on us." It was a plausible expectation, that the monkeys would pack up their infrared and move out, leave them for the Khorbaks. Maybe the big stuff had already pulled out, nothing left but that damn machine gun. "We stay hunkered down, get through the night. Then we slip out of here, go a few miles along the rim, and when we've got enough

261

daylight we look for a way down. We go for that village of friend-lies the General was talking about."

Tess nodded, agreeing. It was their most sensible option. She called across to Thurl. "Sounds good, Thurl. Stay put a while, we'll move out together."

Thurl was silent a moment. "It's a tough trip into that gorge. Where you think it's gonna take you?"

"We'll look for the village," Simon repeated, realizing as he said it that he was still relying on Trask, making an act of faith in him. Trask dead was as powerful as Trask alive, still reaching into his life, controlling, giving the orders. "It's there," Simon said. "It's got to be."

For a long time Thurl said nothing. Then his clear, firm voice came through the dark. "I'm movin' out," he said, and Simon knew, from the determined way he said it, there was no dissuading him.

"Don't do it, Thurl," Tess called, in a pleading tone. But he was up on his feet.

"Look me up in Detroit," he said, "that's where I'm heading. I figure I'll start a car wash. I'll do that for a while, then maybe I'll get into used cars. My real ambition, though, is to be a pimp. I want to have a lot of cool, sumptuous ladies working for me." He was out of the hole he had dug, moving, on his way. "Good luck, you guys. It's been sweet music, real sweet." He raised his weapon over his head in a gesture of farewell, and was off, into the moon-drenched woods.

"Yeah," Simon said. "Sweet music."

"Take care, Thurl," Tess called after him. "You hear? Take care out there."

He didn't answer. They heard the snapping of twigs and a faint rustle as he pushed off through the fallen branches.

There was no more shelling, no more mortar, though a few times the machine gun opened up, harmless chatter of bullets tearing

262

away at the trees. They waited through the night. With Thurl gone, they felt abandoned, specially vulnerable, and in a moment of self-doubt Simon wondered if they shouldn't have gone with him. But the gorge was the only way. Maybe Thurl, being black, would get through, past the Khorbaks, but even for him the chance was slim, if it was a chance at all. For them it would have been a form of suicide.

"He shouldn't have gone," Tess said. "He'll break a leg in the dark."

"Thurl has cat's eyes. He's a survivor."

"Yeah," she said flatly, with no conviction.

They tried to get some sleep, but sleep was impossible. Waiting there, wondering if the monkeys were gone, or if they were loading up for another shelling. Then the machine gun, just to remind them that it was still there. Simon felt strange, not himself. The long march, the firefight on the way in, the shelling, the firefight the night before at the lake, the lack of sleep. Weird, as if he had been popping pills. He yawned, but sleep was something he couldn't reach. Tess yawned, and she too felt peculiar, off balance, as if she were looking on, watching her life happen.

They were still in the big hole she had dug, Simon leaning back against a pile of dirt, and she sitting cross-legged, picking at her fingernails. "I guess the plain truth, Simon," she said gently, but with a degree of firmness, "is that I really don't want to marry you. Is that all right? I mean, just because of what happened last night, I don't want you to imagine we're somehow tied to each other."

"It's all right," he said. "I wasn't imagining. Last night was last night."

"It has nothing to do with you, you understand. It's me, the way I am. That was nice, what happened, and I'd like for it to happen again, I really would. I'd like to lock myself in a room with you, in a hotel, one of those hotels we saw at the lake, and do nothing but have sex for a month. And then home, back to

Philadelphia. Am I terrible? I can't believe I actually spent time in a convent. I don't want to marry anybody, and I don't want children. Yours or anybody else's. It's awful, I know it is. I guess I'm just a very mixed-up person. Maybe I'll go home and try the convent one more time, if they'll have me. Simon, I may never see you again."

She was overwrought, strained beyond her limit. "It's all right," he said, calming her.

"It's not all right. Don't you see? Everything is terribly, terribly wrong."

"I wasn't thinking about getting married either," he said, feeling strangely relaxed. It was as if, after the weeks of stress on the trail, and after the ordeal they had been through in the last hours, he had passed through some sort of barrier and no longer needed rest or sleep. He felt easy, comfortable, the words coming slow and untroubled. "I've thought about it," he said, "but it's something far off. I'm not sure I want kids either. There doesn't have to be a kid named Pearl, or a kid named Jewel. I'll lock you in a hotel room for a month, if you want, then we'll go our separate ways."

"Simon, we're going to die up here."

"Not up here, and not for a long time." He tossed a stone and hit a tree. "We're indestructible."

"You said Falling Stone was indestructible."

"He was. But he made a gift of himself. He lost his mind."

"Simon, I'm losing *my* mind."

"Not yet," he said. "Not yet." She had taken her helmet off, and he put his hand up to her hair, running his fingers through. "Get some sleep. We got a hard day."

Then the machine gun was going again. Somebody on the other rim was drunk on cheap wine. Drunk, or deranged, like Sugg. Or sane, rational, cool, simply practicing meanness. It went on for a while, and then it stopped.

The silence that ensued was unusual, unlike the patches of

silence they had experienced earlier. It was as if they had sunk into sleep: no noise of the gun, and no noise of anything else either—no breeze, no rustling of leaves, no night insects, no crickets. Simon thought it was a trick that his ears were playing, but it wasn't. Tess noticed it too, the vast, unnatural silence, as if they had been drawn up into a vacuum.

And then it was not just the silence, but the light—dim at first, faint but definite, then growing, intensifying, quickly brightening, and with the light there came a hum, a muted whirring sound.

"What's happening?" Tess said.

"I don't know."

It was something down in the gorge. Warily, uncertain what to expect, they left their dug-in position, and, moving from tree to tree, fearful of being picked up on infrared, they made their way toward the rim. Near the edge, where there were no trees for cover, they kept close to the ground, worming along, and when they were close enough to see down into the gorge, what they saw was the UFO, rising slowly up from the bottom. They hadn't seen it, or hadn't noticed it, for quite some time, and now it was back, closer than ever. It rose slowly up out of the gorge, then it paused, hovering between the two rims, roughly at the point where the bridge had been. It was very large, and it was slightly flattened, like an egg.

Tess and Simon were mute. They watched, stupefied. The UFO simply hung there, humming, illumined with its own white light, shedding its light everywhere, filling the gorge with its brilliance. It was overwhelming—a beginning and an ending, luminous and real. Simon felt it, and Tess felt it, an extraordinary resilience, a sense of everlasting calm.

"This isn't happening," she said distantly.

"I know it isn't."

"It's a dream. Wake me up, Simon."

They watched as it rose slightly, then descended again, and moved along slowly between the two rims, coming opposite the

265

bluff where they were situated. It hovered in front of them, vast and strange, otherworldly, conferring an enveloping sense of repose and tranquility. "It's a hallucination," Tess said, absorbed. "I know that now. I have no doubt in my mind that what we're looking at does not exist."

Simon had come to the same conclusion. "Still, it's very pleasant, while it lasts."

"While it lasts. But if we could reach out and touch it, there would be nothing there."

"No. Nothing there," he said hazily. "Do you think it's some form of monkey treachery?"

The stunning white light that emanated from the craft shaded off to lavender, green, rose, a bright weaving of pastels, and suddenly there was music, vivid and strong, echoing in the gorge. It was not as if the music had just been turned on. It seemed always to have been there, but only now did they become conscious of it, a lively sally of trumpets and horns, balanced against an ocean of strings.

"I know that music," Simon said. It was classical, symphonic. Densely orchestrated. "I've heard it before, plenty of times. Is it Liszt? Is that what it is?"

It was familiar to Tess too, but she was uncertain about Liszt. "Isn't it a great sound?"

It was a fantastic sound, the horns belting away, weaving and counterweaving, climbing, climax on top of climax. The gorge resonated with it, the sound building, rushing, blending with the vivid play of pastels, an eruption, a silvery gush of color and tone. Simon was caught up in it, smiling, and as he smiled he realized it had been a very long time since he had smiled with such vigor and conviction. Tess too, smiling— caught, held, energized. A spell was upon them, something was happening—and it was unreal, the best kind of happening there could be.

Simon felt himself closing his eyes. And then, as if only moments later, Tess was shaking him, pulling him out of sleep, and it was not the hum of the UFO that he heard, not the faint whir, and it wasn't music, the richly laminated symphonic tones they had heard in the night, but something completely different, raucous and tough, loud, the sound of a stick raking rapidly across a picket fence. They weren't on the rim of the gorge, but back in the deep hole that Tess had dug. Simon blinked his eyes open and looked into the pale morning sky, stars fading, the sun not yet up, light oozing across the sky as if it were a fluid seeping out of the horizon. The noise drew closer, and soon it was right on top of them, straight up, palpable, and no dream: the rainbow chopper, circling, moving around, inspecting. And in it, who else but Meyerbeer, still (unbearably, and incredibly) alive. Sweet, desperate Christ: *Meyerbeer!*

26 □ A Pink Cloud Shaped Like a Whale

OR WAS IT? They had seen Meyerbeer killed, the chopper smashed to pieces when Trask shot it down, after it had fired on them. And here, now, another rainbow chopper. They huddled close in the deep hole, wet smell of dug earth, hardly knowing what to expect, hoping against hope it was a different Meyerbeer who had tried to kill them. Simon unholstered his .44, and Tess reached for her rifle, feeling, both of them, an instinctive need to be ready.

The chopper circled for a while, then it came down on the flat stretch of rock at the edge of the gorge—and, when it was down, there was no longer any room for doubt. It was Meyerbeer, nobody else. Cigar in mouth, unlit; fluffy brown mustache; casual as ever, and friendly, leaning out of the chopper and calling over to them. "Anybody need a lift?"

Simon waited for the guns on the other side of the gorge to act up again, but there was nothing.

They ran and climbed in.

"It's you," Tess shouted, making herself heard over the roar of the engine. She was still a little astonished to see him.

"Who'd you expect? Douglas MacArthur?"

"Move it out," Simon shouted. "Get it the hell out of here before they start shooting again."

"They're gone, Simon. There's nobody there."

"Really?"

"What do you mean, *really*. Haven't I been flying around, checking it out?"

It was hard to believe. They weren't getting shot at. The monkeys were gone, and Meyerbeer wasn't dead. Everything was hard to believe. "We're *alive*," Tess said.

"That's very nice news," Meyerbeer said, not quite shouting, but getting his voice up just loud enough to be heard above the engine. They were still on the ground, Meyerbeer savoring his role as guardian angel and grand deliverer. "Relax," he said, "get yourselves comfortable, strap in. I happen to be alive myself, you see. A lot of people thought I was dead. And now a lot of the people who thought I was dead are dead themselves. That ought to teach them something, I guess."

"But how?" Simon asked, baffled. "We saw the chopper go down."

"It wasn't me, Simon, and it wasn't this chopper. Damn lucky the General shot that bastard down. That was a copycat chopper the monkeys sent out to blow you people away—they got it from the same damn Arab I got mine from. The fucker'll sell to anybody! But hell, that was one crazy bugger, the monkey in that chopper, dedicated as the devil, hunting the jungle for days on end, weeks, trying to spot you guys. Even had a tape of my voice, the bastard. How in the hell'd he manage that—huh? I do wonder. Anyway, Simon, congratulations, terrific work you did on the bridge. Very fine work indeed. Of course, if you had done it in daylight it would have made my job a lot easier. But we work with what we've got, don't we." He checked his dials, touched a few buttons, engaged the controls, and they were off.

Simon looked at Meyerbeer with amazement. "You were there? You saw the bridge go down?"

"You're damn right I was there. I had to use supersensitive fast film because of the dark. Expensive stuff, Simon, and lucky we at least had that little patch of moon. Wouldn't have missed it for the world. It's the climax of the movie, Simon, the raison d'être. It gives sense and meaning to all the shit and death and fucking around. If the bridge doesn't go down, what's it all for?"

"I don't know," Simon wondered. "What's it all for?" As he said it, he realized he wasn't talking, he was shouting. It was like the night before, during the shelling, you had to shout to make yourself heard. But now it wasn't guns, it was the noise of the chopper that he had to shout against.

"It's for life, Simon. And freedom. You know what for." There was that flat, twangy tone in Meyerbeer's voice again, accentuated and made more obvious because he was talking louder than usual. The twangy tone that Simon could never interpret or understand. When Meyerbeer talked like that, it was hard to say if he was being serious or flippantly ironic. He was up and down, in and out, you couldn't trust the things that he said. Impossible ever to know exactly where he was. "What the hell," he added ringingly, "freedom is a damn big thing. People die for freedom, Simon. You two folks came through a hard time."

Simon bristled. "Meyerbeer, are you serious? Or are you screwing around. If you're screwing around I'm going to blow your brains out, even if it means we crash and all get killed."

"Serious? Of course I'm serious. You don't think I'd fuck around with things like life and freedom, do you? So we crash and get killed, if that's how you want it. What can I say? Nevertheless, you have to admit that was a beautiful thing Falling Stone did out there. Does Tess know?" He turned and looked at Tess, who was wedged into the small space behind them, on a jump seat. "Did he tell you? Falling Stone got right out there on top of that arch and offered a gift to the moon. The moon means a lot to Apaches. The moon and plenty of other things. The Apaches are very good to their gods."

"Trask is dead," Simon said.

"That figures. They're all dead. Aren't they?"

"Thurl is out in the bush somewhere, trying to get back the way we came. I don't think he has a compass."

"He'll be all right. Thurl's a winner. If he doesn't make it back, he'll find some village to settle down in and a broad to shack up with. A whole bunch of broads. He really digs these native types."

"You never got shot down," Simon said.

"Never."

"They were taking bets you'd get shot down."

"I know they were. They lost."

"How come you never got shot down?"

"Why should anyone want to shoot at me? My friends, maybe, might shoot me down. Like you, Simon. You blasted away at me with that Magnum and nearly got me killed. But the other guys, the monkeys—well, they know a good thing when they see it. They know they're in the picture, and they like the idea of being on film. I sold them shares. They'd be very upset if I got shot down." There was that tone again. It could be real, or he could be making it all up—inventing, fabricating. Simon imagined him among the monkeys, the monkeys bowing and scraping, bending over backward to accommodate him, because as far as they were concerned he was no enemy, just a man with an unlit cigar and a camera, a good, solvent business partner whom they fired on and always carefully missed. "Speaking of shares, Simon—now that

270

the General is dead, I've got all these shares you might want to buy in on. How about it? You too, Tess. It would be a terrific investment. There's a monkey colonel down there thinks it's the best thing he's ever run into."

Tess spotted some ground fire. "Somebody's shooting. I think they're shooting at us." She could see them—peasants with straw hats, firing rifles. Aiming and shooting. Small puffs of smoke from the rifles, like white flowers. "They're peasants," she said. "I thought the peasants in this country were on our side. Why are they shooting? Don't they know who we are?"

"The peasants change sides a lot. I tried to sell them some shares, but they couldn't come up with the cash. I threatened to cut them out of the picture, so I think they're mad at me. Don't worry, though. They couldn't hit the side of a barn."

He swung the chopper in a wide arc, then sauntered around, back and forth, teasing, daring the peasants to hit him. He was out of range. He swung in another arc, and Tess went dizzy with the centrifugal force. "For God's sake, Meyerbeer, don't get us killed!"

"How can I get you killed? I'm life! I'm strength! I'm film! I'm Meyerbeer!"

"You're a son of a bitch," Tess said, dead serious.

"That too. Yes. I am a son of a bitch. Buy shares, Tess. I'm worth investing in."

He was a wilderness, a jungle. You talked with Meyerbeer, and it was like walking miles and miles into a forest: you're lost, you can't find your way out, and suddenly it no longer matters, you just wander around, looking at the trees. Simon was thinking again about the bridge, strung there across a meaningless gorge, unused, silent, gleaming in the sun, existing only to be blown apart. He looked at Meyerbeer, trying to fathom the truth, but all he could come up with was a terrible awareness of the way in which reality does not explain itself.

"You arranged it," he blurted, guessing, knowing that he

would never have the facts. Not, at least, in a solid, tangible form that he could document and verify. "You arranged the whole damn thing. You picked out the bridge. It was a nothing bridge that wasn't worth shit. Nobody ever used it."

Meyerbeer smiled. "Simon, I could have picked out for you a very strategic bridge armed to the teeth, and you would never have got near it. Is that what you would have wanted? I picked a bridge you could blow up. After all, you're just out of training, you realize. You're not one of the super blower-uppers of the Western World. That doesn't damage your pride, does it? I gave you an easy bridge, and you knocked it down. It's footage, it'll be great for the box office. I got some terrific shots as that sweet mother went down." Again the tone, lazy and deceptive, tantalizing. Truth and fiction, for him, were hopelessly mixed in everything he said, there was no sorting them out. Always the clever stance, the agile shifting from mask to mask. "A different bridge, Simon, and every last one of you would have been killed. The bridge would still be there. Imagine how it would demoralize the American public. Is that what you're looking for? I realize that you're suffering, at this moment, from exhaustion and mental anguish. Thirty-three days in the jungle—that's something, my hat is off to you. Did you know it was thirty-three days? I can't blame you for being crusty and out of sorts. But you have to admit, Simon, it was a gorgeous bridge. You, a novice at bridge-blowing, you couldn't come by one better. I selected it for its aesthetic value."

Simon crashed his fist against the control panel. "They died, dammit. That whole bunch down there got killed. For nothing. And this is the shit you give me?"

"We're all going to die, Simon. Just go easy on the panel. It's sensitive. Dying is what life is all about. Don't you know that? It's one of the things I came to grips with when I was seven years old. When you're seven, they say you reach the age of reason. Well, that's when I reached it, or maybe when I was ten. And I knew

272

right then, when I was seven or ten, that we are all going to die and there's no sense fighting it. You still don't believe you're going to die, Simon. That's why you're so uptight about so many things. Just think about it for a while and adjust your head. You'll see. You'll feel a lot more relaxed. Join the good guys. Join the winners."

"Are we the winners," Schlumm said, "or are we the losers?"

"I don't know," Eikopf said, "Sometimes it's hard to tell. If anybody knows, I think God knows. But God is not saying."

"It's no fun being a loser," Merlin said. "What do you think, Falling Stone?"

Falling Stone just sat there. He said nothing.

"You sound very strange, Simon," Meyerbeer said. He whipped the chopper around and up, to avoid a sudden cliff. He had been skimming along very low, and now he took the chopper up to a fairly high altitude. "Is that you talking, or is it someone else? Sometimes I think I hear voices."

"You know what I found out?" Simon said. "I found out the black box, *our* black box, talks to *their* black box. Merlin told me, I pried it out of him. The box is a traitor." The box was down near his feet. He had had the presence of mind to grab it and bring it along when they left the gorge.

"You mean you didn't know? Simon, you impress me. What kind of a war can you have if your black box isn't a traitor? A damn dull war, that's what."

Simon opened the cabin hatch.

"What the hell are you doing?" Meyerbeer called, shouting above the rush of wind and the drum of the motor.

"I'm getting rid of a traitor. This is an execution." He tossed the box out, and it sailed away, twirling. Simon watched. Tess watched, leaning over. It twirled, spun, speeding earthward. It struck a wide ledge of rock, bounced, and broke apart, pieces scattering, fractured chips and diodes. Simon pulled the hatch shut.

"I tried to work it last night, but all I got out of it was pi."

"Pi is an important number," Meyerbeer said. "I don't know why, but it is. You shouldn't have destroyed that, Simon. It's an expensive piece of government equipment. And it's classified. You could get shot for that. Or subpoenaed. They could put you in jail."

"Are you going to inform?"

"Me? Inform? I'd never rat on you, Simon. I want to hire you. I need a good advance man. Now that you're not a walking bomb any more, I think we can strike an arrangement. What do you say? I need somebody with a boyish, innocent face like yours, a quiet, nonthreatening manner. That's what you have, Simon, a terrific face and a terrific manner. But down deep you're all iron and you know how to hate. Right Tess? That's what you found out about him back there in the woods, down by the lake. See? I know a lot of things. How about it, Simon? I can have my man in Toledo draw up a contract."

"Are you never serious?" Tess said.

"Never."

They swung in the wind, turning, and, as they turned, they saw, far off in the direction from where they had come, a huge mushroom cloud going up. It had the look of something nuclear.

Meyerbeer was thrilled. "There it is," he sang out. "They finally did it!"

Simon gazed at the mushroom. "Did what?"

"They hit it. Wiped it out. There was another force out there, Simon. While you were wrecking the bridge, they were out for that munitions factory, and they got it. There it is." He had a camera rigged to a bracket outside the cabin, and while he talked he threw an extension switch to get the film rolling. He stabilized the chopper, angling it so that the camera was aimed at the mushroom. "Look at the size of that. Isn't it terrific?"

Simon understood. The bridge had been a diversion. The munitions plant had been the main target all along. All those people dead, and a good bridge gone, just for a diversionary maneuver. He wondered if Trask had known, or if Command had kept him in the dark about it. If he had known, he had been very good at never letting on. Simon was on the point of asking Meyerbeer if Trask had known, but he didn't bother. Meyerbeer was a maze, no point in asking him anything.

"So you see, Simon, it wasn't all for nothing. Who knows, you may even get a medal for this. You and Tess. For doing the impossible. Did you think all of this was just for the boob-tubers back home, the technowar voyeurs? Hell, we made some progress here, we socked it to the monkeys where it hurts."

He looked at Simon and smiled, the special Meyerbeer smile that meant yes and no, maybe and perhaps, all in one package, and for Simon, looking at him, seeing the smile, it all fell into place as it never had before, all of it opening up for him, like some medieval mosaic, a vision of hell. But no snarling devils in this hell, no tails and pitchforks; it was zoom lenses and film, magnetic tape, TV pixels, silver screens, megasound, ultravision, long shots and medium shots, all mixed up with bombs and snipers and mushroom clouds, and Meyerbeer—yes, Meyerbeer, who may not only have selected the bridge (for its aesthetic value, as he beguilingly phrased it), but may also have had a hand in choosing the main target, the munitions factory, picking it because that too was something he needed footage of, the immense black mushroom filling the sky. Which meant, of course, that he wasn't just filming the war, recording it, but inventing it, creating it, or at least co-creating it with the ones who had the detonators and knew how to blow things up. And Simon, seeing all this as it flashed through his mind, drew back from it, thinking it was (had to be) just another fantasy, another of his wild, paranoid imaginings. Meyerbeer, whom he had considered a con man, a sleight-of-hand artist reaping a harvest off the war, but whom he now saw as a wizard, a sorcerer, part of a vast celluloid system in which ideas like heroism and freedom were being recast, changed utterly—a system of images and icons into which Trask and old warriors like Trask, and war itself, had been subsumed, in which even Meyerbeer was only a small part, the tip of the iceberg, because there were other Meyerbeers, as there were other Trasks, the Trasks and the Meyerbeers hating each other but locked together, feeding off each other, and while the Trasks marched to death the Meyerbeers zoomed in and got the footage for the right price, silverscreen sunburst vistacolor, videotube look-at-my-blood wondervision, closeup forget-me-not magnitube splendor. And Simon, seeing this, all of it flashing before him, knew that he and Tess were part of it too, inextricably caught up, webbed and tangled in it. There would be a medal, a hero's welcome—speeches, champagne, reporters, they were news. Meyerbeer would make sure about that.

"It isn't nuclear," Meyerbeer said, holding the chopper stable so that the camera could target the mushroom cloud, "just a hell of a lot of TNT, and other stuff. But when I splice it into the movie, it'll pass for nuclear. It sure is big. You think it will pass, Simon?"

"Meyerbeer, you're immoral."

"Of course I am. Isn't everybody? That's because I'm alive. You're too much in love with death, Simon." He riveted his eyes on Tess. "What do you love, Tess? Do you love Simon? Simon of the innocent face, the iron interior? Or is it something else that you are in love with?" He gave a knowing wink, then switched off the camera and they were off again, moving, heading for Base Blue. Behind them the mushroom towered, vast and dense, a cloud that knew about sudden pain and death. "I think you're a sweet couple," Meyerbeer chirped. "I wish you the best of luck, I really do. I think you make a great team. I've seen the two of you in action. Send me an invitation to the wedding. Is that what this is? Is this a wedding? Name one of the kids for me!"

"Not just immoral," Tess said. "Meyerbeer, you completely lack reality."

276

"I pay you a compliment, and this is what I get? One calls me immoral, the other says I'm unreal. I just saved your lives, folks. That's what you think—immoral, huh?" He jerked the chopper around, up and town, a few quick turns.

Simon held on. Tess held on, and she was furious, verbalizing to beat the band: "Treacherous, deceitful, double-dealing, monstrous, motherless, fuckshit charlatan!"

"That's all? Is that all? Nothing else?" There was the barest hint of wounded pride, and it quickly veered over into that other tone, the tone Simon couldn't deal with, half teasing and half sincere, authentic yet somehow fake, fake yet mysteriously in earnest: "Charlatan, huh? Is that what you say? Well, let me tell you something, I'll give it to you straight. It's film, folks. Film and videotape are remaking the world. Haven't you simpletons noticed? Image. Appearance. What you see. It's here to stay, so you might as well get used to it. It creates. It makes and remakes, twists and turns, shapes and reshapes. It's the divine energy—pulse and power. It gives life and takes it away. Film is God, Simon. Is that news to you?"

"That's what he thinks," Eikopf said.

"I can't hear you," Meyerbeer called. "Simon, you're mumbling to yourself again."

"I said you're an incredible phony," Simon said.

"Oh. That's what I thought you said. Yes, I'm a phony too. It's a fascinating way of life. A career, actually."

"He's the way he is because he's the way he is," Schlumm said to Eikopf. "It's in his mind, the structure of the neurons. Structure is all."

"In the mind, or someplace else," Mickey Kabuki said.

"Sure," Emma Sue remarked. "In his testicles."

"She has a mouth," Sugg noted. "Doesn't she have a mouth?"

Emma Sue brushed her hair. Sugg exercised his hand, the one with the missing middle finger. Schlumm worked on a crossword. Merlin picked his nose. Mickey Kabuki made book that Meyerbeer would crash before he got back to Base Blue. Falling Stone kept an eye on the clouds. Sugarman drew up a menu, the menu to end all menus, including billi bi au cari, escargots, profiteroles aux crevettes à l'indienne, asparagus in beurre blanc, poireaux au gratin, poitrine de volaille pochée, moules ravigote au vermouth, and chocolate mousse.

"Is this God's world, or Meyerbeer's?" Eikopf wondered.

"Or General Trask's?" the Major said, nodding blandly.

"What did you say?" Meyerbeer shouted.

"I said it looks like somebody is shooting at us again," Simon said.

"Really? Actually shooting?"

"Yeah," Tess said. She had spotted it too. "Really shooting."

"Some people have no consideration." Meyerbeer yanked the chopper up and headed for a low-hanging cloud, a big one, shaped roughly like a whale. The morning sun colored it pink. If they got to the cloud, they would be safe.

It was Thurl down there on the ground, firing away, thinking it was only Meyerbeer in the cabin. The chopper was too far off to hit, but then again, he might get lucky. Shooting was good, you aimed and pulled the trigger. Or you didn't aim, you just pulled the trigger. It was a good feeling, knowing he was alive.

He fired, and, as the bullets went up, he saw the chopper entering the cloud, disappearing into the vast pink fluff. He felt like shit, because up ahead of him the trail divided, he had no idea which way to go.

Breathtaking Suspense...

from St. Martin's Press

THE KING'S COMMISSAR by Duncan Kyle
In a gripping blend of fact and fiction that moves between Revolutionary Russia and contemporary London, this thriller goes from top secret missions to the heart of a mystery that could destroy the entire Western World.
"Tense, sustained fascination."   —*The New York Times*
—— 90212-3 $3.95 U.S.

WALKING SHADOWS by Fred Taylor
In 1942 a group of German officers approach British Intelligence with a startling proposition.
"Sizzling, gripping."   —*The New York Times*
—— 90377-4 $3.95 U.S.

AIRFORCE ONE IS HAUNTED by Robert Serling
A dazzling sequel to the bestselling *The President's Plane is Missing*.
—— 90029-5 $3.95 U.S.   —— 90031-7 $4.95 Can.

BLOOD OF THE CZARS by Michael Kilian
What begins as a cultural mission to the Soviet Union soon involves beautiful Tatiana Chase in a byzantine web of murder, espionage, and betrayal.
"Riveting suspense."   —*The Washington Post*
—— 90079-1 $3.95 U.S.   —— 90080-5 $4.95 Can.

NOW AVAILABLE AT YOUR BOOKSTORE!

Get the Inside Story—
It's Stranger than Fiction!

THE MAN WHO KILLED BOYS:
THE STORY OF JOHN WAYNE GACY, JR.
by Clifford L. Linedecker

As horrifying as *Helter Skelter*, this reveals the hidden horror amid the daily lives of ordinary people. "A sensational crime story that evokes both curiosity and revulsion." —*Chicago Tribune* With 8 pages of photos.

_____ 90232-8 $3.95 U.S.   _____ 90233-6 $4.95 Can.

LOVERS, KILLERS, HUSBANDS, WIVES
by Martin Blinder, M.D.

These blood-chilling true stories are case studies in the intimate passion of murder—from the most shocking files of a top legal psychiatrist.

_____ 90219-0 $3.95 U.S.   _____ 90220-4 $4.95 Can.

TOO SECRET, TOO LONG
by Chapman Pincher

The astonishing and infuriating story of the man who was called "the spy of the century" and the woman who controlled him. "Remarkable..." —*Newsweek* With 8 pages of photos.

_____ 90375-8 $4.95 U.S.

SIDNEY REILLY by Michael Kettle

This true story of the world's greatest spy is the first account based on wholly authentic sources—with 8 pages of extraordinary photos.

_____ 90321-9 $3.95 U.S.   _____ 90322-7 $4.95 Can.

THE LAST ENEMY by Richard Hillary

The devastating memoir of a dashing pilot who, after he is shot down and horribly burned, learns the true meaning of courage. "A deeply affecting account of courage in fighting the enemy and in fighting oneself." —*Publishers Weekly*

_____ 90215-8 $3.95 U.S.

NOW AVAILABLE AT
YOUR BOOKSTORE!